The Light
Never Lies

Book Two – Crater Lake Series

Also by Francis Guenette

Disappearing in Plain Sight – Book One of the Crater Lake Series
(2013)

The Light
Never Lies

Book Two – Crater Lake Series

FRANCIS L. GUENETTE

HUCKLEBERRY
HAVEN
PUBLISHING

Author's note: This book is a work of fiction. Names, characters, places and incidents either are the product of the author's imagination or are used fictitiously and any resemblance to actual persons living or dead, events, or locales is entirely coincidental.

ISBN
978-0-9920770-0-6 (Softcover)
978-0-9920770-1-3 (Kindle)
978-0-9920770-2-0 (epub)

Cover Photo & Design: Bruce Witzel

Huckleberry Haven Publishing
Box 309
Port Alice, BC
V0N 2N0
disappearinginplainsight.com

For my father: Joseph Pierre 'Leo' Guenette. 1937-2009
Thank you for showing us how to approach death
with courage and dignity.

Convergence

ONE

THE LAST WEEK OF APRIL

L isa-Marie paced the crowded depot platform. She looked up towards the turn in the road, desperate to catch the first glimpse of the Vancouver bus. The flip-flop of her sandals on the pavement echoed in her ears. She shivered and hugged her arms close to her body. Late April mornings were cold midway up Vancouver Island. She wondered if she had time to run inside and find a bathroom. She glanced at her watch ... probably not.

She sat down on a bench that looked like a beat-up church pew. She thought about praying. If prayer could help her get through the next hour, she would throw herself on her knees, clasp her hands in front of her body and beg for help from any deity that might be tuned in. Tugging the sleeves of her sweater down over her hands, she decided it was far too late for divine intervention.

A grubby-looking guy shuffled up to her. He reached out his hand in a well-understood plea. Lisa-Marie looked pointedly at the no panhandling sign and shook her head. She shifted her gaze to stare at her suitcase. It lay on the curb beside the bus that would leave soon for Dearborn and Cedar Falls. One step at a time – if she thought too far ahead, she would lose her nerve altogether. She rose to pace the length of the platform once more.

A Greyhound came around the corner and glided down the hill. It pulled in beside the up-Island bus. Her hand, held against her thumping heart, shook. She could see Justin moving down the aisle of the bus, turning his head as he scanned the area outside the windows. He was looking for her.

1

The overhead speaker came to life, crackling and spitting out words. *All passengers heading north were to proceed to bay three.*

Justin was off the bus. He glanced around and his gaze slid right past her. He shook his head for an instant. Then he looked back to where she stood. He had been in mid-motion, hoisting his pack over his shoulder and grabbing his duffel from the curb. He froze. His pack fell from his shoulder to the ground. The duffel, halfway off the curb, crashed back down, as well. He straightened up and stared.

Lisa-Marie walked across the space that separated them and smiled up at him. "I've been waiting forever. The bus from Victoria got here ages ago." She leaned over and grabbed his pack to pass it up to him. "I hope we can get on the other bus right away." She stamped her feet and rubbed her arms, "Grab your duffel. Let's get in line. We want to get a seat together."

Her long, brown hair blew across her face as she turned. She got a few steps ahead of him before he grabbed her arm. "Leez ... wait. Come over here." He pulled her away from the line-up. "Why didn't you tell me?" He stared at the drooping sweater that stretched down the girl's thighs, the black leggings below that, and her exposed feet fidgeting on the ground. He frowned, "Why are you wearing flip-flops? It's cold out here." Then his eyes returned to the sweater; for all its oversize it could not hide the obvious bulge of her stomach. He finally gazed at her face with a look of pity mixed with horror. "Why didn't you tell me?"

Lisa-Marie shook off his restraining hand. Her voice cracked as she pushed her hair out of her face, "Can't we just get on the bus?" To her horror, tears filled her eyes.

"Okay," Justin put his hands on her shoulders as if to steady her. "We'll get on the bus. Have you got your ticket?" She nodded as they walked over to the slowly moving line-up.

An older woman smiled at Lisa-Marie, "You're happy now that your fellow is here, aren't you? When are you due, hon?"

"Ummm ... end of June," Lisa-Marie's face turned a dark shade of red as she added a full month onto her due date.

"Not until then? I would have thought you were due any day. This will be your first, I guess?" The woman's smile shifted over to include Justin.

Lisa-Marie imagined herself reaching out and wrapping her two hands around the old woman's throat.

"You're both so young. Well, everyone looks young to me these days." The woman moved ahead to chat with the driver before she boarded the bus.

Justin and Lisa-Marie waited their turn and were soon squeezed, shoulder to shoulder, into adjoining seats. Lisa-Marie pulled out her iPod and rummaged through her purse for her ear buds. She grabbed her lip gloss and applied it. She found her water bottle and had a long, slow drink. Then she stood up and pushed past Justin, "Sorry. Better do this before we get moving." She waddled down the narrow aisle to the bathroom at the rear of the bus.

Settled back into her seat, she searched her bag for the pack of gum she had bought earlier. Justin watched her every move with a look of stunned disbelief. Finally, he reached over to grab her hand, "Stop fiddling around and tell me what the hell is going on."

She cleared her throat and said, "I'm pregnant."

"Ya, I can see that. Why didn't you tell me? All these months we've been messaging and talking. Why didn't you say something?"

"I would have told you, but I didn't even know myself forever, then I felt so retarded." She bit one side of her lower lip and looked down at Justin's hand where it still rested on her own. "It's kind of embarrassing."

A large woman maneuvered down the aisle, pushing a small child in front of her. They sat right behind Lisa-Marie and Justin. As the child kicked the back of her seat, Lisa-Marie made a face, "Great, this is going to be a fun trip." She glanced over at Justin, "It's all going to be fine. I can take my provincial exams at the Dearborn high school so I won't lose any of my grade eleven credits –" Justin pulled his hand away. She felt the tears coming as she whispered, "Don't be mad at me."

"Don't cry. I'm not mad." He pointed at her stomach straining against her sweater, "It's the shock. You understand that, right?"

The engine roared to life and the bus backed out of the bay. They were on their way. One more step accomplished. She was sitting beside Justin and the bus was heading to Crater Lake. With the almost-comforting, steady thump of two small feet against her back, Lisa-Marie rested her head on Justin's shoulder and closed her eyes. "I'm so tired. Is this OK? Can I lean on you like this for a bit?"

"Ya, of course." Justin folded his arms over his chest and stared at the stained upholstery of the seat in front of him.

✻✻✻✻

Robbie sat on the front steps of his aunt's house. He could hear his cousins screaming and chasing each other around inside – playing some stupid, little-kid game. His clothes were packed into an old suitcase his aunt had gotten from someone over at the church.

Everything else Robbie needed was stuffed into his packsack. He had

3

chosen some of his best comics – Ultimate Spiderman and a few X-Men. He'd thrown in some good pencils, a blank notebook, a couple of matchbox cars, and his favourite action figures. He had also included two beach rocks polished smooth by the waves of the Miramichi Bay and a feather he thought might have come from a hawk. He had stuffed his mom's small wallet deep down in the pack. Robbie remembered the way she tucked it into the back pocket of her jeans whenever they went to town. She'd smile and say, "Better not forget this." Her driver's license was still inside. Last of all, he had with him a sealed, brown envelope that his aunt had told him was important. She had said it like she was speaking in capital letters. The envelope contained his birth certificate, Status number, and Medicare card.

He spotted the camper truck in the distance as it inched forward on the gravel road. He looked out to the rolling water of the bay. The sun shone bright on the waves and he had to squeeze his eyes so they wouldn't water. The truck got closer. The screen door creaked open and his aunt's footsteps came to a stop on the porch behind him. Together, they watched the vehicle become life-size as it pulled up and parked in front of the house.

A tall man got out of the driver's side and walked over to push open the rickety gate that hung off one of its hinges. His grey hair, closely shaved on the sides and spiky short on top, ran to a long braid down his back. Dark sunglasses covered his eyes. On his belt he carried a leather sheathed hunting knife. Robbie tilted his head to one side and narrowed his eyes. He nodded slowly as he watched the man come closer.

Alexander Collins pushed the sunglasses up on his head and glanced at the woman who stood on the porch. He thought she resembled an older, more tired version of Marsha. But it had been years since he'd seen Marsha and the memory of a woman's face could play tricks on a guy. He hunkered down near the steps to bring himself eye-level with the boy. Alex reached out and held the boy's face in his hands. He leaned close to touch his forehead to Robbie's. "It's good to see you, Son." Moving back, Alex saw his own dark eyes staring up at him. He shook his head in wonder as he glanced at the woman, "He's the spitting image of his brother when he was this age."

He moved up the stairs and pulled Robbie's aunt into a tight hug. "I'm sorry Ginny – sorry I couldn't make it in time for the funeral."

The woman nodded, shooing back into the house the three kids who were hiding behind her legs. "He's ready, Alex. I packed up all his things. I made sandwiches for the trip. But come inside first. The coffee's on."

Alex disappeared into the house. Robbie sat on the porch and waited. They would be talking grown-up things. His aunt would be telling his father all about the accident, how Robbie's mom had drowned when the *Jodie Lynn* went down so fast no one could believe it. His mom had always said that lobster boat was an old bucket that would end up at the bottom of the bay someday. His aunt would be saying how everyone had come to the funeral, how the church and the hall afterwards, had been packed with people. She'd start crying. She'd been doing that a lot over the last few weeks. She would say that life could sure be a bitch sometimes. She'd tell his father all about the important brown envelope. Robbie held onto the handles of his packsack and waited.

In less time than he thought it would take, his father came out of the house and grabbed the suitcase. "Let's hit the road. We've got a lot of miles to cover." Robbie got up and shrugged his pack over his shoulder. His aunt hugged him, tears streaming down her face. He waved goodbye to the three grubby, little faces pressed against the glass of the living room window. He took a deep breath. Things were finally moving.

Settled in the passenger seat of the truck, Robbie looked out his window and watched the familiar landscape disappear behind him. "Which way are we going when we get to the highway?" he asked in a flat voice.

"Up toward Bathurst. We've got quite the drive ahead of us. Clear across the country. We'll stop in Montreal. There's someone there I want you to meet. Getting over the Shield will be a long haul but once we hit Manitoba, we'll fly across the prairies. There are at least a dozen places we can stop and get a good home-cooked meal. Then we'll see the mountains. It's quite the sight, to come on the Rockies after you've spent a time looking at open prairie." Robbie's small body slumped against the far door. "Do you know what's happening here?" Alex asked him.

"I know you're my dad." Robbie continued to stare out the window before he turned to look at the man behind the wheel. "I know I've got to go with you because my mom is dead. That means she's never coming back and I'll never see her again."

"How did you know that I'm your father?"

Robbie shrugged, "The light was right."

Alex had no idea what the kid meant about the light. He hadn't seen Robbie for close to eight years, not since the kid was a baby. It was a stretch of time that would erase any memory of an absent father and yet the boy's eyes had held total recognition.

"Here's the plan," Alex grabbed two road maps from the dash. "One map is New Brunswick. You can find where we're at right now and figure out how long it's going to take us to get to Quebec City. The other map is the whole damn country. Check out a good route across to Vancouver Island in British Columbia. You're going to be the navigator on this trip. We've got those sandwiches, so I don't want to stop until later. Figure out a place we can get to by around ten o'clock tonight."

❧❧❧❧

Maddy punched at the keys on her phone. *Where the hell are you?* This was her sixth text to Jesse in less than fifteen minutes. She knew he'd have his cell phone with him wherever he was at Micah Camp. Why didn't he answer? She dropped the phone on the bed and reached for the small, sterile-wrapped package from the night table. She gripped the razor blade in her shaking hand. The cuts from an hour ago had stopped seeping bright-red drops of blood. The ones from an hour before still stood out in stark lines across the skin of her forearm. She put the package back on the dresser and grabbed the phone. She held it tightly to her chest and watched the hand on the clock above her bed click each second away.

When it finally rang, she fumbled to answer. Jesse's voice shot right into her skull, "For fuck sakes, Maddy, I can't drop everything and call every time you text me." She sobbed with relief. She could barely get her breath, let alone respond. Jesse went on in a quieter tone, "Okay, stop crying."

After a few moments of hitching, sobbing gasps, Maddy said, "I'm sorry, Jess. I got freaked out when you didn't call back. I needed to hear your voice, talk to me ... tell me anything. What are you doing right now?"

A muffled snort of laughter came down the phone line before Jesse said, "Ya right ... the excitement of being a resident at Micah Camp never gets old. Remember that joke you told me the first day I got here? Where do you send a foster kid who's past the *best-by-date*? You must be feeling nostalgic or something. I was working with Jeremy on the website. He thought someone I knew was dying or something, the way you kept texting. Don't start crying again. It's good to take a break from Jeremy. Our cooler than cool tech instructor has got quite a hate going for his wife right now. He keeps bitching about her. I think they split up or something. I'm walking out through the breezeway – you know the one in front of the soap and paper shop. The kids are slaving away in there. And guess what? It's not pissing down rain here, for once. Sunny skies with a nice little chop out on good old Crater Lake."

Jesse kept talking. The sound of his voice made her earlier panic seem unreal. Maddy moved off the bed. She put the blades and the disinfectant wipes away in a jewel box she kept in the bottom drawer. She walked into the kitchen of her apartment and plugged the kettle in. She opened the curtains to reveal an expanse of clear, blue sky. The sun sparkled off the waters of Vancouver's False Creek.

Still holding the phone, she opened the sliding glass door and stood out on the small deck, breathing in the roasted coffee aroma coming from below. *The Grind* was doing a great trade; all the tables along the sidewalk were taken. In front of the Chinese grocery, the fresh flowers flaunted their bright colours like be-feathered dancers on the Vegas Strip. The day was perfect for sketching the street scene. Soon the tea was steeped and she had her drawing things out on the deck table.

"Jess," she broke in on a monologue about his latest attempt to refine the computer game module he had been designing, "I'm good now. I'm going to sketch for a while. Sorry I bugged you."

"Forget it. I needed a break, anyway. I'll call you later tonight."

❧❧❧❧

The silence in the A-Frame cabin on Crater Lake was charged with tension. Bethany tried to meet Beulah's eyes without flinching. She wanted to run, bolt out the sliding glass door which was open to the afternoon breeze, and keep right on going.

Beulah stood frozen in the middle of a half-turn towards the back door. She stared at Bethany in disbelief. Her mouth opened and closed. She banged the palm of her hand against her forehead as if her brain had gone into a stall and might just be restarted with a sharp smack.

"Let me get this straight," Beulah demanded. Her voice rose as she continued, "Jesus jumped up Christ. I can't believe you have the nerve to break this to me right before I have to go." Beulah's finger jabbed towards Bethany, "Your niece is pregnant, the baby's coming in two bloody weeks and you've known about this since February."

Bethany walked over and sat down on a chair by the table. The way Beulah kept barking out the word *you* made her feel like a bug being pinned to a board. She folded her hands in her lap and willed herself not to cry. The timing of this conversation couldn't be worse; Beulah had that part right.

"I only found out last night that she was coming up today. It wasn't supposed to work out like this. I knew you would be angry with me for keeping it all a secret. Lisa-Marie made me promise I wouldn't say anything. The whole thing has made me feel sick." Bethany pressed her hands to her flaming cheeks.

"You've been stupid before, Beth, but this time you've outdone yourself. I thought I'd heard it all, but this takes the fucking cake."

7

"I guess I deserve that, but stop shouting Beulah. I'm sorry. What more do you want?"

Beulah walked back across the room to put her hands on the table in front of Bethany as she leaned in close, "There is a hell of a lot more I want. You haven't pulled your weight in the bakery for months. You hardly do a thing around here. You can't make the bed or put a decent meal on the table one day out of five. So, ya ... I do want more from you." Beulah stood up straight. With a steely coldness in her blue eyes she stared at Bethany, "No one in her right mind would have kept a sixteen-year-old kid's pregnancy a secret. We're responsible for her. Did you forget about that little fact?"

Bethany rocked back in her chair with the force of Beulah's words. "That isn't fair. You don't know how it was with Lisa-Marie. You have to let me explain."

"You're wrong about that. I don't have to let you explain a damn thing. As far as I'm concerned there are no extenuating circumstances here."

Bethany lost her battle against the tears that now flowed unchecked. She got up from the chair and walked around the table towards Beulah. "I thought you would be happy that things were getting back to normal between us. Last night was good, right?" She reached out to touch Beulah's arm.

Beulah shook Bethany's hand off, "Don't do me any favours. I've learned to get along without your help in the bakery and in other places, too."

Bethany stiffened at the last remark and turned away, stumbling against the edge of the coffee table before she managed to collapse onto the couch. As she raised her eyes, tears clouded her sight, "I bet you wish I had died on the beach last year ... that you and Liam hadn't tried so hard to bring me back."

Beulah ignored any attempt to elicit her sympathy. "I could never wish for someone to be dead ... not after Caleb. But I'll tell you one thing, the way I feel right now, I wish I had never gone into that Fields store the night I met you or ever brought you out here. Now you drop this sobbing, poor-little-me-act and get over to Izzy and Liam's and tell them what the hell is going on before Lisa-Marie arrives on their doorstep. Because that's where I'll be taking her."

Shock stopped Bethany's sobs. "Oh God, no ... you have to come over there with me. I can't face them all by myself. And you can't just go there with Lisa-Marie. What will they think?"

"What do you suggest? Wait until she has the baby and then tell them? She has to face them the same as you do." Beulah grabbed her keys and headed for the door.

TWO

THE PREVIOUS OCTOBER

Bethany came awake in a hospital bed with the sound of a crying baby so loud and real in her ears that she shook her head in confusion. She raised herself half off the bed to look around the room.

"Slow down there, Beth. Take it easy." Dr. Rosemary Maxwell leaned over to touch Bethany's shoulder. She flipped open the chart in her hand and studied it before pulling up a chair beside the bed. "Beulah's over at the coffee shop. How are you feeling?"

Bethany's hand went to the painful lump on her forehead. "What happened, Rosemary? I remember falling out of the boat. What happened? Is Dan okay?"

The doctor reached over to take her pulse, "I'll let Beulah fill you in on all the details. You've had a close call. That bump on your head knocked you out. From what I've heard, if it weren't for Beulah's strong swim and Liam's unshaken determination to stick with the CPR, you might not have made it." She dropped Bethany's wrist back onto the bed with a nod of approval. "You have a slight concussion but, other than that, you're fine."

Beulah came into the room carrying a coffee. Rosemary nodded at her and went on, "I'll leave you two to catch up. I'm going to keep you here one more night, Beth, but you'll be as right as rain to leave tomorrow."

Beulah sat down in the chair next to the bed and reached for Bethany's hand. "Jesus Christ, Beth ... you gave me a scare."

"Tell me what happened; all I remember is falling out of the boat. What happened to Dan?" Bethany shook her head, "No wait, Beulah ... wait ... I had this dream. It was so real. I could hear a baby crying and crying. I was trying to get to the baby to help, but I couldn't find it." Bethany looked around the room, her eyes wide and frantic.

Beulah put her coffee down on the hospital tray and leaned over the bed. "Beth, lie down. We'll talk about everything later."

Bethany rested back against the pillow and clutched at Beulah's hand. Her eyes closed as she murmured, "It was so real ... the baby crying ... so real."

Beulah sipped her coffee and watched as Bethany drifted into a fitful sleep. As if the shock of her partner's near drowning hadn't been enough, Beulah now struggled to make sense of the brief phone conversation she'd just had with Izzy. Beulah had asked Izzy the same question about Dan that Bethany had asked from her hospital bed. It seemed Dan was fine and long gone on the early bus out of Dearborn. He had caused the boat accident when he had tried to kiss Bethany. She'd pushed him away with a force that had knocked him right out of the boat. Bethany had tried to help him but she'd fallen into the water, as well. The boat had tipped over in the rising waves and something heavy had smacked Bethany in the head, knocking her out.

It was all Beulah could do to stop herself from blurting into the phone that, if this was Izzy's idea of a joke, her timing stunk. She found it almost impossible to believe that Dan could have harboured that type of feeling for Bethany. Surely he couldn't have been so addled by passion that he would try to make sexual advances to someone in a rowboat.

Beulah had befriended Dan without hesitation; everyone at Crater Lake had taken to the man who rented Izzy's guest cabin. He had dropped over to the A-Frame several times a week – usually when dinner was being served. He and Beulah had watched ball games and had drunk beer together. She had never had second thoughts about Dan and Bethany fishing together. The man was a priest, for God's sake. How could she have been so wrong about the guy?

※ ※ ※ ※

The sound of Bethany's voice forced Beulah to glance across the table of the A-Frame to confront the faraway, vacant expression on her partner's face. It had been three weeks since the accident.

"I've been thinking a lot about the baby I gave up for adoption years ago." Bethany stared at her hands as she spoke, "Remember how I told you I woke up in the hospital hearing a baby crying?" Her eyes fluttered up to search Beulah's face, "I dreamt about it for a couple of nights. It seemed so real."

Beulah had to admit that her expectation of life returning to anything that looked like normal was getting fainter with each passing day. In addition to the crazy talk, Bethany refused to be alone in the A-Frame. She and Beulah had spent their mornings as they always had, working together in the organic bakery just behind the cabin. In the afternoons, Bethany got into the habit of either walking over to nearby Micah Camp to hang out in the kitchen with Cook, or tagging along with Beulah to Dearborn for the bread deliveries. Beulah would drop her off at the library where she occupied herself doing God knows what.

Beulah fiddled with the invoices on the clipboard in front of her and forced her voice to remain in the neutral range. "I'm not sure dwelling on the past is such a great idea."

"I keep thinking there should be more. I feel like I've wasted most of my life."

"Ya, well, thanks for that glowing analysis of our fifteen years together." Beulah knocked back the last of her coffee.

"There are so many things I've never done." Bethany's voice choked with emotion as she looked up at Beulah, "I want us to have a baby."

Beulah barked out a sharp laugh. "Good luck with that."

The flush in Bethany's cheeks deepened, "Don't laugh at me, I'm serious."

"Considering that I'm your partner, I find that hard to believe."

"I've been looking into it – googling things. Lots of same-sex couples have kids together."

"Is that the kind of stuff you waste your time on at the library? It would be better if you stayed home and made the bed now and then." Beulah held up her hand before Bethany could protest. "I know I've told you that I understand how you don't want to be alone here, but come on. This is ridiculous."

Beulah switched gears, "What does your research say about how to pull something like this off? I'm sure immaculate conception isn't on the table. I'll tell you flat out, I'm not into a threesome if one of the three is a guy."

"There's no need to be crude. We could get a sperm donor. There are all kinds of instructions on the internet for doing it yourself."

"Enough, already, I don't believe you're sitting there suggesting this like you're saying we should get a new couch or something." Beulah slammed a hand down on the table, "Don't go into that whole baby-I-gave-up-is-crying thing again. Do you think a few dreams can justify this kind of talk? You're going to be forty this year. That's too old for you to have a baby and I'm sure

11

as hell too old to raise a child. Even if we were younger ... a sperm donor ... like who? Do sperm donors advertise on the internet, too? And how do you get the donation?"

She sat back in her chair and crossed her arms over her chest, "Do you have any idea how much it costs to raise a kid and how much of a major pain-in-the-ass kids are at every single stage of their friggin' lives? We're already saddled with Lisa-Marie. Paying for her to board down south for high school is expensive enough. I bet she's going to want to go to university. We'll be saddled with that bill, too."

"But I don't care about any of that. I want something else in my life. I want to have a baby." Tears washed down Bethany's face.

"Forget it. If you wanted to have a baby, you should have thought about that before you decided to sleep with me. You probably wouldn't even be able to get pregnant."

Bethany got up from the table and sniffed loudly as she cleared the dishes. With the kitchen counter between them, she added, "I bet I could get pregnant. My periods are regular and I always know exactly when I ovulate."

Beulah stuffed the invoices into her battered, brown briefcase and pulled her glasses off to point them at Bethany. She wanted to tell her to make an appointment with the doctor because the concussion must have scrambled her brains. Instead she shook her head, grabbed her things and walked out of the cabin. There was no point in arguing with a lunatic.

THREE

THE LAST WEEK OF APRIL

Izzy came around the corner of the orchard path and saw Liam sitting in a chair on the deck that hugged the front of their large, cedar-shake cabin. He was enjoying the spring sunshine and the expansive view of Crater Lake that stretched before him. A plate of sandwiches and two mugs of coffee sat on the nearby table. Daffodils, in a planter that ran the length of the deck, were in full bloom, clustered together in bursts of bright yellow.

Dante, Izzy's Irish Setter, and Pearl, Liam's Golden Retriever, jumped up to greet her. She reached down to pet each one of them in turn before she sat down beside Liam. "Where's my dad? Isn't he joining us?"

"He said he ate earlier. Last I saw of him, he was out on the sun porch up to his ears in photos and pages from his book. I left him to it."

Liam shrugged as Izzy reached over to lift a corner of bread on the nearest sandwich. He told her, "It's just chicken salad." Izzy picked up the sandwich and had a closer look, as he continued, "With new lettuce from the greenhouse and fresh chives."

She took a large bite and dedicated herself to chewing. Finally, she smiled at Liam, "Delicious. I think this might be why I keep you around."

"No doubt it is; I am a man of many talents. By the way, I heard back from Cynthia St. Pierre today"

"The author ... did she say yes?"

"She's confirmed for the entire six months with an option for more. It'll be strange to see someone staying over at the guest cabin again."

"She can't possibly turn out to be worse than the last renter we had."

The pained look on Liam's face showed he agreed. The memory of the way things had turned out with the Reverend Daniel Patterson wasn't one he was keen to recall. "Let's steer clear of priests in the future. Ms. St. Pierre will arrive in the first week of June. I've ordered a couple of her books from the library."

"Murder mysteries, right?"

"I thought maybe we could do a book club night with one of her books. Her bio says she was a nurse before she turned to a writing career. All her novels are set in hospitals."

After eating half a sandwich, Liam pushed his chair back and drank his coffee. He watched Izzy polish off everything left on the plate. He couldn't get enough of looking at her, even though they had been living together for months. When she finally sat back and cradled her coffee cup in her hands, he asked, "How was work?"

Her eyes were on the white caps that marched down the center of the lake. "I had two back-to-back intake sessions this morning; they always take longer than I think they will."

"Have all the new residents arrived?"

She relaxed in the chair and stretched her legs out in front of her. "Yes. Looks like one of the guys will want to do work experience in the kitchen. That would be a convenient placement, with Cook down to only two days a week. And who knows if Jillian would be willing to pick up the slack?"

Liam took his cue and asked, "How is Jillian?"

"She's grating, as usual. I heard her complaining to Roland about Cook's old cabin. She thinks it's too small to be a combined research office and living space." Izzy rolled her eyes and changed the subject, "Cook seems happy with the retirement complex in Dearborn. Maybe we'll have to start calling her Elsie now that she's semi-retired." They both shook their heads in unison; no one was ever going to call Cook anything but Cook.

Izzy's eyes sparkling with sudden humour, "You won't believe what Jillian did to Roland this morning, right in front of everyone. She brought him a cup of coffee and he took it from her and started walking over to the fridge. She asked – *What are you doing, Roland?* He told her he was going to get some cream for his coffee, and she said – *You don't need any cream* – in exactly that tone – *you don't need any cream, Roland.*"

Liam frowned, "What did he do?"

"Drank his coffee black."

"Do you still think there's something going on between them?"

"I'm not sure why he would let her tell him what to do if there weren't. But he's always professional around her. Roland takes seriously his role as Director of Micah Camp." Izzy frowned, "I do find Jillian grating, but one-on-one, when she talks about her research, she's quite fascinating. Some of her initial conclusions on resiliency factors, based on these concept maps she gets the residents to make, are brilliant. Her research could make a difference, and you can't say that about a lot of PhD work."

Liam moved his chair closer so he could reach out and hold Izzy's hand. His eyes rested on the brown of his skin against the lighter shade of hers. He remembered the night out on the cliff deck when he had first held Izzy's hand – the night after Bethany had almost drowned. He would never forget the moment on the beach when he knew that Izzy thought Bethany wouldn't make it. The words he had spoken then had become a mantra for him – *we don't give up on each other anymore.*

Izzy's words broke through Liam's memories, "I ran into Reg this morning. He was meeting Josie for coffee at the Camp. Are you feeling okay with some of the changes he's made up at the sawmill?"

Liam slouched back into his chair with a deep sigh. When he spoke, his voice was as lazy as his posture. "I couldn't be happier. We both know the job never suited me; seeing how Reg is running things, like a military operation, really brings that truth home. I have no ego problem with hanging out here, looking after a few chickens and being your gardener, Izz. It's one step away from being a kept man, but what the hell."

Izzy grinned, "Speaking of work, your old cabin is all spiffed up for Justin. The job at the sawmill is going to be perfect for him. If he's interested in forestry, the next four months will give him a chance to see what he's getting himself into. I hope ...," Izzy's voice faded away.

Even without words, he understood. "Are you worried about how things were with him last summer?"

Liam was being tactful and they both knew it. Justin had fallen for Izzy and she had let him go right ahead and fall. It had been an unprofessional ego indulgence that still made her cringe. She would never have allowed the situation to go any further, but still ... she had been his counsellor and later, his boss. She should have put a stop to his infatuation.

Izzy shook off the memories of the past, "He called me to ask for a job. He didn't sound resentful on the phone. Maybe kind of desperate after the job he had lined up fell through at the last minute. He was glad we had something for him. He needs to make some money over the school break. Nothing is the way it was last summer. Reg is going to keep him busy. And there's the reality of you and me being together."

Liam nodded his agreement, "Justin's a damn good worker. We're lucky to have him. I'll get him out in the old Dodge right away to practice for his driver's test. If I know Reg, he'll want the kid to have his license, like yesterday."

"That reminds me, we have to start thinking about buying a new truck. That Dodge was old, ten years ago. It has now passed into another realm."

Izzy immediately regretted such an offhand remark as she watched sadness flicker across the face of the man she had fallen in love with. Liam would want to drive Caleb's old Dodge forever if he could. Caleb's friendship had changed Liam's life. She knew that. Caleb's death, almost three years ago now, was still as painful for Liam as it was for her – a best friend and a wife left to find consolation where they could. It wasn't surprising they had turned to one another. She let the subject drop and reached out for his hand.

Liam leaned over to put his coffee cup on the table. "Are you going back to the Camp this afternoon?"

"I probably should. I have a ton of paperwork."

His mouth twitched at the corners as he let his gaze sweep over her, "That is too bad. A long and lazy afternoon is just about the best time for a kept man to earn his due."

That look made Izzy feel warmer than the April sunshine warranted. She thought she might drag him to the bedroom right that second. But as she smiled into his dark eyes, his gaze shifted across the deck to the tree-lined pathway. Izzy turned and saw Bethany coming towards them.

✂✂✂✂

Roland walked into the skills lab where the four new residents were awaiting his appearance. He placed a pile of handouts on a chair near the white board. Grabbing a black marker from the board's ledge, he wrote in block letters – MICAH CAMP'S RESIDENT CONTRACT. He flipped open the file in his hand and said, "Take a seat, let's get started."

The skills lab was one of the few rooms in the Camp's main building that didn't have a window. The architects had compensated by placing three large skylights in the ceiling. Light spilled into the room, drawing stretched, oblong patterns on the carpeted floor. From where he stood, Roland could see through one of the skylights to the dark evergreens marching up the slope of a distant mountain.

He studied the open file in his hand. Comfortable in his knowledge of clinical psychology, Roland tended to think of the residents in terms of diagnostic shorthand. Mark Jonavich clicked a pen in his hand as his body twitched about on the chair he sat in. Obsessive-compulsive, Roland told himself. Willow Donaldson chewed on the side of her thumb in a rodent-like manner that turned his stomach. Clearly, she had an anxiety disorder. Dylan Sullivan was a typical jock. The young man took up a lot of space with his long legs stretched out in front of his chair and his muscular arms folded over his chest. He looked like a good candidate for oppositional-defiant disorder. Then there was Arianna Delaford. Roland watched as Arianna chatted with Mark, shoved Dylan on the arm playfully, pulled up a chair beside Willow and turned her cheerful gaze to him. He wondered if being overly friendly in such a setting could be an indication of a delusionary personality type.

"We are here to review the basics of the resident contract –" Mark's hand shot up in the air, "Yes, Mr. Jonavich?"

"Is there a handout? I won't be able to understand what you're saying without a handout."

"All in good time. Now, as I was saying," with a pointed stare, Roland forestalled Mark's hand from shooting up again. "It's important for you to understand the responsibilities you take on when you become part of this program. Once you sign the contract it will become the reference for guiding your actions while you are here at Micah Camp."

Roland handed out copies of the contract, "Pair up, please. Ms. Delaford, you sit with Mr. Jonavich, here," he pointed to one corner of the room. "Mr. Sullivan, you and Ms. Donaldson, over there." When the four residents had regrouped themselves, Roland continued, "Read over the contract with your partner and come up with a list of questions for discussion. I will return in exactly twenty minutes."

Roland walked out without a backwards glance. He passed through the living room area with its massive stone fireplace and large windows facing the view of Crater Lake. He carried on under the vaulted ceiling of the spacious foyer and pushed opened the double glass doors that led to his office. Jillian was at his desk, leaning back in his chair and talking on his phone.

She ended her call and jumped up, "I'm sorry, babe. I know you asked me not to use your phone but I can't seem to find a place where I can make a private call."

"The office next door is empty." Roland slid past Jillian, picked up her papers from his desk and handed them over to her.

"That office is dinky. You don't have that perfect view of the lake that Izzy's office has, but this is nice." Jillian pointed out the large window that faced the circle drive in front of the building. The spring bulbs were in full bloom, splashing colour across the flower beds. The sun cast jagged patterns of light through the tall evergreens at the far side of the drive.

"Call me Roland when we're at work. We've discussed this before."

"We're alone in here, babe ... in case you hadn't noticed."

"I don't want you to get into a habit of being overly familiar. It wouldn't be appropriate if people knew that we were intimate. I say this more for your sake than mine."

Jillian took a moment to straighten Roland's suit jacket, brushing the shoulders flat and adjusting the way the fabric fell in the front. She sat down in the chair across from his desk. "So, Mr. Campbell, what is on your agenda this afternoon?"

"I've got about fifteen minutes before I have to instill a decent level of respect in the minds of our four new guests for their resident contracts."

"Sounds better than what I'll be doing. I was on the phone with my supervisor at the university. He's on my back again about the methodology chapter of my dissertation. I just want to do the research. I'm not sure why I have to keep explaining how I'm doing it." Jillian slumped in her chair, a look of pained forbearance on her face.

Roland had little sympathy for her. It hadn't taken him long to conclude that she was a rule breaker who did whatever the hell she wanted to do with no regard for established practices. As far as he was concerned, she was her own worst enemy.

Having to deal with both Izzy and Jillian on a daily basis caused Roland to wonder how he managed to escape cowering about the Camp like a beaten-down dog. He knew what his father would have called the pair of them in a bygone era of political incorrectness – a couple of real ballbreakers. Izzy paid mere lip service to the fact that he was the Director of Micah Camp, theoretically her boss. She consistently refused his counsel. And Jillian was about as high-handed as a woman could be and still lay claim to the title.

The previous fall, Roland had received Jillian's letter expressing her interest in Micah Camp as a research site. She had explained that her dissertation was focused on how youth in care transitioned beyond high school to the next phase of their lives. Her proposal claimed that Micah Camp would be an ideal site because so many of the young people who left the place moved on to successful careers. It was a chance to study a program that was getting it right. Roland had taken her request to the Board and they had approved.

On the afternoon of Christmas Eve, Roland had been sipping from a well-deserved glass of Cabernet Sauvignon, enjoying a peace and quiet that his on-site living conditions at Micah Camp seldom offered him. He jolted out of his easy chair at the sound of a loud knock on his cabin door. He swore as he blotted at the red wine stain spreading relentlessly over the leg of his new trousers.

He walked across the room and wrenched open the door to be greeted by a tall woman in a bulky coat. Her face was framed with a wind-swept tangle of wildly disarrayed, black hair. She had stomped her feet to remove the snow from her heavy boots and smiled, her dark blue eyes crinkling beneath thick, black lashes. "Whew, you're a welcome sight. I was banging on the door of the big building for a while before it occurred to me that people might not be here at Christmas." She had thrust her hand out to him, "I'm Jillian Matthews, the researcher from the University of Victoria. I decided to come up a few days early. You must be Roland." Spotting the stain on his pants, she added, "Quick, let's get some club soda on that." She had cocked her head to one side as she entered the cabin, "Do you actually enjoy classical music? I can't say I've ever developed a taste for it."

Roland had assumed Jillian would be younger; he hadn't expected a woman his own age to be still pursuing her education. He had imagined himself giving sage supervisory advice to a young and dewy-eyed student. That was not to be the case. In the four months since her arrival, Jillian Matthews had done whatever she pleased. As a complement to her research, she was happy to have a part-time job working in the kitchen. She had taken up residence in the cabin left vacant by Cook and had thus solved the ongoing problem of needing two adults on-site every night. But it wasn't just the Camp that Jillian had infiltrated. Roland had to admit that the woman had swept into his life with the crushing weight of a tsunami, and he still hadn't managed to claw his way to higher ground.

As he came back into the skills lab, Roland saw the four residents sitting in a tight circle near the white board. Arianna was finalizing their list of five questions in a neat, bullet format. Roland's eyes scanned the list while he mentally answered the first four questions. No alcohol or recreational drug use meant just that. There were no exceptions to the parts of the contract that defined the resident's responsibilities – educational upgrading, counselling, work experience, and involvement with fund raisers. Leaving the Camp was permitted, under certain circumstances and with permission. There would be no negotiation in relation to cabin assignments. The fifth question was the one that he wished would not come up, though it always did. *What is meant by the words, sexual relationships between residents are strongly discouraged?* He had told Izzy a dozen times that this part of the contract should be reworded to eliminate choice. But she was adamant that a hard-and-fast rule would cause more problems than it would solve. He wished she were in here explaining the nuances of the words *strongly discouraged*.

Roland elaborated on the answers to each of the first four questions; then he stopped to collect his thoughts. Arianna, having taken on the role of spokesperson, raised her hand and Roland nodded at her to speak, "Some of us –"

"Moron," Dylan muttered the word as he glared over at Mark. He then slumped down in his chair and stared at the floor.

Arianna said, "It's a bit confusing ... like ... is it allowed or not?" She looked over at Mark whose arm was up in the air. She nodded her head as if to say alright, before continuing, "And if it's not allowed, why does the contract say that condoms are available in the washrooms on the upper floor?"

Roland looked over the heads of the residents to a point on the far wall as he spoke. "Most of you are nineteen – legally you are adults. Our purpose here is not to dictate your personal lives. As a general rule, sexual relations between residents cause problems; they are unnecessary distractions. Most residents appreciate that. Your time here is short. I would urge you to take full advantage of the opportunities being offered to you at Micah Camp and to allow nothing to get in the way of what you are here to accomplish." Before Mark could get his arm up, Roland looked over at him and added, "You have been informed as to where to obtain a condom, Mr. Jonavich, in the interest of harm reduction. Is that clear?" Mark gave a satisfied nod. Arianna and Willow burst into giggles. Dylan got up and scrawled his signature on the bottom of his contract. He handed it to Roland and walked out of the room.

❧❧❧❧

"Hi, Beth." Izzy's easy smile turned to a look of startled concern, "Are you okay? You'd better sit; you look as white as a ghost."

Bethany sat down, her eyes jumping from Liam to Izzy and down to the cedar boards of the deck. She clutched her hands tightly in her lap to keep them from shaking.

"What is it, Beth?" Anxiety edged Liam's voice.

Tears brimmed in her eyes as she said, "I need to tell you guys something." She took a deep, ragged breath and stared at the flower bed of dancing daffodils. She forced herself to speak, "Lisa-Marie is coming up on the bus this afternoon with Justin."

Izzy and Liam exchanged puzzled glances. It was only the end of April; school wasn't out for another six weeks. Why would Lisa-Marie be coming home now? Something must be wrong.

Bethany turned to look at Liam as the words tumbled from her mouth, "I'm so sorry. I should have told you guys before. She's pregnant, Liam. She's pregnant from that night with you last summer. I'm so sorry."

Izzy sat up straight, her eyes wide. She watched the emotions race across Liam's face – disbelief, panic, and finally a look of shock that made his skin turn a sickly shade. He sprang out of his chair which tipped over behind him and skittered across the deck. He managed to reach the railing where he leaned over and spewed his lunch into the flower bed below.

Izzy stood up, confused about which way to turn. Liam leaned against the railing holding his stomach. The sound of Bethany's sobs filled the space between them. Liam settled the matter when he held up a hand to ward Izzy off as he turned and walked across the deck towards the cabin.

FOUR

THE PREVIOUS NOVEMBER

"**I**'m thinking about asking Liam to be the baby's father."

A heavy rain lashed against the exposed front of the A-Frame. The noise carried through the cabin to the back bedroom. Bethany lay close to Beulah, cuddled inside the crook of her arm. The sound of the nearby waterfall dropping to the stream below, roared through the closed window. Rushing waters surrounded them.

Beulah had been floating in a relaxed state, relieved that Bethany wanted to be available in the bedroom again. Six weeks since the accident had been a long time. She stiffened and withdrew her arm. "You want to have Liam's baby? You are nuts, this proves it. What do you think Izzy will say?"

"Of course, Izzy would have to agree. But think about it for a second. It's the perfect solution. The child would be connected to all of us – one family. Izzy's not going to give Liam a baby. She's older than I am. This could be his one chance to have a child."

Beulah got up and sat on the edge of the bed with her hands pressed flat to her thighs. She looked back over her shoulder, "There is nothing perfect about this idea. What makes you think for one friggin' second that he would want any part of this; or that Izzy and Liam would want to help raise a child? I told you to forget this crazy idea, and I meant it."

"I'm not going to forget it, and I mean that. You don't have the right to tell me what to do." Bethany clutched a pillow to her body and glared at Beulah.

Beulah pulled on her jeans and grabbed a shirt from the chair in the corner, her movements quick and jerking. "Drop it. If you don't like the life you have here, you know the way to town." Beulah left the bedroom, crossed the cabin to the back door and walked out to the bakery.

⁕⁕⁕⁕

Beulah threw a log on the fire that roared in the A-Frame's stove. The rain had stopped but the temperature had fallen. She'd seen frost on the back steps that morning. She sat down on the couch and looked towards the recliner where Bethany had curled up to read a book. "How long is this going to go on?"

It had been a week since Beulah had stormed out of the bedroom. Since that night, she had not been welcome to return. Bethany had not spoken to her. She had not appeared in the bakery, nor had she lifted a single finger anywhere else. The cabin was a disaster zone. Beulah was run ragged from handling the baking every morning and the bread deliveries every afternoon.

Bethany set her book down on the table and took her time answering. "I'm trying to get you to take me seriously."

"Acting like this is hardly the way to go about it."

"I could leave you." Bethany hated that no matter what she said or did, Beulah could find a way to make her feel stupid.

"Where would you go?"

"I don't care ... I don't know ... it doesn't matter. You never listen to anything I say. You're making fun of me, as usual. I'm a lost cause, right? Couldn't look after myself if my life depended on it, right?" She drew in a ragged breath, "Too incompetent to make a decision about anything. That's me, right? What was it you called me? Your lesbian lover by default; I'm too scared to be with a man and too scared to be alone. I don't measure up to your standards in any way, do I?"

Beulah shook her head and slumped further down on the sofa. Here it comes, she thought, guilt trip number whatever, she'd lost count. "What's the point of dragging all of that out?" Looking up towards the ceiling, she massaged her temples. "When I thought you were gone, that day on the beach, I didn't know how I could stand it. Now it seems as though you're losing your mind and dragging us both down. It's as if my whole life drowned in the lake that day, even if you didn't."

Bethany rose from the recliner, knelt down on the floor and gripped Beulah's hands. "If you don't want to lose me, then care about me enough to listen. Tell me you'll think about the idea of our having a baby. We could make this work. A baby would be good for us."

Bethany sat in the passenger seat of the truck and kept her eyes straight ahead, "I left you alone to think about things."

Beulah's grip on the steering wheel tightened. She glanced at Bethany before returning her eyes to the twisting road out of Dearborn. "A week to think about something that would change both our lives forever, your generosity overwhelms me."

Beulah's mind raced in every direction. Bethany was almost forty years old. What were the chances she could actually get pregnant? The odds must be stacked against her. Beulah wondered about the success rate of something as unnatural as do-it-yourself insemination. It couldn't be high. Would Bethany actually go through with talking to Liam about her crazy idea? The thought of that conversation was so damn uncomfortable, Beulah could hardly consider it. If Bethany did manage to ask for Liam's help, he and Izzy were bound to say no. Why should they want to raise a child? Surely they would feel the same way Beulah felt about the idea. Even if they did agree, Liam could be shooting duds for all anyone knew. The odds that this crazy idea would end up producing a baby were slim-to-nil. Why should Beulah be the bad guy?

As she maneuvered the truck around the tight corner, off the pavement and onto the narrow gravel road that led out to Crater Lake, Beulah looked over at Bethany and shrugged. With her eyes back on the road she said, "If this is what you want, I can't stop you. I don't have the kind of control over you that you think I do. The whole thing could be one big disappointment. Liam and Izzy might say no and, even if they do agree, you might not get pregnant. You realize all of that, right?"

"I know all those things, Beulah; I know it's a long-shot."

FIVE

THE LAST WEEK OF APRIL

"Try to calm down, Beth." Izzy reached out to take Bethany's hands in her own.

Bethany choked back a sob as she said, "Lisa-Marie made me promise I wouldn't say anything. She was so sure she wanted to stay in Victoria, have the baby there and give it up for adoption. She said she didn't want you guys to know. She kept saying she would take care of it. I didn't know what to do."

Izzy held her hands over Bethany's and tried to make her sympathetic nod seem convincing. What she really felt like doing was yelling at her friend, the way she was sure Beulah must have done. How could Bethany have hidden this from them? She kept her voice neutral as she asked, "What changed her mind, do you think? If she didn't want us to know, why is she coming here now?"

"All she told me on the phone was that she would be here today with Justin. I couldn't believe it." Bethany struggled to hold back a fresh onslaught of tears. She pulled a tissue from her pocket and blew her nose. Sitting up a bit straighter, she said, "Beulah is so angry at me. We had a huge fight when I told her. She said she's dropping Lisa-Marie off here to talk to you and Liam. I know I've made a mess of everything. I couldn't figure out how to tell Beulah, then I blurted it out just when she was about to leave."

Izzy's eyes widened in disbelief, "Oh, Beth."

"Things haven't been great between us, and now I don't know if she'll even come back to the A-Frame. And if she does ... well ... you know how Beulah is. She's going to be ranting and raving about how stupid I am. I don't know how I can face that with Lisa-Marie there. And the baby is due so soon." A look of panic crept into Bethany's eyes, "It's all such a mess. I can't even think straight."

Izzy frowned. Something wasn't right about Bethany's inability to grasp the true gravity of the situation. What they were all facing was a hell of a lot more serious than one of Beulah's temper tantrums. Someone had to step up to the plate and take responsibility for a pregnant teenager and her soon-to-be-born baby.

She made the type of quick decision that was the hallmark of her personality. "Lisa-Marie could stay here with us. We have lots of room. Liam is going to have to adjust, but we might as well all face the problem head-on." She got up and put her arm around Bethany's shoulder, "Why don't you go back to the A-Frame and have a rest. Try to relax. I'm sure Beulah is going to come home and maybe you can talk things out when she does."

Bethany stared down at the cedar deck, "I've botched-up everything. It breaks my heart to see Liam like that."

Izzy glanced towards the door of the cabin. She could only guess at the tangle of Liam's emotions. After the initial shockwave, they had never spoken about what had happened between him and Lisa-Marie. Izzy assumed Liam had put the ghost of it to rest, as she had. Well, that ghost was out of the closet and rattling up a storm now.

After Bethany left, Izzy studied the early afternoon sun as it sparkled over the rippling lake. A stellar jay perched on the edge of the railing and preened its midnight blue feathers, eyeing her without concern. She shook her head at the bird's boldness and wondered how she was going to feel when she saw Lisa-Marie carrying the evidence of that one night with Liam, the man that she herself now loved so completely.

❧❧❧❧❧

Liam walked through the cabin and past Izzy's father as if he weren't there. He continued out the back door, through the garden and beyond. He passed the guest cabin, walked down the hill and crossed over the bridge to his old place. It was as clean and tidy as Izzy had claimed. He climbed the stairs to the loft and stood at the foot of the bed.

It had been a hot August night last summer when Lisa-Marie had come up the loft stairs and taken off her clothes in front of him. Liam had been in love with Izzy and he had wanted it to be her coming to him. He had stared at Lisa-Marie with lust, confusion and sympathy, all mixed together in a transparent and pathetic mess of emotion. He hadn't been able to reject her

26

so he convinced himself that making love to her was the best he could do under the circumstances. Later, he had examined his behaviour from every possible angle, including what Izzy would think. The situation had been complicated. Lisa-Marie's emotional state was a factor he hadn't been able to ignore. But in the end, he had been honest enough with himself to see past the paradox. What he had done had been wrong. Hindsight is always twenty-twenty.

Liam checked Caleb's gold watch on his wrist; despite the removal of two links by Izzy's jeweller, the band was still loose. Any minute now the bus would be arriving in Dearborn and Beulah would be on her way back to Crater Lake with Justin and Lisa-Marie. Liam didn't know when the moment of confrontation might come, but come it would and there wasn't a thing he could do to avoid it. He was like a deer standing on the highway, blinded by the headlights of an oncoming transport truck. All he could do was wait to be flattened by the impact.

※ ※ ※ ※

Justin felt the bus slow down to make the turn off the highway. They would be in Dearborn in a few minutes. He nudged Lisa-Marie. The time she hadn't used to eat or run to the bathroom, she had spent dozing against his shoulder. He'd had little else to do but think about her condition. What the hell could have happened? He kept asking himself that question as he studied the dark smudges under her closed eyes. If the baby wasn't due until the end of June, Lisa-Marie got pregnant soon after the school year started. Why didn't she do something smart – like make sure the guy used a condom or, failing that common sense measure, have an abortion?

Lisa-Marie came awake slowly and smiled up at Justin. She couldn't believe he was right beside her. She hadn't slept so well in ages. The bus pulled up in front of the Dearborn Hotel. She had a distinct sense of déjà vu as she stepped off to see Beulah leaning against her truck at the side of the parking lot. It was last summer all over again.

Beulah pushed herself away from the truck to help Justin with the bags. She glanced sideways at Lisa-Marie and narrowed her eyes. Pulling a five-dollar bill from her wallet, she handed it to Justin, "Run across the way and pick me up a jug of milk, will you?"

As Justin crossed the street, Beulah grabbed Lisa-Marie's arm and dragged her over to the far side of the truck. "What the hell did you think you were doing, making your aunt keep this whole thing a secret? Has pregnancy addled your brain or something?"

27

Lisa-Marie tried to shake off Beulah's hand, "I thought it was the best thing to do. I didn't want anyone to know."

"Then what the hell are you doing here?" Beulah's eyes drilled into hers, demanding an explanation.

"I changed my mind." Lisa-Marie looked away, her thin veil of bravado almost in shreds.

"You changed your mind?" Beulah ran her free hand through her spiky, grey hair and barked out, "Do you have any idea what showing up like this will do to Liam and Izzy?"

Lisa-Marie glanced across the road to see if Justin was in sight. "Give me a break. I couldn't have the baby all on my own. I got scared." She tried to get past Beulah to stand in front of the truck where Justin could see her, but Beulah still had hold of her arm.

"You're going straight to Izzy's and you're going to explain to her and Liam why you're here. Got it?"

"No, no, no," Lisa-Marie shook her head wildly. "Let go of my arm. You can't force me to go there and talk to them all by myself."

Beulah dropped the girl's arm and shook her head, "Oh, you won't be on your own. I'll be right there making sure you get the job done. Izzy and Liam have a right to know what your plans are. No use delaying the inevitable. Not another word about it." Justin had crossed the street and was heading for the truck. "Do you want to carry on this conversation in front of him?" Lisa-Marie shook her head and moved toward the passenger door.

The drive out to the lake was marked by a heavy silence. When the truck came to a halt at the bottom of Izzy's driveway, Justin hopped out and grabbed his bag from the back. He turned to see Lisa-Marie standing beside him. Beulah was out of the truck and waiting.

"What's going on, Leez? I thought you'd be going over to the A-Frame."

Lisa-Marie felt her face turn hot-red. At the same time, icy fingers ran up and down her back, making her shiver. Her mouth was dry and she had to clear her throat a couple of times before any words would come out. "I have to go in and talk to Izzy and Liam."

He looked at her with surprise, but smiled all the same, "So do I. Let's go." He headed across the gravel drive, past the greenhouse and towards the door to the cabin.

She stumbled along behind him, trying to keep up, knowing she couldn't do anything but move forward. She could almost feel the weight of Beulah at her back.

"Wait, Justin –"

The sound of Lisa-Marie's voice made Justin turn on the bottom step, in the shadow of the large oak door. She was staring at him. Her eyes darted back and forth in a face that had gone from flushed to white. Her expression reminded him of the way his mother used to look when she was over the edge of sanity. He shivered and shook his head to remove the image.

Lisa-Marie's words rushed out, "I have to tell you something. It's about the baby's father." At that moment the door opened and Liam and Izzy were standing there, side by side at the top of the three stairs. Lisa-Marie continued, "The father is," Justin glanced up at Liam in the exact instant that he heard Lisa-Marie say, "Liam." Everything fell into a nightmare kind of order.

Justin had one of those moments when time slows down. He turned from Liam and saw Lisa-Marie place her hands on her bulging stomach. Tears tracked down her face. His gaze went to Izzy. She was as beautiful as she had been the day she told him that she blamed herself for the boyish way he had fallen in love with her. She didn't see him at all. Her eyes were on Liam, and there was an expression of compassion on her face that made Justin's hand curl into a fist.

Time resumed its normal course and, without awareness of having moved, Justin was up the steps in a single leap. As he drew back his fist, he grabbed at the front of Liam's shirt to pull him away from Izzy. The momentum carried the two men backwards through the door and into the entry. He heard Lisa-Marie screaming, "No, Justin, no, no," and he felt hands pulling at him from behind. He was shaking with anger.

Izzy got in front of him as Beulah continued to hold his arms. Izzy's eyes locked onto his, pleading. "Stop it. That's no way to handle this. I know this is a shock. It is for all of us."

He shook Beulah off and backed away. He had no idea what to do. He was reeling, and he felt like he couldn't catch his breath.

For the second time that day, Izzy wasn't sure which way to turn. Liam was visibly shaken, Lisa-Marie was frighteningly pale, and Justin seemed on the verge of tackling a twelve-kilometer hike back to Dearborn. Beulah simply stood to the side, her arms folded over her chest, her eyes going from Liam to Lisa-Marie.

Izzy pulled Justin out of the cabin and down the steps, "I need to get Lisa-Marie calmed down. Help me out here. Go to Liam's old cabin as we planned. Get settled in. I'll come over soon and we can talk."

"Talk can't make any of this okay."

"What are you going to do? There's no bus out of Dearborn until tomorrow. Take some time to think ... please." The power she had always had over him won out. With one last glance of concern at Lisa-Marie, he headed down the garden path.

Izzy walked into the cabin. Her concern for Liam smashed up against impatience as she noticed him staring at Lisa-Marie as if he had never seen a pregnant girl before. Why was it her job to deal with the emotions of every bloody person in this mess? But if someone didn't do something, it looked as though Lisa-Marie might collapse and, in her state, that couldn't be good.

She turned away from Liam and reached out to put her hand on the young girl's arm, "Lisa, I think you need to lie down. Will you do that?" Lisa-Marie nodded wordlessly. Izzy looked over at Beulah and said, "I'm going to take her upstairs."

Beulah shrugged. She did a silent study of Liam's face before walking out of the cabin and heading for the driveway.

※·※·※·※

Beulah maneuvered the truck down the twisting road to park it at the back of the A-Frame. It was still a novelty to drive right down to the cabin. She had made do with the steep ATV trail for a long time. When Reg took over running the sawmill, he had insisted that she let him use the excavator to push a road through. The job of supplying the wood-burning bakery oven with fuel could be accomplished in less than half an hour a week if Beulah had a proper driveway. Reg was a force to contend with when it came to efficiency, so Beulah had agreed.

She couldn't count the number of times Caleb had begged her to let him build a road down to the A-Frame. But Beulah had been stubborn on the issue. She liked things the way they were. Hauling the bread up the trail was part of a romantic idea she had about the rustic way they ran the bakery. She could still see Caleb rubbing his hand along his jaw and shrugging his shoulders in the face of her bull-headedness. Then he'd smiled that crooked smile of his and she'd know everything was just about as right with her world as it could be. It was going on three years since Caleb had died and she still thought of him every single day.

Beulah jumped out of the truck, a few steps away from her back door, and told herself that romantic ideas were not for a woman who was pushing fifty. She jingled her keys and frowned. She knew she had been harsh with Bethany earlier. It was true that the woman had hit a new mark on the stupidity meter, no doubt about that. At the same time, she did owe Bethany a chance to explain. Things had been better between them lately; she had to give her that.

Beulah walked by the wood-burning oven and past the bakery building.

30

She felt a nagging guilt that had kept constant company with her of late. She had to break things off with Abbey, and she had to do it soon. With Bethany back in their bed the way she had been the previous evening, Beulah admitted what she had known for some time. The affair with Abbey had run its course.

SIX

THE PREVIOUS DECEMBER

B ethany poured the coffee and sat down across from Liam at the kitchen table of the A-Frame. "I want to talk to you about something." She took a deep breath and forced her hands to relax around the coffee cup. "I wonder if you would be willing to do something for me ... for me and Beulah, really."

Frowning slightly, Liam nodded. Please God, don't let there be anything wrong with either of them, he thought. His heart was racing and he tried to take a deep breath. He had just moved in with Izzy. Beulah had finally stopped blaming him for Caleb's death. He was happier than he had ever been in his life. It made perfect sense to him that something would come along to ruin everything.

"I want to have a baby." Bethany paused to take in the look of surprise on Liam's face. "I can't accomplish that on my own or with Beulah's help." She rushed on, "I was thinking that you could be a sperm donor for us." The room was quiet. Bethany realized she was now speaking into stunned silence. She blurted out the last of her prepared speech, "Using a total stranger for a donor is hard. Sperm banks charge a lot of money and there are all kinds of issues that make the process complicated." She forced herself to take a sip of her coffee and swallow before she said, "I know you'll have to talk to Izzy. I know it's a big decision."

❧❧❧❧

Izzy and Liam lingered over dinner. The flickering candles on the table enhanced the beauty of the first snow of the season as it collected on the branches of the trees outside the window. Liam had been unusually quiet through most of the meal. Izzy sipped her tea and studied his face in profile – the high cheekbone that caught the light when he turned his head, the sweep of dark hair against his collar.

Sensing her silent gaze, he looked over at her and said, "Bethany told me today that she wants to have a baby. She would like me to be the father." Seeing Izzy's astonished stare, he quickly added, "She asked me to be a sperm donor."

Later that evening, Izzy cuddled against the warmth of Liam's body in the bed they now shared. The hush in the cabin was broken by the crackling of the fire in the living room stove and the sound of the wind in the trees. Some days she could hardly believe how things were between them. Her love for him was different than what she had felt for Caleb. Already she knew she was essential to Liam's life in a way she had never been in Caleb's. That sense of being necessary had a powerful effect on her. It wasn't that Caleb hadn't loved her. It was more that he had never needed anyone to complete him. He had been the gravitational pull that kept all of them in orbit.

She wrapped her arms around Liam and rubbed her hands over his lower back. She spoke softly against his chest, "Are you ready to talk?" She was still getting used to Liam's need to think things through before talking to her. The moment he had spoken the words about Bethany's request, she had wanted to discuss the situation point by point. But she had let the evening pass, Liam reading a novel while she wrote a couple of letters, a *Van Morrison* CD playing in the background.

"I was stunned by the whole thing. I didn't know what to say."

"Hmmm," Izzy continued to rub small circles into Liam's lower back. "It must have been a shock."

He stretched and let out a soft moan of satisfaction, drawing Izzy closer. "What do you think of her asking me something like this?"

She was quiet in his arms. After a moment, she moved away, pulled herself up in the bed and shoved a pillow behind her back. "Beth nearly died. It's normal for her to be reassessing her life. But as a counsellor, I'd have to say it's too soon after the accident for a decision of this magnitude."

Liam propped himself up beside Izzy. "Go on. You're not only a counsellor. She's our friend."

Izzy nodded thoughtfully and stretched her arms over her head. Liam's eyes went along the clean line of her arm to the spot where her arm pit gave way to the rise of her breast in the sleeveless T-shirt she was wearing.

"If things were different for her, if the timing weren't so questionable, I wouldn't object."

"What?" He reluctantly tore his gaze away from Izzy's curves to look at her face.

She met his stare, her eyes lit by the moonlight coming in through the skylight above their bed, "I'm forty-five. I'm never going to have a baby. I know that. We both have a lot to offer. We could afford to push our love out into the world a bit ... open it up to something more. The baby would already have two moms, but I could be a good aunt and it would be your child, Liam. I would love any child of yours." Izzy sighed before saying, "But it sounds desperate on Bethany's part. I suspect that when some time has gone by, she won't feel the same about wanting a child."

A flurry of snowflakes skittered across the deck of the A-Frame. The backdrop of sky, water and mountains was draped in shades of grey. Liam glanced up at Bethany. He remembered the day he had sat at this table and faced up to Bethany's knowledge of what had happened between him and Lisa-Marie. His gut had twisted with fear until he realized that she wouldn't turn her back on him. She never even considered the possibility. His dark eyes met hers. "I don't want to hurt you, Beth. Your friendship means a lot to me."

Tears gathered thickly under Bethany's lashes. "I know what you're going to say."

"Before you asked me to think about this, I would have said there was nothing I wouldn't do for you or Beulah. I was wrong, though. I'm sorry ... I have to say no."

"I understand. It's okay, don't feel bad."

"Let me explain."

"You don't have to. Beulah said you and Izzy would say no and Beulah's always right."

Liam reached out to cover Bethany's hands with his own. "It would mean a lot to me if you would let me tell you why." Bethany nodded her head without raising her eyes.

"A long time ago - so long ago it seems like another person's life - I drank a lot. One day I passed out on a couch and everyone went out and left me alone in the house. There was a newborn baby sleeping upstairs. A fire started in the baby's room. I got out of the house but the baby didn't. I blamed myself for that child's death for a long, long time. I knew it was eating me up inside, but I spent years feeding the guilt by telling myself I could have saved the baby if only I hadn't been drunk. Izzy helped me let go of that; she made me realize I couldn't know what would have happened if I had been sober that day."

Liam paused to draw a deep breath. He squeezed Bethany's hand in his, "Letting go of the guilt doesn't change the fact that the baby's death made me into a different person."

The tears fell unchecked down Bethany's cheeks. Liam pulled her hands closer to him. "I've never thought about being a father. Not until the other day. Then I realized just how much I am changed. I know I can't make up for what happened by not having a child of my own. It's hard to explain, but I feel like I owe that baby something, a sacrifice of some kind." As Liam's story came to an end a deep silence hung between them.

Liam waited patiently for Bethany to look at him, "I've got nothing against two women raising a child; you would be a fabulous mom, I'm sure of that. You and Beulah would do a great job."

Liam watched the snow-storm pick up strength and turn the sky from shades of grey to steely black, until only the swirling snow provided any light. "I thought about how I'd feel if it was Izzy who wanted to have a baby. I love her with everything in me. For her, I would try to get past all of this. I can't do that for anyone else."

"I understand, Liam. I know how much you love Izzy. I understand what you're saying. Thank you for explaining all of this to me."

Liam got up and walked around the table. Bethany rose and he pulled her into a tight embrace. Please be alright, he thought as he stroked his hand down the back of her head and through her soft hair, warm under his touch.

꙳꙳꙳꙳

Beulah came home to a silent cabin. "Are you here, Beth?" Her words had a strange echo. She felt her stomach twist. There was no way she could relive what had happened in Edmonton when Julie had left her high and dry. If Bethany was gone, Beulah would go after her, she'd bring her back kicking and screaming if she had to. She pushed open the bedroom door and saw the bulge of a body under the blankets. She let out a sigh of relief, "Why are you in bed at this time of the afternoon? Why didn't you say something when I called?"

Bethany raised her head to stare at Beulah. Her face was swollen from crying, "There isn't going to be a baby. Liam said no. I know you agreed only because you were so sure it would never happen. You never took me

35

seriously. You never have. Keep the lunatic quiet, right Beulah?" Tears welled up in Bethany's eyes and she doubled over in the bed, sobbing.

Beulah walked out and closed the door. There was nothing for her to say. Bethany was right and for once they both knew it.

❦❦❦❦

"Beth, what would you think about taking Lisa-Marie to Ontario to visit your mom for Christmas?" Beulah broached this idea while she was washing the dinner dishes. Bethany sat on the sofa flipping through the local newspaper. She had gotten out of bed for dinner but she hadn't eaten much. During the meal she hadn't offered more than a nod or two in response to Beulah's attempts at conversation.

Bethany looked up, "Don't talk crazy. You hate my mom and we never go anywhere."

"I don't hate your mom. For Christ's sake, Beth, I've never even met the woman. Anyway, we have Lisa-Marie to think about now. She must miss her grandmother. This will be their first Christmas apart."

"What about the bakery?"

"We can do a few double orders and let people know we're going to be away."

"Three plane tickets to Kingston wouldn't be cheap."

"Like I said, we have to think of Lisa-Marie."

"You're serious?" Bethany stared at Beulah with a puzzled look on her face.

Beulah looked around the tidied kitchen and gave a satisfied nod as she said, "Have you ever known me to suggest spending a large amount of money if I wasn't serious?"

SEVEN

THE LAST WEEK OF APRIL

Lisa-Marie relaxed on the bed and took in every detail of the loft she had named the sunflower room. The warm-toned, cedar-planked ceiling sloped down over her head. A print of Van Gogh's *Sunflowers* hung on the butter-yellow wall to her right. The soft cotton cover of the duvet was bright with yet more sunflowers.

She closed her eyes and breathed the fresh air that drifted in through the open window. It smelt of the lake. She heard a crow squawking in one of the tall evergreens that rose up behind the cabin. The sound of the chimes in the garden carried on the breeze. She felt comfortable with her legs propped up by the pillows Izzy had scrunched under her knees and calves. A cool cloth that smelled of lavender lay on her forehead, soothing her blinding headache.

The baby kicked and rolled around inside her like a circus tumbler. Sometimes she had trouble breathing. It was like the baby was trying to strangle the air right out of her before she could even give birth to it. Izzy had said she would return soon with tea. Lisa-Marie's thoughts rewound to the last time the two of them had seen each other.

❧❧❧❧

It was well into September and Lisa-Marie was in love with everything about her new life in Victoria. She heard Marlene calling up the stairs to say she had a visitor. She hopped off her bed and bounced down the hallway. The restored Queen Anne home on a thickly tree-lined street was a beautiful place to board. Her spacious bedroom, on the upper floor, overlooked the

37

landscaped yard that backed onto a park where a duck pond was visible in the distance. Marlene and her husband, Ted, owned the house and they were great – content to be interested in her life without being pushy.

Then there was school; the biggest and best surprise so far had been the high school. She had to pinch herself every day to believe she wasn't dreaming. She'd had no idea that school could be fun. Much to her shock, she'd quickly and easily made a bunch of friends. Classes were great and the teachers were nice.

As she rounded the corner, Lisa-Marie expected to see Meghan from drama club, stopping by to wail about the upcoming auditions. She was hard-pressed to hide her shock when she saw Izzy standing at the bottom of the stairs.

She recalled the wave of anger that had followed her surprise. Her face flushed and she felt her skin go clammy. "Give me a minute," she said. Turning back, she walked to her room and grabbed a parcel from the top shelf of her closet.

Izzy was waiting for her in Marlene's downstairs office. The huge Gary Oaks that lined the driveway shaded the room with dappled light. Lisa-Marie clutched the parcel to her chest as she closed the door. She glared at Izzy who was as gorgeous as usual. The hem of her dress brushed the top of a pair of stylish leather boots that Lisa-Marie would have killed to own. "What are you doing here?" she asked.

Izzy pushed away from the roll-top desk she had been leaning against. "I saw the letter you wrote to Liam. I need you to tell me what happened between the two of you. What did you mean when you wrote – *don't worry about the sex?*" She pushed a strand of her dark hair away from her face and met Lisa-Marie's eyes.

"Isn't reading other people's mail against the law or something?"

"It was an accident. It doesn't really matter how it happened." Izzy moved a couple of steps closer to Lisa-Marie and her voice dropped, "I need to know if you're alright."

"He didn't rape me, if that's what you think." She saw Izzy wince and she thought she might have gained some advantage. Perhaps she could outstare the older woman. She quickly lost that battle. Izzy might be shaken but she was determined to get an answer to her question. Lisa-Marie broke eye contact and stared down at her feet. "I came onto him, it happened just once and he regretted it. There, are you happy now?"

Lisa-Marie walked over and thrust the parcel at her, "You might as well have this. It's an album of pictures I took of your garden. I'm sure you'll love the ones of Justin." Her resentment and bitterness filled the shortened space between them. "You wrecked everything for me. I wanted to pay you back by being with Liam, but it turned out he worships you, too." Before Izzy could see her tears of humiliation, Lisa-Marie ran out of the room and up the stairs. She had been sure, at that moment, that she would hate Izzy forever.

❦ ❦ ❦ ❦

Lisa-Marie realized she must have dozed when her eyes fluttered open at the sound of Izzy slipping back into the sunflower room carrying a tray. She watched her place it on the top of the dresser. As the older woman turned to her, Lisa-Marie felt a wave of icy panic collide with her ever-present heartburn.

Izzy smiled, "Is it alright if I share a cup of tea with you?" Lisa-Marie shrugged; the look on her face reminded Izzy to proceed with caution. She poured the tea and watched as Lisa-Marie pushed herself up into a sitting position. She couldn't help but stare when the fabric of the girl's bright-pink T-shirt bulged outwards with the baby's movement. Handing her a cup of the tea, Izzy pulled the stool over so she could sit with her back against the dresser. She settled down, sipped and asked, "Is it okay?"

Lisa-Marie nodded. She kept her eyes down, staring at the sunshine colours of the quilt. Her voice was barely audible, "You're not angry ... about this?" She pointed to her stomach.

Izzy's eyebrows rose sharply, "I'm shocked, I won't try to deny that. But I am certainly not angry with you. I wish you had told us earlier. We could have helped. It must have been difficult for you to go through all of this on your own."

"It's sort of funny ... it wasn't bad at all until a little while ago." Lisa-Marie relaxed as she confided in Izzy, "I was taking pictures for the school paper and, even though I didn't get a part in the big play like I wanted, I got to do all the promo photos and cover it for the local paper." A slight frown flitted across her face, "I didn't even know I was pregnant until November. I got a home pregnancy test and it came up positive. I had only been with –" Lisa-Marie stared down at the bed. "Well, you know. He was the only one since way before I left Kingston, so I knew I must have been close to twelve weeks gone."

She set the tea cup down on the night table beside the bed and rubbed slow circles around her stomach with her hands. It felt good finally to explain why she had delayed dealing with the pregnancy. "The guardianship stuff was supposed to be all done by the middle of November. I didn't want to go to the school counsellor or tell anyone until that was settled. What if they thought my being pregnant made Auntie Beth a bad guardian? I was scared they might send me back to Kingston. All the papers weren't signed until the end of November. I had the play coming up. I was so busy," She looked up suddenly at Izzy, "And I didn't want to be *that girl*. The new girl who was so stupid she got pregnant. What if everyone turned against me? So I just kept putting things off."

Shifting around on the bed, Lisa-Marie inhaled sharply. "Crap, it's so hard to breathe some times." Shaking her head she continued, "I didn't want to ruin the big trip back home to see Grannie at Christmas, so I didn't say anything to Auntie Beth. I could still hide my stomach with baggy shirts and stuff. Then Marlene found out. She saw me coming out of the bathroom in a nightie one morning. She made me call home and tell all. I know I shouldn't have made Auntie Beth promise not to say anything, but I didn't want to cause trouble. She and Beulah both kept saying how happy you and Liam were."

Lisa-Marie pulled at the quilt and traced her finger around the edges of the sunflower design. "I thought I could have the baby on my own and give it up for adoption. I still had all my friends and I was busy making plans for next year."

"What changed your mind?"

"I got scared and I thought that maybe Auntie Beth was right when she said it was wrong not to tell. You guys would probably want the baby. It would be better if I had it up here and you could take it right away ... no stupid social workers poking their noses into things and causing trouble."

Her story seemed to have wound down. The room was quiet except for the sound of the squirrels chattering in a nearby tree. Suddenly, Lisa-Marie blurted out, "Justin told me he was coming up here for the whole summer to work at the sawmill. I wanted to see him again."

Izzy poured herself more tea. She wasn't surprised that the reality of giving birth had scared Lisa-Marie. She was a kid. The statement about her and Liam taking the baby sent Izzy's mind spinning. For the moment, she set aside all the implications of that. She chose, instead, to follow a different lead. "You still like Justin, hey?"

"As if it matters ... look at me." Lisa-Marie's face crumpled and tears appeared in the corners of her eyes. "I'm a beached whale."

Izzy bit her bottom lip, "Why don't you rest a bit. I've already talked to your Aunt Beth. She agrees with me that it would be better if you stayed here for now."

Lisa-Marie's eyes widened in surprise, "You want me to stay here?"

"I do. Supper will be in an hour or so. I think you'll enjoy meeting my father. He's taken up long-term houseguest status while he finishes his memoirs. I'm sure you'll have lots of photography things to talk about. Don't worry about anything, Lisa. You don't have to go through this on your own."

"I'm sorry I didn't say something to Justin about Liam before we were right on the doorstep."

"Don't worry about any of that, now. It's all going to be okay."

Izzy had her hand on the door to leave the room when she heard Lisa-Marie murmur, "It's a girl, by the way ... the baby ... it's a girl."

❧❧❧❧

Izzy sat down in the chair across from the table where her father was jotting quick notes on a yellow legal pad. She looked around the sun porch and shook her head. Her father had asked that most of the furniture be removed. He had then transformed the spacious room into an effective work space and sleeping area. Against one wall stood a large white board that was layered with various photographs, papers and post-it notes. A table, now covered with books and papers, had been created from an old door and two sawhorses.

Izzy knew her father had a hip injury that had never healed properly and he was obviously a man who liked to be comfortable. He had an expensive reclining chair installed in one corner and in another, a single bed with a number of mattress configurations available at the flick of a switch. She had accepted the loss of the sun porch space for the foreseeable future and had ordered some elegant wood blinds for the French doors that led from the dining room. The man might as well have a bit of privacy.

Edward Montgomery pushed his work stool back and studied Izzy's face. "The tea is almost steeped. Will you join me?"

"No thanks, I just had some."

Her father fixed his tea, sat back in his chair and took a sip. Holding the cup and saucer on his knee, he asked, "Well, Isabella, do you want to tell me what's going on?"

The way her father always used her full name made her feel like a child being called to account for a breach of some rule or another. She ignored his question. "Have you seen, Liam?"

"After you took the pregnant young lady upstairs, he said he was going to the sawmill and that we shouldn't expect him to join us for dinner."

Izzy nodded and looked past her father to the view of the lake. The water spread out in front of the cabin like a sheet of quicksilver. "Her name is Lisa-

Marie. She's Bethany's niece. She spent last summer here at the lake with Bethany and Beulah."

"Is the young man who arrived with her the father? Though that wouldn't explain why he took a swing at Liam."

"No, it's not Justin." Izzy looked down at her hands folded in her lap. It was awkward and embarrassing to be the one to put words to this situation. She felt a twinge of anger. Best to get it over with, she thought. "Liam is the father."

Edward's eyebrows went up. He placed his cup down on his saucer and waited for Izzy to explain.

"It happened before Liam and I were together. Neither one of us had a clue she was pregnant until Bethany told us this afternoon." Izzy got up from her chair, "I've got to get some dinner started. Maybe we can have trays down here with you. I think you'll like Lisa-Marie; she's quite interested in photography. You'll have lots to talk about."

"Will she be staying on for a while?"

"She's made up her mind that we will want the baby. The best thing we can do right now is have her here where we can keep an eye on her and see what happens."

"I should think that will be hard on Liam."

"Well, he'll have to get used to it, won't he? She can't stay with her aunt right now. Bethany and Beulah have to work out a few things, and they don't need a pregnant girl under their roof while they do it."

Edward studied Izzy's face, "Are you up to this?"

"I honestly don't know. Now I've got the unpleasant task of going over to talk to Justin and try to convince him to stay. If he leaves, I'm worried Lisa-Marie might bolt as well. He seems to be one of the main reasons she came back here."

※※※※

Izzy knocked on the door of the small cabin that perched right out on the edge of the cliff. It felt strange to wait outside the door. When Liam had lived here, Izzy would knock and walk right in. She heard Justin's voice snap out, "What?"

She pushed open the door, almost expecting to see Pearl on the carpet in front of the stove. But, of course, Pearl had moved over to her cabin along with Liam. Justin sat at the kitchen table staring out the window. His duffel bag was tossed carelessly on the floor. She walked across the small room and sat down.

42

Justin refused to look at Izzy. "I'm not staying. Save your breath if that's what you've come to talk about. I'll get Beulah to take me to the bus tomorrow."

"You need this job, we both know that. It's a perfect opportunity. Don't throw it away."

He got up with such force that the chair rocked back behind him. "You want me to work for you - see that guy every day - after what he's done?"

"I'm not here to make excuses for what Liam did. I will say this much, he didn't force himself on her. If you don't believe me, discuss it with Lisa. I'm here to talk about you." Izzy got up to face Justin, "It's almost the beginning of May. You aren't going to find another job that pays what this one does. I'm guessing you don't have any other place to stay for the next four months. Where are you going to go? You need to think about what's the best choice for you."

"I thought I knew you. I was wrong. I thought Liam was a decent guy. Wrong again." Justin raked his hands through his hair. His voice was filled with bitterness when he said, "That guy screwed a sixteen-year-old kid and now that kid is going to have a baby. You might be okay with that, but I'm not." He could see Izzy wince at the force of his words and he knew he had hurt her. He was glad that he could make her feel anything, though hurting her felt like hurting himself.

He leaned over, grabbed his duffel bag and threw in onto the couch, "You're right about one thing. I'm shit out of luck if I don't take this job. So, ya ... I guess I'll have to think about myself." He turned his back on her and stared out the window at the glittering surface of the lake.

He heard Izzy say, "I filled the cupboards and fridge with a few things." Then the silence in the cabin dragged on until it was broken by the quiet sound of the door closing behind her.

EIGHT

Lisa-Marie pulled a cream-coloured, leather-bound journal from her bag. She sat up on the bed in the sunflower room and struggled to adjust the pillows behind her back. The journal had been a birthday gift from Liam the previous summer – a way to welcome her to Crater Lake. She shrugged at the irony of that as she ran her fingers over the soft cover with its intricate design worked around the edges. Flipping the book open she smiled at the pages of entries, all of which started with the words, *Dear Emma*. She had addressed her journal to Jane Austen's character because the spirited, young woman named Emma always seemed to land on her feet no matter what came along to upset her life. Lisa-Marie grabbed a pen and started to write.

Dear Emma:

Well, I'm here, but what a total gong show. When Justin found out about me and Liam he almost punched Liam right in the face. It was horrible. Do you think it could mean Justin was jealous? Still, it was really awful. And Liam looked terrible when he saw me. But he'll have to get used to seeing me. I'm staying here at Izzy's – well, I guess I should say Izzy and Liam's place. Beulah was so angry with me for making Auntie Beth keep the baby a secret that I thought she might slap me right across the face. I guess Auntie Beth can't handle Beulah's snit fit and preggo me all at the same time.

It seems like Auntie Beth has just pushed me off on Izzy. Don't get me wrong, Emma, I'm happy to stay here – I love this room and Izzy isn't mad at me or anything like that. She's as beautiful as she was last summer and, of course, she wouldn't be jealous of me if I slept with Liam twenty times, especially when you consider that I now look like a fat cow because of it.

I promised I would always tell you the truth, Emma. Well, here it is ... I want someone to look after me. I'm scared about having the baby. I never, ever thought I'd want that person to be Izzy, but there's something about the way she says everything will be okay; I believe her.

ೊೊೊೊ

Lisa-Marie came down the stairs from the loft, following her nose. She could see Izzy ladling beef stew onto three plates. A bowl of mashed potatoes steamed on the counter beside a green salad.

"Hey, Lisa. How are you feeling?" Izzy smiled at her and then turned to call down the stairs to the sun porch, "Dad, could you set up those TV trays for me."

Lisa-Marie heard a man's voice say, "I've got to get something sorted here first, Isabella."

She raised her eyebrows at the sound of Izzy's full name. "Can I help with anything?"

"Everything's done. Go down and introduce yourself to my dad. I'll be right there."

Lisa-Marie walked out to the sun porch. She stopped near the elderly man who sat on a rolling stool in front of a work-table. She considered the mock-up page of photos and words he had before him. "I think this one," she leaned forward and pointed at a photo near the bottom of the page, "Should be closer to the top, on the left maybe." She reached out to switch the two photos in question. "There, that's better."

"What is your reason for the change?"

"The way the light is hitting the lion's mane – putting it at the bottom of the page – it kept drawing my eye off to the side. This way it leads me into the writing."

"Well done, young lady." He swivelled around and put his hand out, "My name is Edward Montgomery and you are Lisa-Marie. I am delighted to meet you." Lisa-Marie studied Izzy's father, a man with grey hair swept back from his face and black bifocals perched low on his nose. He wore dark pants and a light-grey turtleneck topped by a cardigan sweater. He looked dignified, like a rich, old man in a movie, and the slight British accent contributed to the effect.

Lisa-Marie shook his outstretched hand. "You took all these photos?" She gestured to the page and turned to the collection of images that were taped on the large white board and spread over the rest of the table. "What kind of a lens did you use to shoot the lions?" Lisa-Marie walked over and studied the board. "Did you use a polarizing filter on this river shot? Is that why you can see the rocks on the riverbed so clearly?"

Edward pulled camera cases out from under the makeshift table as he said, "I did indeed." He shrugged at Izzy when she came into the room carrying dinner for three. She set up on her own while Edward and Lisa-Marie leaned over the camera equipment.

"Let's eat before everything gets cold."

Sometime later, Edward pushed his chair back. From the look of the three plates, Lisa-Marie was the only person with a healthy appetite. He smiled across at the young girl and asked, "Do you have a portfolio I could see?"

"I'll go get it," Lisa-Marie got up and moved toward the stairs.

Izzy watched as she left the room; she marvelled that from behind she would never know that Lisa was pregnant. She smiled at her dad with gratitude, "I knew you two would hit it off." Izzy rose and went up to the dining room where she opened the bottom door of the china cabinet and pulled out an album. When Lisa-Marie reappeared, Izzy handed it to her, "I thought you might like to show Dad this, as well."

Lisa-Marie took the book from Izzy's hand. She stroked her fingers across the soft leather binding. Liam had helped her make the cover. She remembered each of the photos she had placed inside and the gossamer thin paper between the pictures – paper she had made over at Micah Camp between her shifts working in the paper and soap shop. The album had been a gift for Justin. But then it became part of the painful memory of the night he had rejected her. When Izzy had shown up in Victoria to confront her about Liam, she had been more than happy to push the photo collection onto her.

Izzy looked at Lisa-Marie and an unspoken message passed between the two of them – whatever you thought I wanted from Justin last summer, all of that is definitely in the past.

"I have something to show you, too, Izzy." Lisa-Marie took a magazine out of the portfolio. She flipped it open to a full-page black and white photograph of an old woman digging in a dumpster. "Remember the picture I told you about, the one the teacher sent to the contest? It won first prize."

Edward reached over for the magazine and nodded his approval. "An award winning photograph is a jolly good start."

※※※※※

Izzy pulled a thick flannel shirt out of the closet by the door. She walked through the garden and out to the cliff deck where she could see Liam sitting in the swing chair in front of the outdoor chimney stove. The fire was crackling and glowing as she settled down beside him. The motion of the chair carried them back and forth. Izzy leaned into Liam and studied the night sky. It was the dark moon time; the velvet darkness, littered with pinpricks of sparkling light, seemed to press down on her. A steady wind caused a light chop out on the lake. The waves echoed as they smacked against the rocks of the cliff below.

Liam sat forward, "It never once entered my mind that she would be pregnant." He looked over at Izzy, the anguish on his face obvious. "It all happened so suddenly. I never thought of anything like that. I don't know how I'm going to get through this, Izz. I feel like such a bastard, putting it like that ... making it about me. I'm not the one having a baby. She's just a kid, for God's sake." He grabbed Izzy's hand as he went on, "And the worst part is that when Bethany told us, I didn't think about Lisa-Marie at all. She didn't seem real. All I could think, over and over, was that I couldn't stand it if this came between us."

Liam stood up. He dragged Izzy to her feet and into his arms to hug her close with a desperate strength. "I can't lose you. Not now, when I feel I can't even breathe without you."

Izzy pulled back from Liam's arms to look up at him, "I have no intention of being lost. I promise you that." She stood in the dark of the night, surrendering herself to an embrace that made her feel like a life preserver to a drowning man.

✻ ✻ ✻ ✻

Liam sat at the kitchen table and watched the morning rain sluice over the deck. Dark clouds hovered low on the lake and nestled between the mountains. Lisa-Marie came down the stairs from the loft. She wore the same tight, pink T-shirt from the day before. It pulled across her body and emphasized the round bump of her stomach. She shoved her arms into a sweater that didn't stand a chance of making it around her body.

"I thought I could smell coffee." She grabbed a mug from the cupboard and poured herself a cup. She walked over to the table and lowered herself into a chair. She sipped appreciatively and asked, "Where's Izzy?"

"She's already gone to work."

Lisa-Marie sighed loudly, "Okay ... let's get this over with. It's all so embarrassing and I feel like a total dork. I know I should have told you about the baby sooner. I'm sorry. I know it was wrong to make Auntie Beth keep it a secret. Beulah's already taken my head off on that one. Maybe you wonder if it really is your baby. I wouldn't blame you if you did – the way I acted that night – but it is yours."

Liam looked more than uncomfortable, avoiding her eyes to stare down at his hands. "Come on, kiddo. I know you're telling the truth."

Lisa-Marie reached over to pull Liam's bowl of cereal towards her, "Can I finish this if you don't want it? I'm starving and, for frig sakes, don't call me kiddo." She raised a spoonful of cereal up to her mouth, saying, "It pushes the concept of irony over the edge to absurdity."

She ate quickly and pushed the empty bowl aside. "I didn't come here to cause trouble. I don't want anything to do with this baby. I have all kinds of plans for next year. There's a photography exchange trip to Europe in the fall and I'm going. It's your baby, too. Oh crap ... I should get used to saying, she ... she's your baby, too. You're the one who told me you shouldn't get off the hook for what happened."

"The baby's a girl?" Liam asked in surprise.

"That's what the ultrasound showed." Lisa-Marie rose and clutched her belly with one hand as she side-stepped past the chair to get around the table. "I need to talk to Justin."

Liam crossed his arms over his chest and looked away. Lisa-Marie took in his reaction. She threw up her hands in surrender, "I suppose you want to know how I could have waited until the last second to tell him you're the father. Well, pardon me for thinking it wasn't something either one of us wanted to brag about. Geez, can this be the end of my having to say I'm sorry?" With her palms in the air and her stomach pushed so tight against the fabric of her shirt that her protruding belly button stood out, she said, "Aren't things bad enough for me without everyone expecting me to beg for forgiveness?"

Lisa-Marie hurried out of the cabin and into the garden. She stopped to get her breath in front of the Nike of Samothrace statue that graced the covered porch of the garden house. The small, glass-enclosed building stood half-way down the length of the expansive garden. All around her, everything dripped, lush green and wet with the rain. The flower and vegetable beds which had been overrun with colour last summer when Lisa-Marie had spent hours taking pictures, now appeared empty in comparison. Wildly-waving, bright yellow daffodils, multi-coloured tulips and dark-purple hyacinths with their heavy scent, were making a valiant attempt to pick up the slack. The rhododendrons that bordered the outer edges of the garden were in full bloom – giant blotches of pink and red and white. Bright yellow forsythia bushes poked up here and there, their delicate branches bending under the

48

weight of the water drops. Dotted across the garden, clumps of rhubarb, ruby-red, stood tall and straight, their bent umbrella leaves directing the rain down to the earth. Buds sprouted everywhere. The garden was still magic to Lisa-Marie. Its spring face begged to be photographed, as its summer one had the year before.

As she started down the path towards Liam's old cabin, Justin came around the corner. Lisa-Marie's mind raced as she tried to think of how she could possibly explain herself to him. She knew she had to try because she couldn't bear it if he left Crater Lake because of her. She shouted out his name and walked towards him as fast as her protruding belly would allow.

He turned, saw her on the path and called out, "Leez, go back, you're getting soaked. I can't talk right now. I want to get to work early."

She pushed her hair out of her face and let out a sigh of relief. He must be planning to stay if he was on his way to work. Her momentum shortened the distance between them as she tried to keep the begging tone from her voice, "Please don't be mad. I can't stand it if you're angry at me."

The sight of her, standing in the pouring rain, pleading with him, caused Justin to shake his head in resignation. He walked back, took her arm and led her towards the overhang of the greenhouse roof. "Come under here, you're getting soaked."

Lisa-Marie tried to twist her stomach out of Justin's sight. He looked even better than he had last summer. His honey-coloured hair was still long. What had been scruffy whiskers had grown into a well-trimmed beard. It made him look older. She was not over him; she would never be over him.

"I'm sorry for the way the whole thing about Liam came out. I should have told you sooner. I didn't know how to say it." Tears filled her eyes.

"Come on, Leez, don't cry. I'm not mad at you," Justin placed emphasis on the word, *you*, as he stepped closer and put his arm around her shoulder. She scrunched in close, sniffing pathetically. She hated crying around people but lately, she was an unstoppable fountain.

Justin looked over Lisa-Marie's head to the rain-soaked garden. When he spoke he didn't bother to hide the edge of bitterness in his voice, "I blame Liam, and I blame Izzy for acting like the sun rises and sets on him when she knows what he did to you." Justin shook his head, "It's their fault, not yours, Leez."

Lisa-Marie stepped back. She was reluctant to do it but she couldn't let him continue to believe this version of her story. "It wasn't Liam's fault. I went to him ... it was my doing."

While she spoke, she wiped the tears from her eyes with both hands in a sweet little-girl gesture that caused Justin's heart to thump in an odd way. He reacted as he might have if he saw a puppy run out into the street in front of a car. Then he comprehended what she had said. "Come on, Leez, I don't believe that. Why are you protecting him?"

She hung her head, "It was the night I made such a fool of myself with you down on the beach and said all those awful things. I was so angry at you and jealous of Izzy. I went to Liam's. I threw myself at him."

A wave of regret made Justin suck in his breath. He shouldn't have left her alone that night; it was his fault. The guilt hit him like a punch in the gut and made him defensive. "He's old, Leez. No matter what crazy thing you did, he shouldn't have touched you." Justin clenched his hands at his side and tried to control the anger in his voice, "Look, I'm not mad at you, and I don't blame you ... no matter what you say. That bastard ruined your life."

Lisa-Marie drew herself up as tall as she could, even though gravity and the size of her stomach seemed to bend her towards the ground. She answered him back with indignation, her voice rising as the words poured out of her mouth, "Who the hell says my life is ruined?"

Her reaction surprised him. She had gone from beaten-down puppy to spitting hellcat in a few seconds. "Hey, don't get all worked-up. I'm sure that isn't good for you."

Lisa-Marie stamped her foot and wiped at her running nose with the back of her hand. She stared him down, "My life is not ruined. I have a ton of exciting plans for next year. This whole thing," she pointed at her stomach, "It's a temporary setback. In a couple of weeks I'll have the baby, Izzy and Liam can take it and I'll be me again getting on with my life."

Justin studied her tear-stained face; the delicate, bruised shade under her eyes cast shadow marks down her cheeks. He glanced down to the stomach that jutted out from under an impressive bust, totally unlike the one Lisa-Marie had sported the previous summer. He would know; he'd seen her in a bikini enough times, lounging out on the raft with her summer-light hair drying in the breeze. His gaze went down to her swollen ankles and sandal-encased feet. Despite the changes the pregnancy had wrought, he could still recognize his summer companion. All of a sudden, he was glad to see her.

Justin smiled and Lisa-Marie felt as though the sun had burst through the clouds. She looked up at him, "Can we be friends, like last summer before all the bad stuff happened?" She watched a small frown flit across his face and she thought that if he said no, she would throw herself sobbing into his arms and beg. But he didn't say no, not exactly.

"Things aren't like they were last year. I've got a full time job now. I'm taking a distance education course to bring up my English grade and that won't be a walk in the park for me. I'm booked to do my driver's test up here and I need to practice. I've got a lot to do."

Lisa-Marie nudged him with her shoulder, "You have to relax sometimes. You don't want to end up spending all your time over at that cabin by yourself."

A worried frown settled in and narrowed Justin's warm-brown eyes, "You're sure about the just-friends thing, Leez? You need to be sure about that. I don't want to hurt you again."

"I'm over the silly crush I had on you. I promise. I want us to be friends like we were before I messed everything up."

Justin gave her a quick hug. "Okay, I'd like that. Now go back inside before you get a cold or something."

Lisa-Marie waved goodbye over her shoulder and headed back to the cabin. Only two weeks until this baby is out of me, she thought. A few more weeks to get my figure back, and then we'll see about being friends. She had the whole summer to change his mind about that.

NINE

"Should I tell you about it?" Willow sat cross legged by the small table in Izzy's office with a collage in front of her. Her fingers traced over the edges of the cut out magazine photos, pressing them down in spots and trying to shift other images before the glue dried.

"That's up to you," Izzy said as she studied Willow's head of blonde curls bent over the work she had created.

For a first session, the collage activity was one of Izzy's favorites - low key, creative and fun for most of her clients. She sat nearby, almost in a meditative space, listening to the soft shuffling sound of paper as Willow sifted through the boxes of cut out images. The creative flow of energy reached out to include her.

Willow pointed to a small picture of a piano stuck in one corner, "I've taken piano lessons for years ... since I was six. After my mom left, my aunt kept paying for the lessons. Even when they took us all away from my dad, she kept paying for lessons. No matter where I ended up, I always had piano lessons." Willow's hand smoothed over a picture of an open journal that partially concealed the face of a young man. "What I really want to do is write poetry," her fingers stroked along the arm of the leather jacket that the man in the picture wore. Her voice shook, "He said I had a real gift ... that I had wasted my time on the piano. I should have been writing poems all those years." A tear slipped down Willow's cheek. "He was my boyfriend, but it didn't work out."

After Willow left the session, Izzy held the photocopy she had made of the collage and let her mind wander over what she saw. She tried to allow a sense of the whole to sink in without getting caught up on any one image. She wrote up her case notes for the session, a slight frown nestled between her eyes. Something about the collage made her uncomfortable and she had no idea why.

§ § § §

The woodlot wound up the mountain, a vast tract of wilderness. Bouncing along beside Reg in the company pickup, Justin learned that Crater Lake Timber did selective, sustainable logging. "All of the roads you see up here," Reg gestured around with his free hand, "we build them and we decommission them when we're done. We leave as small a footprint as we can."

Reg had been in the logging business since he was a kid. He'd been a faller, a log scaler, a sawyer and had even worked in construction. He knew trees, logs and lumber. "Being a betting man myself, I'm going to tell you, that's the fuckin' triactor of the business." Reg bounced his ball cap up and down on his head and laughed. He had been one of Caleb's first hired hands back in the 70's, when the whole operation consisted of a portable saw that Caleb used to cut his own lumber. He had watched Caleb build Crater Lake Timber up from nothing. "Then I went away for a few years and wouldn't you know that son-of-a-bitch would have to go and get himself killed. Getting squished up against a tree by a fuckin' run-away boulder was no way for a man like him to die."

Reg glanced over at Justin, "I got nothing against Liam; I've known the guy for years. He's the best damn right-hand man you're ever going to find. He's hard-working, honest and quiet. He's not the kind of guy you'll ever catch running his mouth off. That is number one in my book. But he was never cut out to run this operation." He pulled the truck over to the side of the road and jammed it into park. "I've got production up thirty percent since I took over."

Reg hopped out of the truck and pointed up at the trees, "If you want to run a profitable sawmill, the most important thing is a reliable supply of logs." He broke into a wide toothy grin, "That's why this place is almost fuckin'-A perfect. This woodlot is a goldmine."

Reg walked over to a large excavator that was parked nearby. A few guys were gathered around the back end of the machine, drinking coffee; the steam from their thermos cups rose into the crisp morning air. "Sons of bitches don't have enough work to do today, I guess," Reg smiled as he smacked one of the guys on the back. "Come over here, Justin, and meet two of the laziest bastards on the North Island. Have the nerve to call themselves fallers. And don't even get me started on that guy who operates this machine."

One of the loggers pointed up the hill, "Got out of the truck this morning to see three cougars sitting pretty as a picture up on that ridge. It gives you pause, that's all I'll say."

Reg told Justin, "The cougars love the roads and the ATV trails. They treat them like their own personal highways."

The other faller shook his head slowly, "The cougar you see is not a problem. It's the cougar you don't see that you better be worried about. Now the bears crashing through the bush at about forty clicks, they can scare the shit plumb out of a guy." As Justin looked around warily, the guys smacked their knees and laughed at his display of nerves.

The fallers soon moved off toward the bush, hauling their huge saws. Justin followed Reg as he pointed to the trees that surrounded them, talking all the while, "Second growth – the whole mountain was logged back in the forties, right after the war. When I first worked here with Caleb, there were lots of stumps and fallen cedar left everywhere. You'd never see anything like that nowadays. Caleb had us get most of the cedar out. Shake blocking, now that was ball-breaking work, let me tell you."

Reg pointed out Yellow and Red Cedar, Hemlock, Douglas Fir, and Sitka Spruce. Some Alder trees were mixed in, near the streams, and he told Justin that they even cut those now for finish flooring. A large pipeline ran through the bush bringing down a steady flow of water to power a micro-hydro turbine that generated enough electricity for the needs of the cabins, the bakery and the sawmill. Reg pointed to the other side of the rough road, "We've got some selective cutting to do over on that section in the next few weeks."

Coming down from the woodlot a few hours later, Justin could see the whole sawmill operation stretched out before him. Everything was surrounded by a chain link fence with gates that opened to the gravel logging road.

Reg pulled into the yard and jumped out of the truck. "Come on, let's tour this mill."

They entered a building that contained a couple of large circular saws. A beat-up first aid box hung on the wall near a sign that read, *Don't Panic.* Reg kept up a constant commentary as they walked through the building, "I always say, keep costs down by balancing manpower against production." Reg stroked his hand over the base of one of the saws, "I got this baby installed in here last month – it's a heavy-duty beauty queen."

When they walked out of the saw shed, Reg led the way to another building that had large, sliding, metal doors along the front. They were pushed back to reveal more equipment and lumber stacked everywhere. "This is where all the finesse happens. We've got our resaws, the moulder, the planer, the chop saws. And over there is where I take care of all the blades."

Reg leaned back against the rough wooden counter and pulled a toothpick from the pocket of his shirt. He worked it in and around his mouth. "That's my secret to kick-ass production – knowing how to sharpen the saw blades." The look on Reg's face told Justin he was just getting warmed up. "You'll be opening a Pandora's Box of shit if you don't stay on top of those saws. Dull blades will screw you over six ways to Sunday. If you have to get someone to come out here to do the sharpening ... well ... you can kiss your profit bye-bye birdie, as it heads south for the winter. It's like this," Reg pointed over toward the shed that held the large circular saws. "That saw is going to be down way too fuckin' long; production will be in the crapper before you can say Jesus H. Christ in a handcart. You got these guys standing around just whistling Dixie while their sky high wages and benefits make your bottom line bleed like a stuck pig."

He dropped the toothpick back in his pocket, "Come on, I'll show you some of the finished product." Tromping past various lumber storage areas, Reg kept right on talking and pointing, "We carry a lot of inventory so we can meet immediate customer demand. For larger or custom orders we might need one to three weeks of lead-in time. We've got dimensional lumber, timbers, siding – bevel, tongue and groove, and channel. You get some excellent panelling, siding, and soffits from some of that stuff stacked over there. We do custom profiles and fence panels. The sky's the fuckin' limit. Whatever the customer might come up with, we can make."

Reg led the way to a small, two-story building. He looked over his shoulder as he spoke, "What sells the lumber is quality. We have our share of buyers coming to us because we deliver quality at a fair price." He stopped to point out an open shed at the edge of the yard, "That's where the bark gets trimmed from the logs before we haul them over to the saw. That pile of scrap wood there – some of it goes down to the bakery. We chip up the rest, it's good for trail mulch."

Justin followed Reg into the sawmill office. Wooden desks lined three walls, and a large metal filing cabinet stood against the fourth. Reg's desk overflowed with invoices and papers. A stack of magazines perched on top of the file cabinet; the words *Sawmill and Woodlot Management* were emblazoned on the top cover. A satellite dish, visible through the window, hung off the side of the building.

Two very large dogs lay on the floor partway under Reg's chair. He pushed one of the dogs away with his foot, "Don't be overly familiar with these two.

They stay in the yard at night and I don't want them losing their edge." Reg pointed to the desk that looked like the place where everybody threw things, "That'll be yours. Arrange it anyway you want. I put some stuff there for you to read. Come on, I'll show you the lunch room."

Justin caught sight of a framed poster on the wall. Two fallers, with chainsaws in hand, stood beside a massive tree. The caption read:

It will be a sorry day when the forest industry consists chiefly of a very few companies, holding most of the good timber to the disadvantage and early extermination of the most hard working, virile, versatile, ingenuous element of our population: the independent logger and the small mill man. Our forest industry will be healthier if it consists of as many independent units as can be supported. - H.R. MacMillan.

Reg spoke as he watched Justin reading, "No one ever wrote truer words, I'll tell you that for free." He looked around the office suddenly, his face comic with his eyebrows shooting up in an arc and his mouth dropping open. "Holy Mother of God, saying that gave me a goddamn shiver. Caleb used to say that exact thing whenever anyone noticed that poster."

Justin glanced around the lunch room while Reg poured himself a coffee and gave a speech on appropriate behaviour in a co-ed work environment. "I cuss a bit now and then." Reg laughed, "No denying that. The girls who end up working with us teach me a new word or two. But that's where it ends. No sexist remarks, no skin pics on the walls or girlie magazines in the toilet. We don't tell dirty jokes or wear T-shirts with questionable slogans on them, and we don't come on to our fellow employees - got that?" Justin nodded, keeping a serious look on his face.

Reg pointed out the window to the yard where a young woman was hopping into the forklift. She wore black coveralls and work boots, but there was no denying the female figure inside those coveralls or the long hair that fell down her back in a twisted braid. "You see that little lady out there, Justin? She's as pretty as pie and just as sweet." Justin heard Reg's voice slide off the words pretty and pie like syrup dripping from the open spout of a bottle. Then his voice turned business-like, "I think of her as my own daughter, and I've got a few, so I know just what the fuck that means. If you know what's good for you, get used to thinking of her like your sister. And take it from me, she doesn't appreciate it when the guys think she's going to clean up the kitchen or scrub out the toilet. I learned a few new cuss words from her last week on that score." Reg laughed as he grabbed his coffee, "Come on, follow me ... there's plenty more to see."

✻✻✻✻

Justin spotted Liam walking across the sawmill yard. His fists tightened in his gloves as he rose to his full height from bending to stack lumber. He debated turning his back, but there was something in the look of Liam that made him reconsider. Maybe it was the way the guy's dark eyes met his in a steady, unwavering gaze. Maybe it was something left over from the previous year when he and Liam had worked side-by-side in Izzy's garden, joking and laughing together.

Justin stood his ground, "I know I need this job and I know that means I have to see you around here, Liam. Don't think I like the idea."

Liam dug his hands into the front pockets of his jeans. "It's good you've decided to stay. I came to arrange a time to get you started on practicing for your driver's test."

"Forget about that." Justin's spoke through gritted teeth, "I'll ask one of the guys here for help. The less time I have to spend with you the better, man. Let's try to avoid one another wherever possible."

"No one else has the time. This is a pretty tight operation now that Reg is running things. And if you're going to understand the accounting side of the business, you'll have to let me explain the books. Don't let your anger mess up this job for you. You can't judge me any more harshly than I judge myself."

Justin stared at Liam, a cold look in his eyes, "Don't be too sure about that."

"Izzy says to ask you to come for dinner tonight."

That's the last fucking straw, Justin thought as he punched one gloved hand into the other. "I guess we'll all sit together like one big happy family, hey? You make me want to smash you up against this pile of lumber. And don't get me started on how Izzy can even bear to look at you. Don't you two get it ... Leez is only a kid."

"If I could go back and change things, I would. But that isn't how the world works, is it? I'm not asking you to forgive me. I wouldn't ask you to do something I can't do myself. I'm asking that you try not to make things worse than they already are."

Justin still wanted to smash the guy but he had to admit that Liam had a point. No one could change the past. And there was something about his complete acceptance of the responsibility that got to Justin.

"Don't come to dinner for us, come for Lisa-Marie. She needs a friend."

Justin saw the flicker of pain that crossed Liam's face when he said Lisa-Marie's name. The guy's suffering was definitely getting to him. "Shit ... ya, okay. But can you just get out of my face and leave me alone now?" Justin turned back to stacking the lumber. Leez did need a friend, that sure as shit was true. Part of liking her the previous summer had been his desire to look out for her. He couldn't imagine what might happen to her with Liam and Izzy in charge, to say nothing of her aunt and Beulah, if they decided to take over.

As the lumber flew through his hands to the orderly stacks in front of him, Justin's mind went back to the night of his going away party. If he could change the past, he would have slept with Leez, himself. That was what she had wanted. Shit, part of him had wanted that, too. He could still picture how she looked when she threw off her top and shorts and stood with her back to him, out in the water, wearing nothing but her thong underwear. If later, she had figured out it hadn't made him care for her the way she wanted him to care, that still would have been better than what did happen to her. At least he would have had the sense to use a fucking condom. Justin shook his head and continued to stack the lumber with a vengeance.

TEN

Beulah made herself sit patiently on the couch as she urged the woman across from her to talk. "Calm down, Beth, and tell me why on earth you kept Lisa's pregnancy a secret."

"You'll think I'm even stupider than you already do."

Beulah shook her head in exasperation, "I shouldn't have said you were stupid."

"I was in shock when I saw her. I panicked. What if she wanted us to take the baby?" A touch of hysteria edged Bethany's voice, "She's only sixteen. She can't care for a child. It was perfect, right? A baby – it was even Liam's baby. It was everything I begged for a few months ago." She stared at Beulah, "I didn't want that anymore. I was terrified when I saw her." Bethany dropped her face into her hands. After a moment she took a deep breath and reached out for a tissue. She straightened her shoulders, "I went along with Lisa-Marie's plan to give the baby up for adoption because I was scared of the alternative. I knew it was wrong. I didn't say anything to you because I felt as if all the things you've ever thought about me were true."

Beulah had little patience with the way Bethany had bounced from wanting a baby, to throwing herself into her research job with Jillian, to her current pursuit of higher education. Living with the woman was like being inside a fucking pinball machine. But she forced herself to focus on the bigger picture. She would not allow Bethany to slip back into the depression she had suffered the previous autumn. "I'm going to ask Izzy to find a kid from the Camp to work in the bakery." She held up her hand to stop Bethany's protest, "I'll still need you out there for the early hours, but there's no reason you can't start kicking off by nine o'clock. That should make it easier for you to do the research job and start taking a couple of those courses you've been talking about."

Bethany moved over into Beulah's arms and clung to her. She raised her head and asked, "What about Lisa-Marie and the baby?"

"Izzy seems determined to keep Lisa over there for now. I'm not exactly sure why."

Bethany shrugged, "She could tell I was a basket case the other day. She suggested Lisa stay there and I said yes."

Typical, Beulah thought. Izzy liked to control things and Bethany was ever the one to let someone else pick up the pieces. She tightened her arm protectively around the woman beside her, "If Lisa thinks we can take the baby, we'll just have to cross that bridge when we come to it. But look, it might never come up. It's Liam's child. Isn't it more likely he and Izzy will want the baby?"

Bethany shook her head; a frown of concern drew her brows together, "Liam told me he has some issues with being a father."

"It's one thing for him to say that when there's no child to consider. Things are different now. Let's wait and see what happens."

※ ※ ※ ※ ※

Beulah parked her truck at the bottom of the driveway and grabbed Izzy's mail. She tucked it under her jacket to protect it from the drizzling rain and headed over to the place where she had spotted Izzy, sitting on the porch of the garden house, staring at the wet foliage. She seemed lost in thought.

"Hey," Beulah handed over the mail. She pulled up another chair and sat down. "Got a minute?"

"That depends on whether you plan to drop another surprise guest on my doorstep." Izzy gave the woman beside her a cold, sideways glance.

Beulah shrugged, "It was all bound to come out, right?"

"Oh ya ... right. If I'd had a choice, I would have staged things differently. It wasn't a picnic to see Justin try to smash Liam in the face."

Beulah changed the subject, "I wanted to talk to you about something else. Is it possible to get one of the kids from the Camp to work in the bakery?"

Izzy sat up straight and stared at Beulah. "Why? What's going on with Bethany? What's going on with the two of you, for that matter?"

Beulah shrugged with impatience, "Nothing. Bethany and I talked things over last night. It was stupid what she did, keeping everything secret, but she had her reasons. I've got to face the writing on the wall with the bakery. Bethany's got other things going on in her life. Her wages from the research assistant job with Jillian will balance out the cost of hiring a kid."

"A kid part-time isn't going to compensate for losing Bethany. She's worked in the bakery with you from the start."

"She's not going to quit, only stop a couple of hours early each day."

Izzy folded her arms over her chest and nodded as she considered the request. "We can always use suitable work placement sites. I'm sure I can find someone."

"Do you think you could do it soon?"

"I have a session with one of the new residents tomorrow. I'll let you know."

"Is Lisa-Marie, okay?"

"She's very pregnant, but you knew that, right?" Izzy's legs were crossed at the knee and her foot jerked up and down with her own impatience, "Ask her yourself at dinner tonight."

"Are you sure a dinner with everyone together is a good idea?"

"I don't much care if it's a good idea or not. We'd have to do it sometime. Better to get it over with." Izzy could be as stubborn as Beulah when she set her mind to something.

"How is Liam?"

As this question registered, Izzy stared at Beulah, "He's probably feeling exactly the way you'd expect him to be feeling right now."

"What about Lisa-Marie staying here ... is he going to be alright with that?"

Izzy dodged the question with one of her own. "Do you know what her plans are?"

Beulah shifted in her chair and frowned, "No, Lisa-Marie and I didn't talk about that, and Bethany has no idea."

"She expects us to take the baby. She talked about it like it was a done deal and we didn't have much of a choice."

Beulah took a deep breath as she digested this latest piece of information. "It makes sense for Lisa-Marie to stay here then, doesn't it?"

Izzy raised one shoulder in a shrug of resignation, "For now, I suppose. We'll have to see how things turn out."

After Beulah had gone, Izzy studied the garden that stretched out around her. She'd have to get busy dividing some of the perennials and moving them around. A hydrangea bush had grown much faster than she had imagined it would. It now shaded a bed of poppies that were leafing out. The rain splattered down in a steady stream. The bright red and pink rhododendron blossoms bowed under their own increasing weight, as the glossy foliage of the plants gathered the rain and sent it down to the ground in a steady stream.

The statue of St. Francis, at the edge of a flower bed, held a bowl that overflowed with water. A robin flew down to land on the bowl's edge. It sat there for a moment before hopping over to a freshly dug area of the garden to poke its bright yellow beak into the earth.

With a deep sigh, Izzy got up. She had to start dinner. The meal was bound to be a trial but, as she had told Beulah, it would be better to get it over with. Either they would all come together to make things work, or they wouldn't. It was better to know sooner rather than later what choice they would make.

⚜⚜⚜⚜

Lisa-Marie walked out to the kitchen deck where her aunt sat. The late afternoon had brought an end to the rain, and the sky was a bright, washed blue. She plopped down on the bench beside Bethany and went into her open arms. "Oh, Auntie Beth, I'm so sorry about everything." Lisa-Marie pulled back to meet her aunt's eyes, "I thought I could handle things on my own. I was so wrong and stupid."

"Well, sweetie, it seems like I wasn't much smarter."

Lisa-Marie reached down to rub her lower leg. "Oh, for frig sakes; these leg cramps are driving me crazy. I can't breathe properly. I have heartburn every time I lie down. This maniac baby is kicking the hell out of my bladder so I have to pee every five minutes. I can't wait for this to be over. Look at my feet and ankles. Aren't they the grossest things you've ever seen?"

"I'm sorry you're feeling so uncomfortable." Bethany cleared her throat and asked, "How did Liam take the news that you're staying here?"

Lisa-Marie made a face, "He's acting like his dog died or something, but Izzy says I should stay. It's all going to work out." Lisa-Marie glanced to the side and asked, "Is Beulah still super pissed at me?"

"I don't think it was ever you she was upset with. Things have been up and down with us for a while. I've got this job over at the Camp now, as a research assistant, and I've been spending a lot of time studying to write my grade twelve equivalency exam."

"Hey, that's great." Lisa-Marie gave her aunt a quick high-five; their hands smacked together as they smiled at one another.

"I took the test the other day and I know I did well. I'm going to enroll in some university transfer courses. The research job has got me thinking about so many different things and I'm excited about learning stuff." She took a deep breath before going on, "All that hasn't been easy for Beulah. You know how she likes things a certain way."

62

"Do I ever, like her way or the highway. You shouldn't let her stop you from doing what matters to you."

"Well, we're working it out."

Lisa-Marie sat up and grabbed for her aunt's hand, "Feel her kick."

Bethany held her hand over the warmth of Lisa-Marie's stomach and felt the movement of the baby. She blinked back the tears that threatened to spill from her eyes. How could she have wanted something so desperately a few short months ago and now be so terrified at the prospect?

☙☙☙☙

"Jesus Christ, Liam, you're the only guy I know who has the best luck," Beulah gestured to where Izzy stood at the kitchen counter mashing potatoes, "and the worst." She stared pointedly out the window to where Lisa-Marie and Bethany sat together on the deck.

Beulah drained the can of beer in her hand. She gave up even the guise of helping Liam set the table. She flopped down into the rocker in the corner of the kitchen and stared at her feet. Speaking in a low tone, she said, "About that Waverly Street thing ... it's over."

A pained expression crossed Liam's face. Beulah's words were a vivid reminder of the secret he had been keeping now for over two months. He found out about Waverly Street when he went into Dearborn to see Reg and iron out the final details about the management of Crater Lake Timber.

They met for coffee at the house Reg and Josie had just moved into, on the corner of Hampton and Waverly. When Liam left their place an hour later, he felt like a million bucks. He was about to hop into Caleb's old Dodge when he saw Beulah's truck pull up and park in front of the house across the street. She jumped out of the truck and headed up the walk, swinging her keys and whistling. Before she got to the door, it opened and a redhead bounced out onto the front step. Beulah picked up her pace and Liam saw her snake her arms around the woman and pull her close before they entered the house together.

Later that day, Liam watched from the window of the sawmill office for Beulah's truck to return from town. When she drove up, he walked out to the gravel pull-off and waved her down.

"Hey, Liam. What's up?" Beulah tapped her hands on the steering wheel.

"Did you hear that we decided to hire Reg Compton to manage Crater Lake Timber?"

"Ya, Bethany said something about it. It'll be good to see Reg around again."

Liam shoved his hands deep into his pockets. "Did you know that Reg and Josie are living together now?"

"For Christ's sake, is this your gossip hour, or something? I've got things to do even if you don't."

Liam continued undeterred, "I went over to their place this afternoon, to talk over a few things about the job." Beulah took her foot off the brake; the truck moved forward. He raised his voice, "They're living on the corner of Hampton, right where it crosses Waverly."

The truck braked. Beulah jammed the vehicle into park and got out. "Waverly Street, hey," she gave Liam a cold stare. "I'm only going to say this once. Mind your own goddamn business." She walked back to the truck and turned to add, "If you think it's a good idea to tell anyone about Waverly Street, I'm warning you straight out – think again. I mean it, Liam."

Liam shook his head to clear the memory of that day. He watched Beulah as she rocked back and forth in the chair. "Good to hear," he told her.

Izzy glanced over the table. All looked in order, the bright orange of the baby carrots in their mustard glaze, the large bowl of garlic mashed potatoes, the fresh green salad, and the roast chicken flanked by the gravy boat. She reached out to straighten the centerpiece. A crystal bowl contained one perfect, white rhododendron blossom; its waxy flowers, edged delicately in pink, glistened with moisture. Izzy felt everyone's eyes on her as she sat down beside Liam.

Justin moved his chair closer to Lisa-Marie. He stared at Izzy and Liam and shook his head in a way that indicated his disgust. Lisa-Marie squirmed and her face turned red with embarrassment when she saw the way Justin glared across the table. Liam's expression of regret and suffering didn't help. Beulah sat staring up at the ceiling while Bethany darted glances back and forth, her hands nervously clenched in her lap.

The table was silent. No one seemed able to make the first move. Edward got up, leaning on his chair for support. He raised his wine glass, "I propose a toast – to family, to new life, and to kindred spirits," he smiled first at Izzy and then at Lisa-Marie. An awkward moment of indecision and silence followed before people raised their glasses.

⁂⁂⁂⁂

Jesse stood outside the large, front doors of Micah Camp's main building, his cell phone clutched against his ear. "Oh for fuck sakes, Maddy ... the plane gets in at noon. I don't know exactly how long it's going to take to get to your place from the airport." He listened for a moment before he shouted, "Hey, hold it right there. I didn't raise my voice until you started screaming at me. Stop being so crazy all the time."

Jillian came around the corner of the building. Jesse heard a noise down the airwaves that sounded as if Maddy had smacked her phone up against a wall. He pulled the device away from his ear to stare at it, "Well, that's great." He shoved the phone into his pocket.

Jillian stopped by the door, "Sounds pretty intense."

"A chick I'm going to visit in Vancouver this weekend. She's acting like a fucking basket case. I wonder sometimes if she should be in the psych ward." Jesse shrugged, "Sorry about the language."

"No big deal, but will she be alright? The call ended abruptly."

Jesse looked up at the early evening sky as if he were waiting for something. His phone rang. He nodded his head, "Oh ya, this shit will probably go on half the night." He grabbed the phone and answered it as he walked around the corner of the building. "Don't cry, Maddy. I'm going to try to get there as soon as I can, I promise. Ya sure, I can talk now ... whatever you need."

✳ ✳ ✳ ✳

Dylan sprawled on his bed reading a magazine. A quiet knock on the window had him scrambling up to tug on his jeans. He pulled back the curtain just as Arianna jumped up to deliver another knock. He opened the window.

"Do you want to come for a walk down by the lake?"

He frowned. The chick was over-the-top friendly. He thought about telling her to beat it, but since it was still early and he wasn't tired, he nodded and slammed the window shut. He tugged a sweatshirt over his head and walked out of his room.

Jesse stretched out on the living room couch texting on his phone. He looked up in surprise as Dylan headed for the doors. "Got a hot date or something?" Jesse laughed and returned his eyes to the small screen.

Dylan left the cabin and a split second later, Mark's bedroom door shot open. He pulled on his large glasses over sleepy eyes. "I thought we weren't supposed to go out at this time of the night."

Without looking up, Jesse said, "Go back to bed, Mr. Owl. There's nothing going on out here for you to be concerned about."

Dylan shoved his hands deep into the pockets of his hockey jacket and walked over to where Arianna stood, hopping up and down. When she saw him she called out, "Whew, it's colder out here than I thought it would be." She was wearing a thin shirt over a tight T-shirt. He slid out of the jacket and handed it to her. She snuggled into the warmth of the coat, "There's a walk down by the lake and it's bright enough in the moonlight. Come on." Dylan followed her, as if drawn by the long, black flow of her hair.

Arianna scrambled onto the top of a picnic table near the water. Dylan climbed up beside her. She stroked her hand down the sleeve of the jacket before asking, "You played hockey before you came here?"

"Ya ... Junior A ... for the Port Alberni Bulldogs."

"The little kids back home on the reserve are crazy about hockey. They all think they're going to be drafted to the NHL and become the next great Native hockey star."

"Most kids are never even going to make it to Junior A, let alone the NHL. I hate little kids – they're irritating. Look, did you get me out here to talk about hockey?" Dylan felt cold without his jacket and he had no idea what this chick was after. She could get any guy's attention with her large, dark eyes and smooth brown skin. She had a body that reminded him of the girls who used to work out at the gym. They were strong and powerful, their muscles small and well-defined. He had watched the way Arianna's pants clung to her butt, not much of anything shaking there.

She smiled over at him, "What do you think of the place so far? I hear you might be working in the kitchen. Are you signed up for any courses yet?"

"Seems okay ... the food is good. I'll probably be in Math and English upgrading."

"Hey, I'll be in Math and English, too. Maybe we can study together or something"

"Ya, maybe." Dylan wondered how the hell to end this conversation and get back to his warm cabin.

"How come you ended up with a job in the kitchen?"

He snapped out his response. "I asked to work there. I want to be a chef someday."

"That is so awesome. I bet you'll end up being famous with your own TV show, like that guy who swears all the time. I'll be able to tell everyone I knew you before you were a big star." Arianna pushed Dylan in the arm and laughed before adding, "You're rooming with Jesse, right? I met him in the computer lab this afternoon. He seems cool."

Dylan jumped down from the picnic table, "Hand over the jacket. I'm going back; I've got things to do."

Arianna slipped out of the coat and passed it over to Dylan with a smile and a shiver she couldn't hide, "Sure ... well ... I'll see you tomorrow." Dylan walked off toward the resident cabins, leaving her alone in the dark.

ELEVEN

Izzy studied Liam as he sat on the side of the bed staring out the window. Up the hill behind the cabin, the rain drilled steadily into the pond with such force that the drops jumped and skittered over the surface. She enjoyed the fine line of him, his body naked above his jeans, his muscled shoulders hunched forward. She rose on her elbow, "Morning," she said as she slid across the bed to sit beside him.

Liam put his hand on her knee. "Lisa-Marie says we can take the baby. She thinks a baby would be good for us. God, Izz, she acts as if her baby is something she can drop off somewhere, like a parcel."

"She said the same thing to me. It's something we need to talk about – the possibility that we could adopt the baby and raise it as our own child."

"It already is my child." Liam got up, pulled on a T-shirt and left the room.

꒰⁎꒱꒰⁎꒱

"What are you going to take away from the counselling work we've done?" Izzy glanced at Jesse's face, curious about how he would answer the question. They sat at a picnic table overlooking the lake. Today was the last of their formal sessions.

"Aside from the fact that you don't like being jerked around and that you aren't coming on to me?" Jesse leaned back on the bench and laughed.

Izzy raised an eyebrow as she remembered the August day when Jesse had pushed her up against a tree by the side of the trail and kissed her. She had shoved him away with a vigor that he couldn't mistake. When he'd had to answer for his actions to Roland, he had claimed that Izzy was fair game because of the way she had been fooling around with Justin. It had taken a bit of finesse on both their parts to get beyond a rough start like that.

"And what about how you've adjusted to taking your coffee without sugar because you've stolen mine so often?" Izzy smiled across the table before adding, "Seriously, Jess."

Jesse relaxed and took his time. "The biggest thing I learned is that I don't have to be on guard twenty-four-seven. I'll always be wary – it's who I am – but I know I don't have to manipulate all the time. I've got other survival skills. I'm not a little kid anymore. No one's going to knock me down the stairs."

Izzy sipped her coffee. After almost eight months of counselling, Jesse was walking away with a gem of an insight.

He cleared his throat as his voice caught with the threat of emotion, "You pushed me to a point where I had to trust you or walk away. I knew I didn't want to leave. That turned things around. I couldn't have connected with Jim and his family if you hadn't shown me it was worthwhile taking a chance on trust."

Jim, Micah Camp's maintenance man, had asked Jesse to come out to his house one Saturday to help his wife set up her new laptop and a wireless router. Jesse had acted like a big-time operator, bragging to everyone about how much money he'd charge Jim for his expert assistance. He had come back from that afternoon a different young man. The relationship with Jim and his family had grown since then.

"Pretty potent stuff ... trust and the doors it can open. So, what comes next? You have another couple of months here. What are your plans?"

A wide grin spread across Jesse's face, "Great segue, Izzy. I've heard back from the computer tech company in Palo Alto – the gaming guys – they want to fly me out for an interview this Friday."

"The day after tomorrow? That's great. Can you manage on such short notice?"

"I'd crawl there on my hands and knees if I had to. It's all arranged. I've got a flight out of Cedar Falls first thing tomorrow morning with a connection in Vancouver for San Francisco. They're sending a car to meet me at the airport."

"They're pulling out all the stops, hey? It sounds serious."

"I sure hope so; it feels great to be wooed. Anyway, I'll stay at Jim's tonight. His wife is going to take me out to the airport in the morning."

"When are you coming back?"

"I'm getting a flight first thing Saturday morning, as far as Vancouver. I'll spend the rest of the weekend with Maddy and catch the bus back here on Monday morning."

"Hey, that's great; tell her I said hi." Izzy noticed a flicker of uneasiness pass over Jesse's face, but he was already hopping over the picnic bench and grabbing his coffee cup. As they walked back towards the Camp, she asked, "Have Dylan and Mark settled in okay?"

"Ya, right. I must be high on everyone's crap list to get saddled with those two dudes for roommates. I guess this is payback time."

"Are you guys not hitting it off?"

"The weird, dark-haired kid ... Mark ... he informed me the other morning that he would be using the bathroom from exactly six-forty-five until seven-fifteen each day. He insisted that he did not want to be disturbed during that time and, furthermore, that no one was to enter his room or touch any of his things."

"How did you respond?"

Jesse chuckled, "I said I wasn't likely to drag my ass out of bed before eight and, even if I did, I had no intention of disturbing his private bathroom time. I told him no one goes into anyone else's room without being invited ... that he shouldn't hold his breath for an invite into mine ... and that if he didn't want anyone to touch his things, he better not leave them lying around."

"How did he take that?"

"He thanked me and said he thought we would get along fine."

"And Dylan?"

"Ya, well ... he's another story." Jesse replayed the moment a few days ago when he had come out of the bathroom, wrapping a towel around his waist and heading for his room. Dylan had been sitting on the sofa. He had glanced at Jesse. That glance had been a subtle thing, hard to pin down, except to say it didn't land where it should have and it went on a fraction of a second too long. He wasn't about to try to explain a glance like that to Izzy. She probably wouldn't have a clue. It would take another guy to understand what he meant. Besides, when Dylan found himself in the counselling room, he'd be spilling his guts as fast as the rest of them. There was no need for Jesse to circumvent that process.

Izzy respected Jesse's silence. They came off the trail in sight of the Camp's main building. She reached across to shake his hand, "Good luck with the trip and the interview. Remember Jess, my door is always open if you need to talk."

"Sure, thanks for thinking I was worth a second try."

Izzy felt tears come to her eyes. She blinked them away, "Thank you for being willing to do the work. It was all you."

ᵔᵂᵔᵂᵔᵂᵔᵂ

After making the final bread delivery, Beulah turned the truck in the direction of Waverly Street. She thought about the number of times she had driven this route feeling quite different than she did today. Beulah knew why she had gotten involved with Abbey Greene. She had needed a distraction from having to face up to the fact that her entire life had gone down an outhouse shit hole. Bethany's conduct after Christmas had made Beulah seethe with frustration.

The trip back east for Christmas, on first blush, appeared a stroke of genius. Bethany pulled out of her slump. She started eating again. She even held up her end of a conversation now and then. And most importantly, she stopped talking about wanting a baby. Beulah felt confident that when they returned home, their lives would get back to normal.

But she didn't factor Jillian into her assumptions. Bethany went over to Micah Camp right after the holidays. Before Beulah knew what was happening, Bethany had a part time job working with Jillian. Then it was *Jillian says this* and *Jillian says that* until Beulah became nostalgic for the days of Bethany's complete silence.

Never once in the fifteen years that she and Bethany had been together had Beulah ever been jealous of another woman, but she was bitterly jealous of Jillian. It didn't matter at all that Jillian wasn't a lesbian. Beulah came to the conclusion that she would rather see Bethany in bed with Jillian, than have to hear, day in and day out, what Jillian thought of every goddamn thing. It was Jillian's idea that Bethany study to take her grade twelve equivalency exam. It was Jillian's brainstorm that after Bethany passed that, she could start taking university courses and work towards getting a degree. The studying, combined with the part time research job, meant Bethany was always distracted or tired when they worked in the bakery. She was also behind on everything around the A-Frame.

As if things weren't already bad enough, when it came to any action in the bedroom, Bethany made a face and said she would do it for Beulah's sake but, to be honest, she wasn't all that interested in sex at this particular time in her life. This statement was followed by a summation of Jillian's thoughts on a woman's right to choose sexual abstinence within a committed relationship. Beulah remembered looking at Bethany in stunned disbelief.

A few days after this conversation, Beulah spotted an ad about the spring bowling league. An excuse to be out of the A-Frame a couple of nights a week

70

was worth its weight in gold. She signed up that afternoon. Abbey, with her long red hair, dark green eyes and a body that didn't stop, played on the team. She sat beside Beulah that first night as they unlaced their bowling shoes. She complained about how her husband took the car all the time and left her stranded. She didn't like walking home in the dark, but maybe she could get a cab. Beulah had offered to drive her. Abbey was a first-class flirt, sliding across the seat of the truck to kiss Beulah on the cheek and thank her for the ride.

Beulah was an excellent bowler. Abbey jumped up to hug her whenever Beulah made a strike, pressing in tight against her body. That sort of thing wore Beulah down. When Bethany went to Victoria in February, Abbey's husband was out of town, as well. Beulah spent the entire weekend at the house on Waverly.

The affair chilled near the end of March. Beulah didn't like the idea that Liam knew about Abbey. The thought that he would tell Izzy made Beulah squirm. Then there was the issue of the sex itself. What seemed hot at the start, got to be a chore. Abbey made an effort only when she could turn things rough, and Beulah was sick of slapping Abbey's ass every time they were in bed together.

Beulah jerked her thoughts back to the present moment as she swung the truck into Abbey's driveway. She would just end the thing – quick and clean.

The sound of the rain dripped from the eaves of the house and filled the silence of the living room. "What makes you think I won't tell Bethany?" Abbey purred out those words as she wrapped one of her thick curls around her finger.

Beulah's shook her head, "What would you have to gain by doing something as idiotic as that? It's over. I wouldn't come back to you. You're not in any position to throw out threats. What if I decided to tell what's-his-name?"

"What if I don't care if he finds out? What if I want to see you lose her?"

"You don't know Bethany. She wouldn't leave me. Cut the crap, Abbey. You aren't going to tell her, and we both know that." Beulah got up and walked over to the door. "We had some good times and now it's over."

Beulah left the house and got into her truck. She took a deep breath as relief flooded through her. She backed out of the driveway and headed along Waverly thinking she would be happy if she never went down that road again.

⚜ ⚜ ⚜ ⚜

Arianna walked into Izzy's office. On her way to the two chairs near the window, she veered off to examine a small goddess statue that sat on a bookshelf, "Oh man, this is cool." Then she stopped at the window, "Wow, you have a great view, but it sure rains a lot here doesn't it?" Finally, she plopped onto the chair and leaned forward to touch the edge of a tulip in a vase on the table, "Aw ... these are so pretty." She straightened up and smiled.

Izzy smiled back at Arianna as she pulled out the collage materials, "I have a project I'd like you to do. It's something I find helpful and most people enjoy it."

Toward the end of the session, Izzy sat forward in her chair, "Arianna, I'm going to stop you. I'm sorry if that seems abrupt." Arianna held her collage in her hands. She glanced at Izzy with a puzzled look on her face.

"I understand that you're quite concerned about other people. You've talked about Dylan," Izzy pointed to the picture of a hockey player. "Willow," her finger moved to a small blonde-haired girl holding a doll under her arm. "And now you're talking about Mark." Izzy sat back in her chair, "Here's my dilemma – you're the only person in this room with me right now. The only person I can help is you. Does that make sense?"

"Sort of, but it would be a help to me if Dylan liked me and if that teacher, Jeremy, would give Mark handouts when we're in the computer lab. He keeps saying he'll do it and he doesn't come through."

Izzy got up and moved the chair from in front of her desk, so it was sitting close to Arianna. "Let's try something. I want you to close your eyes and think about the first time you remember feeling like you had to help someone." Izzy glanced at Arianna. She saw that her eyes were closed and she was nodding. "Think about that situation for a moment. Think about the person you needed to help ... what did that person look like ... what was that person doing ... what were you doing ... where were you? Now, I want you to imagine that the person you needed to help is sitting in that empty chair. When you open your eyes, I want you to talk to him or her. Tell that person what it was like for you when you had to help."

Arianna opened her eyes; she seemed confused. Izzy gestured toward the chair with her hand and nodded her encouragement.

"It's my baby sister, she's just a baby. She'll fall off that chair."

Izzy bit her bottom lip, "Hmmm ... why don't you imagine you've picked her up. Talk to her, Arianna – tell her how you feel about needing to help her."

Arianna reached over to pick up the imaginary child. She cradled the infant in her arms and said, "Don't cry. Mama will come back soon. Please don't cry anymore. Take your bottle." Rocking back and forth, she hummed softly to herself. After a moment, she shook her head, her eyes flew open and she stared at Izzy.

"How old were you then, Arianna?"

"I was six. Noah was four and Jenna was a baby."

"Where was your mom?"

"I don't know. We never knew where she went. Only that she was gone and that she'd come back sometime."

"And you looked after Noah and Jenna when she was gone?"

"I got way better at it, lucky for them. No wonder Jenna cried so much that first time. I didn't even know I was supposed to heat the bottle up. The poor kid, hey?" Arianna smiled but sadness filled her large, dark eyes.

"Our time is almost up for today. How are you doing?" Izzy asked.

"I'm good. It's been a while since I've thought about being so little."

"I have an idea for your work placement that I want to discuss with you. Next door to the Camp, two women I know run an organic bakery. They're looking for someone to work with them part time."

Arianna perked up, "That sounds cool. I was hoping I would get a job away from the Camp. I like seeing new places and doing new things."

Before Arianna left the office, Izzy said, "I'll talk to Jeremy about the handouts." That comment put a huge smile on the young woman's face.

TWELVE

Lisa-Marie knocked on the door before going into Liam's old cabin. She called out Justin's name. The place looked the same, except it wasn't as neat as it had been when Liam lived there. Dishes cluttered the sink and a knife stuck out of an open jar of peanut butter on the counter.

"Hey, Leez. Don't mind me, I can barely move, I'm so stiff." Justin sprawled on the sofa that sat against the back wall of the cabin. He still wore his work clothes but his steel-toed boots were thrown off to the side.

Lisa-Marie smiled at the sight of him, "I brought you some of the chicken pot pie we had tonight for dinner. I made the crust."

"You're a life saver. I'm starving to death but too tired and sore to move my ass off this sofa to cook anything." Justin groaned as he got up.

As he passed her to grab a carton of milk from the fridge, Lisa-Marie inhaled deeply and asked, "What's that smell?"

"Yellow Cedar. I helped out on the saw this afternoon for a big order. The smell gets right into your clothes."

Lisa-Marie wandered over to the rocker and sat down gingerly. Her altered centre of gravity made even simple operations a chore. She watched Justin demolish the food in front of him. "I thought I saw you cutting across from the Camp earlier. Did you go over to say hi?" She kept her voice casual so she wouldn't sound like a stalker.

His reply came through a mouth full of food, "I had to get set up for my online English course. Maryanne, one of the teachers, helped me out, and there's a new girl there named Willow who can tutor me. I'm so sore and tired I have no idea how I'll manage to study, but I've got to do it."

At the name, Willow, a ping of alarm went off in Lisa-Marie's head. "I can help, too. I'm good at English."

Justin got up to put his dirty dishes in the sink. He dumped the empty milk carton in the garbage. Lisa-Marie gestured to the trash can, "You better rinse that out. If you don't, it's going to stink up the place and when you leave the garbage out in the bin over at Izzy's, the smell of it will attract a bear or something."

Justin made a face before pulling the milk carton out of the trash and rinsing it. "I suck at this domestic stuff, Leez. You can't believe how my back and shoulders are hurting. I thought gardening was hard work. I fell into bed last night like a corpse." Justin flopped back onto the sofa.

"What's the sawmill like? I've never been up there."

He leaned back and stretched his arms up to clasp his hands behind his head. "It's loud, lots of machines and sawdust. Reg is the guy who runs things. He lives with Josie. He says she's as pretty and spunky a little lady as he's ever had the pleasure to bed." On the last bit of information, Justin did an amazingly accurate impression of Reg's folksy drawl.

Lisa-Marie burst into a fit of giggles. "Oh geez, don't make me laugh like that. I'll pee myself. Wait a minute, I'll be right back." She struggled out of the rocker and headed towards the bathroom. After she returned and settled back into the chair, she said, "Okay ... what else?"

"I've got my own desk with a ton of stuff thrown on top of it for me to look at, if I ever get a chance. They want me to take some Work Safe BC training courses and Level One First Aid."

"Wow, your own desk. That's cool."

"You remember when I told you about the forestry course I was taking first semester? How I thought it might be easy after spending a year up here in the trees?" He grinned at her before going on, "It turned out to be one of my favourites. This job gives me a chance to see it all in action." Justin sat forward and moaned, "If only that action wasn't such muscle-humping, back-breaking, mother-fuckin' hard work." Lisa-Marie's eyes widened at his language and he told her, "That string of words is courtesy of Reg. The guy has turned swearing into an art form and, to tell you the truth, it's a bit contagious. By the end of the summer, I'll sound just like him."

"I bet you'll get used to the hard work pretty quick. Then you won't feel so stiff all the time."

"Ya, no doubt. There's this girl named Misty working up there; she's from the Camp. She was doing her Math homework instead of eating lunch. I guess that'll be me soon with my English stuff. I helped her out so she'd have at least a few minutes to eat. I wish English was as easy as Math."

If a ping had gone off at the mention of Willow, it was like a five-alarm fire in Lisa-Marie's head when she heard the words – *there's this girl named Misty working up there.* She looked out the window at the gathering dusk in the sky. "I better get back."

Justin pushed himself up from the sofa, "I'll walk you over."

"You don't have to do that when you're so tired."

"Hey, I'm not going to let you walk back on your own. You're not exactly in any shape to outrun a bear, are you?"

A blush coloured Lisa-Marie's cheeks. She looked so forlorn that Justin walked over and gave her a quick hug. "It's the least I can do after you saved my life with that chicken pie. Come on. Let's get you and that baby bump home for the night."

Lisa-Marie tried to catch her breath. The baby was making it hard enough to breathe without a little hug from Justin making her heart do this crazy thumping. She glanced up, "Why don't you start coming over to Izzy and Liam's for dinner. It's awkward with just the two of them and me around the table – Edward eats down in the sun porch half the time. If you're there, I won't be stuck trying to think of what to talk about over the main course every friggin' night. I won't have to trudge through the bush to bring you leftovers and you won't have to worry about domestic stuff." She smiled, "Win, win, win – right?"

Justin pondered the idea for a moment and then common sense and expediency won out over righteousness. "Ya, I guess. The food's bound to be better than anything I'll be able to make for myself, and I don't like you walking over here by yourself in the evenings."

⁂⁂⁂⁂

Lisa-Marie tried to get comfortable. She was in bed reading a novel by Cynthia St. Pierre. Izzy had told her that the author would be renting the guest cabin for the summer. The book was intense, all about a crazy nurse who killed off preemie babies in a neo-natal intensive care unit. The woman's life had gone right down the toilet. She found out she had the gene for Huntington's disease; then her sister got hit by a car. And to top it all off, her hot doctor boyfriend dumped her. She was pretty bummed about that since he was hot *everywhere.* Lisa-Marie had turned the pages a few times with her face red up to her ears. There were obviously more than a few things about sex that she had yet to learn.

She closed the book and frowned. No matter how she crunched the numbers, things didn't look great for her – another week and a half until the baby came and then another four to get in shape. These girls, Misty ... *what a stripper name* ... and Willow ... *who would name their kid after a tree* ... had six full weeks to get their claws into Justin and there wasn't a thing she could do about it.

Izzy knocked on the door of the loft and pushed it open. A quick glance around the room made it clear that Lisa-Marie had settled in. Her laptop and camera were on the desk, along with her journal and a bottle of perfume. Some clothes had been tossed haphazardly into the corner and over the back of the chair; Izzy assumed that the rest were tucked away in the small dresser. On the night table, she saw an iPod, a necklace, a few colourful bracelets and the tube of moisturizer she had given Lisa-Marie the other day.

"Thought I'd check-in. How are you feeling?"

"Like a big, fat blubber puss." Lisa-Marie made a face, "I'm so sick of peeing every two minutes I could scream."

Izzy leaned against the door jamb and smiled in sympathy before asking, "Did Justin like the chicken pie?"

"He inhaled it like he was starving to death," Lisa-Marie laughed and then she frowned.

"What's up?"

"He's already got a bunch of followers, after only a few days. Can you believe that?" Izzy looked puzzled so Lisa-Marie explained, "Girls – someone named Misty from up at the sawmill and another one named Willow to help him with his English course." Lisa-Marie pushed her hand against her lower back and shifted around awkwardly on the bed. "I can't wait to get this baby out of me."

"Do you want me to get a hot water bottle for your back?" Izzy was happy to face a problem she thought she could solve.

"No, I'm fine. I'm going to turn out my light. I'll see you in the morning."

"Night, Lisa. I'll wake you up around eight o'clock so we have time to get to Dr. Maxwell's office in Dearborn by nine. I think you'll like her. She's been our family doctor forever."

※ ※ ※ ※

Izzy got into bed and turned toward Liam. He had his back to her but she could tell he was awake. "I don't want to harp on about this subject, but we should talk about the baby before she's on the doorstep." Liam rolled over and stared at the ceiling.

Izzy put her hand on his chest, "What did you mean when you said the baby is already yours?" As the words came out of her mouth, she frowned, "Well, that sounded stupid. I know the baby is yours, but the way you said it this morning ... it seemed as if you meant something more."

The silence stretched out between them. Finally, Liam said, "I'm not ready to talk about any of this."

The pain and anguish in his voice was obvious. Izzy backed off. If she pursued it, Liam would only withdraw further. The last few months hadn't been all one big honeymoon. She'd pushed Liam a couple of times and she had regretted it. The way he turned in on himself and slipped away from her, even though they were still in the same room, had been infuriating. She'd ended up saying things she wished she hadn't. It was her attempt to pull him back, believing that even his anger would be preferable to the silent treatment. But she learned that he wouldn't get angry and that her words - words that tripped off her tongue in frustration - had the power to hurt him far more than she ever intended.

She sat up and pulled her shirt over her head. She slid astride Liam's body, stroking her hands up his bare chest and caressing the side of his face. She leaned over and kissed him.

He held her arms tightly for a moment, then twisted his body away from her, "Izz, I can't do this. I'm sorry."

THIRTEEN

The camper truck was parked in a pull out just off the side of the TransCanada Highway. An outcropping of rock drew attention to the endless waves of Lake Superior. Alex stood by a picnic table, sipped his coffee and kept an eye on the boy. Robbie sat on top of a large rock, his knees drawn up close to his body. Wind ruffled through the dark hair that covered the collar of his thick sweater.

Alex thought back to the first night he and Robbie had spent in the camper. He made up Robbie's bed on the small sofa. Everything seemed fine. Alex had dropped off to sleep in his own bed at the top of the camper much as he always did - awake one minute and dead to the world the next. He woke up to the sound of screaming - a sound that made the hair stand up on the back of his neck. His knife was in his hand before his eyes were open. He jumped down to the floor of the camper and saw Robbie's small body thrashing. The poor kid wasn't even awake and yet he was screaming like that. Alex still cringed at the memory. He had leaned over to shake Robbie. When the kid's eyes locked onto Alex's, the terror going straight down to their depths was obvious. Robbie had turned his head away and whispered, "I thought I was under the water."

He had scooped Robbie up and deposited him on the upper bed. With that change in sleeping arrangements, the following nights had been quiet. Robbie slept next to him like a small dog curled into a ball.

He walked over to the rock and sat down beside the boy. Robbie shifted his eyes from the water to his dad and back again before he spoke. "Father Jack said God has a big plan, and my mom dying is part of it. He said we can't figure out a thing as big as that." Robbie paused to pry up a small rock with the toe of his shoe. He reached down to examine it. After a moment, he threw it out towards the waves. "I've been thinking about that. Buddy Joe was out on the *Jodie Lynn* that day, too. He told me he could have died instead of my mom. He could have been the one close to the wheel-house and stuck in there, instead of her. I don't think Father Jack knows jack shit about God's big plan." Robbie continued to stare out at the water.

"Well, a priest can get in the habit of thinking he knows what's going on with God. Doesn't mean he does. We've got to get moving ... you ready?" Robbie nodded and they headed for the truck.

⚜⚜⚜⚜

Izzy walked into the kitchen of Micah Camp's main building carrying her black leather journal. She said hello to Jim as he poured himself a coffee, and asked, "How are Jeannie and the kids?" Izzy filled her own coffee cup as Jim grabbed a large cinnamon bun from the plate Cook had set out on the counter.

His eyes sparkled as he ran his hand over his bald head and hooked his thumbs under the bib of his brown overalls, "Really good. We've got all the boys in baseball, seems like we're out at the ball field more often than we're home. The wife thinks it's too much, but I say we've got to keep those kids busy." Jim waved the cinnamon bun at her and wandered over to the long table set up in the dining room for the staff meeting.

Jillian entered the kitchen from the direction of Roland's office. She spotted Izzy and waved hello. The woman's hair – a wild mane of soft, black frizz – always caught Izzy's attention. It took up a lot of space.

Izzy walked through to the dining room. Roland sat at the head of the table with multiple files and binders in front of him. He passed around copies of the agenda. He dressed the part of the boss by wearing an expensive suit and a Windsor knot tie in honor of the staff meeting. Roland didn't let working in the middle of the wilderness interfere with his personal dress code. His sandy coloured hair, balding at the temples, was neatly trimmed. In fact, everything about Roland was neat – from his clean-shaven face to his well-kept fingernails.

Roland glanced pointedly at the clock on the wall and stared at Maryanne, the Camp's English teacher, who stood chatting to Jillian. Maryanne's theatrical style of attire revealed her drama background. She wore a patterned dress that almost swept the floor. A long, silk scarf around her neck competed for attention with numerous strands of dark glass beads that swung to and fro as she talked.

Jeremy, the Camp's computer technology instructor, slumped over the table and slammed back his coffee. His knee and sneakered foot bounced up and down. He didn't look all that much different to Izzy now than he had years ago when he had been one of Micah Camp's first residents. He still had the wispy blonde hair tied back in a pony-tail, scruffy whiskers and penetrating green eyes behind thick black-rimmed glasses. She thought she even recognized the T-shirt that declared – *The Clash Forever* – from those long-ago days. Jeremy now ran a successful computer business in Dearborn and volunteered his services part-time at the Camp.

Izzy pulled out her chair. As Roland cleared his throat to hint that people should come to order, Darlene Evans, Micah Camp's local board member, made her appearance. She served on the town council in Dearborn and was married to the town's former mayor. A woman in her late fifties, Darlene cared passionately for the work done at Micah Camp. She had been a foster caregiver herself for many years. Giving back to the community was big on Darlene's agenda. Izzy noted that most things about Darlene were spacious. A large woman in height, breadth, attitude and presence, she carried all of those attributes well.

Josie moved quickly into the room, pulling Reg behind her. She sat down and shook her head at Reg when he headed towards the coffee pot. Her dark hair was pulled into a ponytail that seemed to vibrate with a life of its own. Reg shrugged at Jim and plopped into the chair beside Josie. He was dressed in his work clothes and if they weren't enough to convince everyone he had just come down from the sawmill, the fresh-cut-wood smell that surrounded him sealed the deal.

In partnership with the board, Josie ran the *Micah Camp Paper and Soap Company*. Working to crazy deadlines with a high-turnover staff that consisted exclusively of Micah Camp residents, suited Josie's hyperactive personality. The business did well, with the Camp's share of the profits allocated to scholarship funds.

Izzy thumbed through her journal. She felt a pull in the line of tension that ran the length of the table between her and Roland. All eyes were on her. Izzy snapped the journal shut, folded her hands in front of her and raised her eyes to Roland.

He frowned, shuffled his papers and stared at the large clock hanging on the dining room wall, "I'll dispense with my opening remarks in order to compensate for our late start. We'll go straight to our first order of business. Darlene, would you please present your Board of Director's Report."

Darlene rose to her feet. Her gravelly voice boomed out, "Good to see all of you again. First off, the annual fund-raiser in Vancouver went off without a hitch. The mayor and I had a blast. There was excellent attendance, good PR for the work you do here and, most importantly – plenty of money was raised."

Izzy caught herself wondering if Darlene addressed her husband as the mayor when they were in bed together. She tried to hide her amusement and forced herself to focus.

"The Alumni Giving Program has taken off. I want to thank everyone who spoke with past residents on our behalf." Darlene paused to look at Izzy and Jeremy with a smile. "And, of course, the board discussed expansion."

Izzy sipped her coffee and zoned out while Darlene reported the details of what Izzy considered to be the neverending debate over the pros and cons of expansion. Growth was always considered a possibility but it never became a reality. Micah Camp currently had a maximum limit of twenty-four residents and, as far as Izzy was concerned, that was more than enough.

When Darlene sat down, Roland called on Maryanne to give the Fundraising Committee Report.

With her dress swishing one way, her scarf and beads the other, Maryanne rose and threw her arms out, "People ...," she paused for dramatic effect. "The planning for our own local fundraising event is upon us." She held her hand to her heart, raised her eyes to the ceiling and sang the opening lines of a Broadway show tune. Into the stunned silence that followed, Maryanne explained, "A talent night is what I have in mind. You will dig deep, people; you will draw from the depths of yourselves, those hidden talents I know you all possess. With our current allocation of young people, we will organize a show not only to boggle the eyes and ears of the people of Dearborn and Cedar Falls, but to open their wallets, as well." After a bow, Maryanne took her seat, oblivious to the collective moans and raised eyebrows that surrounded her.

Roland waved Jillian up to report on her research. Looking briefly at her notes, Jillian began, "We've completed the first round of interviews with all residents and staff. Recorded sessions have been transcribed and we've begun preliminary analysis of the data. Some very intriguing themes have emerged." She paused to smile broadly.

Roland cringed. He had told Jillian a number of times that themes do not emerge from data, that whatever is discovered in a given data set is the work of interpretation, especially given the nature of her research. The word *emerge* made it sound as though Jillian waved a magic wand over a collection of transcripts and, lo and below, her findings floated out. Roland pinched the top of his nose and closed his eyes for a brief moment of respite.

Jillian continued, "Time spent in foster care, contact with family of origin after entering care, history of abuse and type of abuse suffered ... we are finding all of these factors. But these aren't new and the literature supports much of this. The unique themes that we are seeing here is the role of the natural environment along with the combination of counselling, education, work experience and peer interactions, all examined in relation to the length of time spent in the program." She looked around the table in triumph.

Darlene raised a hand, a frown on her wide face, "For those of us who don't speak the research lingo, could you translate?"

"Everything you do here is bang on." After a smattering of congratulatory applause, Jillian reported that she would soon begin a round of follow-up interviews.

The teachers reported on aspects of the educational program. Maryanne complained at length, as she did at every meeting, that she could not be expected to tutor everyone in English and also follow up on post-secondary applications. Micah Camp needed a full-time career counsellor. Although Izzy agreed wholeheartedly, the look on Darlene's face told her they weren't likely to see such a position filled any time soon. And it was typical of Maryanne to complain about a task that Izzy did the lion's share of.

Roland ushered Jesse into the room to give the Residents' Report. Izzy admired the way Jesse handled himself. He was now the golden boy of Micah Camp and the role suited him. He tabled the work the residents had done on the recreational budget, then he sat by while Roland said, "We have to crack down on the amount of internet bandwidth that is being used by residents downloading items to their personal computers. Three times last week, I couldn't get on the net at all. That has to stop. Tell them to monitor themselves or I'll have to start turning the service off at night."

Jeremy rolled his eyes and winked over at Jesse. When Roland turned to stare at him, he slumped down in his chair like a misbehaving teenager.

"Jeremy, do you have anything to report on the website overhaul?"

"Jesse and I have been working on it every minute we can spare. There are some tricky issues related to access – what's in the public realm and that sort of thing. But it's coming."

Roland turned back to Jesse, "Please bring up the issue of the boat shed at your next residents' meeting. If it continues to be used as an after-hours liaison spot, tell everyone that Jim will be calling a meeting to present a health and safety talk."

Jim straightened in his chair and gave Roland a look of disbelief, "Why me?"

"Are you not the head of the Health and Safety Committee, Jim? You were the last time I checked the list of committee heads." Jim stared at Jesse; the look on his face was clear. If Jesse knew what was good for him, Jim had better not have to address all the residents on health and safety issues regarding the use of the boat shed for anything other than boat-related activities.

Roland waved Jesse out of the room and Izzy gave a brief report related to the new residents' work-assignments. Then the floor was opened for other business. Jim reported that the rider mower wasn't going to make it through another year. Darlene took note. Roland advised the four teachers to work out a schedule so that someone would always be available Monday to Friday from nine to three to meet any educational queries. He had long since given up on trying to organize their part-time schedules himself – better to let them work it out themselves. Cook's reduced hours were discussed and she was given yet another round of applause for her many years of service at Micah Camp.

As Roland launched into what were clearly his closing remarks, Reg poked Josie in the side, and her hand flew up into the air. Roland raised his eyebrows at the woman's sudden bid for attention. He had suggested numerous times that Izzy meet separately with people who were only invited to attend staff meetings because they supervised resident work placements. Naturally, Izzy had not agreed to this. Apparently, she preferred to have the regular staff meetings bogged down with issues that could have more easily been dealt with elsewhere. He nodded at Josie to speak. She squirmed on her chair and blurted out, "I'm going to have to dismiss someone from working in the paper and soap shop."

Izzy frowned, "What's up?" She looked over at Jillian's digital tape recorder which hummed away on the table and added, "There's no need to mention any names. I think we all know who you mean."

"It's the first time I've ever had to say I don't want someone working in the shop, so it's kind of hard." Josie looked miserable. "He did something to a vat of soap the other day and it ruined the whole batch. I can't have stuff like that happening."

Izzy held her pen between the first two fingers of her right hand and tapped it against her thumb, "Everyone makes mistakes. Maybe with more supervised training he would do better."

Josie shook her head and her ponytail slapped from side to side. "It was a deliberate attempt to destroy a whole batch of soap. There's really no other way to look at it. I caught him red-handed." Josie's voice almost faded away to nothing on the last few words.

Roland frowned and asked, "What on earth did he put in the soap that could have caused so much damage?"

Josie glanced at Reg and elbowed him hard in the side, "Get that stupid grin off your face." She turned to Roland, "I'd rather not say."

As speculation ran unchecked around the table, Reg leaned over to Jim and whispered something that made Jim choke with laughter.

The meeting was getting out of hand. Roland exercised iron control over his voice as he told Josie, "This is obviously a disciplinary matter. You could have saved us all time simply by filling out a yellow form as per procedures outlined –" Roland stopped talking with a snap as he bit back his next words. The tape recorder whirred away on the table. "Jillian, I'm going to ask you for the last time to shut off that device." He turned to Reg, who wore a look of bemused innocence, "I trust you're not having similar issues with the residents who are working up at the sawmill?"

Reg stroked his hand down his moustache a couple of times. Then he jammed the ball cap on his head up and down. Finally, he cleared his throat and spoke, "Well ... no one's gotten all hot and bothered and tried to crank their shaft anywhere near the saws ... if that's what you mean."

Cook had been dozing off. Jim's burst of laughter almost caused her to fall off her chair. Darlene, who had taken a sip of coffee, choked, coughed and made a valiant effort not to spew coffee out of her nose. As the meaning of Reg's words sank in, Roland's face became dangerously pinched.

Josie punched Reg in the arm, "Oh thanks a lot. You promised you wouldn't say anything."

Maryanne shook her head and whispered to Darlene in a voice that carried around the entire table, "When you've worked with young people as long as I have, nothing surprises you. I can't tell you the number of times I've been witness to displays worthy of a triple x-rating."

Roland got up and took the digital recorder out of Jillian's hand. He clicked the off switch and dropped it into the pocket of his suit jacket. Acknowledging her outrage, he said, "Do not say one word. I will return it to you when I have erased the latter portion of this meeting." He looked slowly around the table, defying anyone to crack so much as a grin, "I think we have covered the agenda for today. The meeting is adjourned."

Jillian scribbled away at her notes to ensure she had an accurate description of anything Roland planned to erase. She then set her notebook aside, smiled at Roland and got up to clear the dishes and cups from the table.

Izzy walked over to her and said, "I heard you'll be going down Island on the weekend, Jill. I was wondering if I could ask a favour."

"Sure. What can I do for you?"

"Let me grab Darlene. I need her advice on a couple of things. Can you pop by my office as soon as you finish up here?"

When the three women had gathered in her office, Izzy turned to Darlene, "I know you have a ton of experience with babies. Can you give me a list of supplies a person would need for a newborn?"

"What does the mom already have?"

"Nothing."

"When is the baby due?"

"Ten days or so."

Darlene's eyes widened. "You'd better get some paper and start writing." She settled herself in a chair and ticked off a long list of items, one after the other.

A few minutes later, Izzy stared in dismay at the paper in her hand. She looked over at Jillian, "I planned to ask if you could do the baby shopping for me when you went down Island, but I can't ask you to get all this stuff."

"I have quite the reputation for being a power shopper. I could probably find everything on that list in an hour or two, tops. There's a massive Babies R'Us in Nanaimo. I bought my niece a gift there."

Darlene heaved herself out of Izzy's desk chair and asked, "What's up? Who's having a baby?"

Izzy folded the list in half, "The mom is staying with us. We're going to help out a bit."

"Sounds like a hell of a lot more than a bit. But it's your dime. I've got to get moving. I'll see you at the first planning meeting for this talent show thing. Sweet baby Jesus, I wish Maryanne wouldn't always get so elaborate with her fundraising schemes. The mayor is going to blow a gasket if I try to rope him into any kind of public performance that doesn't involve the polka. He still hasn't forgiven me for that dunking tank incident last year. Maybe I can hide away on the food committee." Darlene made a face and waved as she left the office.

Jillian stood up and said, "The new mom-to-be ... Bethany's niece, right?"

Izzy nodded as she handed over the list, "I'll call the store and make sure they have my credit card number. Let me know if you have to go somewhere else to get anything and I'll pay you back. Are you sure this isn't too much?"

"It'll be fun. Roland will get a hoot out of it."

Izzy wasn't convinced about that, but she needed Jillian's help. She didn't have the time to shop. Lisa-Marie refused to think past the moment when she wouldn't be pregnant anymore, and Liam wouldn't even discuss the reality of a baby. No one but Izzy seemed able to tackle the practicalities of the situation. If it were up to the so-called parents, the baby would be sleeping in a crate and wearing tea towels for diapers.

As Jillian left the office with the list in hand, Izzy called out, "Jill ... there's no need to skimp. If you see anything else we'll need, go ahead and get it and maybe pick out some pretty things, too. The baby's a girl. She should have some pretty things."

FOURTEEN

Edward sat in Dr. Rosemary Maxwell's waiting room and his thoughts naturally went back to the last time he had been in such a situation.

"Well, my friend ... here we are again." His London doctor of many years had sat on the edge of his desk and tapped a medical file against his leg.

Edward had asked, "What are my options?"

"The cancer is back and it has spread to the bones. At this point, surgery is not a viable option. We can do a round of radiation. The overall statistics are not good. Only five percent of men with cancer such as yours are still alive within two years of diagnosis."

Edward frowned at the doctor's way of framing that statistic. Anyone else would have talked about what became of the other ninety-five percent. "Do the chaps who take the radiation live longer?"

"Not necessarily."

Edward straightened in the chair. He had already fought one battle with cancer during which he had taken full advantage of all that modern medicine could offer him. He had promised himself that he wouldn't go through that ordeal again.

"How long would I have if I forego treatment?"

"Again, a difficult thing to predict – worst case scenario six months; best case, perhaps a year."

Edward had walked out of the doctor's office and onto a busy London street with a copy of his file in hand and a script for morphine tablets in his pocket. He had dealt with his affairs, leaving most things in the hands of his solicitor to be sorted out later. A phone call to Isabella was received with the degree of surprise Edward had expected. Three weeks later he was set up on the sun porch of her cabin with the view of Crater Lake spread out before him and the work on his book progressing according to schedule.

The sound of his name being called brought Edward back to the present moment. He followed the receptionist down the hall to an examining room where he sat in an uncomfortable straight back chair and waited for the doctor. She wasted no time in making her appearance. Giving his hand a firm shake, she introduced herself, pulled a stool forward and sat down.

Dr. Rosemary Maxwell glanced down at the file in her hand, "The last time you saw a doctor was in London –" she looked up at the man sitting across from her. "Almost two months ago?"

"Yes, that's correct. I'm running low on the morphine prescribed at that time and, to be frank with you, Dr. Maxwell, the dose is not what it could be."

"I can help you with that." She gestured for him to lie down on the examining table, which he did with care. After a brief exam she gave him time to return to his chair. She looked directly at him and asked, "Do you have any questions?"

"Not particularly. Opting out of treatment put an end to most of my inquiries."

The doctor studied Edward's face before saying, "A higher dose of morphine should take care of most of the pain and still allow you to function. Will you be staying on here in the Dearborn area?"

Edward was silent as he looked out the office window to the blue sky and scudding clouds. He saw a seagull come into view and watched it bank to the side, its bright yellow beak outlined against the white of the cloud. "I haven't made up my mind yet."

"There are a few things to consider if you decide to stay. Dearborn has only this clinic and nothing like adequate hospice care. There is a hospital in Cedar Falls, about thirty minutes from here. It could handle an end-of-life patient. A bigger center would offer far more. Have you discussed this with Izzy and Liam?"

"When I've decided, I will speak to them."

"Well, my advice is don't wait too long. Families appreciate some time to get used to the thought of losing a loved one. I'll write you a prescription for a higher dose of morphine. Come back and see me next week and we can discuss how you're doing with pain management."

※ ※ ※ ※

Edward's mind drifted as he sat back in his recliner. The chair was a blessing. It had both massage and heating options as well as a mechanism designed to move him to an upright position with the mere push of a button. Isabella had laughed when she saw it. His old hip injury proved to be an effective excuse for such indulgences.

He had taken his first increased dose of morphine and it was, indeed, dealing with the pain. He was exhausted from the trip into Dearborn and he felt more than content to spend a couple of hours in the chair dozing. Whenever he did choose to open his eyes, the view of the lake was before him. The cabin was quiet this fine Saturday afternoon, with Izzy and Liam working in the garden and Lisa-Marie giving Justin a driving lesson.

Edward had heard Lisa joke with Liam when she grabbed the keys from him, "I can teach Justin how to drive that old truck all by myself. I was getting pretty decent at it by the end of last summer, remember?" Liam had looked pained, as he did in every exchange that Edward saw him have with Lisa. Well ... it was no surprise. How Liam managed to carry on, with the evidence of his indiscretion before his face on a daily basis, was more than Edward could have done.

He had lied to Dr. Maxwell when he said he was still making up his mind about his plans. He had decided. He was going to die right here, in this cabin, in this chair, with the view of the lake in front of him. He had a plan in mind for when his work on the book was completed. Before Edward left the doctor's office, he held up the prescription and asked, "Hypothetically speaking, how much of this morphine would it take to end things early?"

The doctor had studied him, her face quite expressionless. "I'm not comfortable answering such a question but, the internet being what it is, I'm sure you could find the answer yourself." And, of course, she had been right.

⁂

A young man in a leather jacket approached the front door of a house on a quiet Kamloops street. He knocked and waited. A woman shooed a toddler behind her as she opened the door. The man smiled and stuck out his hand, "I phoned earlier about the job. My name's Jonathan."

The woman shook his hand and ushered him into the house. "You caught me right in the middle of making bread."

He followed her through to the kitchen. She opened a drawer, drew out a clean tea towel and threw it over a mound of dough on the counter. She turned and pulled down a piece of paper that was tacked up on the fridge with a magnet.

She handed him the list, "My husband said to ask if you think you can manage all of this, once a week."

Jonathan's eyes moved down the list. "No problem, ma'am. The ad said you'd have all of the equipment I'll need ... right?"

"Oh yes, everything's in the garage. We're a bit bogged down right now and the yard work is over-the-top for us. We're foster caregivers. We're getting a couple of new teens settled in and that takes a lot of energy."

He smiled at the woman as she turned to pull the toddler out of a lower cupboard. Jonathan scanned the kitchen area. He spotted the other pieces of paper on the fridge and the note pad sitting by the phone. He was in the house. That was a start. He'd make sure he kept on getting in. Someone would let something slip. That was all he needed, one small clue. When he had seen the sign appear on the lawn of this particular house, asking for someone to do yard work, he had felt a thud in his chest that almost knocked him over. He knew it would be only a matter of time until he discovered where Willow had gone.

꙳꙳꙳꙳

Roland watched Jillian maneuver the large cart through the baby store. "You seem to know a lot about babies," he told her.

"My sister has three little girls. I love babies but, of course, everyone loves babies," she flashed him a huge smile before turning to a display and squealing with delight, "Oh, let's grab this, too. Isn't it the cutest thing, babe. Feel how soft it is." Jillian held a small pink bunny.

He reached over to look at the price tag and shook his head, "Good Lord, Jillian ... you've already spent a small fortune of Izzy's money. Maybe you should stop soon."

"She said to get some pretty things," Jillian tossed the bunny into the cart and looked over her shoulder at Roland, "I bet you anything Izzy and Liam are going to adopt this baby. Why else would Izzy be springing for all this stuff? And why is Bethany's niece staying with them instead of with her own aunt?"

"It's none of our business, Jill."

"Well, I'm just saying ... it's odd, right? Aren't you the least bit curious?"

"If Izzy wanted us to know what was going on, she would have discussed it with us."

"Oh, you're insufferable, Roland. It doesn't hurt if you and I speculate a bit. No one is around to hear us."

"Whether anyone else can hear or not is beside the point. I don't want to speculate about Izzy's private life and neither should you." Roland walked along behind Jillian in silence as she continued to toss items into the cart. He

91

looked to his left and saw a display of tiny dresses. One caught his eye. In the sea of baby pink frills, this dress stood out – a cheery red fabric dotted with white flowers – a simple, tiny, sleeveless dress. He picked it off the rack and called out to Jillian, "Maybe we should get the baby a gift. After all, Bethany works with you and it is her niece's baby. What do you think of this dress?"

"Oh, Roland, it's so cute. Should we get a white sweater to go with it?"

Roland considered the idea, "Yes, I suppose so. We'd want the outfit to match."

FIFTEEN

Dylan sat on the sofa in the living room of his cabin, an open binder on the coffee table in front of him. He was having a hard time concentrating, but he forced himself to do one last check of the grocery list for a butter chicken recipe Cook had said she would let him try out later in the week.

A tall, dark-haired girl walked out of Jesse's bedroom and strolled across the living room. She lazily buttoned what looked like one of Jesse's shirts over her naked body; its long sleeves drooped down past her hands. She smiled at him and said, "Hi. I'm Maddy."

Dylan closed the binder with a loud snap and got up off the sofa. He grabbed his coat and books and left the cabin without saying a word.

Maddy stared at the door with a perplexed look on her face. She turned to see another guy emerge from the bathroom; black hair stuck up wildly around his head. He wore a long bathrobe and he was clutching a toothbrush and tube of toothpaste. He squinted as he craned his head forward to stare at her. He reached into the pocket of his robe, extracted a pair of thick-lensed glasses and put them on.

"Who are you? Why are you in this cabin and why are you wearing Jesse's shirt?" His voice was squeaky and his eyes were magnified and distorted.

"My name is Maddy. I'm a friend of Jesse's. He said I could borrow this shirt. Who are you?"

"I use the bathroom from six-forty-five to seven-fifteen each morning. I don't like to be disturbed during those times. All my things are clearly marked so I would appreciate it if you would not touch anything that belongs to me." He started to turn away, but then he shook his head as if he had forgotten

93

something. Turning back, he said, "I'm Mark." He stuck out his hand, "I'm glad to meet you, Maddy. You're very pretty. Have a nice day." He walked into his bedroom and closed the door firmly behind him.

When Jesse joined her in the shower a few minutes later, Maddy slowly moved her body against his and looked over her shoulder, "Your roommates are sort of weird."

He laughed as he kissed her neck, "Ya, tell me about it."

ﷻﷻﷻﷻ

Arianna walked across the dining room and sat down beside Dylan. "I heard Jillian saying that you're going to do some Indian, curry-chicken dish for dinner this week. I love Indian food, the spicier the better."

Dylan pushed his plate of pancakes away and pointed with his fork towards the dining room doors. Jesse and Maddy had just come in. "He had that chick in our cabin all night. Who the hell is she, anyway? I was trying to sleep in the friggin' room right next to him. Does he think I want to hear that kind of shit going on?"

Arianna looked curiously innocent. "What shit?"

"Baking-a-fucking-angel-food-cake shit ... what the hell do you think? He was banging her half the night and she was moaning like a ten-dollar hooker. That shit, Arianna. Do you have to be so dense all the time?"

Arianna cringed at Dylan's words, but put on a sympathetic look, "Oh, gross ... yuck." But as she watched Maddy and Jesse walk over to a table and sit down, she caught herself thinking how perfect they looked together. Maddy was exotic, tall and graceful. Her hair was dyed so dark it framed her pale face like a shroud. "She looks pretty, though, doesn't she?"

Dylan gave her a scathing look before he got up and left. Arianna walked over to the table where Maddy was sitting. Jesse had been pulled aside by Roland. "Hey, my name's Arianna. You're new. How do you know, Jesse?"

Maddy rolled her eyes and a mischievous smile lit up her face. She waved her hand to an empty chair and grinned as she said, "Let me tell you about the ways I know Jesse."

ﷻﷻﷻﷻ

Izzy was in the hallway outside her office when Jesse caught up with her. "Hi, Jess. What's up? How was Palo Alto?" She entered the room, dropped her briefcase on the desk and tossed her coat over the back of a chair.

"I need your help. It's Maddy. I brought her back to the Camp with me

94

last night. You need to see her. She's a mess. I didn't know what else to do."

Izzy tried to hide her shock as she drew Jesse over to the chairs that faced the lake. "Maddy's here? Sit down. Tell me what happened." Izzy perched on the edge of her chair.

"She's been going downhill for a while. I know I should have said something but she didn't want me to. She said she could handle it. When I got to her place, she was talking crazy. She begged me not to leave her there alone." Jesse slumped in the chair, "Can you talk to Roland? He was on my case first thing this morning when he saw Maddy. This place is huge, right? There must be somewhere she can stay until you can get her straightened out."

"Does she want to talk to me, Jess?"

"She says she won't talk to anybody else."

One thing at a time, Izzy thought. She turned her attention back to Jesse. "How did things go on the interview?"

"They want me ... bad." Jesse got up from the chair and headed for the door. "I've got a ton of things to do, but I'll come by and tell you all about it – maybe tomorrow." Halfway across the room he stopped and said, "I knew you wouldn't turn your back on Maddy. I told her you would work everything out." He smiled with relief as he left the office.

ᵛᵉᵛᵉᵛᵉᵛᵉ

"I hope you have an explanation for why Ms. Sinclair was in the dining room for breakfast today. Mr. McAlister knows the policy related to inviting a guest to stay at the Camp; and, I for one, have not seen a request form pass by my desk." Roland looked over the top of his computer screen at Izzy as she came into his office and closed the glass doors behind her. He had been completing an online grant application, a particular kind of hell that did not put him in a good frame of mind.

"I am here to talk about Maddy." Izzy sat down and waited for Roland to finish up whatever he was doing and give her his full attention. "I've spoken with Jesse. He brought her here because she needs help and he didn't know what else to do."

"For someone who needs help, she certainly seemed in fine spirits at breakfast." Roland leaned back in his chair and studied Izzy. She had a pair of glasses pushed up into her hair; the bright red frames glinted against her dark curls. She wore a dress that fell down around her long legs – legs that were wrapped in the shimmer of sheer stockings. The dress was a designer piece in an expensive fabric. Roland prided himself on knowing the value of upscale

95

clothing. The cross-over front of the dress was revealing enough to be sexy but restrained enough to be professional. She wore a necklace of overlapping silver medallions. A thin, black silk blazer topped the outfit and the sleeves were pushed up her forearms. Izzy had crossed her legs at the knees and the toe of her foot in its Ralph Lauren black pump, moved up and down. Her left hand, somewhat naked without the gold ring she had worn until recently, rested on the arm of the chair.

Izzy exuded the confidence of a woman who knew she possessed a powerful presence. Roland felt relieved that she was not his type. Wanting a woman like Izzy could be likened to being drawn, quartered and forced to watch your entrails dragged through the public square. He felt sorry for Liam.

"I want Maddy to stay at the Camp for a while. I need a chance to work with her and see if she and I can get to the bottom of what has gone wrong."

Roland leaned over his desk to steeple his long fingers in front of him. "Three points, Izzy. One – we have no precedent for residents returning to the Camp. Two – I was under the impression that your schedule was full. Three – where would you suggest she stay?"

"There's an empty room in the cabin that Arianna and Willow are using." Izzy sat up straight in the chair; the stiffness of her posture an obvious sign that she intended to stand her ground.

"There's a long waiting list for every room at Micah Camp. You know that."

"And yet, that room is empty. She needs my help and I'm not turning my back on her." The tapping sound of Izzy's nails on the arm of the chair was loud in the quiet office.

"I have a budget to think about. I'm sure that seems like an inconsequential thing but, trust me, it is not. She's not receiving any funding from the Ministry. How am I to explain that to the board?"

As she took a deep breath, Izzy tilted her head back to gaze at the ceiling. "The room is sitting empty. I'm sure one more person eating here isn't going to make a difference to your budget. I'll be seeing her on my own time." She looked over at Roland and raised an eyebrow, "If that isn't good enough for you, then tell me how much extra money you need and I'll write you a cheque."

Roland held up his hand and continued in a more conciliatory tone, "Let's keep in mind that we are on the same side. I'm trying to do my job as I'm sure you are trying to do yours. We'll see how things work out. She can use the extra bed but, as soon as the board approves a new female resident, she'll have to vacate that room. See her on your own time and we won't worry about the funding issues for the present. As you say, she isn't likely to eat that much."

After Izzy had swished out the door, Roland sat back in his chair and looked out the window to the drive. He shook his head. He knew that he took a low-minded delight in bringing the woman to the verge of losing her temper. He had never known her husband, Caleb, who had been killed in a logging accident before Roland came to work at Micah Camp. One heard stories, of course. He imagined that a mythic character like Caleb would have been the right type of man for Izzy. He was quite sure Liam was out of his depth. Roland would give Liam a year at the most, before he'd be reduced to a puddle of grovelling misery laid out on a floor somewhere. Much the same as Jillian was determined to do to him.

Roland checked his watch. Jillian was busy with interviews all morning. He could grab a coffee with all the cream he wanted if he nipped over to the kitchen right now. The cost of having that woman in his bed every night was high but, with planning, it could be managed. He pulled a small book from the upper pocket of his suit jacket and jotted down a short note. *What is a normal cholesterol reading for a male, aged forty-eight?*

❧❧❧❧❧

"I think we better try that calming exercise again." Every time Maddy tried to tell Izzy what had happened in Vancouver, she started crying and her slender body shook with each new onslaught of tears.

"I'm good now. I really do want to tell you." Maddy took a deep breath. She held onto the arms of her chair with a death-like grip, her knuckles white with the pressure.

"Take your time. We'll stop whenever you need to."

"Everything started off fine." Maddy gestured with her graceful hands as she spoke, "The courses were awesome and I loved my little apartment. I was on top of all of it, living on my own and managing school. Some days I got pretty stressed out, but I could do it." Tears filled her eyes and she shook her head as if to deny their presence. "Then around the end of November, my mom called me to say that my grandmother had died. I thought I was ready. I thought I could go to the funeral and see my mom and my grandfather again. You and I worked so hard last year on the stuff about him. I thought I was strong enough. But I wasn't. He was standing there smiling at me and hugging me and crying about my grandmother. My mom was right beside him, getting him tea and sandwiches. She kept saying to me, oh your poor grandfather." Maddy dropped her face down into her hands. Sobs shook her body.

Izzy sat forward in her chair, "Let's take a break."

"No ... I need to get it all out. I went home and cut that night. I felt so guilty. I told myself I wouldn't do it again. But things got so hard." She took a ragged breath and practically exhaled her words between hitching sobs, "After Christmas, I got called in for an appointment with one of my instructors. I'd missed a couple of assignments. He was an old guy. When I was alone in his office, he got sort of close to me. He smelled like my grandfather. I totally freaked and ran out of there. When I got home, I cut and cut. I couldn't stop." The sobs were now making it difficult for Maddy to catch her breath.

Izzy spoke in a tone that all her clients recognized as her no-options voice. "We are going to stop for a minute. I want you to breathe with me." When Maddy had regained control of herself, Izzy asked, "You did stop cutting though, didn't you? How did you manage that?"

"Jesse helped me. I phoned him over and over. When I heard his voice, I felt like I could stop. After what happened with the teacher, I started missing more and more school. I was blowing the whole semester. Everything fell apart. Last month my scholarship money got cut."

"What happened when Jesse got to your apartment this past weekend?"

"I don't even want to say, I'm so ashamed. It was all so crazy and stupid." Through the tears, she explained, "He said his plane got in at noon. I cleaned up the apartment and went down the block to get some stuff for dinner. He wasn't there at one, and he wasn't answering any of my texts or calls. I started cutting. He didn't get there until three." Maddy's hands swiped wildly at her tears, "I went crazy thinking he wasn't going to show up at all and even after he got there, I just couldn't pull it together."

Izzy reached across the space between them and put her hands over Maddy's. They sat there like that for a moment; Maddy's sobbing was the only sound between them. "Listen to my voice, breathe deeply." It took thirty minutes before Izzy felt Maddy was ready to leave the office. "I've arranged with Roland for you to have a room in one of the cabins. And if you want something to do with your time, Josie says she'd love to have you back working in the paper and soap shop. Let's meet every day for the next little while."

After Maddy left, Izzy turned her chair so she could look out the window to the expanse of shimmering water, the mountains looming large and solid, tree-lined slopes undulating down to the lake's edge. The view never failed to calm her thoughts and clear her mind. She turned back to her desk and jotted down a few notes in Maddy's file. Her first priority was to help Maddy get control of the cutting. After that, her dependence on Jesse would have to be addressed.

⁂

Izzy reviewed her notes from Dylan's intake session. She had asked him about his interest in cooking. He had told her that it was the only post-secondary program at the College in Port Alberni that fit with his hockey schedule, so he enrolled. Then it turned out he was pretty good at cooking. He liked baking. The precise science of making a cake rise was as challenging as barreling down the ice on a breakaway for the *he-shoots, he-scores* moment.

She closed the file and pictured the young man who had sat in her office, talking about baking. The Dylan she had observed around the Camp this past week did not seem to be the same person she had met with, one-on-one.

Dylan knocked on the open door of Izzy's office. He was five minutes early. She rose and came around the desk, "Come on in," Izzy gestured to the chairs facing the lake. She closed the door and joined him. She watched the tough-guy attitude fall away as he slumped into the chair. He was once again the quiet, young man she had interviewed days ago.

Dylan took a deep breath, "You know what happened to me when I was a kid, right?" A flash of pain swept over his face and a wave of anxiety tightened his whole body. Izzy felt the darkness that crept into the room and hung over them. She nodded. She didn't wince and she kept her composure because that was a vital part of her job. She would not give Dylan the impression that he had to protect her from any of the horrendous details of his past. He needed to know he could talk about anything with her.

But, in Dylan's case, it was a challenge. The monstrous shadow that had entered the room was his father, a pedophile who had abused Dylan for years. His mother had been so controlled by her husband that she was helpless to see what was happening. When Dylan was eleven, he acted out what had been done to him, on a younger boy in the washroom of his elementary school. A teacher came in; he was caught. The investigation revealed what Dylan had suffered. Child services took him away from his parents. He was placed with a pair of skilled, foster caregivers. He got a lot of help. Records showed that he had done well in school and that he'd won several sporting awards. He had never been in trouble again and it looked as though he had been able to put behind him much of what had happened to him as a child.

"Dylan, can I ask you something before we talk about anything to do with the past?" Dylan nodded. "I've noticed you coming and going around the Camp a few times this past week and I feel like I've seen a different guy than the one who sat in my office for the intake interview. When you walked in today a mask seemed to fall off your face. I saw you relax. Can you tell me what that's about?"

"This place is safe, right? Nothing can get at me when I'm here, in your office. I've been to a lot of counsellors. They were all good at what they did. It was always safe. I'm sure it'll be the same here." He grabbed Izzy's attention with a sudden urgency in his voice, "I know you probably have a plan for our first meeting, but I need to talk about some stuff right now or I'm going to explode."

"The only plan I have is to help. If you want to talk, go right ahead."

Dylan sat ramrod straight in the chair. His words came out in a rush, "I went to counsellors for years when I got away from my dad. They all did everything they could to help me." He flexed his shoulders, "I've always had some issues with anger, but the hockey and other sports helped. I wasn't a goon or anything, but it was a good way to channel ... things." He raised his eyes to Izzy's in what looked like a desperate appeal. He seemed to vibrate with tension.

"There's no rush, Dylan. Take your time." Izzy kept her tone quiet and her body posture relaxed.

He got up and paced the room; one hand curled into a fist and pounded against the palm of the other. Izzy's office was not small, but Dylan was a big guy and the energy flowing out of him was intense. The room seemed to contract around them.

The words spilled out at last, "I might be gay. I don't know for sure. I've been with girls before. You know how it is playing hockey." He glanced at Izzy, "Well maybe you don't ... there are some girls who will do anything to be with a hockey player, even a going-nowhere, Junior A Bulldog. There were threesomes and stuff – bang-bang nights we called them. I'd keep doing experiments – checking out if a girl turned me on or if I got more of a charge from one of the guys. Of course, when it came to the guys, I was only looking, and being friggin' careful that no one noticed. So it wasn't really the best of experiments."

Dylan sat back down in the chair across from Izzy; his admission was like a stiff wind blowing all the tension out of the room. "If I am gay, then I need to figure out if I was meant to be. You know, how people say you were born that way? But maybe it's because of what my dad did to me. If it's because of that bastard, then I've got to fight it off. And I'll probably need help to beat it – just like I did with the other crap that happened with him." Dylan's eyes met Izzy's, "I've got to get some answers before I crack up or do something worse."

Izzy leaned forward to hold his gaze, "No one can ever know what was meant to be. All we have is what is ... right?" While Dylan pondered that, she said, "Some questions in life don't give up the goods when you attack them head on. Some questions require a bit of circling around the issue until you find the way in. Do you understand what I'm saying?"

"You're saying be patient."

"Yes, I am saying that, for sure. Sexuality is complicated, like a puzzle. I'll do everything I can to help you find your way inside that puzzle."

"Okay, I do feel better knowing I have someone to talk to."

As Dylan headed out of the office, he turned at the door to ask, "Is there any way I can move to a different cabin? I don't want to share with Jesse now that he's moved that chick, Maddy, in with him."

"Maddy has been given a room in one of the girls' cabins, so I don't think that will be a problem."

After Dylan had gone, Izzy sat at her desk and shook her head. She hadn't anticipated the first session with him going the way it had. Every client and every session was challenging in its own way. Dylan's ability to invest so much trust in the counselling process could only help the work they needed to accomplish together. Her job would be to slow things down, to make sure he was ready for whatever was coming, and to help him realize it wasn't only in her office that he could be himself and feel safe.

She clicked her pen rhythmically as she thought about Dylan's request to change cabins and she recalled the look he had on his face when he said Jesse and Maddy's names. Something was going on, a new triangle that she resolved to keep on her radar.

SIXTEEN

"**M**addy, what the hell happened? Why are you back here?" Lisa-Marie maneuvered her way down onto the couch in the residents' lounge at Micah Camp. "Don't get me wrong, I'm glad to see you."

"Hey, you're one to be asking a question like that, Leez. What happened to me? Look at you. Is it Justin's?"

Lisa-Marie narrowed her eyes at Maddy, "No."

Maddy tilted her head to the side to stare at Lisa-Marie, "It isn't –" Lisa-Marie shook her head wildly. Maddy was the only person Lisa-Marie had told about sleeping with Liam, and now she wished she hadn't. She didn't want anyone talking about Liam being the baby's father. That was bound to make things difficult for Izzy, and staying on Izzy's good side was important. She had discovered that having Izzy in her corner was as comforting as Maddy had once assured her it would be.

"No, no ... some guy I hooked up with when I got to Victoria. It was just the one time. I never thought I'd get caught. Bad luck for me."

Arianna came into the lounge and made a beeline for Maddy. She plopped onto the sofa on the other side of Lisa-Marie and asked, "Mind if I join you guys?"

Maddy quickly introduced the girls to one another and explained, "Leez is staying at Izzy's and she's having a baby. Arianna is going to be working over at the bakery with your aunt's partner. Got any tips for her?"

"Her bark is worse than her bite, that's for sure," Lisa-Marie muttered.

Arianna grinned, "Thanks for the heads up. What do you guys think of Mr. Cool Hockey Dude?" She had her feet up on the table beside Lisa-Marie's and she pointed with her toes in the direction of Dylan as he leaned

THE LIGHT NEVER LIES

over the pool table to make a shot.

"His butt isn't hard on the eyes," Maddy took her time appraising Dylan. "You like him?"

"He's cute."

"If you want him, put the guy out of his misery. He bit my head off when I came out of Jesse's bedroom the other morning. I think he's jealous that Jesse's getting hot sex and he isn't. Want me to tell you guys all about it? The hot sex, I mean."

"Stop talking about sex, okay? It makes me feel queasy. And the last thing any of us wants to hear is what you and Jesse do in bed. I'll never get what you see in him." Lisa-Marie was trying to hoist herself up on the sofa as she talked.

"You never will, since you don't want me to talk about sex." Maddy laughed.

Arianna grabbed Lisa-Marie's arm to help her. "The baby's due soon, hey? Are you scared?"

"More like I'd give a million bucks to pop this thing out of me right here, right now. I don't care how bad it is. I do not want to be pregnant for another second."

❧❧❧❧❧

"So Leez finally snagged you, hey?" Jesse smirked at Justin and nodded towards the sofa where Lisa-Marie was sitting. Her belly protruded away from her body in an arc and her feet rested on the table. Arianna was shoving a pillow behind her back. Maddy sat on the other side of Lisa-Marie, moving her hands to highlight whatever point she was trying to make.

When Lisa-Marie had announced at dinner that she wanted to visit with Maddy, Justin had offered to tag along. They'd found Maddy and Jesse cuddled together on a chair in the corner of the lounge. Jesse had jumped up and done a comic double take as he pointed at Lisa-Marie's stomach. She had told him to piss off before Maddy dragged her away across the room.

Justin hadn't expected to be stuck shooting the shit with Jesse, who still appeared to be the pain-in-the-ass guy that Justin had never liked. "Give it a rest, will you. She's about to have a baby. What's the story with Maddy? Why is she back here?"

"Complicated man, fucking complicated. You were here last year; you know she was on the top of her game when she left. She waved goodbye to me like it wouldn't matter to her if she ever saw my ass again." Jesse paused to tilt his head back and pour half a box of Smarties into his mouth. His words rolled out around the sound of the crunching candy, "Right before Christmas, she starts texting and calling, and she asks me to come for a visit. I jumped at the chance. I mean, she's hot, right? And we had a good thing going before she left. At first everything seemed fine ... fun in the city and enjoyable times elsewhere, too ... if you get what I'm saying." Jesse grinned before continuing, "But we had this major blow-up right before I left. She got hysterical and kicked me out. But then she was calling again right away, saying ... sorry, sorry, sorry."

Jesse drained his can of Coke, "She's been in a fucking decline ever since. I don't have a clue what's happened to her." He cast a worried glance at Maddy who was acting out some dance routine that had Lisa-Marie and Arianna laughing. "I went to visit her after my interview down at Palo Alto and she was a basket case." He saw Justin watching Maddy's antics, as well. "I know ... you wouldn't think it to look at her now, acting as though she doesn't have a care in the world. I was supposed to be at her apartment by one but every fucking thing that could go wrong did – my plane was delayed out of San Francisco because of fog, I got screwed up with the buses leaving the airport and to top it all off my phone was dead and I'd forgotten the charger. When I finally got to her place she'd been cutting for a couple of hours; she was so hysterical I thought I'd have to call 9-1-1. She begged me not to leave her alone. I had to get back here, so I brought her with me. I didn't know what else to do. I'm sure Izzy can get her straightened out."

Justin digested the story. He hadn't pegged Jesse for the type of guy who would help anyone out, let alone stick with a chick through the scene he had just described.

Justin nodded towards the pool table that had become available. He went over and began racking up the balls. He'd known his share of girls who cut and they were always the most difficult to deal with. Maddy had arrived as a resident at the Camp only a week after he had. Right after meeting him, she'd suggested they hook up down at the boat shed. He knew then he'd have nothing to do with her in that way. Girls who act easy with sex are usually not. When Maddy had talked in group one day about cutting, all the pieces had fallen together. In Justin's experience, confessions of cutting were usually followed by stories of having being screwed over pretty early by some guy. In Maddy's case, it had turned out to be her own grandfather.

He felt his shoulder muscles tense and his hands clench when he remembered Maddy telling them what had happened to her and how her mom had stood by, blind to all of it. Justin knew all about how a mother could disappear. He understood that most of those women had been victims themselves at one time. What he didn't understand was how so many men

104

could be such fucking perverts. It was a hard thing to accept. That got him thinking about Liam and Lisa-Marie which didn't help his state of mind.

He forced himself to relax as he stood back chalking his pool cue. Maddy had pulled herself together while she worked with Izzy; Jesse had that part of the story right. She had left Micah Camp to study graphic arts at a school in Vancouver. Justin assumed she was getting on with her life in much the same way he had gotten on with his. He felt guilty looking at her now. She had been a good friend and he'd left Micah Camp and never given her a second thought.

"What's the story with Palo Alto?" Justin leaned across the table to take his shot.

"Sweet ... they want me to start working for them as soon as I leave here. The place is out of this world – a gym, a pool, gaming rooms, gadgets and toys like you wouldn't believe. I'm starting off with a great salary and a signing bonus with all kinds of perks thrown in. They're finding me a place to live. And for the record, California is as perfect as everyone says."

"When do you leave?"

"I'll probably be gone by early August. What about you? How's the job up at the sawmill?"

Justin leaned in for another shot. "It wasn't my first choice but it's working out."

"I hear Willow's tutoring your English course." Jesse's eyes followed the balls on the table. He groaned as Justin made a tricky shot and set himself up for the next one. "What a little doll. Those blonde curls and baby blues – she's hot." Jesse turned to make sure Maddy was on the other side of the room before he added, "Not Misty hot – the rack on that chick makes me want to fall on my knees. But Willow's got something going on."

Jesse took his turn at the table and frowned at the outcome. "What's Lisa planning to do with the kid?"

"How should I know? Izzy and Liam are helping her out. It's none of my business ... or yours, for that matter."

Jesse studied Justin's face, "You over your thing for Izzy?"

Justin walked around the table to take his last shot. He scowled at Jesse, "I won't even dignify that asshole remark with an answer."

Jesse watched as Justin sunk the eight ball to win the game. As they hung up their pool cues, Jesse said, "I've seen Liam over here a few times. The guy's always smiling like he won the lottery. Getting in bed with Izzy every night ... I guess he did, right?"

Lisa-Marie felt the warmth of Justin's hand under her arm as they walked back from the Camp. The path crossed behind the A-Frame and she heard the familiar sound of the stream flowing down the hill. The red glow of the fire flickered in the outdoor oven. The smell of the burning wood carried on the breeze. She missed the A-Frame but, for now, she was better off where she was.

Edward was letting her experiment with a bunch of his photos. She had been shocked to find out that he didn't know anything about digitally enhancing images. He had insisted on having Jeremy install a very pricey bit of photo editing software on his laptop and now he had her working up samples of various techniques for him to study. Time flew by whenever she and Edward talked about lenses and filters, angles and F-stops, and the special feeling he wanted people to have when they saw a particular shot.

Then there was the fact that Justin had given into the lure of coming to Izzy and Liam's cabin every night for dinner. She couldn't miss a daily opportunity like that to see him. She imagined she'd have to go back to the A-Frame sometime after the baby was born.

Lisa-Marie moved to sidestep a branch on the path. "You were pretty friendly with Jesse. I thought you couldn't stand the guy."

Justin reached out with his foot to kick the branch away. "He's still a pain, but not as bad as he was last summer. He's different. We all are. Did Maddy say anything about why she's back?"

"No, she changed the subject when I asked." Justin was too quiet beside her. "Why? What did Jesse say?"

"He said more than enough. Obviously she wouldn't come back to the Camp unless something was wrong. What did you tell her about the baby?"

"I said I had been with some guy in Victoria. I feel like a slut telling her that but I don't want anyone else to know what really happened."

Justin stared ahead on the dark path, "I doubt if Maddy would think any less of you either way. Who else does know ... about Liam?"

"Just Auntie Beth and Beulah."

"That's good. You should try to keep it that way." The bitterness in Justin's voice was obvious.

"Ya, well, I'm not exactly going around bragging about it."

"Sorry." They had crossed the deck to the cabin and he opened the door for Lisa-Marie, "I'll see you tomorrow." Justin forced a smile as he reached out and ruffled her hair

SEVENTEEN

Robbie leaned over the railing of the *Queen of Nanaimo* and inhaled so deeply it looked as if he was trying to pull the smell of the ocean down into his toes. Driving onto the huge ferry, Alex had wondered if the passage to Vancouver Island would bother the boy, but he didn't seem to make any connection between the Pacific Ocean and the waters of Miramichi Bay, or between this ship and the *Jodie Lynn*.

Coming across the deserted deck, Robbie slid down into a crouch near the bench where Alex had settled. He sped two small cars along the edge of the seat and crashed them into each other. "How did you meet my mom?"

"She never told you?"

"Every time anyone ever said your name, she said you must be stirring up shit somewhere since that's what you were good at." Alex let out a loud snort of laughter. "She didn't say it like she hated you or anything."

"No, I never thought she would hate me. I seem to remember my leaving was mutually agreed upon. You know about all the trouble with the commercial fisherman and the lobster?" Alex saw Robbie nod without looking up from the car collision in front of him. "I came out to help. Your mom was right in the middle of all the fuss. That's how we met."

"Did you love her?"

"For a time ... yes, I loved her very much."

"Did you ever think about me?" Robbie held the cars tight in his hand as he waited for the answer.

"Yes, I thought of you many, many times." Robbie looked right into Alex's eyes and paused before nodding his acceptance. He got up and wandered to the end of the bench where he dug in his pocket and pulled out a couple of small toy figures. Before Alex turned his gaze back to the brilliant blue of the sky, Robbie had a game going that involved dropping the figures from the top of the bench onto the miniature cars as he moved them along the seat.

Marsha had told Alex to stay away from her and Robbie. She had said she didn't want to raise a kid with a guy who could only see his way to showing up now and then; and it didn't look like Alex was a guy who could ever do much else. He had agreed with her opinion of him, and he had stayed away. He thought about telling the kid that he had done what Marsha had asked him to do, but that would have been a lie. He knew that she had wanted him to prove her wrong - wanted him to change, for the right woman and the dark-eyed baby she held in her arms. But Alex had been too old to change.

⁊⁊⁊⁊

Izzy leaned forward, holding her hair up while Liam worked his fingers in deep circles around the back of her neck and shoulders. When he had walked into the kitchen earlier, he'd found her frowning over her laptop, papers and books.

He slowed the movement of his hands, "Your neck muscles are still all bunched up in a knot. You need to take a break."

"Ya, maybe you're right. Is there any more coffee?"

Izzy settled into the rocker in the corner of the kitchen with the coffee Liam handed her. She flexed her shoulders and tried to relax. "Things at the Camp are a bit crazy right now with Maddy landing in my lap the way she has. I'm behind on this course planning. They wanted my outline last week."

"How is Maddy?" Liam sat down in the other rocker and watched Izzy's face.

"Not good ... she's lost a lot of ground. I need to see her every day, on my own time - time I would spend doing this other stuff," Izzy pointed to the pile of books on the table. "Roland was on my case about letting her stay. I told him to let me know what it would cost and I'd write him a cheque. I swear to God, he does things like that to get at me. But I would have paid. I can't turn my back on her."

Liam took a sip of his coffee and let Izzy's voice wash over him. Her attitude about money still caught him by surprise at times, but he reminded himself that she had good reason to take a relaxed approach to her finances. He thought back to the first and last conversation he'd had with Izzy about money. It had been an eye-opener.

⚜⚜⚜⚜

The talk had taken place Christmas morning. They took their coffee out to the sun porch where they watched the first flakes of snow come down. Izzy, still in her pajamas with a heavy sweater wrapped around her body, curled up in a chair with a look of wonder on her face as she studied the snow blowing against the window. The time seemed ripe for introducing a topic Liam had wanted to discuss since he'd moved into the cabin.

"How much money do you have, Izz?"

"Geez Liam ... how much money do you have? What kind of question is that? Do you need money?"

"No, as a matter of fact, I don't. Since coming here, I've been able to bank money every month. I only have the government pension coming when I turn sixty-five, but I've kept up my retirement savings. The interest hasn't been the best lately, but in previous years it wasn't bad. I have my wages from the sawmill – it's more than I need. I'm even able to put a decent chunk of that aside. I'm no Jimmy Pattison, but I'm not on poverty road either."

Liam gave Izzy a look that said, your turn. She slumped a bit and pulled her eyes away from the flurried, white landscape outside the window to give him her full attention. She hesitated, "I grew up in a home where discussions related to money were considered vulgar. I've never quite gotten over that, I suppose. When I was with Caleb, we never talked about money because we never had to. Then Caleb died and there wasn't anyone to talk to at all."

"But I had to think about the money and do something with it." She looked back out the window. "I understand why you're asking, Liam, and you have every right. We're together now," Izzy brought her gaze back to his. Her slight smile didn't quite reach her eyes. "I need you to understand something before we talk about this." She took a deep breath, "I don't think of this money as mine, though technically ... legally it is. I did nothing to deserve all of this bloody money."

"It's that much, hey?" He had always known that Caleb and Izzy were financially secure. They never bragged about it or lived in a way that would make it obvious, but they both had a generosity and an easy attitude about buying things that spoke volumes.

"I suppose many people would think so." Now that she had started, Izzy embraced the opportunity to talk, "Actually, I'm glad you brought this up." She grabbed her journal from the seat beside her and flipped it open to a blank page. She jotted down a figure that made Liam's eyes widen. "When Caleb left the States back in the seventies he had this amount in a trust fund

109

his family set up for him." Seeing Liam's reaction, she said, "You knew Caleb's family had money."

Liam nodded. Caleb's mother, Lillian, had visited enough times over the years. He had gotten to know her well. He knew she came from money, had lots of it and enjoyed spending it.

Izzy kept on talking. "Some of that trust fund went towards the capital costs for this place, but land was available for a song back in those days. Setting up the sawmill was an expense, as well. Caleb lived off the interest from the fund and off his quarterly dividend payments from the winery down in Sonoma – everyone in his family had shares." Izzy drew a quick line through the figure she had written down and jotted a new one underneath. "Ten years ago, Caleb and I set up an anonymous scholarship fund over at the Camp, so that reduced what was left in the trust. But it was still a fair amount of money."

She tapped her pen against the journal as she spoke. "Right before Caleb and I met, his dad died. Caleb's uncle and his two sons took over running the winery. Caleb's dad's shares went to Lillian. For years, the profit from Caleb's shares and interest on the capital of the trust fund was more than enough for Caleb and me. We had my salary from the Camp and whatever came in from the sawmill. When Lillian died, Caleb inherited her shares and the controlling interest in the winery. When Caleb died, all of that landed on me."

She cast a quick look at Liam. Mentioning Caleb's death was hard but Liam seemed okay with it. His eyes were sad but he kept his pain under control. Losing Caleb was something neither one of them would ever get over. Together, they had come to accept that.

Moving over to the couch, Izzy sat down next to Liam. "Do you remember when I went away for a month after Caleb died? I had to go down to California to meet with his family ... and a room full of lawyers. The cousins wanted to buy me out of the controlling share in the winery, and that seemed like the right thing to do. I agreed to sell Caleb's shares, the land and the house – all of it as a package." Izzy jotted down another figure in the journal and pointed to it with her finger.

She snuggled in closer, her eyes far away and her voice hushed, "You should have seen that house. I spent hours wandering around the place thinking of what it must have been like for Caleb to grow up there. It was like those pictures you see of sprawling estates owned by Columbian drug lords – well, minus the security walls. Anyway, the cousins were grateful to keep the vineyard and winery in the family. I knew that's what Caleb would have wanted." She sat up straight and pointed to the written figures, "I haven't touched any of the money that came from selling everything down south. The yearly income from the interest alone is staggering; mind you, the taxes on the money can be brutal. But no matter how you look at it, I have way more money than we'll ever need."

Liam tried to hide his shock. He reached over and closed the journal that lay in Izzy's lap. He felt better when the figures were no longer staring out at him. It was one thing for him to know that he and Izzy were comfortable when it came to money. It was another for him to find out that the woman he loved was very wealthy. "So, you and I have no issues with money?"

"Not around needing money. We have plenty. You don't have to live like a pauper, saving every cent you make and worrying about your pension. You don't need to work at all."

"I've been thinking about that. Josie came to talk to me before the holidays. Do you remember Reg Compton?" Izzy nodded and Liam went on, "He and Josie just got together. Anyway, he's back in town and trying to find work. He might be the guy we've been looking for to run Crater Lake Timber. We should talk to him and, while we're at it, think about spending some money to install a satellite phone and internet connection at the sawmill office. Then I can go back to gardening and looking after the chickens. What about that?"

✻✻✻✻

Izzy stretched in the rocking chair before rising. "I'd better get working on this stuff. I have to be back at the Camp to see Maddy before dinner, then I have group tonight. Are you on your way out to the garden? What are you planning to do?"

"I was going to start potting up the hanging flower baskets."

"Oh ... that's my favorite job." The crestfallen look on Izzy's face was comical. Liam just managed to choke back a laugh.

He got up and reached across the table to close the lid of her laptop. "Come on outside with me right now, Izz. You can do this stuff later."

"I should see if Lisa and Dad want any lunch."

"They're up to their ears in the latest version of his galley pages. If they're hungry, they know where the kitchen is. Come on."

An hour later, Izzy smiled as she pivoted a basket to and fro making sure there were no empty spots. It was filled with white alyssum, purple heliotrope, a couple of small geraniums, a pair of trailing fuchsias, all interspersed with blue river daisies. Satisfied, she reached up to hang it on one of the many hooks running the length of the greenhouse rafter.

"Izz, you know that old sofa in the back of the shop?"

She glanced over at Liam. He was looking at her in a way that would have made her blush if she weren't forty-six years old and hadn't already had the pleasure of sharing a bed with him for months. Though some things didn't lose their fascination overnight, and thank God for that, she told herself.

Liam's eyes held hers as he said, "How about you and I go there now ... to the shop. We could lock the door and try out the springs on that old sofa."

Izzy pulled her gardening gloves off and reached for Liam's hand.

Later, with their clothes back in order, Liam held Izzy tight against his chest. "I'm sorry about the other night. Having Lisa right upstairs isn't easy. Sometimes I feel like I can't breathe."

⚜⚜⚜⚜

When she heard the knock on the back door of the A-Frame, Beulah dropped the dish cloth into the sink and reached for a towel to wipe her hands. "That must be the kid from the Camp." She looked over at Bethany, "Can you finish up here while I show her around?"

She pulled open the door. The girl standing on the back step of the A-Frame smiled, thrust out her hand and grabbed Beulah's, "Hey, I'm Arianna. You must be Beulah ... oh crap, am I saying it right ... Beulah? Should I call you that or Mrs. Something? Would it be Mrs.? Or maybe you're Bethany," Arianna looked past her to the woman busy in the kitchen. "I never thought of asking what either of you looked like or what I should call you."

Beulah reclaimed her hand from Arianna's and pointed back over her shoulder, "That's Bethany, I'm Beulah. Your timing is excellent, I'm about to light the oven. Come on."

Arianna flashed a smile at Bethany, waved and followed Beulah down the stairs and across the yard. They walked towards the open shed that housed the red brick oven. The large chimney protruded through an opening in the roof. Heavy metal doors spanned the oven's mid-section. Under those doors, a brick-lined space gaped black and empty. Beulah crunched paper into the space and loaded kindling on top.

Arianna looked beyond the oven shed to the stream that tumbled down through the trees, roaring and splashing over large rocks. It ran past the far side of the A-Frame and poured over the cliff to the lake below. "It's really pretty here."

Yes, Beulah thought, it certainly is. She could still remember the first time she had stood in this space. Caleb had walked ahead of her to open up the A-Frame and show her around. She had seen, in that moment, how her dream

112

of the wood-fired oven and the bakery could fit onto this piece of land.

"Grab a pair of gloves," Beulah pointed to an extra pair on the top of the brick structure. "Make yourself useful by hauling over some wood."

When the fire was blazing, Beulah sized Arianna up. The girl didn't look like a weakling. Time would tell. Hefting bags of flour and removing multiple loaves of bread from the oven were not tasks for a lightweight. She threw some more wood on the flames, "We'll have to babysit this fire for a few minutes." Arianna leaned in against one side of the brick oven. The kid had seemed like a chatter-box at first but she could be quiet as well.

Beulah folded her arms over her chest and stared at the fire. "Baking bread in a wood-burning oven is a combination of science, art and witchcraft. It's not exact, if you know what I mean. More like experience, intuition and sheer luck." She leaned on the other side of the oven and went on, "In the beginning, I thought the whole idea of baking bread outside would be romantic." Beulah snorted at the naiveté of her former self, "I'm not saying it doesn't have its moments ... like when I'm pulling the loaves out of the oven and the snow is falling ... the whole fresh-baked smell and the bread coming right out into the wilderness." Beulah looked away, at the evergreens that grew up the slope and the snow-capped mountains beyond. "It's not so romantic when the wood is wet and the fire's hissing rather than crackling the way it's supposed to."

Arianna patted the oven, "I've seen something like this before, back home. One of the elders baked bannock out in her backyard."

"Baking bread in wood-fired ovens goes way back. Our oven works like this – the fire we've lit will burn out by about midnight. The heat that's trapped in the bricks will hold and the oven temperature will be perfect for baking tomorrow morning."

Arianna walked around to inspect the front of the oven. "How do you know when it's ready for baking?"

"I just put my hand on the bricks. You get a feel for it when you've done it for a while. In the morning, I come out here and rake all the ashes out from underneath the oven before we begin to bake ... just to keep everything neat." She snorted as she added another log to the fire, "That's another myth about wood-burning ovens. People think the wood has something to do with the flavor of the bread, but the wood is long gone before we ever put anything in the oven." Beulah straightened up, "What's special about bread baked in a wood-fired oven is the steam that builds up when the oven is loaded."

Arianna asked, "Steam?"

"That's the secret. When that the oven is full, there's a lot of moisture being pushed out of the loaves. The steam creates the thick, crispy crust."

Bethany came out of the A-Frame and walked over to join Beulah and Arianna. She smiled at Arianna, "You'll be the first person we've ever had working with us in the bakery. It will be fun to show someone else how we do things. Don't you think so, Beulah?"

Beulah nodded and led the way to a rectangular shaped building. The afternoon light streamed through the windows that lined the top of the two longest walls. Beulah pointed out things as she made her way across the room, "That's the commercial oven. We do the cracked wheat buns in there. This is the proof box." She pointed out the large metal box and the double doors swung open with the touch of her hand. "Over there are the mixing vats. We can push them right into the proof box when the sponge is ready for the first rising. The box allows us to control humidity and temperature. That's crucial when you're working with something as delicate as bread."

Beulah laughed when she noticed how Arianna stared dumbstruck at the mixing vats with their massive double, diving arms suspended above the stainless steel. "Wait until you see those babies in action. They can look like something out of a sci-fi movie when they get going." Beulah turned to point out the two upright, cabinets enclosed behind glass doors, "That's where the loaves rise; they're also temperature controlled. Over there is the fridge, the storage bins for the flour, cooling racks for the bread."

Beulah stopped talking to put her hands down on the long butcher-block style table with its smooth, worn surface. This had been the first thing to be installed in the bakery building. She could not count the hours that she and Bethany had spent side by side at this table. "This is where we hand shape each and every loaf." Beulah glanced at Bethany; their eyes met and they exchanged a look of understanding.

Arianna did a full circle as she took in the entirety of the shop. Her eyes came to rest on the chalkboard hooked on the wall. It listed a complete schedule with the hours from five a.m. to noon, with tasks spelled out for each time interval. Her mouth dropped open long before she got to the bottom of the list, "Wow, you two must have to keep moving to get through all of that."

Beulah nodded, "And it doesn't end at noon. We live our lives around the bread. Active baking all morning, deliveries all afternoon and, by the time I get back from Dearborn, the fire has to be lit. Then we nurse that along into the night and fall into bed so the whole process can start again the next day."

"It's a full time job, that's for sure." Bethany walked over to the shelves that held the racks of cooling bread, "We've always concentrated on making a few products and doing those well. A French bread –" she broke off a piece.

"It has a distinct sourdough sharpness and a crisp crust." She handed the piece to Arianna and watched her chew it. "What do you think?"

Arianna spoke around the bread in her mouth, "Yummy."

Bethany was already breaking off a piece of another loaf, "This is whole grain, herb bread, topped with coarse salt." She gestured over to the commercial oven, "We use the regular oven to bake buns. Our recipe uses cracked wheat and honey. It's quite rich with eggs and cream. People are still crazy about those buns, even after all these years."

Beulah pointed to the racks of cooled bread, "We bake the bread one day and it goes to town the next. The whole grains are better when they sit overnight." Pointing to the chalkboard, she added, "We follow that schedule five days a week but we don't bake bread on Saturday; that's a bit of a treat day for us. We make pizza crusts in the outside oven. They fly off the shelves of the stores all of Saturday afternoon and Sunday. The oven gets Saturday night off. We get our break on Sunday - except for lighting the fire Sunday night, that is. We do regular baking on Monday - but make no deliveries Monday afternoon."

Bethany laughed, "But don't think Beulah takes it easy ... ever. Monday afternoons we scour out the whole bakery building."

"So, what will I be able to do here? I'm allowed to work twenty hours a week." Arianna leaned back against the long wooden table and smiled.

Bethany's eyes crinkling at the corners as she returned Arianna's smile. That smile reminded Beulah of the woman she had fallen for so many years before. All of a sudden, it seemed that their life together could return to what it had been. "Bethany is going to be getting off at nine o'clock each morning. So, if you were here from eight to noon, Tuesday to Saturday, that would work well for us. You'll be pitching in on everything."

"This looks like an awesome place to work. Back home on the reserve, we have this gigantic winery and I've been through it a bunch of times. This reminds me of where they make the wine - so clean and shiny. Should I start tomorrow?"

Beulah nodded, "Tomorrow would be perfect."

EIGHTEEN

Izzy opened her umbrella as she walked out of the Camp's main building. She picked her way across the gravel driveway, avoiding the puddles, and walked down the path to the maintenance shed. Poking her head through the door, she saw Jim over by the workbench, tinkering with an engine.

"Hey," Izzy put the umbrella down and shook it out before crossing over to the bench where Jim stood. "I'm looking for Mark, have you seen him?"

"He's in the electrical control room. The kid's a genius, Izzy. I caught him in there the other day and almost freaked out. He had the high voltage box open." Jim didn't see the look of alarm that crossed Izzy's face. With his hand buried inside the greasy motor, he was too busy cranking a ratchet. "I tiptoed across the floor so as not to startle him." He glanced sideways at her, "I didn't want him to fry right there in front of me. But when I got close, I could see he was just looking things over. We got the box closed up and he started tinkering with some of the meters. He's got them all calibrated and he explained a few things to me that I didn't have a clue about."

Izzy glanced around the maintenance shed before asking, "Is there a place around here that I could talk with him?"

Jim put down the ratchet and pointed to a doorway, "Sure, pop into my office and I'll go get him."

Izzy walked into a small room that contained a beat up chair and a couch that sagged dangerously in the middle. A coffee maker sat on the counter. At one time, it must have been white before layers of dirt and grease did their work. An inky, black substance covered the bottom two inches of the pot.

Herding Mark in front of him, Jim came into the room. He reached for an equally smudged cup from the shelf, "Great, I was hoping there would be a

116

cup of coffee left. I'll grab this and get out of your hair." He poured the thick brew into his mug and waved the ratchet in Izzy's direction as he headed out of the room. She shuddered and turned her attention to the young man standing in front of her.

"When you didn't show up for our appointment, I decided to come and look for you." Izzy sat down on the edge of the chair and gestured for Mark to take a seat on the couch. "Can we talk now?"

Mark walked across the room and sat down. He frowned as he checked his watch, "I thought there was a lot more time before I was supposed to go and see you."

"No problem." Izzy smiled. "Would you like me to explain what I do here at the Camp?"

Mark jumped up to get his pack and rummaged around inside it. He came back to the couch and opened the notebook in his hand to a blank page. "I like to write stuff down, so I'll remember –" he looked at Izzy's empty hands, "unless you have a handout?"

"You can take some notes if that's useful for you. When you talk with me, everything you tell me is confidential ... between the two of us. But there are a few cases where I might have to break that confidentiality. I want you to know about those times." Mark looked up, his eyes magnified by his thick glasses. "If you told me that you planned to hurt yourself or that you knew someone else was going to get hurt, I would have to break our confidentiality."

Mark was quiet as he thought over Izzy's words. After a moment, he said, "Like if I told you I heard Dylan saying he will smack Jesse's head against a door jamb if he has to hear him screwing around with Maddy for one more night?"

Izzy kept her facial expression neutral, "Sort of like that, but maybe something more serious, like if you told me you were going to hurt yourself or you heard that Dylan was going to take a gun and shoot Jesse. Do you see the difference?" Mark nodded and scribbled something in his notebook. "So, that's an important thing to remember when you talk to me – what you say is private."

Mark cut in, "Unless I tell you someone is going to shoot someone."

"Have you ever been to a counsellor before?" Izzy's question was answered by a shake of Mark's head. "I'm here to help. That's my job. Can you think of a way I might be able to help you?"

Mark looked past Izzy to the wall behind her. He tapped his pen against his leg. "I've thought of something."

When it became obvious Mark wasn't going to say anything more, Izzy realized she had only told him to think of something. "Please tell me what you've thought of."

Mark's words came out in a rush, "Everyone knows how to do things here. I don't know the rules. You could help me with that."

"Are you thinking of any situations in particular?"

"There are two things. I don't know what to do in the dining room. People come in and they sit together and, unless I see Arianna, I don't know how to figure out where to sit." Mark picked up his notebook and spun it into a tight roll. He banged it on the couch. "I like Maddy. She's funny. I know she's Jesse's girlfriend. I don't like her like that. But I want to know how to talk to her. That's my second thing. When my mom was alive, she would help me learn the rules for doing things."

Izzy leaned forward and asked, "How did she do that?"

"When I was little she would draw it all out for me, like in a picture book. I had a whole bunch of them. When I got older, she would help me write a list of rules for each thing I wanted to do."

"I'm sure we can work together on that. How would you feel if I came out here to meet with you from now on?"

Mark's face lit up, "That would be good. I really like it out here."

"Jim says you've been working on some of the electrical stuff. Would you like to show me?" Mark was up off the couch and talking a mile a minute about shunts, wires and calibration settings as he gestured for Izzy to follow him. She walked after him through the shop, thinking that if he needed a comprehensive list of rules on how to navigate his way through social situations, then she would help him to develop it.

❧❧❧❧

Dylan hurried over to the stainless steel sinks in the kitchen and washed his hands. He adjusted his apron and jammed on his cook's hat. He opened the large fridge, pulled out the glass dishes of chicken and put them on the counter. The spice and lime smell of the marinade wafted up at him.

Cook sat at the table. Her legs were stretched out to rest on a nearby chair and her face was buried in an open newspaper. She barely nodded at Dylan as he moved around the kitchen, setting the skillets on the stove and dribbling oil into each of them.

Bethany and Jillian came in, laughing and chatting as they walked over to the counter to look at the chicken. "I could smell the spice from down the hall. What can we do to help?" Jillian rubbed her hands together as she spoke.

"I need someone to chop all those onions and someone to make the salad." Dylan looked over at Cook, "You got the pita bread, right? We really need that bread."

"Relax there *Galloping Gourmet*, your bread is waiting for you in the pantry." Cook didn't even lift her head from the newspaper.

Dylan grabbed the tomatoes from the fridge. "Great. I've got to get these chopped and pureed."

Looking up from the food processor that was blending the deep red mixture, Dylan spoke over the noise, "Smaller, Beth, I need those onions chopped fine."

Jillian raised her eyebrows as she washed the lettuce in the sink, "Come on, Beth ... get it right or we might have to fire you."

Bethany laughed, "Well at least you can't lower my wages."

Dylan browned the chicken in several batches; the smell of onion, garlic and ginger paste hung in the air. He added chicken broth and the pureed tomato mixture and shoved the large pans into the oven.

With the timer set, he turned to smile at the women gathered in the kitchen. "Now for the fun part," he brought out three large sheet cakes from the pantry and began assembling ingredients from the cupboard. "This is my favorite thing to make and eat – a vanilla sponge cake roll with coconut icing, drenched with dark chocolate and lightly dusted with powdered sugar."

When the pans of chicken came out of the oven, Dylan drizzled on the butter and laid out the cilantro garnish. He stood back to study the effect, "Presentation is everything, ladies. Remember that when you work with me." He grinned at them and moved the pans of chicken out to the dining room. Jillian followed with a giant bowl of salad in each hand. Bethany carried in a large basket of bread.

After the dessert was served, Dylan returned to the dining room to receive a well-deserved round of applause. Arianna rushed up and threw her arms around him. She whispered in his ear, "The chicken was so good ... but, like I said, I could take it spicier."

He glanced over Arianna's head and saw Maddy sitting beside Jesse at a nearby table. She reached over and put a piece of cake in Jesse's mouth. Jesse grabbed her hand and held it while he slowly licked the icing from her palm. Dylan pushed Arianna away, "I've got to get back for the clean-up."

"I'll come with you and help."

Dylan shrugged and turned towards the kitchen.

※⌒※⌒※⌒※⌒

"Hey, Justin, can I tag along to the Camp with you? I'll visit with Maddy while you're being tutored." Lisa-Marie grabbed an old, red windbreaker that at least semi-covered her stomach. Half way to the Camp, she doubled over on the trail and gasped.

"What is it, Leez? Is it the baby? Are you all right?" Justin put his hand on her back and leaned down close to her.

She straightened up slowly and took a deep breath, "I'm fine ... it's these stupid fake contractions. I've been having them all day."

"How do you know they're fake?"

"The baby isn't supposed to come for another week. Come on, let's get going before a cougar flops out of a tree on top of us. Did you know they can climb trees?"

Lisa-Marie lingered at the door to the library as Justin crossed the room to join Willow at a table. The blonde girl smiled up at him as he said hello; then he must have joked about something because they both laughed. Lisa-Marie smouldered with jealousy as she walked away. This was worse than the way she had felt when Justin hadn't been able to tear his eyes away from Izzy. Lisa-Marie had always known that Izzy enjoyed being worshipped; but Izzy would not have allowed Justin to kiss her. There were no such guarantees with Willow. The thought of Justin with his arms around that girl, lowering his lips to her pouty little mouth, made Lisa-Marie feel sick. But maybe she just had heartburn again.

She walked into the TV room and looked around for Maddy. She saw her in a chair, sitting on Jesse's lap. "Oh for frig sakes, can't you guys get a room or something ... the two of you ... over-the-top gross." Lisa-Marie lowered herself onto the couch, clutched at her stomach and leaned over groaning. When she looked up, everyone in the room was staring at her with varying degrees of alarm on their faces. If she hadn't still been gasping to catch her breath, she would have burst out laughing. "It's just the fake contractions, relax."

Jesse scooted out from under Maddy's body, "I'm out of here. Way too much drama in this room for my liking." Lisa-Marie made a face at him while Maddy got up from the chair and came over to the sofa.

"Tell me everything you know about that Willow girl." Lisa-Marie put her feet up on the coffee table and stared at Maddy.

"Pretty, if you like the delicate type. Why?"

"She's tutoring Justin in English." Lisa-Marie's voice was so heavy with sarcasm over the word *tutoring* that Maddy burst out laughing.

After Lisa-Marie punched her in the arm, Maddy said, "Don't worry about her. I heard her talking with Arianna the other night, going on and on about how she'll never get over this guy she broke up with before she came here. *Jonathan this* and *Jonathan that.* She was holding a picture of him and crying." Maddy cautioned Lisa-Marie, "If I were you, I'd be way more worried about Misty."

"Oh shit, I knew it. With a name like that, I knew it. What about her?"

"Well, seriously Leez, have you seen her?" Lisa-Marie shook her head and Maddy said, "She's got an awesome figure, tall like me, but a bust out to here," Maddy was gesturing beyond her own low-cut T-shirt. "You don't want Justin having anything to do with her. No guy could look at her without thinking about getting her shirt off and you can imagine just how fast that little fantasy would go south."

"He already told me that he's been helping her out with her math, on their lunch hours."

Maddy bit her bottom lip and raised her eyebrows. Then she dropped an arm around Lisa-Marie and said, "Come on, cheer up. Dylan made this awesome rolled cake with coconut icing for dessert tonight. Let's go to the kitchen and see if there's any left." Lisa-Marie heaved herself off the couch to follow Maddy out of the room. She was only half listening as Maddy chatted on, "Now that guy, Dylan ... you've got to see him down in the weight room with his shirt off ... hot ... like sizzling. And he cooks, too. Arianna better move on that prime real estate before I think about taking a run at him."

�·✾·✾·✾

Dear Emma:

These fake contractions are killing me. I hope this doesn't go on for the next week until the real ones start, and I hope the real ones aren't a lot worse than these.

Something is so wrong with Maddy. When I ask her what's going on with her and Jesse, she says their friends. Ya right. They're together all the time and they can't keep their hands off each other. And even though they're only friends, Maddy says she'll probably go to California with him in August. She won't talk about any of the things that must have gone wrong so that she ended up back here. All she talks about is sex. For frig sakes, she's becoming a nymphomaniac. When we were walking back from the Camp tonight, I asked Justin if he thought Jesse was going to take Maddy to California with him and he got a weird look on his face. I'm pretty sure that look meant Jesse will be taking Maddy to California when pigs learn how to fly.

I can't write anymore, Emma. I'm so, so, so uncomfortable. I never should have eaten so much of that stupid cake.

NINETEEN

Justin pulled Izzy's Highlander into its parking spot beside Caleb's old Dodge. He hopped out of the vehicle, jingling the keys in his hand and feeling on top of the world. He had enjoyed the trip into Dearborn with Edward. Driving Izzy's SUV hybrid back to Crater Lake, after successfully passing his driver's test, had been pure luxury compared to his practice driving sessions in the old Dodge.

He had been surprised to find that he didn't mind talking with Edward. His first impression of Izzy's father, with his snooty British accent, hadn't been stellar. What's more, he couldn't relate to the boring way Edward and Leez talked non-stop about light and contrast. But it turned out the guy had some interesting stories. He'd travelled everywhere and he'd been in more than his share of scrapes – getting chased by a lion, or accidentally walking in on a major drug-for-diamond swap while doing a photo shoot of a village market in Sierra Leone. His dry sense of humor made light of any real danger, though Justin didn't buy it, especially the part about the lion.

Izzy and Liam came around the corner of the workshop. Izzy smiled at the sight of Justin jiggling her keys. Liam gave him a thumbs-up. Justin's anger at the pair of them had been loosening its grip. It was hard to sit at the table with them for dinner every night and still keep his holier-than-thou attitude stoked. He had begun to accept Izzy's words; the situation was complicated and Leez herself had said Liam wasn't completely to blame.

Edward patted Justin on the back and called out, "Give this young man a big hand. He is now permitted to operate a motor vehicle." Izzy and Liam clapped. Izzy reached out to shake Justin's hand and, as always, the warmth of her smile drew him in.

Izzy felt a lump in her throat as Justin turned from her to accept Liam's handshake. It would be a miracle if they could get by the earthquake that Lisa-Marie's pregnancy had caused within the complicated network of their various relationships – to say nothing of the aftershocks that kept rocking each one of them in turn.

The sound of another vehicle coming down the steep drive from the logging road above grabbed Izzy's attention. She turned to Liam, "Who could that be?" Beulah had already been over with the day's mail. They weren't expecting anyone. Izzy watched as an older model truck with a beat-up camper on top turned the corner. "Who'd drive a camper down here? What part of *private drive* don't people get?"

The truck pulled up in front of them. A man got out of the driver's side and walked straight over to Liam. For the second time in as many weeks, Liam wore a look of utter shock. The man grabbed him by the shoulders and pulled him close, bending until their foreheads were touching – Liam's dark hair resting against the man's greying head.

Izzy had no idea what was going on, but tears blurred her vision as she witnessed the intimacy of the older man's gesture. She thought maybe she should turn away. Watching seemed like a violation.

Liam's head came up. He moved back a step and stared in disbelief at the man before lunging forward and wrapping his arms around him in a tight hug. Then he uttered a word that made Izzy's mouth drop open, "Dad," Liam's voice shook, "What are you doing here?"

"Ah Liam, it's good to see you." Alex turned to wave Robbie forward, "I want you to meet your little brother, Robbie." Liam's father glanced around the circle of stunned faces before he turned to Izzy and reached for her hand, "I'm Alexander Collins, Liam's father."

Liam stepped over to Izzy, put his arm around her and pulled her close, "This is Izzy Montgomery –"

"Liam and I live here together," Izzy added without missing a beat. She looked past Alexander at Robbie who was standing nearby. She walked over and knelt down at the boy's level, "I'm Izzy." Robbie smiled at her. She was about to draw him towards the rest of the group to make some introductions, when movement near the back door of the cabin caught her eye. Lisa-Marie was coming down the steps holding her stomach. She spotted all of them standing in the drive and lurched along the path towards them.

"Oh my God, I think my water broke. Does that mean I'm having the baby?"

Liam stepped back as yet another shock wave hit him. Izzy gave him a fleeting look of sympathy before she threw her hands up in a gesture of surrender, "Why does everything around this place have to happen at once?" Alexander laughed and Izzy saw Robbie grinning. She rushed over to Lisa-Marie.

"Sit down Lisa," with her arm around Lisa-Marie's shoulders, Izzy practically pushed her down onto the bench outside the workshop. "Are you having contractions?"

"Just those fake Brandon Hickley things Dr. Maxwell talked about ... most of yesterday and today. I could hardly concentrate on sorting the pictures on the computer it hurts so much." She looked over at Edward as if to apologize. A grimace of pain gripped her face and she doubled over holding her stomach and gasping, "Shit, shit, shit ... this is friggin' awful ... oh my God. The baby's not supposed to come until next week," she wailed.

"I don't think you're having Braxton Hicks contractions. This looks like the real thing – especially if your water has broken. Does anyone have a watch?" Justin pulled his watch off his wrist as he walked over. Izzy asked, "Can you keep an eye on how many minutes go by before she has another contraction?"

Justin knelt down beside Lisa-Marie. He held her hand, smiling encouragement at her. "Hey, Leez, it's going to be okay. Hang in there." The contraction ended and Lisa-Marie flashed him a beautiful, large smile. She leaned in to snuggle against his arm while she dropped her head onto his chest.

Oh my God, Izzy thought, even now, of all times, that girl can't get her mind off Justin. She turned to Liam, "Better grab the bag I packed. It's in the entry under the table. Give Beulah and Bethany a call on the two-way radio. Tell them what's going on." Liam nodded and headed for the cabin.

Izzy walked over towards Alexander and Robbie. She couldn't help but stare. She felt like she had entered a time warp. She saw Liam as the young boy she could never have known and, at the same time, the man he would be in twenty years.

"Alexander, Robbie ... this is my father, Edward Montgomery," Izzy pointed to her dad who came across to Alexander and shook his hand. "That's Justin over there with Lisa-Marie ... who, as you have probably guessed, is having a baby."

"Call me Alex. It seems like we've arrived at an exciting time." Izzy studied Alex intently. What was happening? Fathers were coming out of the woodwork ... and now a brother ... and soon a baby. Izzy felt as if she, like Liam, might stagger under the weight of family.

Lisa-Marie panted, "Shit, shit, shit ... not again."

"Five minutes, Izzy," Justin called out.

"We'd better get moving. I think we'll be fine, but the hospital in Cedar Falls is over an hour's drive from here." Izzy saw Liam coming back from the cabin with the bag. She called out to him, "I'm going in the Highlander with Lisa-Marie. There's lots of room for her to stretch out in the back." Izzy turned to her father, "Dad, could you drive? And Justin, will you come with us? Liam, why don't you take your dad and Robbie along with you in the Dodge? We can't leave them alone here when they've just arrived. What's happening with Beulah and Bethany?"

"They're ready to go. I'll call them again as soon as we get to the top of the drive." Liam was already moving toward the Highlander to stow the bag. Justin had his arm around Lisa-Marie and was helping her walk.

Izzy caught up with Liam and gave him a quick hug. She whispered in his ear, "It's all going to work out. Try not to worry." She pulled away and gave him her cell phone, "Call Dr. Maxwell as soon as you're in range. Let her know we're on our way to the hospital." She ran to the SUV and climbed in the back seat with Lisa-Marie.

"Have you been here on Vancouver Island all this time, Liam? For years I've been keeping my ear to the ground trying to hear news of you. I'd about given you up for dead."

"I've lived here fifteen years. How did you find me?"

"Now that's an interesting story." Alexander settled back in the passenger seat, "It's nice not to be driving for a change. Robbie's a bit young to have taken a turn at the wheel on our cross country journey." Alex jostled Robbie with his shoulder but all he got for his efforts was a small grunt.

"You two drove all the way across the country?"

"I picked Robbie up in New Brunswick, out at Burnt Church. Anyway, how I found you was inspired, even if I do say so myself. Wish I'd thought of it years ago. I know this woman ... she's tribal police over on the reserve near Orillia ... her name's Kate. She's gotten a wee bit straight-laced, what with being a cop and all, but she's a fine woman. I heard a rumour that you'd been in Vancouver years ago. Then it came to me – I asked Kate to run your name down through the Department of Motor Vehicles in British Columbia, and sure enough, up pops an address for Liam Samuel Collins. All I had to do was find Dearborn on the map, ask around for directions, and Bob's your uncle."

"When did you leave New Brunswick?"

"Three weeks ago, give or take. We stopped in Montreal for a couple of days. There was someone there I wanted Robbie to meet and I took the kid to a *Habs* game. His eyes nearly popped out of his head when the Montreal Canadiens skated onto the ice. We did a side trip into Toronto so he could ride up the CN Tower and go to the Hockey Hall of Fame, then a run over to Orillia to say hi to Kate. We didn't make a lot of stops. I wanted to get out here as soon as I could."

Robbie dozed against his father's shoulder, moving in and out of dreams, feeling the connections of light that enveloped him within the cab of the truck. He heard Liam say, "You're my father and I don't have a clue what you've been doing with yourself all these years."

His dad laughed and answered, "That story is a long one, Son."

"We've got an hour's drive ahead of us. Seems like a good time to make a start and, believe me, I could use the distraction."

Through the chasing shadows of the dream world, Robbie heard his dad's voice speaking of warriors and death, occupations and blockades, names and places that meant nothing to Robbie but somehow held a sacred power. It felt as if his father intoned the prayers at Church, raising a chalice high above them and speaking words of consecration. This power wove its way deep into Robbie's subconscious. He woke up an hour later as they pulled into the hospital parking lot in Cedar Falls, with as full an understanding of their father as Liam now possessed, without being able to recall a single detail.

TWENTY

As long as Robbie could remember, he had been able to see patterns of light around people. When he was little, he assumed everyone saw them. He had been shocked the day he learned that wasn't true. The first time Robbie remembered talking about the light, he was quite small. He had climbed onto his grandpa's lap and patted his head, "Light, light." He moved his hand across his grandpa's chest and repeated the words. Then he patted his grandpa's stomach and frowned, "Dark."

Robbie's grandpa died that winter of stomach cancer. His grandmother kept her eye on Robbie after that. Later she explained to him that seeing light the way he did was special. She told him that it had been the same for her when she was little, but she had outgrown it. He asked if that would happen to him, too. She said maybe, it was hard to tell if his gift was strong enough to last.

Robbie was reading a comic book while he sat in the waiting room of the Cedar Falls hospital. His attention was only half on the Archie Double Digest in his hand. Every now and then he would look up, tilt his head to the side and narrow his eyes as he checked out the light around people.

Robbie would have known Liam was family even if no one had told him. When he glanced over at his dad and older brother, he could see that their light merged together as they spoke. He knew if he were to go and stand with them, his light would flow right into that pattern.

The pregnant girl's light spiked wild colours all around her when she came out to the waiting room to visit. It wasn't long before she doubled over, holding her stomach and panting. When she straightened up, she saw the Slurpee in Robbie's hand. She smiled and told him, "I would die for a drink of that right now." He gave her a sip.

At first, he had thought Lisa-Marie must be Izzy's girl. She clung to Izzy like she was her mom, but Robbie couldn't see any family light between them. He noticed how Lisa-Marie's spiking light reached out for the tall guy named Justin. He was nice. He had brought Robbie the Slurpee and the Archie comic from the store across the street.

When Justin walked around he gave off a bright light. Earlier, Robbie had seen an old woman in a hospital robe, dragging an IV around behind her. He had watched her move right up beside Justin. She was trying to reach his light. Of course, she didn't know she was doing it, but being close to such a bright light made people feel better.

Robbie thought Justin must be the baby's dad, but when he examined the light around the pregnant girl's stomach – the light coming from the baby – he saw something he didn't understand at all. It was faint but it was there, reaching toward him – family light. How could her baby be family?

Robbie watched the pregnant girl hug a woman she called Auntie Beth. He studied this woman. Her light was shaky, like a candle that flamed up all bright and strong, only to gutter back down into its own wax where it flickered off and on. The tall, skinny women next to her had a light that was harsh on the outside and hard to look at. Robbie had to concentrate before he saw the softer tones dancing below the surface.

The next time Robbie looked up from the comic book, he checked out the older man who was sitting across the room from him, reading a newspaper. As his eyes scanned Edward's body, he saw where the light stopped abruptly. Robbie jerked his head up and stared at the man's face. Edward was gazing back at him over the top of his glasses. He raised one eyebrow at Robbie. It seemed as though the man knew what Robbie had seen. The light was still strong around Edward's heart and when Izzy appeared, that light leaped out to meet her.

Robbie hadn't been sure at first, but now he knew that it was Izzy's light he was searching for. His gaze returned to her again and again. When he had stood in the driveway earlier, watching his dad hug Liam, his eyes had been drawn to Izzy. He saw her light reach out and wrap itself right around Liam. Robbie hadn't seen anything like that happen before and it made him feel funny inside – like he might cry, but not because he was sad. Then Izzy's light had touched him and he found that he could take a deep breath for the first time since he heard the *Jodie Lynn* had sunk. Izzy's light made him feel like his mom was there.

Izzy came out of the delivery room to update everyone on how things were going. Robbie heard the sounds that were coming from behind the heavy doors. She sat down in the chair next to his, "How are you doing? Don't get freaked out by the screaming. It sounds way worse than it is."

"I was around when two of my cousins were born. I know it takes some screaming to get a baby out."

Izzy laughed. Her hand stayed on his arm as she smiled at him, "Well, Robbie, Robbie, McBobby ... maybe you should be in there with Lisa instead of me. You've got more experience, for sure."

He shook his head and grinned, "No thanks." He decided that the next time he saw her, he would call her Izzy, Izzy, McLizzy.

⚓⚓⚓⚓

Liam looked up at the clock on the wall of the waiting room. It was after ten and they hadn't heard anything for an hour. Well, that wasn't entirely accurate. Whenever anyone opened the doors to the delivery area, plenty was heard and none of it was reassuring. He looked at his dad, asleep in the seat beside him and nudged him with his elbow, "Do you think it should take this long?"

Alexander stretched in the chair and yawned, "Takes as long as it takes, Liam. You can't rush a thing like a baby."

Liam looked over to see Bethany resting her head against Beulah's arm. Her eyes were closed. Robbie was out like a light, curled up in a chair next to Liam's. Edward was taking a stroll around the waiting room, leaning heavily on his cane. When Justin came in with a tray of coffee from the Tim Horton's across the street, Alexander pushed himself up and smiled, "Thank God for Timmy's, couldn't have made it across this whole damn country without it." He sipped his coffee and asked, "What's the story, Liam? You and your woman seem pretty involved with this baby's birth."

Liam got out of his chair and gestured for his father to follow him. In a private corner of the waiting room he told Alex the truth. "The baby is mine," he avoided meeting his father's eyes.

"I take it from the look on your face that this wasn't one of those planned events like you see on Oprah - a surrogate or something?"

"It was a mistake. She isn't even seventeen. It happened before Izzy and I were together."

Alexander smiled, "Are you saying that I'm about to become a grandfather?"

"I think you're missing the point, but ya, I guess so. I'd appreciate it if you wouldn't advertise the fact."

Alexander pushed Liam with his shoulder, "If that dark-haired beauty who looks at you like the sun rises where you're standing, has it in her to be beside that girl helping her bring your child into the world, then you should be grateful, Son. Some mighty strong force is looking out for your ass. Come on, cheer up. It's bound to happen soon now. I was there when both you and Robbie were born ... Fiona, too. When you hold that baby in your arms, Liam, you won't be thinking of anything but what a miracle a new life truly is."

Before Liam could follow up on who the hell Fiona might be, Izzy came through the door. Her smile softened her features as she walked toward them. She went into Liam's arms and hugged him. She turned and spoke to everyone, "The baby was born about twenty minutes ago. She's perfect, seven pounds, nine ounces. Lisa's doing well. She's tired, but she was a real trooper. She wanted to take a quick shower and the nurses had some things to do with the baby, but you're all welcome to come in now."

Everyone got up and moved around, hugging and laughing. Izzy took Liam's hand in hers and reached up to kiss his cheek. She whispered close to his ear, "Come and meet your daughter." Robbie sat up and rubbed his eyes. Izzy grabbed his hand as well and led them all down the hall to Lisa-Marie's room.

⁂⁂⁂⁂

Justin was stunned at the way Lisa-Marie was walking around taking pictures and joking with everyone. She had dark circles under her eyes and she looked a bit puffy, kind of distorted around the edges, but he would never have guessed she was the same girl he had seen and heard earlier that evening. She reached for a piece of black forest cake and dug into it with gusto. She smiled at Justin, "I guess they don't call it labour for nothing. I'm starving."

The sounds that had come from the delivery room had sent Justin into a panic. When he heard a scream that he knew was coming from Leez, he had selfishly wished they had put her in a room further down the hall. He thought she could die, screaming like that. If it hadn't been for Alex and even Robbie reassuring him, he might have bolted out of the hospital. As it was, he had been the one running around doing errands – getting coffee, grabbing a comic for the kid, picking up a cake and balloons, you name it – anything to get away from the sounds.

Justin had watched Liam's face and he had felt for the guy. The way those screams made Justin cringe, he could only imagine how the person responsible must feel. He didn't understand how any man could embrace the idea of fatherhood knowing he'd have to live through the screaming.

131

His attention came back to the celebrations when Robbie called out to him, "Justin, you haven't held the baby yet." Robbie looked like a real pro, sitting in the big chair with the baby in his arms, singing to her. Justin felt nervous, but he sat down in the space Robbie offered him. Then he let Izzy hand him the small bundle. He looked down into the dark eyes that latched onto his, and his heart lurched. Everything else in the room faded away except the baby lying in the crook of his arm. All he wanted to do was protect her. He would give his own life to keep her safe.

As Robbie moved away to get a piece of cake, he caught a flash of something. He turned back and saw Justin's light reach out to the baby in a crazy splash of brightness. He knew Justin wasn't the baby's dad but he might as well have been. Robbie smiled as he grabbed a chunk of cake. The baby was lucky to be hit by Justin's light like that.

✺✺✺✺

Dr. Rosemary Maxwell walked into Lisa-Marie's hospital room. The remains of a large bakery cake sat on a hospital trolley. A big bunch of pink balloons floated near the ceiling. People were milling around and laughing. Liam sat in the rocking chair with the newborn baby in his arms.

The doctor had seen all these people in the waiting room before the baby was born. At that time, she had assumed that the tall young man was the father. But when the baby's head of dark hair had crowned, all wet and slick, followed by the soft brown skin of her shoulder, Rosemary was certain she had made an incorrect assumption. Izzy had coached Lisa-Marie through the whole thing, calm and steady as if she was the girl's mother. Izzy had cried when the baby was born. The doctor watched Liam now as he gazed down at the child in his arms. His face was filled with an emotion she couldn't quite discern.

Rosemary had been a family doctor in Dearborn for more years than she wanted to remember. She had treated Liam many times for his stomach complaints and she had seen Bethany, Beulah and Izzy for checkups. She had been the one to sign Caleb's death certificate. She remembered how she had stood in the silence of the clinic in Dearborn looking at the stretcher that held his dead body. It was hard to believe that something as mundane as a logging accident could snuff out a life such as Caleb's. He had struck her as the type of guy who should only be brought down while saving the world from imminent destruction.

The doctor turned her attention to the two people in the room she didn't know, an older man who looked like he'd walked off a movie set where he had been playing the role of a First Nations marine, and a young boy. The resemblance of both of these people to Liam was staggering. She walked over to the older man and extended her hand, "Hello, I'm Rosemary."

Liam called out from the rocker, "That's my father, Dr. Alexander Collins. Meet our family doctor, Dad – Rosemary Maxwell. And this guy here is my little brother, Robbie."

Alexander shook the doctor's hand and explained, "A PhD type doctor."

Izzy's eyebrows went up as she stared from Liam to Alex and then back.

Liam shrugged, "I just found out the PhD part myself."

Robbie leaned against Liam's chair and asked, "What will the baby's name be?" Liam glanced over at Lisa-Marie, but she was busy with Justin, laughing about something.

Rosemary stopped at the table to grab a piece of cake and walked over to the two young people. "You look like you're feeling okay, Lisa." Rosemary nodded at Justin, "I'm Dr. Maxwell."

"Justin Roberts. Lisa and I are friends."

Rosemary focused her attention on the young mother. "So, Lisa ... what about a name for your little girl?"

Lisa-Marie raised her eyebrows as she shrugged, "Whatever Izzy and Liam think is fine by me."

Liam studied the baby in his arms. "My mother's name was Sophie. I've always like that name."

Alexander nodded and smiled, "Right on, Son. Your mom had a beautiful name. It means wisdom and that's not a bad way to start out in the world."

Bethany came over to stroke the baby's dark hair. "Lisa-Marie's mom's name was Leanne. That might be a nice middle name."

Liam spoke to the child in his arms, "Sophie Leanne. Do you like the sound of that, little one?" He looked around the room and grinned, "I think she likes it."

Amidst the smiles and nodding, Rosemary put her fingers to her lips and exhaled a loud whistle. When a sea of startled eyes had come to rest on her, she said, "I've been present for a lot of deliveries, but I can't say I've ever seen a group naming before. What's up? If anyone wants to fill me in, I'd appreciate it."

Everyone in the room turned to stare at Lisa-Marie who shook her head, "I'm not saying it."

As the silence in the room became uncomfortable, Izzy found herself thinking, once more into the breach. How often am I going to have to do this?

She put her hand on Liam's shoulder, "Liam is Sophie's father. We hope, for now at least, that this information doesn't have to go any further."

Rosemary got up from the bed and glanced from Izzy to Liam, "Okay, then ... are the two of you going to be helping with the baby?" They both nodded. The doctor turned to Lisa-Marie, "I want you in bed. You need some sleep. Izzy and Liam can stay." She looked over at the other people in the room, "I'd like the rest of you to say your goodbyes."

As Robbie walked out of the room, he said, "If Liam is Sophie's dad that means I'm an uncle."

Alex put his hand on the boy's shoulder, "You're right, Son. Sophie is going to find out soon enough that she's a lucky little girl to have a dad like Liam and an uncle like you.

Divergence

TWENTY-ONE

It was after five in the afternoon and Izzy was exhausted. She had been up with the baby numerous times the previous night, she had missed lunch and her last session at the Camp had gone over time. As she came through the cabin door, the mess in the kitchen caught her like a smack in the face. Dirty dishes were everywhere. The hamburger she had tossed out of the freezer that morning had thawed and was dripping blood through its wrapping, over the edge of the counter to the floor. Someone had slopped the dog's dish over and tracked through the mess. The milk sat out on the table beside a half-eaten bowl of cereal.

Her sinking feeling was followed by a physical cringe at the onslaught of noise coming from the living room. Sophie's screams echoed through the entire cabin. Izzy walked over to the stairs that led down to the main floor. Another disaster met her eyes. Piles of clothes were heaped on the sofa, some folded, most not. Her personal laundry was scattered about and a fancy bra was draped over the arm of a chair. Everything in the room was out of whack, including Liam. He looked like his head might explode as he tried to calm the screaming baby. Edward stood in the doorway to the sun porch, leaning heavily on his cane. Robbie, who had been sitting upstairs at Izzy's desk, came down to the main floor and hung close behind her.

"What's happened to this place, Liam? It looks like a bomb went off. No one could clean up the dishes all day, or start dinner?" Izzy tried to keep her tone light but the stress that edged every word was pronounced.

Liam shifted Sophie to his other arm. Her little face was beet-red from crying and her hair stood up in sweaty tufts. He stared at Izzy with desperation, "I haven't been able to put this baby down most of the day."

Edward threw his support behind Liam, "Believe me, Isabella, we have tried everything. She's been fed and burped and had her nappy changed. Liam's walked her up and down endlessly. Nothing seems to be helping."

Izzy heard the sound of voices in the kitchen at the same time that she saw Lisa-Marie enter through the door that led in from the garden. The young girl's face was flushed.

Liam swung around to face her, "Where have you been? You were supposed to be back here by two. It's after five now."

Lisa-Marie halted mid-step, turned and shot back, "Lay off me, Liam. I was working." The strident quality of the baby's crying ramped up a notch.

Izzy's attention turned then to the top of the stairs that led into the kitchen where she saw Alex standing beside Cynthia St. Pierre. Alex wore his customary smile ... nothing much fazed him; but their new guest's brows shot up at the interchange between Liam and Lisa-Marie. As Cynthia scanned the room, her eyes came to rest on the bra dangling off the arm of the chair. The piece of clothing seemed determined to make a suggestive statement.

Izzy tossed the lingerie under a cushion. She forced herself to smile, "You've caught us at a bad time. Is there anything you need?"

"Nothing special ... just dinner, I guess."

The room was plunged into absolute silence; even the baby paused to catch her breath. All eyes turned in stunned disbelief to Cynthia. A slight frown drew her eyebrows together, "I understood that renting the guest cabin included dinner. I hate to eat alone. I always look for a place that includes dinner."

Sophie regained her breath and howled. Izzy forced herself to remain calm. She imagined only two choices in such a situation – scream hysterically and escape the room, or take charge of things. Being the kind of person who would always opt for the latter, Izzy held her hands up in a gesture that told everyone not to move.

❧❧❧❧

Izzy had let the first couple of honeymoon weeks with Sophie lull her into a false sense of security. She had felt on top of things. She had struggled to get used to the lack of sleep but she believed she had a handle on the baby's schedule. Now her illusions of control were shattered. Sophie, at a month old, bore no resemblance to the passive newborn who did little more than look sweet, eat, sleep and need a diaper change at intervals in between.

Izzy's thoughts flashed back to the morning after Sophie was born. She had known they were probably headed for trouble but she hadn't wanted to dwell on anything negative. Sophie's birth had been an incredible experience. No doubt she had been in the grip of vicarious hormones.

Liam had come in that morning, after installing the car seat in the Highlander, to see Izzy coaxing Sophie to latch onto a tiny bottle. "Where is Lisa-Marie and why are you giving the baby formula?"

"I don't know where Lisa-Marie is. I haven't seen her for almost an hour. The nurse says Sophie has to take some fluids."

"Lisa-Marie should breastfeed. It's way better for both of them." Liam reached into his back pocket, drew out a battered pamphlet and waved it as he continued, "I read up on it last night."

"The nurse was here early this morning talking to her about breastfeeding. She absolutely refused. She said she wasn't going to do it, and nothing anyone could say was going to convince her."

"She has to do what's right for the baby. She can't act as though Sophie's needs don't count."

Izzy stared at Liam. Something had crept into his voice that she had never heard before. "Are you listening to yourself or, for that matter, to anything I'm saying? We can't force her to breastfeed Sophie if she doesn't want to." Izzy nodded down at the baby in her arms, "We are it for this child, Liam. You'd better get used to the idea."

Liam sat down on the edge of the hospital bed. "Lisa is Sophie's mother. She has to accept that."

It was on the tip of Izzy's tongue to tell Liam that he shouldn't hold his breath on that idea becoming reality, but she refrained. "I don't see things turning out that way, Liam. I'm sorry. We are going to end up with the responsibility of looking after this child. We should at least start thinking about the legal implications of that." She pointed to a brown envelope on the hospital tray near the bed, "There's a whole bunch of paperwork to fill out. I know you said you weren't ready to discuss these things, but the baby is here now ... she's real. We have to get a plan A and maybe B and C, if necessary. Figure out what's going to go on all those forms."

Liam took a deep breath before speaking, "We might have to give Lisa time to get used to the idea of being a mother."

"You know damn well that isn't what I'm saying."

Liam's shoulders slumped as he stared down at the floor. "If you love me, Izz -"

The anguish on Liam's face and in his voice was crushing. Izzy had let the whole thing go because she did, indeed, love Liam. She was sure Lisa-Marie had no intention of getting used to the idea of being a mother; but Liam wasn't going to accept that fact until he was ready. There wasn't anything she could do to speed up the process.

Lisa-Marie had shown up an hour later. She had been out on the front steps of the hospital where there was cell service, enjoying the sunshine and texting on her phone. As Izzy had predicted, Liam got nowhere with his insistence on the benefits of breastfeeding. He'd had to settle for wrestling a commitment from Lisa to stay on at their cabin and help look after Sophie. Izzy suspected the girl had her own agenda for not moving back to the A-Frame with her aunt and Beulah; she also believed that the agenda had nothing to do with the baby.

They had brought Sophie home to Crater Lake the next day. Jillian had been over to set up all the baby stuff. They established a schedule of sorts and everyone chipped in during the day. Izzy or Liam took the nine o'clock feeding before they turned in for the night. Sophie was put down to sleep in her rolling cradle and pushed out to the dining room above the sun porch. Lisa-Marie took over until she went to bed after the midnight feeding. Justin usually hung out with her doing his homework. The rest of the time she spent with Edward working on his book. When Lisa-Marie turned in, she left the baby's cradle close to Izzy and Liam's bedroom door. Liam took the three a.m. feeding and Izzy was up by five to handle things from there.

Izzy had taken two weeks off work, which hadn't been easy. She was needed at the Camp and Sophie's sudden arrival in their lives had given her no time to book a replacement. She had told herself Liam would be fine looking after the baby. He had both Edward and Alex to give him a hand and Izzy's schedule was somewhat flexible.

Liam had been left with little choice but to accept Izzy's decision. By the look on his face, she had known he hadn't liked the idea. He had turned his frustration on Lisa-Marie and objected strenuously to her announcement that she was going back to her old job in the paper and soap shop. She had finally screamed at Liam that she needed to get out of the cabin for at least part of every day. Izzy had taken Lisa-Marie's side. The whole birth experience had brought the two of them together in an alliance of sorts. Izzy knew Liam felt as though she had left him hanging out to dry, but she'd had to do what she thought was right. She understood Lisa-Marie's desperation. The girl was like a pressure cooker – if the steam didn't find its way out she would explode.

As Sophie morphed from a sleeping angel to a demanding, squalling force to be reckoned with, Izzy did her best to stay on top of things. If being awakened by a screaming baby had been her only nightly interruption, she might have had a fighting chance. Contending with Liam's nightmares didn't help. The bad dreams started almost as soon as the baby arrived home from the hospital. Izzy could usually shake him awake before he started screaming but he would come out of the dream in a cold sweat, shaking and mumbling. It was a terrible thing to witness. His torment, and the fact that he wouldn't discuss the dreams at all, ate away at her. Often she couldn't get back to sleep afterwards, though Liam seemed to manage by holding her body tight against his own.

Then there were the added responsibilities of trying to cope with a house full of people. At times, the increase in their numbers was expedient; during the day, someone was usually around to help with Sophie. Robbie had moved in from Alex's camper to stay in the loft beside Lisa-Marie's room. He was no trouble but he still needed to be fed and watched over to a degree. Alex didn't seem to take his role as Robbie's father all that seriously. He would disappear for whole days without any sort of by-your-leave. Someone had to make sure Robbie took a shower now and then, brushed his teeth and had clean clothes to wear. Dinner for seven people every night took a degree of planning. Izzy's mind veered away from even considering the growing piles of laundry everywhere. After years of living a relatively quiet life, she had to admit that she felt a bit frayed around the edges.

At the beginning of June, Cynthia St. Pierre had arrived to take up residence in the guest cabin. Izzy took a day off to clean, cook and create a welcoming atmosphere. Everyone, including Sophie, behaved well and the elegant dinner went off without a hitch. Cynthia told them that her first order of business was to take advantage of being so close to Johnstone Straight and the world famous Robson Bight to do some whale watching. Izzy struck Cynthia off her to-do list and got on with all the other tasks that screamed for her attention.

⚡⚡⚡⚡

Arriving back from the whale watching excursion, Cynthia unpacked her things and walked over from the guest cabin to Izzy and Liam's. She spotted Alex as he came down the metal steps of a camper parked at the bottom of the large, gravel drive. As a writer, she enjoyed encounters with people who could prove interesting and Alex certainly fit that bill nicely. He had an air about him that drew the eye ... a dose of edginess that came with the braid and the feathered earring ... a dollop of mystery around the need to dress in what looked like army surplus clothing ... a hint of danger added by the hunting knife on his belt. Cynthia smoothed her summer dress down over her hips as she approached him. As they fell into step together, she asked, "Are you on your way into dinner?"

They heard the baby screaming before they opened the kitchen door. Cynthia stared down into the living room and witnessed the argument between Liam and Lisa-Marie. The black bra caught her eye, as anything so out of place was bound to do.

She was still trying to connect the dots between the people she had met at dinner a few days before. In the absence of any real explanations, she had made a number of assumptions. Lisa-Marie was probably Izzy's daughter from a previous relationship. The angry words she had just heard fit with how she imagined a stepfather might act in Liam's position. Izzy and Liam were apparently housing this daughter, the daughter's baby and the daughter's boyfriend. The boyfriend was a nice young man who worked at the sawmill. Robbie was undeniably Liam's son, though whether Izzy was the boy's mother or not was unclear. Alex and Edward had been easy to peg as they were called Dad respectively by Liam and Izzy.

Cynthia didn't see herself as a demanding person and she had made do in messier houses. Her only real concern, as she stood on the landing and looked down at the mayhem, was that she might have been mistaken in assuming dinner was included with her lodging.

ֆ֎ֆ֎ֆ֎ֆ֎

Izzy studied Cynthia while holding everyone at bay with her raised hands. The woman looked closer to sixty than fifty. She wore her hair in a smart style with well-groomed sheets of silver framing her face and flicking under her chin. Her summer dress showed off her tanned skin. A number of silver bracelets encircled one of her arms. Rings glinted on her fingers.

Emotions raced across the woman's face – confusion was replaced by something close to embarrassment. Izzy lowered her hands, "Hang on a minute, Cynthia." She turned to Liam and took Sophie from him, "Go for a walk or something and try to calm down. You're going to give yourself a stroke."

She handed the baby to Robbie, "See if you can get her settled down a bit."

Liam flexed his shoulders, "Thank you. I've been trying to get the payroll up to the sawmill since early this morning." He walked out the back door of the cabin without a second glance at anyone.

Izzy approached Lisa-Marie and put the back of her hand gently up to her forehead, "You're running a fever again. Are you still taking those antibiotics

Rosemary prescribed for you?" Lisa-Marie had been suffering a low-grade infection ever since leaving the hospital after Sophie's birth. She wasn't eating properly and Izzy guessed the young girl was running herself ragged trying to get back in shape.

"Yes, I'm taking the pills, I'm fine. I wish everyone would get off my back for two freaking seconds," she glared at the door through which Liam had escaped. "I just need a shower."

"Get in the shower, then go lie down." Izzy turned back to Cynthia, "I have no problem with having you stay for dinners; we usually have quite a crowd here anyway. One more won't matter. We are running a bit behind today."

Alex chuckled, "Ya, we noticed. Look, I saw some hamburger out. I make a mighty tasty and, I might add, fast spaghetti and meatballs. I think I could have it on the table in an hour, with a wee bit of assistance." He looked meaningfully at Cynthia who raised her eyebrows in surprise at both the invitation and the smile. She recovered quickly and nodded her acceptance.

Robbie sat on the edge of the sofa singing softly to Sophie who had stopped crying. Izzy turned her attention to her father. Edward hadn't moved since he had sunk down onto a dining room chair. She walked over to the bottom of the kitchen stairs and called out, "Cynthia, could I impose on you for one more thing?" When Cynthia appeared, Izzy asked, "Could you get my father some tea? There's a tray on the counter with everything you'll need."

Izzy turned back to her father and pointed to the recliner in the living room, "Sit down where you'll be comfortable, Dad. You look all done in."

"Yes, I think I will. The hip is playing me up today." Edward leaned heavily on his cane and moved towards the chair.

Izzy scrunched down beside Robbie, "Give me about ten minutes to deal with the laundry and straighten this room up, then I'll take her from you." Robbie nodded and kept on singing. Sophie's eyes fluttered up and down, heavy with sleep.

Izzy grabbed the laundry baskets and separated out the clothes. She got all Sophie's things in one basket and the folded clothes in another. She put Lisa-Marie's stuff near the bathroom and the other baskets in her bedroom behind a closed door. She whirled around picking up the mess in the living room. By the time Lisa-Marie emerged from the bathroom in a robe, with a towel around her hair, the place looked close to normal.

"Your laundry is there Lisa –" Izzy turned toward Robbie, "I just have to go and change." The look on Robbie's face stopped her in her tracks. "Oh gosh, you look pretty glum." She took the baby from Robbie and dragged

Sophie's cradle out to the living room to park it between the two large chairs. She settled the baby down, pulling the soft pink blanket up around her tiny shoulders. She turned back to Robbie and ruffled his dark hair, "What's up?"

"My stomach hurts. Hungry I guess, I dunno. You were late."

Izzy put her arm around his shoulders and squeezed, "I know, stupid work. Come on, we've got those double-stuff Oreos that you like." Izzy walked up to the kitchen to grab Robbie's snack. Cynthia had put the finishing touches on the tea tray. Alex, who wore Izzy's red poppy apron, produced meatballs at a surprising speed from the bowl of hamburger mixture on the counter.

"Should I put out an extra cup for you, Izzy?" Cynthia asked.

Izzy nodded and ushered Robbie back to the living room. Lisa-Marie headed up the stairs to the loft above with her basket of laundry in hand. Izzy called out, "Eat something, Lisa."

Lisa-Marie kept on walking up the stairs, "No, I'll wait for dinner."

Cynthia placed the tea tray on the oak coffee table in the middle of the now tidy living room. Edward nodded his thanks. She smiled and made her way back to the kitchen where Alex could be heard calling for his assistant.

Izzy smiled at Robbie as he wolfed down his snack, "Let's read some Harry Potter." They settled back in an armchair with the book. Edward poured the tea. From the kitchen came the sounds of cooking, talking and laughter.

The first thing Liam heard when he came through the door was Izzy's voice. He walked into the living room. Edward dozed in the recliner, his empty tea cup balanced on his knee. The smell of food wafted from the kitchen. Sophie slept in the cradle. Robbie's eyes were drooping, as well. Liam looked at Izzy with Robbie cuddled next to her and he felt a large fist reach into his chest to squeeze his heart painfully. Something about the two of them – together – made him feel hollow for all the things he was desperately afraid he couldn't hang onto. Izzy stopped reading and smiled up at him. She amazed him. Whatever they piled onto her, she came through it all with dignity and charm. Her smile made his heart lurch back into a steady thumping beat.

He sat down on the sofa, now emptied of the day's accumulation of laundry, and poured lukewarm tea into Izzy's empty cup. He took a drink and said, "Thank you from the bottom of my heart for transforming hell's amphitheatre into this scene of domestic bliss."

Lisa-Marie walked into the living room. She looked better. She had done her hair and put on make-up. She wore a top that emphasized her bust and camouflaged the stomach she was working so hard to be rid of.

Liam glanced at her over the edge of the tea cup, "I'm sorry I snapped at you. Sophie had a tough day and it got to me ... not being able to do anything for her."

A pout pulled the young girl's lower lip down, "You should be sorry. I was working, you know, like I said." She scanned the room quickly, "Where's Sophie's laundry? I'll fold it."

Izzy pointed behind her, "It's in the basket on our bed." Lisa-Marie went into the bedroom, grabbed the basket and headed down to the sun porch to check in with Edward.

Liam reached to adjust the cushion that rested under his arm. His hand snagged a piece of fabric; he pulled out Izzy's bra, hooked on the end of his finger. As the black lace garment swung in the air between the two of them, they burst out laughing. The door in the entry opened and Justin called out hello. With a twinkle in his eye, Liam stuffed the underwear into his pocket.

Justin went straight to Sophie's cradle where the baby was now awake, cooing and gurgling. He leaned over to tickle her under the chin, "Hey, how is little Sophie pie today?" He looked over at Izzy, "Can I pick her up?"

Lisa-Marie came up from the sun porch when she heard Justin's voice. She watched him cradle Sophie in his arms. A small frown settled between her eyes. "Justin, come over here and see the photo I've been working on." He walked toward her smiling. As she took Sophie from him, the baby's little arms waved in the air. Lisa-Marie shook her head at Sophie's apparent attempts to charm.

A short time later Alex appeared at the top of the stairs to the kitchen and called out, "If we could get a hand with the table, we're about ready to rock and roll here."

Izzy disentangled herself from Robbie who dozed in the chair. She made her way out to the kitchen. Someone had managed a trip to the greenhouse. There was a fresh salad on the table and Cynthia had sliced a loaf of bread. Izzy pulled dishes, cutlery, glasses, napkins and serving spoons out of cupboards and drawers. She handed them to Cynthia and did a head count as she looked around the table – her, Liam, Edward, Lisa-Marie, Justin, Robbie, Alex and Cynthia. She called down to the living room, "Dinner's ready. Liam, bring Sophie's blue chair up here when you come."

ﻌﻌﻌﻌ

The spaghetti and meat balls were demolished, the salad bowl was scraped clean and the last slice of bread was eaten. Justin, Lisa-Marie and Robbie had already started on the dishes. They were having fun with the task. The adults were enjoying coffee and dessert – a rhubarb cobbler Izzy had pulled from the freezer and popped into the oven before they sat down to eat. Edward excused himself right after dinner, though he had barely touched his plate. It was on the tip of Cynthia's tongue to ask Izzy what was wrong with her father, but Robbie's voice interrupted her.

"Dad, did you get me that new X-Men comic I told you about?"

Cynthia tried to hide her surprise when Alex answered, "I couldn't find it and no one had a clue what I was asking for. You'll have to come with me to town next time if you want something special." She looked carefully from Alex to Robbie to Liam.

Accurate assumptions about the relationships between people were clearly not Cynthia's strong suit. The fact that Lisa-Marie called Izzy by her first name sank another of her theories. Watching Lisa-Marie and Justin together, she was sure at least about their feelings for one another. Justin might not be Sophie's father but there was something between him and the baby's mother. Lisa-Marie took every opportunity she could to touch him, pushing his arm as he washed the dishes and leaning into him. He returned her antics with affectionate glances.

Sophie started to cry and Izzy reached down to pick her up. She handed the baby to Liam, "Break time's over. Take your daughter." She called into the kitchen, "Can you heat up Sophie's bottle, Lisa?" Izzy's eyebrow went up as she locked eyes with Cynthia and realized what her remark had revealed; then she shrugged and sat back down. Her message was as clear as if she had stated it out loud. Think what you want; I really don't care.

Cynthia sipped her coffee and composed her face into what she hoped was a neutral expression. This was a blended family like none she'd ever encountered before. She hurried to change the subject, "I hope it will be a long time before I live through another embarrassing moment like the one I experienced when you asked me if I needed anything and I said, dinner." She laughed and put her coffee cup down, "Seriously though, I'm more than happy to help out. I can see you guys have your hands full."

Alex said, "Put me on the chore roster, too. I'll take most anything except laundry."

Izzy glanced at Liam before saying, "We're not proud. If you don't withdraw your offer in two seconds, we'll take you up on it." She laughed, "Time's up, you asked for it. Could the two of you take responsibility for the evening meal? I'm not sure why we're all so unorganized over one baby, but there it is. We seem to get buried by the end of the day."

Alex smiled over at Cynthia, "How about we do the grocery shopping, too? That way we'll always have what we need for cooking."

Later that evening, Cynthia sat on the deck of the guest cabin. She was exhausted from three hours of editing – hunching over her laptop, going line-by-line through her manuscript. She took a deep breath and relaxed into the sound of the water lapping against the lake shore below. The memory of Alex's smile came back to her. She felt a rush of warmth as she pictured his black eyes laughing into hers as if issuing a challenge of some type.

TWENTY-TWO

"**D**oes Izzy know her dad is really sick?" Robbie dipped a French fry in ketchup as he looked up at Liam. They were sitting at a picnic table on the deck of the Beach Road Café eating fish and chips. Sophie slept in her stroller parked at the end of the table. The afternoon breeze floated a few clouds across the bright blue sky. The historic boardwalk ran alongside the café. A steady stream of tourists headed for the dock and the multitude of boats moored in the protected waters of Dearborn's harbour. The stacked rock wall of the breakwater could be seen in the distance. Beyond the protective arms of rock, the white caps on the ocean marched along, spraying froth and catching the sun.

Liam's mind had been wandering. He needed to drop off some paperwork for the accountant and he had to pick up the chicken feed. He tried to remember if diapers were on sale at the drugstore. When Robbie's question registered, he choked slightly on his last swallow of tea. Robbie had gone back to reading his comic book by the time Liam asked, "How do you know Edward's sick?"

Liam hadn't yet adjusted to the reality of Robbie. The kid seemed to take most things in stride. He blended in, playing cards with Lisa-Marie and Justin, chatting about his comic book buddies, reading or drawing on his own. He was no problem. Robbie was actually a big help, especially on a trip to town with the baby. Liam wasn't sure how he'd have done everything if he'd had to drag Sophie out of the car seat at every stop.

For the most part, the kid had managed to fly below the level of Liam's awareness. He had noticed that Robbie thought the sun rose and set on Izzy ... he and the boy had that much in common. What role a much older

147

brother was to play in Robbie's life was unclear to Liam. Considering everything else he had to deal with, he hadn't even tried to work out what a relationship with Robbie would look like. So he was surprised that when the kid chose to become a distinct blip on the radar screen of his life, he did it with such a straightforward question.

Robbie was like the lake, one moment crystal clear right down to the bottom where Liam could see the contours of every single rock. Then the wind would come up, the water would start to move and Liam would have no idea what was beneath the surface. At those times, he was liable to stub his toe if he didn't proceed with caution.

Robbie looked up at Liam and said, "Everywhere is light," he waved his hand across his body, "and then black."

"I don't understand what you mean."

Robbie crammed the last of the fries into his mouth and washed them down with a big gulp of Coke. He swiped a napkin across his face and looked out to the small Tri-Island ferry where it was moving through the waves with gulls swooping and banking lazily in its wake. "Gran said I might grow out of it – seeing the light around people. I know stuff because of how the light looks."

"What kind of light do you see when you look at me?"

"Family light ... like our dad."

"Can you see it now?"

Robbie squinted his eyes and turned his head to the side, "Yup, and Sophie, too."

"And the dark you see on Edward means he's sick?" When Robbie nodded solemnly, Liam asked, "How sick?"

Robbie's large eyes bored into Liam's, "When my Grandpa had blackness like that across his stomach ... he didn't last long."

Liam reached over to rest his hand on Robbie's shoulder, "I don't think Izzy knows, but don't worry. I'll talk to her. What would you say to an ice cream cone for dessert? They make a triple scoop here and you can choose a different kind of ice cream for each scoop."

❦❦❦❦

Dear Emma:

I want to shove one of Sophie's dirty diapers in Liam's mouth so I don't have to hear his nagging voice. I've done everything he wanted me to do. I feed the baby when it's my turn. I change her diapers and haul her around as much as anyone else. I listen to everyone go on like she's the next baby Lama or something. News flash – it's just a baby. Now he's getting on my case about work and how it means I'm spending too much time away from Sophie. One day I'm going to tell him that he's nuts if he thinks he's the boss of me.

I feel funny when I look at that baby – I wish I didn't have to. If it wasn't for having Justin around all the time and being able to work with Edward (who is one of the best photographers in the whole wide world – the stuff he has done and the things he knows – I could listen to him talk for days and never get bored) I would get on the bus and go back to Victoria. Well – I would be sorry not to be with Izzy, too. I love having coffee with her in the morning and talking about clothes and makeup and stuff. The other day she gave me this silky cardigan. She said the colour never suited her. What a joke – everything suits, Izzy.

I've starved myself for over a month now, Emma, and it is working. I feel pretty horrible most of the time. I couldn't keep it up except for reminding myself how Justin might be looking at teeny-weeny Willow or gawking at Misty with her bust out to frig knows where. I only weigh a couple of pounds more than I did last summer but those pounds are sitting like a squishy tire right on my stomach. I do sit-ups like a maniac but that belly is still there. I can't wait until the weather warms up enough for swimming. That should help. I go to see the doctor soon for my six-week check. Finally, all of this baby crap will be over. After that, I really hope the next person who wants me to drop open my knees is not wearing a mask and gloves!

If this was last summer, I would be telling you about all the time I spend with Justin. He's here every night for supper and he stays to do his homework. Sometimes we go over to the Camp together and hang out with Maddy and Jesse. But I know that spending time together is not going to make him my boyfriend. He meant that thing about being friends and I don't have a clue how to get him to change his mind.

Maddy's not getting any better at all. You should have seen the fight she and Jesse had at the Camp the other night. She didn't even care that we could hear the whole thing. Justin said we should probably leave, so we did. And get this, Emma – the next day, at work, I asked her how she was and all she could go on and on about was the great make-up sex she and Jesse had. That can't be right – fighting like that and then having sex.

⁕⁕⁕⁕

Izzy sat at her desk, frowning as she flipped through the pages of Maddy's file. They had achieved the first goal – Maddy wasn't cutting anymore. But on the issue of Jesse, Izzy had run into a brick wall.

Maddy would not budge in her assertion that she and Jesse were friends with benefits - nothing more. She was willing to admit that she did turn to Jesse when she felt *crazy,* but she would not go as far as to say that she had become dependent on him. When Izzy confronted Maddy by posing a conundrum - that currently, Jesse appeared to be the cause of the young woman's *craziness* as well as the solution to it - Maddy became agitated. She paced the counselling room with tears running down her face. She told Izzy that she knew she probably should talk about the *craziness* but she was afraid she would start cutting again if she did. That remark spoke volumes.

Since Maddy's arrival, Jesse had steered clear of Izzy. She wondered if Maddy had made him promise he wouldn't talk to her. Testing the waters, Izzy suggested Jesse attend one of their sessions. That idea went over like a lead balloon. Maddy was livid. She told Izzy she would never agree to something like that. Jesse was a guy she was having sex with ... end of discussion. She stormed out of the session and missed her next two appointments. When she came back she was miserable in her regrets and sorrows, but she wouldn't change her mind.

Izzy was sure of one thing - Maddy knew her relationship with Jesse was problematic. But she could not force her to face that reality. That would be a form of therapeutic violence and it could also be dangerous. Things weren't black and white. Izzy shrugged; if life were straightforward, no one would need to come and see her.

She opened her journal and jotted down ideas: *consult with someone (but who?), get at the root of Maddy's fear of losing Jesse (but how?), get tough (not worth the risk), shift the focus.* Izzy gazed at her journal and underlined the last idea. She would try to get Maddy to talk about her future. She would emphasize any aspect, no matter how small, that didn't involve Jesse. A frown settled again on Izzy's face; the clock was ticking. Maddy's stay at the Camp wasn't open-ended and, even if it were, Jesse was leaving in August. Whatever the relationship was, it would soon come to a point of confrontation.

⚜⚜⚜⚜

Arianna leaned close to Dylan. He was standing beside the gleaming counter in the Camp's kitchen, flipping through a cookbook. She pointed to a picture of roast beef and Yorkshire pudding, "That looks yummy."

"It would be impressive, especially the pudding, but it's bound to be too hot at the end of June for a heavy meal like that." He turned to the seafood section, "Darlene says some of the locals will contribute fish ... salmon barbecued on an outdoor grill and served with salads is better than roast beef on a hot day." Dylan checked the index of the book and turned to another section, "I'll show them what I can do with the desserts."

"It's a lot, being in charge of the whole meal. Maryanne says the Talent Night is always sold out. That's like three hundred people."

Dylan narrowed his eyes at Arianna, "Are you trying to freak me out? I can do this, no sweat."

"Of course you can. I didn't mean it like that. I want to help." Arianna nudged Dylan with her shoulder, "Mark and I are working on an awesome song for the talent part. I promised him I wouldn't say a word, but do you want me to tell you about it?"

"You better not say anything if you promised to keep quiet."

Robbie walked into the kitchen and stepped in between Dylan and Arianna, "What are you guys looking at?"

Dylan glared at him, "I thought I told you to stay out of the kitchen?"

"You said to stay out when you're cooking. You're not cooking now." Robbie held up a comic book, "I've got the new Wolverine. It's not as good as Spiderman, but do you want to see it?"

Dylan slammed the cookbook shut. "Go and irritate someone else, I've got more important things to do than talk to a stupid kid about a comic." He walked out of the kitchen.

Arianna took the comic book and flipped through it. "I love Wolverine." She shot her hand out and aimed it at Robbie's face as she pretended that a sharp set of metal claws had sprung from her fingertips.

He giggled and backed up a few feet before turning his palm up and shooting an imaginary spider web towards her, "Spiderman can take Wolverine any day."

Arianna laughed, "Don't be too sure. I'll grab some cookies and we can read all about how Wolverine is way more of a bad-ass than tired, old Spidie."

※ ※ ※ ※

Edward looked up from polishing a telephoto lens. He had been stretched out in the recliner for the last twenty minutes – waiting, always waiting. The morphine had finally taken hold. He luxuriated in the cessation of pain, the feeling of floating. It was as if he were lying on the raft out on the lake with the water rolling under him – moving, always moving. He saw Liam coming down the stairs from the dining room to the sun porch.

This was the man his daughter was in love with. Events of the last weeks had certainly put that love to the test, but nothing seemed to shake it. He remembered that Isabella had been a determined child. He suspected that she had inherited her mother's tenacity; neither one of them ever liked to admit she might have miscalculated in some way.

Edward found it almost impossible not to pity Liam. The man advertised his misery like those poor beggars who wear sandwich board signs over their bodies, hawking for car washes and pizza joints. Edward hated being a witness to the grim lines around Liam's mouth and the pained expression in his eyes whenever he had to deal with Lisa. Still, he had to admit that his sympathies leaned towards the girl.

Lisa had talent and dreams. Edward thought she should take every opportunity to find out how far she could go with that combination. Liam's determination to bind her to the child would only get in the way. She was already a skilled photographer. On top of that, she had an eye for something Edward had never considered. Lisa could see the potential in an image - after it was taken. In his time, good photography was about knowing what a shot could be before pushing the shutter. Digital cameras changed all of that. Editing software opened up another world. Lisa could crop a photo here or there, adjust the saturation level and try out one effect after another until a picture emerged with quite a different feel to it. He was amazed at what she could do on a computer. Her assistance with his book would allow him to take the story to a new level.

"Do you mind if I join you?"

Edward gestured to the free chair by his work table. Liam sat down and watched the soft cloth in Edward's hand swipe over the camera lens. The compassion on Liam's face, and what it probably meant, was easy for Edward to read. He cleared his throat and set the lens down on the table beside his chair. "How did you find out?"

"Robbie asked me if Izzy knew her dad was really sick."

"I'm not surprised. There's something about the way that lad looks at people. Have you ever noticed how he tips his head to the side and narrows his eyes?"

"I saw him do it today. I haven't paid very much attention to Robbie. I probably convinced myself I already have too much on my plate." He glanced back at Edward, "How bad is it?"

"My London doctor gave me a year; that was about five months ago." Edward pulled a small key out of his sweater pocket and reached over to open the top drawer of his file cabinet. He pulled out a bottle of pills. "Dr. Maxwell is keeping me well supplied with morphine. I am getting weaker, though. I'm not going to be able to manage those stairs up to the bathroom for much longer." Edward dropped the bottle of pills back in the drawer and relocked it. "Cancer ... but, of course, you guessed that."

"There isn't anything that can be done?"

Edward appreciated the fact that Liam's voice didn't waver. "I've already gone one round with cancer treatment. I've decided to forego such a desperate and torturous choice again, thank you kindly. Besides, the bloody disease has spread too far this time."

"What can we do for you?"

"I've decided to die here ... preferably in this chair. I want to work until the end. The book means a great deal to me. I find I have become quite obsessed with finishing. And I don't want Isabella to be inconvenienced in any way. I have money; I can pay for the care I require. I realize this is a somewhat remote area, but I've discovered over the course of my years that money paves over many a rough spot."

"Cynthia was a nurse before she became a writer; she might be able to help out. I'll speak to her if you like." Liam met Edward's gaze before he added, "I did some volunteer hospice work years ago - for guys who had drunk themselves right to the edge of the grave - there but for the grace of God and all of that. If you'd like, I can help you when things get to that point."

The respectful way Liam made the offer touched Edward. "I'm more than willing to barter my dignity for the right to have things the way I want them for as long as I can."

"What can we do about these stairs?" Liam pointed up toward the dining room, "You're comfortable here, it would be a shame to have to move you."

Edward pulled a pamphlet from under a stack of papers on the table. He handed it to Liam, "Hydraulic stair lift - it's already waiting at that freight place in Dearborn for someone to pick it up."

Liam looked with curiosity at the picture on the front of the pamphlet. An elderly man smiled as he sat sideways in a small seat attached to a staircase. "I'll get Reg down to help me put it in." He handed the paper back to Edward and locked eyes with the older man, "We'll have to tell, Izzy."

"Yes ... that will be the difficult part, won't it?"

TWENTY-THREE

B eulah twisted her body to squeeze in behind the giant arm of the dough mixer. Using an old toothbrush, she scrubbed at a crevice near the joint of the arm and the motor casing. Arianna looked up from wiping down the surface of the butcher block table, "I've got to up my game with Dylan. I've been making it pretty obvious that I like him but he's not getting it."

"Did it ever occur to you that maybe the guy isn't interested?" Beulah wiggled out from behind the mixer.

"I've got to take a shot. He's so cute, a major babe. He's like the guy version of one of those super models they put in the Sports Illustrated Swimsuit Edition."

Beulah pushed the mixer back into place as a buzzer sounded, "Thanks for making a comparison I can relate to. The bread is done. Come on, *Miss Lonely Heart*, let's get moving."

Beulah led the way out of the bakery. She grabbed a long pole that stood by the oven and jammed it into the catch to release the oven door. As it swung open, a cloud of steam escaped and the smell of freshly baked bread filled the area. Arianna passed Beulah one of the large bread boards which she slipped inside the oven. She edged the board under the first row of baked loaves, pulled it out and balanced it on her shoulder as she headed for the bakery shed.

On her way back for the second load, Beulah caught sight of Alex coming down the trail. She called out, "Man of the moment, come on over here and give us a hand." Beulah jammed the wooden bread board back into the oven and pulled it out loaded, "Both of you," she nodded at Arianna and Alex, "take this." She watched them raise the board and head inside with it. Beulah closed down the oven and followed her helpers into the bakery.

Arianna placed the loaves on the cooling racks. Alex leaned against the wall and asked, "Where you from, kid?"

Arianna glanced at him and smiled, "The Osoyoos Band, up in the interior."

"You wouldn't happen to know Muriel Abbot would you?"

"She's like my auntie's best friend." Arianna's face lit up.

"You tell her, the next time you see her, that Dr. Collins says hello."

"I will, for sure." She turned to Beulah, "Mind if I go now? I've got a math test this afternoon and I still need to study."

Beulah waved her off and took over the job of getting the rest of the bread onto the racks. Alex made himself comfortable, lounging on an old sofa that sat against the bakery wall. Without turning from her task, Beulah said, "You just happen to know a friend of that kid's aunt? Quite the coincidence wouldn't you say, Dr. Collins?" She couldn't help the sharp edge with which she rolled out the word *doctor*. It was hard to believe that the guy sitting on the sofa, wearing faded jeans and combat boots, could be a doctor of anything.

Alex laughed. "Not a coincidence at all. There aren't many Aboriginal people with PhD's in this country. I'm in high demand to serve on graduate student committees. I was an external examiner at Muriel Abbot's doctoral defense a couple of years ago. She did some outstanding research on economic development." He changed the subject, "Liam tells me you have some enthusiasm for baseball. I've got a proposition for you."

Beulah leaned back against the solid weight of the long wooden table and folded her arms across her white-aproned chest. She nodded at Alex to continue.

"There's this bunch of kids from the reserve over at Cedar Falls. They'd like to go to the All-Native Slow Pitch Tournament down in Courtenay on the August long weekend. The Band has agreed to get them to Dearborn a couple of nights a week to practice and I said I'd organize them up a bit. I'm looking for a coach."

"Doesn't a proposition mean you do something for me and I'll do something for you? I'm not hearing the part about what's in this for me. Do these kids even know how to play baseball?"

"Let's say they are long on enthusiasm and short on skills."

"Ya right ... still not hearing what's in it for me."

Alex pulled a small knife from his pocket. He flicked the blade out and began to clean his nails. "I heard this joke the other day." He glanced up at Beulah and went on, "A young couple - let's call them Sally and Hector -

they want some time to themselves, so they rent a hotel room in town. You know those houses on the reserve can get mighty crowded, not enough room to swing a rat without smacking your grannie. After they check-in, Sally gets worried. What if she gets pregnant? She sends Hector out to buy a box of condoms. Then she shuts out all the lights and hops into the bed."

Alex warmed up to the joke and chuckled to himself. "Hector beelines it for the drugstore but when he gets there, he realizes he left his wallet back at the hotel. He digs in his pocket and finds a toonie. He asks for a single condom. The man behind the counter says – *What quality do you want? The white one is okay. It'll cost you two bucks. The purple one is better, but it'll cost you three.* Hector gets the white condom and rushes back to the hotel room."

Alex looked over at Beulah and dropped his voice down a notch, "Now, while Hector is out on his mission, this old white dude walks into the wrong room. It's dark and all, so Sally can be excused for thinking he's her man. That geezer gets more than he's bargaining for. Afterwards, Sally falls asleep and the old boy wanders off. When Hector gets back ... well, he jumps right into the bed and he and Sally get at it."

Alex studied his nails then flicked his knife closed before he continued, "Nine months later, Sally gives birth to a bouncing baby boy. He's a kid that looks like a cup of coffee with a whole lot of cream. When the boy gets older, he asks his dad – *How come I look part white when you and Mom are both Indian?*" Alex paused, barely holding in his own amusement, "Hector shouts – *You are damn lucky, kid. One more loonie and you'd have been purple.*"

Beulah hadn't seen the punch line coming; she hooted loudly. Watching Alex laugh at his own joke only added to the hilarity. When he quieted down and wiped the tears from his eyes, Beulah said, "You're quite the comedian. Don't be waiting around for me to share any girl-on-girl jokes with you."

Alex held up a hand, "No problem. I've heard my share." The expression on his face changed as he switched to another topic. "Let me tell you something, Beulah. When I get invited into a community – Dr. Alexander Collins, Professor of Indigenous Governance, a founding member of the Native Warrior Society – there isn't one person out of a hundred who understands what the hell it is I do. Some think I'm going to make a speech or give people orders, like a bloody Indian agent. Others think I'm some shit disturber who's going to whip people up to blockade the main road into town." He shook his head, "I've been in on protests, but they're the end product of a journey, not the beginning. What I do is hang out. I go to meetings and community events. I talk to people, drink a lot of tea, I tell a few jokes and stories. I'm looking for a common cause, a way to bring people together – especially young people – doing something that creates a sense of belonging. It's a fine thing to be part of."

Beulah pulled her apron over her head, "Let's have a coffee and you can tell me more about how coaching a bunch of native kids would involve me in any sort of a common cause."

An hour later, after coffee and a couple of sandwiches, Beulah ushered Alex out the back door of the A-Frame. As she loaded the bread into flats and carried them out to the truck, she found herself thinking that practices are all well and good, but a game is what really gets the juices going. Maybe she'd see about reuniting the Crater Lake Timber Wolves to serve as the opposing team for these kids. Heading out to the ball field was an idea that had Beulah whistling as she started the truck and barreled up the driveway.

✄✄✄✄

"You'll never guess what happened this morning," Maddy reached past Lisa-Marie to grab some raffia to twist around the bar of soap she had just wrapped. She held up the finished product, straightened the *Micah Camp Soap Company* label and stacked the bar in the box she and Lisa-Marie were filling for shipment.

The shop's tall windows were open to a view of Crater Lake that stretched from one end of the Camp to the other. The afternoon sun shone in and bounced off the vaulted ceiling, making the entire work area bright and inviting. Seated at one of the long, butcher block work tables, Lisa-Marie grabbed a piece of wrapping paper and a bar of soap as she listened.

"Mark walked right in on Jesse and me –" Maddy stopped talking when she saw the puzzled look on Lisa-Marie's face. "You know Mark ... the short kid with the big glasses and funny hair. He's in the same cabin as Jesse and Dylan."

Lisa-Marie kept wrapping, "Oh ya, that kid. He did what?"

"He walked into the bedroom this morning when Jesse and I were in the middle of –"

"If you're going to talk about sex, stop right now."

"You are seriously ruining the drama of this story. Anyway, it isn't actually about sex, except that Jesse and I were having sex when he walked in."

"Ick ... the poor kid. He's probably traumatized for life. What did he want?"

"I don't know. He had this paper in his hand and he kept looking down at it all the time like he was checking a list of instructions or something. He asked me if I would be going over for breakfast soon. When I said ... ya, I guess ... he said he wondered if I would like to sit with him in the dining room."

"Weird. What did you say?"

"I didn't get to say anything. Jesse threw a book at Mark and told him to get out."

"I wonder why he couldn't see you guys were ... occupied."

"All he seemed to be thinking about was that piece of paper."

"Embarrassing ... did you sit with him at breakfast?"

Maddy laughed, "Ya, of course. Seemed like the least I could do after all of that."

Lisa-Marie slid off her stool and walked to the back of the shop to get another bin of soap. Josie was leaning over a vat of paper pulp and giving instructions to a couple of kids who were standing beside her. She smiled brightly at Lisa-Marie. When Lisa-Marie had asked Josie if she could have her old job back, the woman had welcomed her with a big hug, saying, "You couldn't have shown up at a better time."

Lisa-Marie plonked the soap bin down on the table and got back on her stool. Maddy had been watching her as she walked across the shop. "You look terrific, Leez. I can't believe you were humongous and pregnant ... what was it? Like a month ago."

Lisa-Marie leaned back to poke at her stomach, "Exactly five weeks and six days. I can't seem to get rid of this gross roll and look at this," she tugged up her T-shirt and pulled her shorts down slightly to reveal what looked like scratches running along her side. "Stretch marks. I'll never be able to wear a bikini again." With a scowl on her face, she tugged her clothes back into place and reached for a bar of soap.

Maddy pulled her long sleeved shirt up to her forearm to show line upon line of scars - most faded to dull silver, but some still as red and vivid as Lisa-Marie's stretch marks. "We all have scars. You won't be seeing me in a bikini any time soon, or even a short sleeved shirt."

"Oh shit, I'm sorry for whining on about myself. It's just that I'm so totally jealous of Willow and Misty and their perfect never-had-a-baby bodies. I can't stand the thought of Justin comparing me to them."

Maddy scrutinized Lisa-Marie, "Well, you're better in the bust department than you were. You must be happy about that."

"Ya, I guess," Lisa-Marie smoothed her T-shirt down before changing the subject, "What do you think of being a backup singer for Izzy's song at the Talent Show?"

"The song is lame, but I love her idea of matching black dresses, pearls and stiletto heels."

※※※※

"Hi, Mark. Do you mind if I walk along with you?" Izzy was on her way over to Jillian's cabin to have coffee with Bethany. Mark fell into step beside her. "I noticed that you were sitting with Maddy in the dining room this morning. Did you try the list of steps we worked on?"

"Yes ... it worked okay ... except for the part when Jesse threw a book at my head."

"Why on earth would he do something like that?" Surprise made Izzy blurt out the question.

Mark stopped on the trail and kicked at a rock with the toe of his sneaker. With his head down and his dark hair sticking up, he reminded Izzy of Robbie.

"I followed the list exactly."

Izzy waited, trying to keep her own thoughts in check. It wasn't likely that Jesse would be jealous of Mark sitting with Maddy at breakfast. She finally asked, "Are you going to tell me what happened?"

"I knew Maddy was in Jesse's room, so I knocked on the door and went in. I asked her, the way you and I practiced," Mark hesitated and his face turned red. "I didn't know they were ... busy. I was trying to follow the list of steps and get everything right."

Izzy wanted to reach out and hug Mark, but she didn't. "You know what? I blame myself for not thinking of something like that. Here's what we'll do. We'll add a step to the top of the list. Something like ... wait until the person is in a public spot. Do you think that might work?"

Mark gave Izzy's proposal serious consideration. "Good idea. A public spot, not a bathroom or a bedroom. I'll write that at the top of the list as soon as I get back to my cabin."

He walked away with a bounce in his step. Izzy shook her head at the image his story had created. It was true that she was to blame for not anticipating such an eventuality.

Bethany sat in a chair near a table cluttered with a laptop, printer, books, and papers dotted with coloured post-it notes. The headphones that she had been wearing when Izzy came in were tossed aside. She looked different – professional – dressed in neatly cropped pants and a crisp, button-up shirt. Izzy realized that she hadn't taken the time to notice how Bethany had changed since she took on the research assistant job.

Izzy pointed to the desk and asked, "How is the work going?"

"The transcribing is a bit tedious. I wish people wouldn't mumble as much as they do, but I can mix it up with all kinds of other jobs, so it's not too bad. Everything Jillian gets me to do is fascinating." Bethany picked up a thick book. "I've been reading about a bunch of research on what Canadian young people have to say about school and work." She handed the book to Izzy, "Jill asked me to look it over and take some notes. It's really interesting." Bethany pulled out another piece of paper from a pile and passed that over as well, "I got this email today. I had to print it out. I might even frame it. I am now officially registered as a distant-education student at the University of Victoria. I've enrolled in my first course, too – psychology."

Izzy smiled at Bethany's enthusiasm and studied the paper. "Sounds like your reduced hours at the bakery are working out well."

Bethany nodded, "I have most of my mornings free. I've been doing a study skills course that Roland put together for me, learning how to take notes and do other things that will help me when I get into my first university course."

Bethany set her coffee cup down on the table and sat up straight. "I wanted to talk to you about Lisa-Marie. I feel ashamed about how Beulah and I have dumped her on you and Liam. And now there's Sophie to think about. It must seem like we've washed our hands of both of them and we never meant to do that."

"You're her legal guardian. Do you think she should move back to the A-Frame?"

"I did talk to her about that. She told me that Liam wouldn't want her to because he thinks she needs to spend time with Sophie. I asked her what she wanted, but she couldn't say. It seems like she's confused. All she talks about is getting back to normal."

"I'm not surprised she's confused. I think we all are. Lisa's been through a lot and I understand how she'd like her life to get back to the way it was." Izzy shrugged, "I suspect the attraction of staying at our place is more about my dad and Justin than it is about Sophie. But she does her share of caring for the baby and that is a help. We have the space - it isn't a problem. I just don't want you to feel as though we've stolen your niece."

"No, it's not like that. She stops over at the A-Frame all the time and I see her here when she's working."

Izzy studied Bethany's face, "Between you and me, what do you think she should do? She could walk away from all of it - let Liam and me adopt Sophie. She doesn't have to be a mother at her age. She's got her whole life in front of her."

Bethany looked down at her hands, now gripped tightly in her lap. "I don't know, Izzy. There's no walking away after having a baby ... it doesn't matter what any of you decide to do."

It was silent in the small cabin as both women contemplated Bethany's words. Finally, Izzy said, "I think we'd better leave things as they are for now. Maybe we'll just have to think of all our places as one commune with a few different buildings."

Bethany smiled suddenly, "Caleb would have loved that."

"Yes, I think he would have."

⚜⚜⚜⚜

Arianna stood outside Willow's bedroom door. Through the wall between their rooms, she had heard the muffled sounds of desperate sobbing. She took a deep breath, knocked on the door and went in. Willow was curled up on the bed; a mess of blonde hair covered her face. She held a framed picture close to her.

"What's wrong?" Arianna asked this question as she walked over to the bed.

Willow raised her red-rimmed eyes; her voice shook with emotion, "I'll never see Jonathan again and I still love him so much. I can't stand how much I miss him. I'll never stop loving him."

Not this again, Arianna thought. "What happened between you guys? You didn't tell me the last time you talked about him." Willow sat up on the bed and reached for a tissue.

"Jonathan is special -" she hesitated; then her words ran out together in a rush, "He has a terrible temper, he can't help it. I left him. I knew that if I didn't leave, he would probably kill me one day."

The absolute certainty in Willow's voice made Arianna shiver. "How did you know?" Arianna scooted across the bed to sit cross-legged with her back against the wall. "Tell me everything."

Willow held tight to the framed picture. "I met him right after I moved into the foster home in Kamloops. I had to go to a new high school. It was horrible. I didn't know anyone. Everyone was snotty and mean. Jonathan was in grade twelve." A sad smile flitted across Willow's face, "He found me one day, all by myself in the courtyard. After that, we were always together." She looked up at Arianna, "It wasn't what you think. He didn't even touch me for what seemed like forever - only kissing and stuff. He said I wasn't ready. I thought I would go crazy, I wanted him so badly."

Willow fidgeted with a hangnail on her thumb as she continued, "After Jonathan graduated he moved in with his older brother. They both worked at the pulp mill. I would go over and watch Jonathan paint and he would get me to read my poems out loud while he worked. He said I inspired him; I was his muse. He could be so sweet."

Arianna reached over to stop Willow from picking at her finger, "What about the dark side?"

"Jonathan could get crazy jealous. It was all so stupid because I never once gave him a reason to be jealous. He would get all worked up in his own mind about things." Willow chewed on the side of her thumb. "It got way worse after we started doing it. He would grab me around the throat and choke me. I blacked out a bunch of times and I always had to wear turtlenecks to cover the bruises." When Willow saw the horror-stricken look on Arianna's face, she shook her head, "You don't understand. I forgave him. I hoped that if he got to trust me, things would be better." Tears ran down Willow's face. Arianna reached over to pat her on the arm. "One day when things were bad, he told me - *no one but me will ever touch you. I'll kill you, I'll kill the guy, I'll take down everyone I see near you and then I'll kill myself.* I knew he meant it. His brother had all kinds of guns. Jonathan showed me. They were always going out in the hills to shoot at stuff."

Willow locked eyes with Arianna and asked, "Do you believe in God?"

A puzzled look flashed across Arianna's face. She took her time answering. "My mom took me to this Church once. People were falling on the floor and talking crazy. She said they were sharing a message from God. You'd think if God wanted to get a message out, he'd at least give it to someone who speaks so that people can understand. I don't know. The whole thing scared me. If that's what God's about, you can count me out."

"I've never heard of anything like that. I'm Catholic. The Church teaches that all life is sacred. If I stayed with Jonathan, it would be a terrible sin. I'd have been risking my own life, maybe the lives of other people as well, and putting Jonathan's immortal soul in danger. I left him because of that."

"So you broke up with him?"

"Not exactly ... I ran away to Vancouver. I stayed with a friend of a friend in this real dump of an apartment for a couple of weeks. Someone told me I should go to Social Services for money since I wasn't nineteen yet. When I did, they got in touch with my worker up in Kamloops. She said I could stay in Vancouver if that's what I wanted. They'd find a new foster home for me. No one knew why I ran away and my foster family didn't know a thing about Jonathan. Anyway, a social worker called my aunt and she flew out from Toronto to see me. She spoke to them about me, how I'm a classically trained pianist and that something should be done for me. That's how I ended up coming here."

"I didn't know you play the piano. Why haven't you ever said anything?"

"I hate the piano. When I applied to get in here, my aunt made me say I would try for a music scholarship. I want to be a poet."

Arianna asked, "You never saw Jonathan or talked to him again?"

"No ... my aunt got the whole story out of me about his temper. She made me promise I won't ever go back to him or let him know where I am. I wasn't going to anyway. Like I said ... it would be wrong. I don't want him to get into trouble. Jonathan can't go to jail or anything like that. He's an artist. It wasn't his fault." A note of desperation crept into Willow's voice, "He loves me, I know that. He suffered so much for the way he hurt me. You'd have to see his paintings to understand. No one knows but my aunt and now, you. Don't tell anyone, promise."

"I won't say a word. I think it's so brave the way you have tried to protect him. I don't know if I could have been strong enough to leave someone I loved so much." Willow smiled through her tears. Arianna knew she was only saying what Willow wanted to hear and she squirmed a bit inside, knowing her real thoughts. The guy sounded like a psycho and Willow was lucky she got away at all. There was no point in saying that, though. She could see Willow felt miserable enough as it was.

TWENTY-FOUR

I zzy congratulated herself on having had a productive Saturday. In the morning, she took Lisa with her to Dearborn. The two of them had their hair done, their eyebrows waxed, pedicures and a superb lunch at *The Sea Shed*. When she returned to the lake, she strapped Sophie into the baby carrier and went for a long walk, tramping along the lake trails with Dante and Pearl romping ahead of her. After that, she spent a couple of hours in the garden and greenhouse, puttering but making progress all the same.

She was surprised to come into a quiet cabin. "Where is everyone?" She directed this question to Liam who was sitting in the living room reading a book.

"Sophie's still sleeping ... all that fresh air, I guess. Robbie, Justin and Lisa-Marie are over at the Camp for dinner and a movie afterwards. Our official cooks decided to eat Chinese food in town. They're still stuffed. They brought us the leftovers."

After a quick shower and a change of clothes, Izzy carried a glass of wine and a shot of whiskey down to the sun porch where Liam now sat with Edward. She handed the shot glass to her father. Izzy sipped her wine and let out a contented sigh. "What a perfect day. I planted a whole new crop of lettuce. We'll be eating a lot of salad this summer."

Edward drained the alcohol from his glass and sat forward in the recliner. "Isabella, I want to discuss something with you and this seems like a perfect time. Heaven knows it isn't easy to get a quiet moment in your home these days."

Izzy agreed with her father's assessment of their reality. She looked over at Liam, ready to share a smile with him. His face was turned away. She glanced back at her father. A split second before he spoke, she knew what was coming. With lightning speed the pieces of a puzzle slipped into place. She could almost hear the click, click, click, click as they snapped together. Her father didn't eat, he had lost weight, he was becoming weaker and he had never announced an end to his visit. She had noticed all of these things over the past weeks with a deliberate, hazy awareness that kept her from seeing the whole picture. Of course her father was dealing with much more than a bad hip.

"I have cancer. The disease has progressed to the point where no treatment options are possible. I have about six months."

Izzy stared at her father; then her eyes sought out Liam's. The concern on his face completed the circle of reality that suddenly closed in on her. She forced herself to breathe and loosen the grip she had on her wine glass. Her free hand went up to her mouth as if she would hold back any inane comment that might slip out.

Edward removed his glasses and tapped them on the arm of the chair, "I have made plans. I want to die here, working as long as I can on my book. As I've explained to Liam, I have money. It's essential to me that you are not burdened by my condition, Isabella."

Izzy stiffened at the words *die here*. It was too blunt, too real. And what exactly did *here* mean? Questions popped into her head – if *here* meant *right here* – wasn't dying of cancer a painful process? Wouldn't a hospital be more appropriate? How could her father get the attention he would need this far from town? What if something went wrong? Then again, what more could go wrong? Dying was dying, after all. She raised the glass to her lips and took a drink.

Liam could read the doubt that raced across Izzy's face. He walked over, put his hand on her shoulder and waited until she raised her eyes to his. "I've spoken to Cynthia. She's going to help with any nursing care. I can manage the other things. We can do this, Izz."

Tears filled Izzy's eyes. She blinked to stem the flow. She felt the strength in Liam and it braced her. She straightened in her chair and looked away from both men to watch a small Junco sparrow hop along the edge of the deck railing. The black head and the eyes circled in white made the bird look as though it was staring back at her from under an executioner's hood. She pushed away such a morbid thought and took a deep breath. Turning back to face her father, she drained the wine and struggled to keep her voice steady, "Yes, of course. Tell me what you need me to do, Dad."

❧❧❧❧

Liam found Izzy sitting on the small deck of the garden house. The glass walls behind her reflected the dark shapes of the taller plants. He had given Sophie a bottle, bundled her into a sweater and carried her outside with him. Dusk had turned the sky midnight blue. Edward and Lisa-Marie had talked about this colour, one evening when they had tripods set up and cameras pointed out the open windows of the sun porch. Izzy had yelled that they'd better get the screens back on before bugs filled the cabin. They ignored her, immersed in what Edward had called the blue moment, that liminal time between light and dark when the intensity of hue could be captured.

Liam settled himself and Sophie into the chair next to Izzy. Secure in Liam's arms, Sophie shifted her eyes, like tiny chips of black obsidian, from his face to Izzy's in the gathering dusk.

Izzy reached over to adjust the baby's sweater, "I knew something was wrong. Before he said the words, I knew what he was going to say." Liam nodded and sat the baby up in the crook of his arm. Izzy stroked Sophie's head as she asked, "Why did he tell you before me?"

"He didn't. I confronted him with it."

"You guessed something was wrong?"

"No. There's something else I wanted to talk to you about or ... rather, someone else – Robbie."

A frown crossed Izzy's face, "I suppose we'll have to tell him and all the others, won't we?"

"Robbie knows; he's the one who told me."

"How could Robbie know?"

"He told me that he sees light around people and that the light tells him things. He knew from the light around me that I was his brother and from light around Sophie that she was family, too. He saw, I guess you could say – an absence of light on Edward's body. He knew he was sick because of that." Liam continued, "When Robbie told me about the light, I remembered something I heard way back when I was little. It was something my grandmother told my mother about a kid who visited us. She called the child a *light-seer*. At the time, I thought – *seer*, like a wizard and *light*, as in lightweight ... starting out." Liam laughed and Sophie turned her head to stare at him. "Oh yes, little one, even I – cranky old man that I am – manage a chuckle now and then."

Izzy smiled despite her sadness, "Are you sure we can do this for Dad, along with everything else we have on our plates?" She reached over, took

166

Sophie from Liam's arms and brought the baby up close to her face to touch their noses together.

. "We don't have a choice, Izz. He's your father ... family. The living owe the dying something, there's no way around that."

✻✻✻✻

Cynthia took a quick look at Alex as he lounged on the deck of the guest cabin, sipping a drink. The time they had spent together over the previous week had made her reassess her first impression of him. She had pegged him as a grown-up playing at little-boy games of military swagger. But Alex was not playing at anything. What had seemed like swagger, she now recognized as a kind of dangerous intensity under the surface of all his actions. He was like a large cat, lazy and sinuous, until that split second when he would gather his strength and pounce.

After their Chinese food lunch, they had completed the week's shopping, hauled the groceries back to the lake and packed them away in the cupboards at Izzy and Liam's. Relieved of dinner duty, Alex had invited Cynthia to join him on a boat trip to explore the lake. Sitting on the seat in the prow of the small boat, Cynthia had watched Alex lean over the motor and yank on the engine's pull cord. The sharp action made the muscles of his arm and bicep stand out in stark relief against his brown skin. As the motor jumped to life, a cloud of blue exhaust had drifted toward her on the wind, reminding her of summer camping trips and water skiing. She hadn't thought of water skiing in years.

Alex had taken the boat out in an arc from the beach near Izzy and Liam's, then he steered back along the shore, tracing the curve of the cove. At one end, Justin's cabin appeared, as if floating over the cliff edge. Set further back, the guest cabin was next in line. All Cynthia could see of her current home was a bit of the roof and the edge of the deck railing. Izzy and Liam's place spread out from the center of what looked like a huge park with gardens giving way to the greenhouse and workshop behind the cabin. She caught a mere glimpse of the sawmill further up the tree-lined hillside. The clean lines of the A-Frame came into view, visible above the beach and finally, the sprawling buildings of Micah Camp. For the first time since her arrival, Cynthia was able to get a full picture in her mind of each place in relation to the others. Then Alex had opened up the motor and sped across the width of the lake. They cruised by the summer cabins located on the more populated side of Crater Lake, distaining the extravagance of what neither of them would . ever own or even want.

Later, as they hiked up from the beach, Cynthia had said, "I have an expensive bottle of scotch in my cabin. Would you like to stop for a drink?'

Alex had smiled like a Cheshire cat, "Well, that has to be the second most popular thing any man would want to hear a woman say." Cynthia had felt herself blush and it seemed that Alex enjoyed her discomfort before adding, "The first thing being – I'm fine if you spend all day on the golf course, dear."

"I don't see you on a golf course, Alex," Cynthia had relaxed and smiled back at the man walking beside her.

"You would be surprised the places a guy like me could end up."

So, Alex had accepted her invitation and had ended up on the deck of the guest cabin. Cynthia savoured the scotch in her own glass before she cleared her throat to say, "I'm not sure if you know this or not, but curiosity is a writer's stock-in-trade." She smiled at him, "An occupational hazard, so to speak. Do you mind if I ask you a personal question?"

Alex rolled the liquor around the bottom of his glass, "Ah, Ms. St. Pierre, are you sure you want to hear the answer? Remember what the feminists always say ... the personal is political. I find much truth in that statement."

She pointed her own glass at Alex, "You will call me Cynthia or that will be the last drink you have on this porch."

"Cynthia it is," his voice purred out her name.

She shivered and rubbed her arms before asking, "Where is Robbie's mother?"

Alex sat forward and studied the concentric ripple pattern that had just appeared on the surface of the lake. He pointed out towards the water, "Best time for fishing. Did you see that fish jump?"

Cynthia spoke quickly, "I didn't mean to pry."

Alex dismissed her comment with a shake of his head. "Robbie's mom died a few months back. Her name was Marsha. There was an accident on the lobster boat she crewed on – it sank. She was trapped in the wheelhouse; she drowned."

Cynthia's eyes widened, "Oh my God, Alex ... I'm so sorry."

"Save your sympathy for the kid, it's a hell of a thing for him. I hadn't seen Marsha since Robbie was a baby. I'll tell you this – she was a damn good woman who didn't deserve to die so young."

"How old was she?"

"Not even thirty-two, if my memory serves me."

Cynthia tried to hide her surprise with a nod of her head. She had already surmised that Robbie's mother had to be younger than Alex. But geez, she would have been around twenty-three and he in his fifties when Robbie was conceived. That warranted at least a raised eyebrow. Alex was watching her again, as if he could see the calculations that were running through her mind. May as well be branded for a lion as a lamb, she told herself, "And Liam's mother?"

Alex relaxed back into his chair and drained his glass. "I better keep my chronology straight if you want me to walk back through time. There is Kate to consider."

"Hold that thought." Cynthia got up. "Shall I pour you another?" She waved her empty glass at his and saw him nod. By the time she settled back into her chair, twilight had given way to dark. She tugged a light sweater over her sleeveless blouse and nodded at Alex to continue.

"I met Kate at the University of Toronto. She was a kid, getting a degree in criminology and big as a house, pregnant with Fiona. Robbie and I visited Fi in Montreal on our way here. She's doing a medical internship at McGill. She always was a smart kid. Fiona spent a lot of time with me when she was growing up. But me and Kate - that wasn't going to work. We drifted apart after a time. She was bound for a career in law enforcement - tribal police. What my life was all about didn't fit for her. Kate went her own way down the straight and narrow but Fi was like my own by then. We've stayed close." Alex frowned and added, "If you count time spent with a kid, then Fi is more mine than Robbie or Liam."

"I wouldn't think that, to see either of them with you. The three of you seem quite close."

"When I arrived here a month ago, I hadn't seen Liam for close to thirty years." Alex was quiet; a contemplative stillness wrapped around him. "It's a frightening thing when you think about the way your life goes by. Years of following a certain path - no matter how momentous or righteous one thinks that path might be - it means the loss of other things."

They both sipped their drinks in silence. Eventually, Alex resumed his stroll down memory lane. "Liam's mom and I got together when we were young, full of righteous Indian rage and wanting to change the world. She was full-blood Cree, from Northern Manitoba. My mom was Mi'kmaq but my dad was a white guy - Scottish. We were a military family ... lived on Canadian forces bases all across the country. We landed at Shilo, near Brandon, when I was in high school. Liam's mom had come down south for school; that's how we met. As soon as I graduated, we lit out of there, travelling all over, stirring things up - even after Liam was born. We'd leave him with his grandmother up north. But Sophie's mom took sick with a heart condition that kind of dragged on and Sophie went home to be with her and Liam. Something of the rage burnt out of her as she got older. Our paths separated. I never stopped loving that woman. She died some years back."

It was silent on the deck then, only the sound of the waves carried up the cliff face and the creaking sound that old snags make when the wind catches the tops of them. An owl hooted mournfully in the distance. Cynthia heard Alex ask, "Is there a Mr. St. Pierre hanging his hat somewhere?"

She studied her left hand as it rested atop the arm of the deck chair; her fingers curled around a now empty glass. The always unadorned third finger made an empty statement. "There was a young man, years and years ago. We were in love and wanted to marry. It didn't work out for a number of reasons that seem insignificant now. My life moved on." Cynthia could hear the loss in her own voice as she said, "I never thought of marrying anyone else."

Alex rose then and set his empty glass on the railing. Cynthia felt the shadow of him come close in the dark as he leaned over her chair. He stroked the side of her face and brushed his lips against her cheek. "Good night, Cynthia."

Her breath caught sharply as she watched him walk off into the dark.

TWENTY-FIVE

"**D**ad, can I get you anything before I head over to the Camp?" Izzy hated the way her voice sounded, strained even to her own ears.

Edward glanced up at her, "No nothing, dear. I'm fine. Do you know when Lisa-Marie will be home? I'm becoming quite dependent on that young lady." Edward frowned, "You've told her?" Izzy nodded. "Good. I'm sorry to have burdened you with that. I would have asked Liam to do it but I knew it would be better coming from you."

When Izzy had said the words – *Edward is dying of cancer* – Lisa had reacted with a look of incomprehension. She hadn't cried, though and Izzy had been relieved. If Lisa had cried, she was sure she would have, too. Would that have been such a terrible thing? She now wondered. When she had talked to Lisa, Izzy knew that she'd behaved as her own mother would have done in a similar situation – controlled, matter-of-fact. Having to talk about a father dying is an event that warrants tears. By not letting her own emotion show, she had denied Lisa the opportunity to share how she felt. It was shitty modelling and Izzy knew it.

Her thoughts bounced away to a conversation she'd had with Cook right after her father arrived at Crater Lake. They had been in the kitchen of the cabin getting refreshments ready for a book club gathering. Cook had said, "Your dad is quite the British gentleman."

"He does seem more British than Canadian now. He's spent so much time in London it's all rubbed off on him."

"I was a bit surprised to see him so settled in. I thought you said once that you and your dad weren't close."

"We weren't. Out of the blue, I got an email saying he was coming for a

171

visit. It totally floored me. The next week he arrived, set up his writing things in the sun porch and started working on his book. As far as I can tell, his visit is quite open-ended ... he hasn't said a word about leaving."

"Are you and Liam okay with that?"

"Liam thinks it's great that I have this chance to get to know my dad after all these years. I'm enjoying having him around. We don't have cozy little father-daughter chats or anything like that ... he uses that British politeness quite effectively to keep people at a distance, me included. I'm fine with that. I don't think I'd know how to handle him if he wanted to be overly affectionate."

As Izzy looked down at Edward sitting in his recliner, she realized that her father's politeness with her was a barrier, as effective as any ocean had been. She had no idea how to break through to a place where she could say the things she wanted to say. So instead, Izzy contented herself with making lists of things she could do to help – arrange for a masseuse, inquire about reflexology, research vitamin therapy and find out how to coax a dying man to eat.

⚜⚜⚜⚜

Lisa-Marie walked down to the sun porch. She avoided Edward's eye, mumbled hello and took a seat at the work table. Edward studied her from beneath his black rimmed glasses, "I'll accept none of that, Lisa."

Startled, she replied, "None of what?"

He took off his glasses and leaned forward in the recliner, "No moping around because I'm dying. We have no time for such indulgence." He saw the tears come quickly to her eyes – tears she tried to blink away. He sighed, "I'm seventy-two years old, Lisa. I've lived a full life. I've been able to do the work I love, to travel everywhere I've wanted to go. I feel as though I'm leaving something of value behind me." Edward glanced over to his worktable where he kept a framed picture of Izzy as a child. "As I've gotten to know Isabella again, I see the talented woman she has become. She's a force for change in this world. I'm proud of her and I feel a small measure of satisfaction that I've had something to do with that. And this book – the opportunity to gather the best of my life's work together and to share some of what I've learned with you – this book is essential, for both of us. We do not have time to waste. Do you understand?"

Lisa-Marie sniffled a couple of times before she said, "I want to learn as much as I can. I want to help."

"Excellent. Let's start with the group of photos we were working on

172

yesterday. I think we were almost there. What had you done to the one of the two boys by the river?"

"I layered out some of the background scene and brought up the shadow on the faces. It seems like the feeling you're after ... what was it you said?"

Edward smiled, "I said I wanted a surreal look – something akin to Joseph Conrad's *Heart of Darkness* which you, uninitiated to the classics, had not read or even heard of."

Lisa-Marie found herself grinning, "Ya, it's top of my reading list now for sure." She had the photo program open and was pulling up the image in question. Soon she was immersed in the work.

⁕⁕⁕⁕

Dear Emma:

I used to be tough. Now I'm a total wimp. I don't know how I can stand this – Edward is dying – not dying like any old person is dying – dying like soon. He has cancer. When I think about how he must feel, knowing he will die, it makes my stomach hurt. I don't ever want to die. I know that's stupid. Everyone is going to die someday. I guess I mean that I want to live and live and live. There's so much I want to do. I pour over Edward's photos and see all the places he's been to – the world is way bigger than I ever imagined. Did you know, Emma, that there are icebergs that are striped deep-blue? It's because of the way the algae and krill get stuck in the ice when it melts and refreezes. Edward has a photo of a bunch of guys in a Zodiac boat right beside this huge iceberg with all these incredible blue stripes.

When there are things like that in the world, maybe Edward could be the person who wakes up one day and all his cancer is gone. That happens. Or maybe some doctor will find a cure for him. I don't think he should just give up and accept that he's going to die. He should fight. I don't want to be as hopeless as Izzy seems to be.

⁕⁕⁕⁕

Robbie knocked on Lisa-Marie's door and pushed it open to poke his head into her loft, "What are you doing, Leez?"

Lisa-Marie was sitting on the edge of her bed. She was using her foot to push Sophie's cradle, hoping to rock the baby back to sleep. It wasn't working. She looked at Robbie and asked, "Why are you still up? It's late."

Robbie walked over to the cradle. He searched around for the baby's soother, put it back in her mouth and tucked her blanket up under her arm,

173

close to her face. She sucked avidly on the pacifier and settled down. With his back to Lisa-Marie, Robbie asked, "Were you crying because of Edward?"

"They told you about him?"

Robbie sat down on the floor. "I knew he was sick, the first time I saw him."

"How would you know something like that?"

"Did Liam and Izzy want you to have Sophie for them?"

Lisa-Marie's eyes widened as she stared at Robbie. After a moment, she said, "Not at first but I guess it worked out that way."

Robbie pulled a deck of cards out of his pocket and shuffled them before he laid out the pattern for a solitaire game of *Clock*. With his head down and his eyes on the cards he asked, "Why are you afraid of Sophie?"

Lisa-Marie slammed her journal shut. "I'm not afraid of Sophie. She's a baby. Why would you say something so stupid?"

Robbie kept flipping the cards, "My friend Jamie ... he was afraid of his dad. Well, his dad was sort of scary, especially when he was drinking. When you look at Sophie, you have that light around you, like Jamie had with his dad ... like you're afraid she'll hurt you."

Lisa-Marie eyed Robbie suspiciously, "What has light got to do with me and Sophie?"

Robbie slid a King under the stack of cards in the middle of the circle, "My mom is dead. My dad said it's never easy when anyone dies but I think it has to be easier if someone old is dying, like Edward ... easier than if the person has a kid and loves fishing and stuff."

Lisa-Marie stroked her fingers over the smooth leather of the journal cover, "My mom's dead, too."

Robbie flipped the last King. He threw it down in disgust. He picked up the cards. "When I look at people, I can see light around them. It's different for different people ... shapes and colours." Robbie grinned up at her, "When you were in the hospital having Sophie, your light was crazy. It flashed everywhere and was coloured like a rainbow. I knew, even before anyone said, that Sophie was family."

"That's totally freaky; knock it off, saying stuff like that. People will think you're nuts or something. You've read too many comic books. You're not a superhero, you know."

"Ya, I know that. I wish I was, though." Robbie's voice was wistful.

"Is it scary?"

"Nah, I'm used to it. I've always been able to do it." Robbie had the cards laid out again. He flipped through the pile in his hand, "Do you like living here with Liam and Izzy?"

"I love this room and I like being with Izzy. Liam's a bit of a pain. It's only until I go back to school in the fall, anyway."

"Do you go to the same school as Justin?"

"No ... he's in university. I'm still in high school."

"You like Justin, right?"

Lisa-Marie threw a pillow at Robbie's head. "Don't be such a snoop. Stop using your light-sensing power on me." Robbie grinned at her and threw the pillow back. Lisa-Marie dodged it and surprised even herself by asking, "Does Justin like me?" She felt like a total fool as the question hung out there. She made herself shake it off. Robbie was just a weird kid, for frig sakes. It didn't matter if he thought she was an idiot.

"He loves you and Sophie." Robbie didn't even look up as he gathered the cards and shuffled them.

Lisa-Marie's heart thumped wildly.

"You know that picture that Izzy has up on her desk ... from when she married the guy who died ... Caleb?" Lisa-Marie nodded and Robbie went on, "Justin has a light like that Caleb guy. He wants to protect you and Sophie. Nothing bad will ever happen when Justin is around."

Loves me like a big brother, that's what the crazy kid means, she thought. Well, crap to that and crap to this kid who was probably unhinged because his mom up and died on him. Then he got carted all the way across the country by Indian GI Joe. No wonder Robbie was showing signs of being delusional. "Are you trying to say your super powers get light off a picture of a dead guy?"

"Sometimes a part of someone hangs around, if the light was strong. Hey, Leez, do you want to play Rummy?

"Ya sure, come on up here on the bed and don't make any noise. I don't want to end up with a screaming baby before I get to take her downstairs."

TWENTY-SIX

Lisa-Marie couldn't believe her eyes. Justin was walking along the trail through the apple trees with Willow at his side. She brought her hand up to steady the tray she held. She continued to circle the deck, offering appetizers to the guests while her thoughts seethed. Who did Justin think he was? How could he decide, on his own, to invite Willow over to Izzy's for the book-club potluck?

Izzy moved across the other side of the deck with a basket of fresh bread chunks and a bowl of spinach and artichoke dip. She looked gorgeous. Her tousled curls fell loosely down her back and the fabric of her dress clung to her curves. The silver medallion necklace glinted around her neck. Lisa-Marie remembered a similar gathering, last summer, when the sight of Izzy's perfection had thrown her down to the bottom of a well of self-conscious confusion. She took a deep breath and let the relief of being free of those feelings wash over her.

Edward held out his empty wine glass to Lisa, "Be a dear and get me a refill, would you?" She grabbed Edward's glass and walked off towards the beverage table.

Justin led Willow across the deck. "Izzy, I was sure you wouldn't mind if I invited Willow for dinner and the book club. I told her about Cynthia being a writer and she wanted to meet her." Justin grabbed a large chunk of bread from the basket in Izzy's hand and swiped it through the bowl of dip. He chewed with appreciation. "This is good. I'm starving." As Beulah walked by with a couple of beers in hand, he reached out for one. He smiled at Willow, "I'll get you something to drink. What would you like?"

"There's a non-alcoholic punch on the table." Izzy wasn't about to allow a resident of the Camp to drink alcohol right under Roland's nose. She had a flash of memory from the previous summer – Justin lounging on her deck drinking a beer ... more than once. Well, that had been different. Justin had been near the end of his time at the Camp, he was over nineteen and he worked for her. A sharp poke from her conscience reminded her that offering Justin a beer so he could sit and keep her company, hadn't been right.

Izzy turned her attention to Willow, "Try the dip. I'll introduce you to Cynthia as soon as she makes an appearance."

Justin brought Willow a glass of punch and grabbed for another chunk of bread. He spotted Liam coming out of the cabin carrying Sophie. "Come on Willow, you have to meet Sophie-pie."

Lisa-Marie was hard pressed to control her growing annoyance as she watched Justin take Sophie from Liam and hold the baby comfortably. He and Willow stood together looking at Sophie as though they had discovered a pot of friggin' gold. She walked over and took the baby from Justin.

Willow glanced from mother to daughter. She giggled and said, "What a cute baby. And wow, she looks just like you, Lisa." Even Justin raised an eyebrow at that remark.

Cynthia emerged from the kitchen and Izzy called Willow away to meet her. Roland, Jillian and Cook arrived from the Camp. With a sigh of relief, Lisa-Marie passed Sophie into Jillian's willing arms. She didn't like anyone to notice ... but Sophie wasn't a big fan of having Lisa-Marie hold her. The feeling was mutual. She wandered over to the drink table, poured herself a splash of wine and topped the glass up with soda water. She took her glass and the tray of appetizers across the deck to stand near Justin.

Cook disappeared into the cabin carrying two pies. Roland was right behind her toting the large bowl of English Trifle that Jillian had made. After they had placed the food on the counter, Cook pointed out the window to Jillian who was cuddling Sophie, "Better watch it, Roland. At Jillian's age, holding a baby makes the tick tock of the biological clock mighty loud." Before Roland could make any kind of protest, Cook grinned and walked out the door.

Roland went outside and took the seat next to Jillian. "She's wearing the outfit you picked out, babe. Isn't she just so infant chic?" The simple lines of the dress and the colours were perfect on the baby. Jillian leaned over to Roland and whispered, "What a stroke of luck for Izzy and Liam that whoever fathered this little one was native. Adopting her and raising her as their child will be so much easier for them. I mean look at her; she almost looks like Liam."

"Jill, keep your voice down," Roland whispered. "What if someone overhears you?"

"No one can hear me, babe. You're so paranoid sometimes." Jillian laughed and rocked Sophie in her arms.

Roland shook his head in frustration. Jillian's refusal to heed his repeated directives about not calling him by that ridiculous nickname was trying his patience to the breaking point. On top of that, it was unfortunate enough that he had to hear her speculate about people's personal lives, without others having to listen to her wildly inappropriate assumptions.

Roland suspected that if the situation with this baby were as straightforward as Jillian supposed – a teenage girl caught up in a pregnancy she didn't expect, two middle-aged people who would love to raise a child – Izzy would have made some kind of announcement by now. The baby was almost two months old. Something else was going on and the last thing he wanted to do was think about what it might be.

Izzy sipped her wine. The weather had turned out to be perfect – a stunning blue sky and the suggestion of a breeze. The lake spread out before her like a swath of lamé fabric. She glanced across the deck at the tear drops of deep purple wisteria that hung through the open lattice of the arbor. The afternoon light caught the blossoms, highlighting and shadowing a myriad of shades. The honeysuckle draped over the top of another section of arbor. It was budding up beautifully. The pots on the deck and the hanging baskets were filling out. There was nothing of the rich, abundant colour that would be seen in the coming weeks, but the intensity of the green foliage and the different shapes and textures of the plants were tantalizing signs of what was to come. The last of the late tulips splashed red and pink from the raised bed along the back of the deck.

Izzy watched her father as he sat in the armchair Liam had carried out to the deck for him. His face was in the shade of the cabin overhang. He looked comfortable enough. Roland was chatting to him. Edward's hair fell forward on his face and he raked it back with a snap of his wrist. Izzy looked closer and realized that his usually neat style now brushed the back collar of his sweater.

Cynthia and Willow stood beside Izzy, chatting about Willow's poetry. Willow handed over a tattered journal and Cynthia said, "I'm no expert on verse but, sure, I'd be happy to read your poems."

"Willow, I have something to ask you." Willow and Cynthia stopped talking and turned to Izzy. "Sorry to interrupt. I overheard some of the girls at Camp saying that you cut hair. Would you be able to come over tomorrow afternoon and trim my father's hair? He's ...," Izzy's voice faltered for a moment. "He's not interested in going into town for such things these days."

"Oh sure, I'd be happy to."

"When did you learn to cut hair?" Cynthia asked as she ran her hand through her own hair, "This style gets out of control so fast."

"I did a year of training while I was in grade twelve – a school-work internship thing. I wasn't all that serious about making a career out of it but, boy oh boy, has it ever turned out to be a terrific thing to know how to do. I could give you a trim and get your reverse bob back in shape."

Robbie came out to the deck and Izzy called him over. "Robbie, have you met Willow yet? Robbie is Liam's younger brother," Izzy pointed across the deck, "and Liam is my partner." Robbie looked down at the cedar boards and mumbled hello as he sidled closer to Izzy. She kept him beside her as she excused herself and made another round of the deck, handing out appetizers, filling glasses and chatting. Robbie wasn't a moody kid but there were times when something came over him. When this happened he chose to be near her. She had no idea why, but the relief in his dark eyes tugged at her heart.

Alex strolled over to Cynthia who stood sipping her wine. "I'm certainly looking forward to this book club discussion. I have so many questions about the logistics of some of the steamier scenes you've written."

She looked up to see the playful glint in his eyes and shoved him hard with her elbow, "Don't you dare." He laughed and walked away to talk to Beulah, as Cynthia called after him, "I mean it, Alex."

⚜⚜⚜⚜⚜

People gathered around the table and heaped their plates with food. Izzy pointed to a dish and told Jillian, "Be sure to try those dilly beans. They're something new that Bethany and I experimented with this year. We're crazy about them."

Jillian popped one into her mouth, chewed and said, "Delicious. I'd love to have some of these propped up in a large Caesar."

Izzy laughed, "I like your style, Jill."

Justin's attentiveness towards Willow didn't surprise Lisa-Marie though it bugged the hell out of her. He waited for Willow to fill her plate; then he found her a place to sit in the living room. He beckoned at Lisa-Marie to join them. Robbie followed along and sat on the floor nearby. He crammed forkfuls of lasagna into his mouth at breakneck speed while he told Justin all about a book he was reading on how to be a spy.

Lisa-Marie nudged Robbie with her foot, "Slow down, you'll end up choking. I know Justin has first aid training but I don't think he wants to whip a Heimlich maneuver on you."

Robbie ignored her warning and stuffed a large chunk of bread in his mouth. He scanned the room, counting the people. Without looking at Willow, he said, "Good you invited someone else, Justin. Otherwise, there would have been thirteen for supper. Bad luck for sure. Back home, Father Jack said only stupid people were superstitious about numbers and other stuff, like getting the same seat at the bingo hall every night. But my auntie said he was so crazy to say something like that about bingo."

Willow laughed a small, tinkling sound, "I'm glad to have saved the group from bad luck." She turned to Justin who was wolfing his way through his food. "The bonfire later should be lots of fun. Someone told me that you play the guitar. I hope you'll play tonight."

Justin nodded. He had been eating just as fast as Robbie, but he had a bit more going on in the manners department. He wouldn't try to respond with his mouth full. Lisa-Marie had noticed that Justin was eating a lot lately. She assumed he must be burning the calories off because there wasn't an ounce of fat on his tall frame. She noticed the way his arms and shoulders were bulking out. This sawmill job was doing wonders for the guy's position on the sizzling-hot scale. She couldn't wait for the weather to warm up enough for swimming. Then she could really check him out.

Most of the adults had pulled up chairs around the dining room table. Alex laughed at Robbie's comment about bad luck. "I'm not one to get too caught up in biblical references, but thirteen people for supper ... that idea is a bit sobering."

Izzy relaxed and enjoyed the meal. Sophie had conked out earlier, leaving her free to eat dinner without the burden of balancing a cranky baby on her lap. She took a sip of wine and glanced over at Beulah, "How is Arianna working out?"

Beulah scooped up another serving of lasagna as she replied, "That kid is great. She's a hard worker and catches on quick. Hiring her was the best thing we could have done."

Bethany smiled at Beulah and helped herself to more dilly beans. "These are good, Izzy. We have to make them again this year."

Jillian and Bethany got into a side discussion about the more complicated aspects of pickle making. Edward talked with Roland about the finer points of producing a lavish coffee-table book. Alex and Cook discovered they were both Atlantic Canadians and they chatted on about the distinguishing features of such a reality. Liam sat beside Izzy, eating slowly. She caught his eye and smiled. Hosting a social gathering with someone she loved was a pleasure she had missed since Caleb's death.

Beulah rapped on the table for attention. "Listen up, I've got an idea." To a chorus of groans, she said, "The Tricksters – the native kids Alex and I have been working with – would like to challenge the Crater Lake Timber Wolves to an exhibition ball game."

Izzy's eyebrows shot up in surprise. "But Beulah, there hasn't been a Crater Lake Timber Wolves team for over three years." She frowned, "Don't you think we'd be a bit rusty?" To say nothing of being short-handed, she thought to herself. When Caleb died, they lost the heart and soul of their team as well as the best catcher anyone had ever seen in a beer league.

"Come on, it's for fun. They want a real game experience before they go down Island to play in the tournament." Beulah was warming to the topic. "I know we're out of practice but it's like riding a bike, right? Reg is back. We still have Josie, Cook, you and Liam and I've got some new blood in mind." Beulah raised her voice so it carried over to the living room, "Have you ever played any baseball, Justin?"

"Ya sure, I wasn't a half bad catcher back in the day."

Izzy choked slightly, though she was not really surprised to learn the baseball position Justin had played. She noticed the look Liam gave her. He reached over to cover her hand with his own. They were developing an accurate sense for knowing what the other was thinking.

Lisa-Marie walked over to the dining room table and refilled her bowl with salad. She stared at Beulah, "Aren't you going to ask me to play in your stupid game?"

"Have you ever played baseball?" Beulah asked the question in a way that suggested she was sure the answer would be no.

"Of course I've played baseball. I didn't grow up on the moon."

Bethany shook her head, "I'm not so sure Kingston isn't somewhere in the vicinity."

Robbie had come over to the table. He was digging a piece of lasagna out of the pan with the serving spoon, heavily assisted by his fingers. Liam relieved him of the task, "Don't use your fingers, kid. This is a semi-public gathering." He flipped the square of lasagna onto Robbie's plate.

Robbie called over his shoulder to Justin, "When people are lying they look up and they move their hands a lot, just like Leez did when she said she knew how to play baseball. I read it in that book I was telling you about. Spies know all kinds of things like that."

Lisa-Marie glared at Robbie. "Hey, why don't you shut-up? You better watch it, or I'll sneak into your room one night and steal your precious Spiderman comics."

Robbie gave Lisa-Marie an appraising look, "My room is totally booby-trapped. You'd be so sorry if you tried anything like that." With a smart-aleck look he chanted, "Liar, liar, pants on fire. You've never played baseball."

Izzy frowned at Robbie. She touched Lisa's arm, "Of course you can be on the team. Now, take the bickering away from the table, both of you." Lisa-Marie stuck out her tongue at Robbie as she walked away.

Picking up where she'd left off, Beulah announced, "I've got Arianna lined up and another jock kid named Dylan. All we need to do is choose a night for the game."

The next ten minutes were taken up with the difficult task of finding a time that suited everyone. Izzy finally said, "Look, we all keep the third Wednesday of the month open for the book club. Let's have the ball game instead. The Tricksters are available on Wednesdays ... right Beulah? Reg and Josie will make it work." As everyone nodded, Izzy added, "For those who feel a literary deficit, I suggest reading W.B. Kinsella's novel, *Shoeless Joe.*"

Alex hooted out a laugh and raised his glass to toast Izzy, "Excellent choice." He looked over at Liam to ask, "Have you read it?"

Liam rolled his eyes, "I've not only read it, I've attempted to teach it on more than one occasion and, I'll tell you, the significance of that book is lost on high school kids."

Izzy quickly covered her look of surprise at Liam's words. The fact that he could so comfortably allude to his past teaching career proved he was a different man than he had been a year ago.

Beulah's face wore a comic look of puzzlement, "Have we done this book before? I don't remember it. Why is it so perfect?"

Izzy let out a loud sigh. "You and Caleb ... the two of you make me laugh. *Shoeless Joe* is the ultimate baseball book – baseball as a metaphor for life. I couldn't believe it when I found out Caleb had never read it and wasn't particularly interested in doing so. He said he'd seen the movie, *Field of Dreams*. I told him that wasn't the same at all."

Robbie was back at the table waiting for dessert. He leaned into Izzy and asked, "Who is Shoeless Joe?"

Alex explained, "He played ball in the major leagues for the Chicago White Sox way back before any of us were born. Well, Edward might have been around then," Alex grinned widely. "Shoeless Joe and a bunch of other players on the team took money to throw the World Series. They got banned from ever playing major league baseball again."

Edward crossed his arms as he spoke. The worn, black leather patches on the elbows of his sweater were a dated, yet dignified fashion statement. "A bit before my time, I think. Wasn't it 1919 or something?"

Robbie gathered up a pile of empty plates, hoping that he could speed up the serving of dessert. "I like hockey best but can I play in the game, too?"

Alex said, "I'm sure we'll find something for you to do, Son."

"What was the name of that book, Izzy? You've got me all wrong," Beulah insisted. "I'll read a book about baseball being a metaphor for life."

Izzy burst out laughing in the face of Beulah's sincerity. "We have a copy in the library. I'll grab it for you after dinner." She smiled over at Robbie, "I think it must be time to get the dessert out here. What do you think, Robbie, Robbie, McBobby?"

🌾🌾🌾🌾

"Before we get into this, I want you guys to know that I'm feeling a tad intimidated." Cynthia looked around the group of people in Izzy and Liam's living room. "Maybe I should offer a bit of an explanation as to what *genre fiction* is," she frowned before adding, "and what it isn't."

Alex waved his copy of Cynthia's book at her, "I'll tell you this. Whatever *genre fiction* might mean, this book is quite the page turner. There were times I could not put it down."

Cynthia gave him a warning glare and ignored his interruption. "My books aren't about to be nominated for a Governor General's Award or anything." Her voice rose, "Don't get me wrong. I'm not denigrating what I do. I'm damn proud of my work."

Izzy leaned forward in her chair to ask, "How would you define the term *genre fiction*?"

"Easily enough ... shorter than a more literary novel, a bit formulaic, action driven; you don't get into the heads of the characters all that much. My genre is crime stories set in hospitals. I try to shake it up a bit by always having the reader know who committed the crime before anyone else in the story does." Cynthia sat back and smiled at the group. "So, given that explanation, tell me what you thought of *The Preemie Killings*."

Alex cleared his throat to get Cynthia's attention, "I think you're leaving out one important aspect of the work – an aspect that involves a lot of action. I confess that in all my long years, I've never encountered some of the action you have described."

Izzy raised an eyebrow and Liam frowned over at his father. A withering stare from Cynthia was followed by the warning, "Alexander –" The combined censor of the others made Alex sit back. Apparently, he had been chastised into silence.

Cook leaned forward, "I usually get the feeling I want to throw any book this group chooses against a wall before the end of the first chapter. But your book," Cook smiled over at Cynthia, "first-class. I couldn't put it down."

Izzy raised her eyebrows as she glanced at Liam and smiled. She couldn't wait until later to say, "Who knew that Cook's penchant for throwing books against the wall had to do with literary excellence?"

Edward shifted uncomfortably in the recliner chair and a grimace of pain flickered across his face. He spoke apologetically, "The setting confirmed my hatred of all things associated with hospitals. You describe it all too well. To be honest, I couldn't finish. I admit to feeling somewhat ... what is it you always say, Lisa?" He looked over at Lisa-Maria, "Right, I remember, creeped out."

Cynthia seemed surprised, "I've spent so many years working in that environment, I never thought about the hospital setting turning people off. Going into a hospital feels like going home to me."

"Aha, yes ... so much of life is what we're used to. I have felt that way about travelling, the hustle and bustle of an airport or train station. Even the thought of such places makes me nostalgic." Edward sipped at the drink in his hand, a far-away look on his face.

Alex called out, "I had a question about –"

"Did you have a comment, Roland?" Cynthia asked.

Roland leaned forward with a copy of *The Preemie Killings* in his hand. He flipped the book open to a page he had marked with a small sticky note. "I'm not meaning to be critical, Cynthia, but on page one hundred and ten you mention that your jilted, homicidal, neonatal nurse is a vegetarian and then on page two hundred and five," Roland turned the pages to the next marker, "you have her sit down and gleefully order a steak dinner to celebrate getting away with yet another murder."

Cynthia had her hands up in the air before Roland finished speaking, "I wish I had a dollar for every time I've had that discrepancy drawn to my attention. I'd be living on a tropical island somewhere. *The Preemie Killings* was one of my earlier books. I have improved over time. My books have also become popular enough so that I warrant an experienced editor instead of the junior variety."

Alex crossed his arms, "There seemed to be a lot of –"

Cynthia looked pointedly over at Lisa-Marie, "Let's hear what someone younger thinks."

Lisa-Marie's eyes shifted from Cynthia to Alex before she said, "I found it kind of hard to believe so many terrible things would happen to one woman. You know, getting dumped and finding out she has a horrible disease and the whole thing with her sister." A thoughtful look crossed her face, "I guess when the bad luck wheel starts rolling, anything can happen. I thought it was a fun read. I liked already knowing what the characters in the story were only finding out. I loved the way you described what she was eating all the time. That whole vegetarian thing ... I missed it completely."

"I have a comment or two, Cynthia." Alex tried to catch Cynthia's eye.

She cut him off again, "How did you like the book, Bethany?"

Justin leaned close to Lisa-Marie's ear, "What's up with her? Why won't she let Alexander talk?"

Lisa-Marie whispered back, "He's giving her a hard time about," she paused and stared at Justin, "... you know." Justin looked blankly at her. She asked, "Have you read the book?" He shook his head, this time sheepishly and smiled the Justin kind of smile that made her heart thump. "I'm not enlightening you on this one." She forced herself to look away as she turned her attention to running her hands over Pearl's golden fur. Wherever Lisa-Marie sat, the dog inevitably found its way to her side.

Bethany smiled at Cynthia, "It was fascinating to read about how each of the characters discovered Octavia was the killer. The cold-blooded way she did away with the babies was hard to read but you made me see her motivation. When she got caught, I felt a bit sorry for her."

Beulah snorted, "You can't have it both ways, Beth. The woman was a ruthless murderer, for God's sake."

Alex had his copy of the book open in his lap. "I'd like to read this passage out loud and see if others," he looked around the room, "especially the men, feel that it might be engorging the truth somewhat."

Cynthia reached over and grabbed the book out of Alex's hands. She snapped it shut with a bang. "Alright, that's quite enough out of you." She looked around the room, "Some genre novels include explicit sex scenes. I honestly don't think our discussion tonight has to dwell on those parts of the book." She glared at Alex and added, "If someone here could control his adolescent humour I, for one, would be appreciative."

Justin had sat up straight at the words, *explicit sex*. He stared at Lisa-Marie with his eyebrows raised, "Geez, guess I missed out big time by not reading her book. Can I borrow yours?"

Punching him in the arm, Lisa-Marie said, "No friggin' way."

Izzy changed the subject, "Your description of the hospital and the ups and downs of a nurse's career, had quite the ring of authenticity. It made me curious about your experience in nursing."

With a relieved look on her face, Cynthia sat back in her seat and explained, "I was a nurse for almost thirty years. I don't think there's one part of nursing I've skipped over - surgical, emergency, obstetrics, neonatal, pediatrics, geriatrics. I liked to move around and I liked to learn new things."

"So why the switch over to writing, Cynthia?" Jillian asked.

"Nursing is hard work, not something you can do forever. Most nurses have problems with their feet and their backs tend to go. I wanted to have something else well-established before retirement rolled around. I gave the writing a try and I liked it. I've been more successful than I ever anticipated and now I have a lifestyle that suits me. I travel a lot, looking for situations like the one I have now - rent a place for a few months while I'm writing ... travel a bit while my editor looks things over ... rent another place while I edit. I've been all over. One year I took a lovely little condo down in Tucson, another year I lived way up north in a house that was built around a tree. I've spent a whole winter in Whistler and an entire year in New York City. It's been great."

꒰ꔛ꒰ꔛ꒰ꔛ꒰ꔛ꒱

With most of the guests on their way, Izzy poured boiling water into a large tea pot and set it to steep. She went upstairs to check on Robbie. She waited outside his loft door for him to give her the all clear. She suspected that boys his age needed privacy as much as anyone else and she didn't want to step inadvertently into one of his spy traps.

Robbie lay on his stomach in the bed with his notebook open. His pencil crayons were spread out in front of him. Dante sprawled alongside, taking up a significant portion of the bed. Robbie sat up and pushed Dante towards the wall. He slid over and made room for Izzy to sit down.

"Hey, Robbie, Robbie, McBobby. How you doing?" He was so cute with his dark Liam eyes and his bright red and blue Spiderman pajamas. She'd ordered those from Sears, as well as a Spiderman quilt that now housed boy, dog, books and writing things.

Robbie smiled up at her, "Izzy, Izzy, McLizzy. I'm okay. Has everyone gone?"

"Your dad and Cynthia are going to have tea with Liam and me out on the deck. Let's see what you're drawing?"

186

Robbie pushed his notebook towards her, "It's a comic book about a kid who has super powers and he uses them to become a world famous spy. He can tell the future."

Robbie flipped through the pages of drawings, all neatly slotted into blocks on the page, complete with thought balloons over each character's head. Izzy kept her eyes on his work as she asked, "When you see light, do you wish you could know what's going to happen?"

"Ya ... sometimes. I would have told my mom not to go out on the boat that day." Izzy put an arm around Robbie to give him a quick hug. He looked up at her, "That Willow girl, she's one of your kids at the Camp, right?"

"She's one of my clients, yes. Most of the kids at the Camp come to see me." Robbie was twirling a red pencil crayon around and around. "Why do you ask?"

"I can't look at her. Her light makes my stomach hurt. I don't know why."

Izzy pulled Robbie into a tighter hug, "Guess what? You don't have to know why. Pay attention to what your body tells you, Robbie." Changing the subject, Izzy grabbed a book off the shelf, "Want me to read a chapter of Harry Potter before I go outside with the others."

A smile crept over Robbie's face, then he frowned, "Won't everyone be waiting for you?"

"Let them wait. Nothing good will happen until I get there anyway, right?" Robbie snuggled down next to Dante. By the time Izzy got up to leave, he was all but asleep. She tugged the blanket up around him, pushed Dante over to the wall yet again and cleared the books and pencils off the bed. She went out and closed the door.

On her way through the now quiet cabin, Izzy thought about Robbie and Lisa-Marie – how they had bickered away like brother and sister earlier in the evening. From what Alex had told her, Robbie was used to being part of a big family. It would be natural for him to see Lisa-Marie as an older sister. They were living in the same house, sharing adjacent rooms in the upper lofts. It made sense. She wasn't surprised she'd been slow to pick up on the developing relationship between them. Izzy had been an only child. Unless she really thought about it, she didn't have much of an idea about how siblings treated one another.

She frowned as she walked out the door of the cabin to join the other adults on the cliff deck. She wondered what on earth Robbie sensed about Willow that would make him so uncomfortable that it caused his stomach to ache.

TWENTY-SEVEN

"That was a fun, right, babe?"

Roland felt his jaw tighten as Jillian reached out and hooked her arm through his. They walked along the trail that wound its way from Izzy and Liam's cabin, through the apple trees, to disappear into the dark of the tall evergreens. Ahead, they could see the beam of a flashlight spiral over the tree tops. The sound of voices was clear on the night air.

Justin, Lisa-Marie and Willow had started back towards Micah Camp a few minutes before Roland and Jillian. No doubt they're all hyped up for the bonfire, Roland thought. He'd have to verify that Jeremy, who had volunteered to provide supervision for the event, was on his toes. Roland had a difficult time viewing Jeremy as an adult, with his penchant for adolescent fashion statements and his exaggerated left-wing political commentaries. But what could he do when someone agreed to provide valuable time, energy and skills, free of charge? Roland was not in a position to kick the board's gift horse in the mouth. But he didn't want the residents burning the whole Camp down while Jeremy stood on the sidelines talking about fake moon-landings and the US government orchestration of the 9/11 bombings. Roland flexed his shoulders, hoping to shake loose the tension that had dug in across his back.

"What's up, babe? You seem tense."

Jillian's accurate interpretation of his mood only increased Roland's irritation. He took a deep breath and tried to keep his voice neutral, "For the hundredth time, Jill ... my name is Roland." To her soft laugh, he added, "Do you think you could stop going out of your way to humiliate me in public?"

Jillian pulled her arm away from Roland, "What are you talking about?"

"You do recall taking the butter dish out of my hand in front of everyone and saying that at my age I should be watching my cholesterol?"

"I didn't say it in that tone and, even if I did, it was for your own good."

"Just because we share a bed does not give you carte blanche to control my life."

Jillian glared at Roland as she reached over to grab the flashlight from his hand, "Fine. If that's the way you feel, I'm going back to my own cabin tonight and you can sleep by yourself." She swung around quickly and stomped off down the trail, leaving Roland in the dark.

He called out after her, "For your information, the doctor says my cholesterol is perfectly normal for a man my age," Roland pulled out his keys and flicked on the small LED light that dangled from the chain. He proceeded along the trail in the wake of the pinpoint stream of illumination.

⚜⚜⚜⚜

"Okay, Alex ... out with it. How did you get to be Dr. Alexander Collins?" Izzy nudged Liam. He was sitting on the swing chair beside her with his legs stretched out to the fire in the chimney stove, his arms folded over his chest. "I've tried to get the story out of this guy but all he'll say is that you would tell it so much better." Izzy snuggled close to Liam and took a sip of her tea.

Liam shrugged, "Honestly, I wouldn't know where to start."

"It's a story that goes way back – to the late seventies and early eighties – an interesting chain of events that launched my academic career." Alex looked over at Liam, "I was home to the reserve out at Margaree for the first time in years. You have to go there some day with me." He stretched his long legs out in front of him in a pose that mirrored his son's.

"I got stuck holding the bag on a break-and-enter at a liquor store in Port Hawkesbury." Alex laughed when he saw the startled look on Izzy's face. "You asked for it. This is how it went down. I was hitching a ride and a couple of white guys picked me up. I didn't have a clue they were armed or what they had in mind when they stopped in the Hawke. The cops pulled the car over before we got ten minutes down the road. The whole time, I was yelling for them to let me out. A big-time heist, alright. I seem to recall the take was a hundred bucks."

Alex shook his head, "They'd ditched the gun and no one at the liquor store could make a positive ID ... or so they said. Those two white jokers had their sentences knocked down to nothing but the cops had their hooks in me. They knew the FBI wanted me for questioning about a bunch of stuff across the line and over in Morley, too. They held that over my head like a club.

They threatened to drive me down to the border and dump me on the other side, with the FBI waiting there to pick me up. I pled out to their bullshit charge. I wasn't about to become another Leonard Pelletier - rotting in some US prison for the rest of my life. My lawyer got the sentence down to five years and I served about three, over at Springhill. They had that mine disaster there. The federal pen is the main employer now. No one goes down underground anymore but more than a few guys go down hard in that prison."

Izzy's face wore a puzzled look, "But why would the FBI want to talk to you?"

"That goes back to Alcatraz in '69 and Wounded Knee in '71."

"Alcatraz? The prison?"

"It wasn't a prison anymore in '69. The American Indian Movement staged an occupation on the rock. Liam's mother and I were there on and off." Alex frowned and added, "Like most ideological stands, it devolved somewhat into partisan politics before the dust settled. It was too bad because those first couple of months were just about as good as it gets. I sometimes wonder if all my moving around since then has been about trying to recapture those moments, like a junkie chasing after that first high."

Izzy tapped her fingers against the side of her mug, her mind sifting through things she had learned. "When you say Wounded Knee, you're saying you were down in South Dakota, at Pine Ridge?"

"You've studied your Native American history."

"I wouldn't say that but I did read Dee Brown's book when I was younger."

"Yes, I was at Pine Ridge. That was a coming-of-age thing for the whole AIM organization. Some good people died while it was all going down and later, in the aftermath, it was even worse. I hightailed it back to Canada and never risked crossing the border again. In '76, AIM came up north and occupied the band offices at the Stoney reserve near Morley, Alberta. That was quite the reunion, let me tell you. The whole thing didn't sit well with the authorities on either side of the line. Let's just say they were biding their time and taking names."

Cynthia leaned forward to pick up the tea pot. She refilled her mug and looked over at Alex, "You went to jail, then?"

He nodded. "Doing time is no picnic; to hell with what the right-wingers say about coloured televisions and golf courses. But I had this Indian warrior reputation going on - bunch of bullshit - but it helped. It was the heyday of educational programming in the federal corrections system. I kept my head down and finished an undergrad degree. When I got out, I walked straight into a graduate program at the University of Toronto, getting scholarships wherever I turned. It was an easy step into a doctoral program. Academia is heads-up on educating Natives. Eyes glaze over with something like reverence at the thought of an Aboriginal getting a graduate degree. They should visit a few of the reserves I've been to. You could count on one hand the kids who were going to finish high school. We've got to get back to basics on the education question and it's all rooted in self-governance. It's all about setting some historical injustices straight, once and for all. But that's another story."

Alex drained his mug of tea and sat up straight in his chair. "I was on the blockade at Oka, at Ipperwash when Dudley George was shot, over to Gustafson Lake for the standoff there, in Burnt Church for all the fisheries bullshit. Those were the big news events here in Canada. There were many other actions that didn't get any media coverage. They all have a place in the greater struggle." Alex laughed as he sang the lyrics from an old Stompin' Tom Connors tune. "I've been everywhere man, I've been everywhere ...," he shrugged. "The last few years, I've been moving back and forth across this country from sea to shining sea. I take visiting professor assignments wherever I can and I do a lot of organizing. Those are all long stories, too."

The look Alex gave Izzy as he sat back was clear – *you know who you're dealing with now.* Izzy glanced at Liam. His father's stories had not fazed him. Liam might not have been aware of all the details of his old man's life, but he had always had an instinctual knowledge of who his father was.

※※※※

Maddy forced herself to look away from Jesse. He was talking and laughing with a few guys outside the circle of the large bonfire that blazed and crackled, zipping orange sparks up into the air. She had seen the way his eyes strayed over to Misty. To be fair, all the guys were looking in that direction, including Jeremy who had no right to be so obviously creepy. But the chick was a total flirt. She was giggling and waving a roasted marshmallow through the air in front of her. Flames licked the edges of the white confection as it bubbled and turned black. She made a show of leaning forward to blow it out before she opened her mouth to push the mess inside; then she licked her fingers slowly. Her tight shirt, with the top few buttons open, afforded quite the spectacle. Give it a rest, Maddy told herself. Jesse was free to gawk at any chick he wanted to, even one as obvious as Misty.

She smiled as Mark wove his way past the people sitting in the log-enclosed circle. She waved at him and patted the spot next to her.

He glanced at a paper in his hand, then stuffed it into his pocket and walked over. He sat down and adjusted his glasses a couple of times before he said, "Hello Maddy. The weather is perfect tonight for a bonfire – no rain and only a bit of a breeze. Are you having a good time?"

Out of the corner of her eye, Maddy watched Jesse walk over to Misty and lean close to listen to whatever she was saying. What a complete bastard. Why didn't he stand up on the log and tell everyone he wanted to bang her? Pathetic. She made herself turn back to Mark. "Oh ya, sure, I'm having a fabulous time. What's new with you?"

Mark cleared his throat and looked thoughtful, "I didn't do well on the English quiz this morning but I helped Jim fix the rider mower this afternoon and he said he couldn't have done it without me. I thought the meatloaf tasted good at dinner." He paused to ask, "Is anything new with you?"

Maddy laughed at Mark's literal take on her question, "Nope, I can't think of a thing that's worth telling."

"Would you like me to roast you a marshmallow?"

"Ahhh ... thanks, that would be so nice." Maddy watched the meticulous way Mark skewered the marshmallow onto the stick and how he paid careful attention to cooking it to a perfect golden hue. Jesse could take a few lessons from Mark on how to make a girl feel special. She glanced over at Jesse again. Now he was sitting beside Misty. She thought about walking right over there and slapping his face. She was about to jump up when Mark's voice interrupted her movement.

"Here you go, Maddy." He held the marshmallow out to her. "I better go now. Thanks for letting me sit with you."

Tears came to Maddy's eyes and she blinked rapidly. The way Mark talked to her made her ache inside. She almost reached out for his hand to make him stay, but stopped herself. She knew better than to act crazy in public by holding Mark's hand. Instead, she waved goodbye and forced herself to swallow the marshmallow in her mouth. Leez came down the trail with Justin and Willow. Hopping on top of the log, Maddy motioned wildly, "Leez, over here, over here."

Lisa-Marie's eyes went from Maddy on the other side of the fire, to Willow who stood close to Justin's side like she was glued there. Joining Maddy would mean leaving the field open for little *Miss China Doll* with her tinkling laugh and golden curls. On the other hand, she'd look like an idiot if she ignored her friend's frantic performance. Justin was already glancing over at Maddy with a frown on his face. Lisa-Marie nudged him, "See you."

She walked away and forced herself not to check over her shoulder. Plopping down on the log beside Maddy, she muttered, "Shit, just look at the two of them. He invited her over to Izzy's book club thing. Can you believe that?"

"Ya, well, if Jesse doesn't stop talking to that slut, Misty, I'm going to slap his face. Then I'm going to drag her by the hair over to the lake and throw her trashy ass in the water."

Lisa-Marie was about to laugh until she realized her friend was serious. Maddy was halfway up, with her leg over the log, when Lisa-Marie grabbed her arm and dragged her back. "Get a hold of yourself. He'll think you're psycho or something. Everyone will. Sit down. What the hell's wrong with you? All he's doing is sitting beside her."

Jesse got up and moved away from the fire to talk with some of the other guys. Lisa-Marie heaved a sigh of relief. She turned to Maddy, "What's going on? One minute you say you and Jesse aren't exclusive and the next minute you're acting like a jealous girlfriend. You can't have it both ways."

"We aren't exclusive. That doesn't mean I like the idea of him slobbering over another girl right in front of me."

"If you aren't exclusive, why would you think of going to California with him?"

"I like being with Jesse. What's wrong with that?

"Besides the fact that Jesse is a total asshole and he drives you crazy? Not much, I guess. Did he say he wanted you to go with him?"

"It's unspoken, Leez. Why wouldn't I go? I can't stay here forever."

"What about art school?"

"I'm sure there are art schools in California. Look, can we talk about something else? I feel like you're an inquisitor or something." Maddy grinned at Lisa-Marie, "Do you have any thumbscrews in your pockets or maybe a red-hot poker hidden somewhere?"

Lisa-Marie giggled. She spotted Justin as he walked around the outside of the log circle, his guitar in hand. He stopped to say hi to Misty but he didn't linger. Lisa-Marie felt herself relax when he came over, sat down beside her and began to tune his guitar.

A moment later, Willow materialized out of the dark to take the seat on Justin's other side. Lisa-Marie was determined to play things cool. Witnessing Maddy's behaviour was enough to give anyone sober second thoughts.

Willow leaned forward to tug at Justin's arm. She asked him to play a song she knew. He smiled over at her and strummed the opening chords. The next thing Lisa-Marie knew, he was leaning his head toward the girl's golden curls as they sang together.

Maddy elbowed her in the side, "I'd be happy to resurrect the idea of throwing a trashy chick in the lake if you're up for it." For a second Lisa-Marie considered the idea, then she elbowed Maddy in the side as she hissed, "Shut up, they'll hear you."

Dylan drifted away from the guys who had been passing around a joint just beyond the glare of the bonfire. He had seen Jesse making his way toward the group; the less time he spent in the same space with that guy, the better. He grabbed a hotdog from the food-laden table and concentrated on getting the wiener onto a roasting stick. Arianna made her way towards him, waving two cans of Coke.

She sat down close and nudged him with her shoulder as she passed him one of the Cokes. "You're burning that hotdog. Want me to fix that bun for you?"

She was halfway up before he could say, "Nah, I'm going to eat it plain. Sit down; stop jumping up and down like a friggin' yo-yo."

Arianna sat back down, even closer, "Smelled kind of skunky over there by the trees. What were you guys doing?"

He chugged the cold Coke and chomped down on the hotdog. He could feel Arianna leaning into him, humming along to the music. Her dark head of hair was heavy against his arm, her thigh pressed into his leg. He thought about putting his arm around her. Why not? He could give it a try and see how he felt. He had almost made up his mind to pull her closer when he saw Maddy walk past, heading toward Jesse. He watched as she locked her hands behind Jesse's neck and rotated her hips against his body in time with the music. When Jesse's hands went around her waist and he bent to kiss her, Dylan got up, "I'm out of here. See you tomorrow."

"Want me to come with you?" Arianna called after him. He waved for her to stay put and kept on walking.

"What were you talking to Misty about?" Maddy strolled along beside Jesse on the path toward his cabin.

Jesse reached out and draped an arm around her. He pulled her closer, "She wanted some music for her iPod."

"That was a lot of laughing and you gawking down the front of her shirt for lining up a little favour like getting her some music."

Jesse stiffened, "Knock it off, Maddy."

"I saw the way you looked at her. I know exactly what you were thinking."

He pulled his arm away, "This is pointless. We aren't a couple, right? That's what you're always saying. You don't know as much about me as you think."

Maddy got in front of him and slammed her hands against his chest, "Why don't you admit you want to screw her. Do you think I'm stupid? Why not just say it? It's real easy ... five little words ... I want to screw Misty. There, see how easy that was?"

Jesse grabbed her hands and pushed her away, "I said knock it off and I meant it." He began walking again. Maddy pushed him from behind, pounding her fists into his back and screaming, "I knew you were too chicken shit to admit it. Do you think I care who you screw? I just wanted you to be honest, for once."

He swung around and grabbed her upper arms, "Get a hold of yourself, right now." He shook her; the seriousness and anger in his voice got the results he knew would follow. They had played out this scene enough times so that they both knew the moves by heart. She crumpled; the anger drained out of her like a swollen river that had breached its banks. A torrent of tears filled the void.

He held her arms while she sobbed and whispered, "I'm sorry, I'm sorry, I'm sorry. I know you can screw anyone you want." He pulled her closer and felt her collapse against him.

He stroked the back of her head, "Calm down. Don't cry. Don't go crazy on me."

Maddy nodded against his chest and mumbled, "I didn't mean any of it, Jess, I'm sorry. You can talk to Misty if you want. I was wrong to say those things, I don't mean them. I'm sorry. You can go and be with her if you want."

Jesse held her tightly as he said, "No thanks, I've got my hands full with you."

⚜ ⚜ ⚜ ⚜

Jillian sat in her cabin and steamed about the nerve of Roland. She was only trying to help. Did he want to drop dead with clogged arteries? He could go ahead and gorge himself with buttered buns and put cream in his coffee every day, for all she cared. Men can be such ingrates. She reached over, pulled a printed transcript from the desk and settled down to read.

A couple of hours later she got up, stretched and decided that it was silly to spend the night in her own cabin. Roland's place was way nicer. He had a full-size bathtub. Plus his bed was far more comfortable than hers and more important than mere comfort was the fact that Jillian liked sharing a bed with Roland. She wasn't one to cut off her nose to spite her face. If he didn't want to heed her advice on the cholesterol, it was his life to shorten.

On her way over to Roland's cabin, Jillian stopped short when she saw Maddy run at Jesse and start flailing on him, screaming accusations in his face. They were visible in the lights that marked the path to the residents' cabins. Jillian considered walking over to intervene. Before she could move, Maddy collapsed, sobbing against Jesse's chest. Jillian watched the tender way he held her and stroked her hair while he bent his head close to hers. They walked off together and Jillian found herself almost doubting the violence she had witnessed.

ɪɾɔɪɾɔɪɾɔɪɾɔ

Cynthia could feel, rather than hear Alex behind her. He didn't make a sound when he walked. Her own sandals clacked loudly across the cedar planking on the guest cabin deck. She stopped short of the sliding glass door and turned. He was standing close to her. She glanced up and past his shoulder to see the crescent of the waxing moon. It hung sideways in the clear night sky, tilting at what seemed an impossible angle. She heard the rushing noise of the stream in the distance. As Alex leaned down to her, she rested her hands against his chest; whether to keep him away or to pull him closer, she was unsure. He kissed her in a way that her writer's pen would have described as *thoroughly* ... and to hell with her editor's caution to destroy all *ly* adverbs.

She saw his smile as he said, "Are you going to invite me in?"

Now she did push back with her hands, "Not so fast, *Mr. Native Warrior*. I'm not quite ready for the battle you have in mind." She dropped her hands to her side, "Maybe we'd better both stand on the blockade for a while and see what happens."

Alex stepped back, "A little blockade standing makes for interesting skirmishes down the road." He waved goodbye and walked off down the path. He was surefooted and silent on the dark trail.

Cynthia stood with her back to the door; a steady, slow pulse of blood pounded through her. Any blockade she might throw up was unlikely to hold if he kissed her like that again.

᛭᛭᛭᛭᛭

Liam pulled Izzy into his arms and leaned close to kiss her neck, his breath was warm as it trailed across her skin. He whispered, "Do you notice how quiet it is in this cabin?"

Izzy brushed his lips with her own, "Hmmm, I do. No crying baby, Robbie's light is off, Lisa is out. Yes, indeed, it's exceptionally quiet in here." She slid her hands up inside his shirt and stroked the skin along the length of his back.

"Come on, woman, there's a bed close by that's calling our names." Izzy went still in Liam's arms. He felt a cold breeze, and the hair on the back of his neck stood up. He looked toward the entry but the door was closed. He was sure the thought struck her at the same time it hit him - *that was something Caleb would have said.*

Izzy shivered and looked behind her. Then she shook her head and grabbed at Liam's hand, "There's no such thing as ghosts, Liam. But don't call me woman, there's no point in tempting fate." She pulled him into the bedroom. As he closed the door behind them, she moved into his arms.

᛭᛭᛭᛭᛭

Lisa-Marie walked along the trail beside Justin. She hoped that the gut-wrenching jealousy she felt would not start puffing smoke out of her ears or blasting fire out of her nostrils as if she had somehow morphed into a dragon girl.

"Leez, I think you should talk to Izzy about how out of control Maddy is acting."

The concern in Justin's voice got Lisa-Marie's attention. "I thought about it but she's my friend. I don't want to rat on her."

Justin grabbed her arm, "Grow up. We're not kids anymore. There's something wrong with Maddy. If you're her friend, you should be telling someone that." He dropped her arm and started walking again.

"I'll talk to Izzy. Geez, you don't have to bite my head off."

TWENTY-EIGHT

"**I**sabella, the solicitor is expecting you at his office in Dearborn at four o'clock. You have to sign those power of attorney papers."

Izzy walked out of the bathroom and checked her watch. She needed to pick up the pace a bit if she was going to get anything done before she went to work. She had forgotten today was the day she had to go to the lawyer's office. She needed another cup of coffee and she couldn't find her hair brush. "Are you sure all this power of attorney stuff is necessary?"

Edward swung his chair away from the work table and looked up at her. He frowned from over the top of his bifocals, "Bloody hell, I could have a stroke tomorrow and grow as dull as your average garden marrow. Then what would you do about my affairs?"

Izzy pulled a face at the picture her father's words conjured up. "I'll be there, don't worry." She turned to call up the stairs, "Lisa, have you seen my brush?"

Izzy walked into the kitchen as Lisa-Marie came down the stairs from her loft. She leaned close, saying, "Feel ... that new shampoo is awesome." She passed Izzy the hair brush.

Touching a strand of Lisa's hair, Izzy smiled, "Nice ... those streaks look pretty but I know they dry the hair out. A good shampoo and conditioner are important."

"Thanks so much for the other stuff you put in my room."

"No problem. I was shopping around a bit yesterday and thought you might need a few things."

Lisa-Marie pulled a soft cotton robe lined with pink flannel around her body and cinched the belt. She grabbed a coffee and popped a slice of bread into the toaster. Izzy had given her the robe the week before. It had been a gift from Caleb. She had laughed as she handed it over to Lisa, "I guess the look on my face told him in no uncertain terms that he was never to get me anything pink again."

As she spread the bread with a hint of butter, Lisa-Marie asked, "I was wondering about Maddy –"

"Wondering what?" Izzy had filled the sink with water and was washing the dishes.

"How you think she's doing."

"I can't talk about how Maddy's doing, I'm sorry." Lisa-Marie nodded and took another sip of her coffee. Izzy dried her hands and leaned back against the kitchen counter. "Why don't you tell me how you think Maddy's doing?"

"We're worried about her ... me and Justin. He said I should talk to you. She's my friend. I don't want to be saying anything against her." Izzy nodded her understanding and Lisa-Marie went on, "Sometimes she freaks out with Jesse. She keeps saying they aren't a couple but then she gets crazy jealous and starts screaming at him; then she ends up crying and saying she's sorry. She doesn't even care if anyone sees her making such a total fool of herself. I promised Justin I'd tell you."

"Thanks, Lisa." Izzy saw Lisa-Marie sigh with relief as she finished her toast and headed up the stairs to get dressed.

Izzy walked out onto the deck and grabbed a pair of clippers. Her gardening chores were now slotted into any spare minutes she could manage. She worked her way along the planter that spanned the entire length of the spacious deck. She clipped off all the daffodil stalks and dumped them into a bucket. She untwisted dead pieces of clematis from the vines and snipped them out.

Her thoughts danced around the issue of Maddy's treatment. The fact that Justin wanted Lisa-Marie to talk to Izzy was serious. Justin had seen his fair share of dysfunction. If he thought there was a problem, there was a problem. She sat down on the bench and focused on the apple blossoms catching the first hints of sunlight coming over the hill. The trees stretched out of sight on either side of the path; blossoms stood in thick clusters on branch after branch. Even the beauty of the flowering trees couldn't distract her. It wasn't like she was unaware that Maddy's relationship with Jesse was a problem. Izzy shook her head ruefully. It was too bad that understanding a problem didn't necessarily provide a solution.

Justin walked into the sawmill lunchroom and saw Misty lounging back on the sofa, drinking a can of Diet Pepsi. She smiled over at him. He reached into the fridge and pulled out his lunch. Lisa-Marie usually threw something together for him after dinner. He opened the bag and saw a big chunk of fried chicken, two dill pickles, a buttered cheese and onion bun, and a giant piece of carrot cake with cream cheese frosting.

Justin sat at the lunchroom table and dug in. He looked over at Misty and asked, "No homework today?"

She got up and stretched her arms over her head as she bent her body back in an arc. She straightened up and sat down at the table across from him, "I should be studying but I'm getting sick of it." She watched him eat for a moment before she said, "We should go out some time. Maybe see a movie in town. Get to know each other better."

Justin wiped his greasy hands on a piece of paper towel and took a drink from his water bottle. "Don't take this the wrong way ... I like to think carefully about whether I want to get to know a person better."

Misty gathered her hair into a pony-tail. She pushed the chair back, "I'm a very nice girl to get to know. I thought I'd tell you that so you can work it into your considerations." She zipped up the front of her coveralls over her low-cut T-shirt, "I've got to get back to work. Reg wants half the yard cleared so the trucks can get in for that big order that's going out this afternoon. See you." She waved at him and strolled out.

Justin finished his lunch and set the alarm on his phone for fifteen minutes. He stretched out on the couch and closed his eyes. He was supposed to oversee the loading and invoicing for the order Misty had mentioned and he couldn't afford to rub Reg the wrong way by coming down late from lunch. He replayed Misty's last words. Not much doubt about what she had meant. He wondered, before he dozed off, why he'd hesitated to take her up on the offer.

The woman behind the café's service counter looked right past the young native girl who stood first in line, bouncing a baby on her hip. She pointed at the man standing behind the girl, "What'll it be?"

As the man placed his order, Alex tapped him on the shoulder. The guy turned with a look of impatience, "Hey, I'm in the middle of something here, buddy."

"Ya, well, this young woman and her child were here first ... buddy. Maybe you should just wait your turn." The man stared down at the girl holding the baby as if he were shocked to see her there.

"Should have spoken up or something, I didn't see you. Go ahead."

The woman behind the counter barely hid the scowl on her face. "We don't give out free water and I won't heat up a baby bottle unless you order something."

Alex stared at the woman until she huffed loudly and looked away. Then he said, "How about you just take her order and cut the crap?" He reached over and tickled the baby under the chin.

Alex, Beulah and Robbie settled down with their food at a picnic table out on the deck. Beulah had to admit, she was enjoying the baseball coaching and the impromptu meals out. Robbie could never seem to make it back to the lake without stopping for some food to tide him over.

Beulah had stood back watching the confrontation inside the café. She took a drink of her coffee and said, "You don't mind sticking your nose into things, do you Alex?"

Alex wolfed through his own burger and reached over to take a few of Robbie's fries. "Like I told you the other day, Beulah, it's not all blockades and protests. It's the little things that matter. Maybe that guy's going to think twice about going along with the status quo next time around. Maybe that young girl walks out of here feeling a bit better about herself because someone cares enough to speak up for her. It's all about modeling a different way of being."

Robbie changed the subject for them, "I'll tell you what I think about that Trickster ball team. Those kids don't know jack shit about baseball and they aren't getting better, even though this is their fourth practice."

Alex pointed his can of Coke at Robbie, "Watch your language; what the hell will people think ... a kid your age talking like that."

Beulah laughed, "I hear you, Robbie. We're still a long, long way from moulding that crowd into any kind of team. I'll tell you this, though – we might just be at the end of the beginning." Beulah narrowed her eyes thoughtfully, her attention caught for a moment by the boats in the harbour. The riggings made a steady thwacking sound as they flapped in the wind that swooped over the breakwater and tossed the tops of the masts to and fro.

She remembered her first sight of the kids as they stumbled off the bus - black and grey hoodies pulled tight around scowling faces, a couple of the guys wearing leather jackets and stomping boots, one girl dressed like maybe she thought she would be trying out for a *Much Music* video. The sneering, adolescent attitude had not fooled Beulah. It didn't begin to hide the aching need the kids had to be part of something none of them could even name. Alex was right about that – helping a kid find out what that something could be, was a project worth taking on. But Jesus jumped up Christ, it would have been gratifying to have a bit more to work with.

That first afternoon, a tall guy – the only one dressed like he was there to work out – had pointed to the rest of the kids and told Beulah, "These losers are the dregs. All the real sports kids are playing soccer and floor hockey."

Beulah had sized him up, "So what gives with you?"

He shrugged and grinned at her, "I've got what the coaches call an attitude problem. I got kicked off both teams."

"Well, *Mr. Attitude Problem*, you are going to be my pitcher. Think twice before you consider giving me any grief because there's no getting kicked off this team. You do what I tell you to do, or these practices will become your own personal hell."

She was brought out of her reverie when Alex hopped up from the bench. He eyed Beulah with a knowing look, "You are a woman who enjoys a challenge. I could tell that from the first day we met."

TWENTY-NINE

J onathan looked up from clipping the hedge along the driveway. The woman had just driven in and was lifting her toddler out of his car seat. Several grocery bags cluttered the back of the car. He ambled over and asked, "Do you want a hand with those?" She smiled at him and nodded.

Inside the kitchen, he put the bags on the counter and scanned the room. The woman came in behind him, wiping her hand across her face, "It's boiling out. Do you want a cold drink? There's juice in the fridge."

"Thanks. I'll get it." He took his time, checking out the front of the fridge for tell-tale notes, glancing at the message pad by the phone, looking at the pile of mail pushed into a corner of the kitchen counter.

He stabbed the tiny straw into the juice box and drained most of it in one drink. The woman hurried around the kitchen, pulling things out of the grocery bags and opening and closing cupboards. Jonathan raised his voice above the noise the toddler was making by banging cans of spaghetti sauce together. "My girlfriend used to have a friend who lived out this way. I can't remember her name. I think she lived on this street." The woman clunked a frying pan on the stove, unwrapped a pound of hamburger and dumped it into the pan. She reached down to relieve the toddler of one of the cans. "I think we might have come to this house to pick her up once." The woman turned from the stove and grabbed the other can from the toddler before he could beat it against the wall. She deposited the kid in his high chair. Jonathan tried one last shot, "Maybe she was one of your foster kids."

The woman smiled at him as she filled a pot with water and turned to put it on the stove. "Sorry, I'm a bit out of it this afternoon. I've got to get dinner going here; I'm running way behind."

Jonathan tossed the empty juice container into the recycling box near the door. He waved goodbye and headed back outside.

⚜⚜⚜⚜

Holding Sophie snug against her shoulder, Izzy opened the door. "Hi Rosemary, it's good to see you."

The doctor walked into the cabin. "Let me see that baby." She took Sophie and stared down at her for a moment. "Oh goodness, she's getting as round as a butterball and so cute with all that lovely black hair. How old is she now?"

"Seven weeks. She is a cute one, for sure. Come in. I'm glad you could free up enough time to come all the way out here."

Rosemary handed Sophie back to Izzy, "No problem. I like a road trip now and then. How are you doing with everything?"

"I think Dad is as comfortable as he can be. We've got the stair equipment installed so he doesn't have to struggle up and down. Cynthia's here to check on him every day, though he doesn't let me hang around and hear what they're talking about. Liam's helping him out with anything else he might need."

Rosemary and Izzy walked through the living room towards the sun porch. Edward was ensconced in his chair. He waved at them and called out, "Isabella, how about some tea for the good doctor?" Izzy nodded and went to the kitchen

Rosemary sat down in the chair by Edward's work table and whistled softly, "No wonder you're partial to this view." She reached over, encircled Edward's wrist with her fingers and took his pulse. She asked, "Are you eating?"

"It's a struggle; I force myself. I know I can't afford to get too weak, too quickly."

"How about the pain?" The doctor pulled the stethoscope from around her neck and hooked the earpieces in place. She rubbed the other end against the leg of her pants to warm it up and then reached inside Edward's shirt to place it against his chest, "Take a deep breath for me."

Edward inhaled sharply before saying, "The morphine is working for now. Isabella has arranged to have a brilliant man give me a body massage with hot stones and oils, three times a week. That keeps me limber."

"That's great. You'll find everything works better if you can get up and move." Rosemary draped the stethoscope back around her neck. "I've set up an automatic refill on your morphine. You just have to call the drugstore a day

204

ahead of time when you're running low."

As Izzy came down the stairs with the tea, Edward said, "I want to hear all about your *Doctors without Borders* work, Rosemary. I suspect we've travelled in the same areas of the world. I have some photographs that I think you'll find fascinating." Rosemary glanced from Edward's face to Izzy's. She accepted Edward's desire to change the subject and reached for a cup of tea.

⚜⚜⚜⚜

Izzy hauled the baby swing out to the garden. Darlene had practically forced her to take the piece of equipment. She went back into the cabin to get Sophie. The thing wasn't a bad device if you ignored all the options for music and lights. She put Sophie in the swing, did up the harness and turned it on at the lowest speed. The first time she had used it, the swing had been set on the highest speed. She had thought Sophie would be pitched out of the contraption like an object from a medieval catapult.

Izzy stood back and watched the baby move gently to and fro. Sophie's hair stuck up on her head like the spines of a hedgehog. Izzy had dressed her in a white, two-piece outfit that made the baby's skin look even darker than it was. Yes, indeed, Sophie was a cute one. At two months, the resemblance the child bore to her father and mother was becoming obvious, at least to Izzy. The dark hair and eyes were Liam's but the bow-shaped mouth and perfect eyebrows were all Lisa. Izzy shook her head as she watched the baby drift off to sleep.

She put on her garden gloves, stepped into the dirt and surveyed the flats of bedding plants she had asked Liam to set out in the vegetable garden. It was going to be a big job to get them all in place. She worked around the edges of a gnawing frustration as she dug rows of holes, banged bedding plants out of their pots and eased them into the soil.

Earlier, when she had walked Rosemary out to her car, she was no closer to understanding how her father was doing than she had been before the doctor arrived. Yesterday, Lisa-Marie had been in the sun porch working with Edward. He had stood up to move from his work table to the stairlift and he had stumbled, grabbing onto the railing. Lisa-Marie had been beside him in a flash, holding his arm, steadying him and reaming him out. Izzy heard her say, "For frig sakes, Edward, use your cane like Cynthia told you. If you end up falling down and breaking a leg or hip or something, that will be the end of working on this book." Her father had smiled and accepted Lisa's help to get him turned around and onto the lift.

Izzy had walked away, resenting the sound of their laughter and the effortless comfort Lisa had with Edward. She tried to imagine her father taking an order from her like the one Lisa had given him, or even letting her help him the way Lisa had. She couldn't picture it.

Izzy moved away from an area of cabbage plants to tackle the broccoli. She thought about the glimpse she had caught of Liam and her father in the bathroom that morning. Liam's hand held a razor. Her father's face was layered with shaving cream as he sat on the sturdy stool that had simply appeared in the bathroom one day. Liam had tipped up her father's face and stroked the razor down in a clean line. Her father had said something she couldn't catch and Liam had chuckled. The intimacy they were sharing caused a lump in Izzy's throat. She had walked away and had barely made it behind the closed door of her bedroom before she broke down, muffling a sob with her hand as she doubled over.

She had grabbed Liam before he left the house and said, "Dad must be getting worse if he needs help shaving." Liam had explained that Edward's hands shook and he didn't want to take a chance with the razor. Liam had then asked her if she'd noticed that her father dictated all of his notes and emails to Lisa-Marie. She hadn't. No one bothered to tell her anything unless she asked and she was frustrated because most of the time she didn't even know what to ask.

Izzy dug the small shovel into the ground with rapid thrusts. Liam had his own dad who'd stayed away for decades and yet, the two of them were thick as thieves. It didn't seem fair. She straightened up, stretched out her back and told herself it was stupid to think like that. She and her father had their own path to walk. If he was comfortable keeping her at arm's length while he allowed everyone else to come close, so be it. She accepted anything that would allow him to cope with what he was facing. There would be things that only she could do. It was just a matter of being patient and letting those things come to her.

❦❦❦❦

Lisa-Marie breathed a huge sigh of relief as she strolled down the wide front steps of Dearborn Senior Secondary. She had been coming into town to write her grade eleven provincial exams and today she had finished off with a bang.

Arianna spotted her and called out, "Hey, am I glad to see you. Beulah's chomping at the bit to get the bread delivered."

"Geez, I'm thirty minutes early. I aced the exam, by the way."

Arianna smiled and hopped into the truck while Beulah snapped her fingers at Lisa-Marie, "Cut the chit-chat, let's get moving here."

After Beulah had dropped them off, Lisa-Marie and Arianna walked into a small shop tucked into the corner of one of Dearborn's three mini strip malls. These shopping venues were laid out like a letter Z across the flat area of the town that opened onto the waterfront. The sign above the door read, *The Fashion Stop.*

"Izzy says they have some nice stuff here." Lisa-Marie told Arianna. As soon as they were in the store, she had her doubts about whether she could afford to be in such a place.

The shop had an exclusive, pricey feel and the woman standing behind the counter was nothing short of terrifying. Lisa-Marie cringed at the sight of her perfect make-up and French manicured nails tapping on the keys of a laptop. The woman studied the two young girls, raised an eyebrow and asked, in a clipped tone, "Is there something I can help you two with?"

Lisa-Marie shook her head as she moved over to a rack of jeans and flipped through them. All the coolest brands were represented. She turned over a price tag and swallowed hard. A couple of quick mental calculations told her she was out of her league.

Arianna strolled up to the counter. She leaned her elbows on the shiny black surface and gestured the woman closer. "My friend needs a bathing suit but here's the thing," she pointed over to Lisa-Marie. "She looks great, right?" The woman smiled and Arianna went on, "She had a baby about seven weeks ago and now she's all freaked out that she looks like crap and can't wear a bikini ever again. Do you think you can help her?"

A knowing look came over the woman's face. She nodded and came out from behind the counter. "Come on," she gestured to Lisa-Marie, who looked up in surprise and followed after the woman's tight skirt and spike heels. The woman stopped in front of a rack of bathing suits and riffled through the brightly coloured spandex. She studied Lisa-Marie, "Have you got stretch marks?"

Lisa-Marie blushed and glared over at Arianna who had buried her head in a display of scarfs. She nodded with a look of dismay on her face and brushed her hand in a scratching gesture high up on her side and stomach.

The woman laughed, "Don't be embarrassed, hon. Look at me." She spun out from the rack with her hand on her hip. "Would you believe this is the figure of a mother of three?" Lisa-Marie shook her head. "I won't say you don't have to work your tail off to get back in shape but, trust me, it can be done and not only by the likes of the rich and famous. Here we go." She pulled out a fuchsia pink, one-piece suit. "High cut here, it'll make you look like a fashion model with legs that don't stop, some nice shirring over the stomach for camouflage, the sexiest low back you'll ever see and just look at this top ... hot, right? It's designed to keep the girls right up where they need to be. Try it on."

Lisa-Marie headed for the dressing room. There wasn't a chance of saying no to that woman. When she had the suit on, she turned to and fro in front of the full-length mirror. She looked good. It wasn't a bikini but it was cute in its own way. She twisted her body around to lift the price tag and her shoulders sagged ... one hundred and twenty dollars. She got dressed and walked out of the dressing room. Ignoring Arianna's pout because she didn't get to see how the bathing suit looked, Lisa-Marie dropped it on the counter and said, "Hold this for me for an hour. I hope I'll be back." She walked out of the store and told Arianna, "We need to find Beulah."

They caught up with Beulah outside the grocery store. She was chatting to a tall man in a green apron embossed with a large apple on the front. Beulah noticed Lisa-Marie's empty hands, "I thought you were going shopping. Couldn't find anything to suit your uptown tastes?" She waved goodbye to the guy in the apron and began walking across the parking lot.

Lisa-Marie caught up to her by the driver's side of the truck. "Wait a minute, Beulah. Geez, this is embarrassing. I need some money."

Beulah studied her with a thoughtful look on her face, "How much and why?"

Words spilled out of Lisa-Marie's mouth, "I'm trying to save everything I make at the Camp for the Europe trip. I have my child allowance money from Auntie Beth. I've saved that up since I got here but it isn't enough. I'm a full size bigger after the baby. I need some jeans and shorts. And I found the perfect bathing suit but it costs a lot."

Beulah pulled out her wallet and tugged a credit card from its slot. "Try to keep it under two hundred."

"I'll pay you back."

"Don't be an idiot. You have to have clothes. You're a kid; someone has to look after you. Don't go hog wild or anything."

Beulah watched as Lisa-Marie and Arianna ran across the parking lot on their way back to *The Fashion Shop*. She got in the truck and drummed her fingers on the steering wheel. What the hell was wrong with Bethany? She was letting the kid slip through the cracks. What else was Lisa-Marie lacking because she didn't want to ask them for money?

❧❧❧❧

Beulah found Izzy on her knees in the vegetable garden. Sophie was fast asleep in the baby swing in the middle of the path. Izzy got up and pulled off her garden gloves. She stepped out of the dirt and sat on a bench near the trail. "Hey, Beulah ... I hope you want to sit down for a minute because I need a break. I kept thinking Sophie would wake up and I would have an excuse to stop. Wouldn't you know it - she's sleeping like an angel."

"And you say you enjoy all of this," Beulah swept her hand to indicate the large garden.

"I do," Izzy said. "But being on my knees for hours is not as easy as it used to be and I feel as though I'm behind all the time." She pointed over to a bed, "Look at that foxglove. Sure, it's pretty when it blooms but it's taking over. I can barely see the toad lilies. I should have been digging most of it out weeks ago."

Beulah sat down and said, "I came over because I need to talk to you about something and I feel as uncomfortable as hell doing it."

"What now?" Izzy leaned forward to brush dirt from the knees of her garden pants.

"Lisa-Marie asked me for money today to get a bathing suit and jeans. It was like I was her wicked stepmother and she was Cinderella wearing rags. It got me thinking about how she's been managing and why the hell Bethany hasn't been over here finding out. What's she doing for personal stuff?"

"It's not a big deal, Beulah. I've been picking up a few things for her. I don't mind. God knows, Liam could care less what kind of shampoo is in the bathroom or what kind of toothpaste is in the drawer. I've enjoyed having someone to shop for."

"So, we've dumped her on you guys in every way. It doesn't feel right."

"Come on, let's not mince words here. She wouldn't be staying with us and she wouldn't need new clothes, for that matter, if it weren't for Sophie. So trying to determine who's financially responsible for her is a bit stupid. And you know damn well that Liam and I are not hurting for money."

"I still don't feel right about it. Don't get her clothes. We can at least do that."

"I've already ordered her a few things for her birthday." Izzy thought about the fancy dress, the cute plaid shirt and sleeveless T-shirts she had ordered. "Oh, for the love of God, Beulah, get that sour look off your face. It was fun. I'm not going to let your misguided sense of responsibility ruin that."

Robbie ran out the back door of the cabin, waved to Izzy in the garden and sprinted past her to the driveway. He fell into step beside Justin, "I saw you from my window. Do you want to go swimming with me and Lisa-Marie?"

Justin smiled down at Robbie in his baggy swimming trunks and high top running shoes with the laces flapping around his bare ankles. "The lake is going to be freezing."

"So what? Lisa-Marie got a new bathing suit and she says she's trying it out today no matter what."

"I guess I can't let a girl and a little kid show me up. I'll meet you guys down there."

Lisa-Marie stood on the beach with her toes in the icy water thinking that the raft had been closer to the shore the previous summer. Robbie was already jumping up and down on it, yelling at her, "Fraidie cat, fraidie cat."

"Race you to the raft," Justin was sprinting down the south stairs and Lisa-Marie found herself plowing into the water and diving under before she could stop and think.

Justin reached down from the raft to pull her up, "Wow, you have really lost your edge, Leez, but it's early days." He watched her push the wet hair off her face as she smiled up at him. She looked a hell of lot more than cute. He dragged his eyes away from the plunging top of her bathing suit.

They stretched out on the raft and watched Robbie cannonball in and out of the freezing water. Lisa-Marie rolled over onto her back and propped herself up on her elbows. "That kid must be part polar bear."

Robbie splashed through the water and clung to the side of the raft, "Come on you guys. It's no fun if you don't get in the water."

Justin grimaced over at Lisa-Marie. He got up and did a perfect dive into the smooth water. Robbie pulled himself up on the raft and called out to Justin, "That was awesome. Can you teach me?"

For the next half an hour, as Lisa-Marie worked on her tan in the warm afternoon sun, Justin coached Robbie in the basics of diving. As Robbie's dark head popped out of the water after yet another modified belly flop, Justin called out, "Okay, I'm freezing, time to head in."

Back on the shore, Lisa-Marie reached for her towel and smiled at Justin, "Same time, same place tomorrow?"

"You guys are nuts. I'm going home to put on long underwear and a sweater. I'll see you at dinner." Justin draped his towel over his neck and waved as he walked away.

THIRTY

"**I**'m not sure about your take on the role of Master of Ceremonies, Roland. It's too late to change anything now. I suppose we'll just have to go with it." Maryanne slapped her clipboard against the side of her leg. She glanced at her watch and called down to the main floor of the hall, "Arianna, Mark ... all of you, your number is now two minutes over the time limit. You'll have to pick up the pace." She glanced over at Izzy, Maddy and Lisa-Marie, "Are the three of you ready? You'll be on as soon as these *Thriller* wannabes wrap it up."

Roland walked off the stage, telling Izzy as he passed, "I'm sure that without my walking stick and tails, she can't imagine the effect I'm after. The woman has probably never even heard of Joel Gray."

The planning committee and performers for the Talent Night Fundraiser had gathered at the Dearborn Community Center for a final rehearsal. Darlene arrived and looked around. She spotted Dylan leaning against a wall chatting to an attractive girl. Darlene pulled up a chair, sat down and waved him over. Her feet were killing her. She had come straight from a standing-room-only meeting that had gone on forever in the town council chamber. Her ears were still ringing from the shouting. It seemed there was no way to reconcile people who supported fish farms on economic terms and those who opposed them on environmental grounds.

She shook her head at the sight of Maryanne swishing about waving her stopwatch in the air. Overseeing the dinner was something Maryanne would not interfere with and that was a blessing. When Dylan was seated beside her, Darlene said, "Let's go through the timing again."

Dylan flipped open his notebook, "Barbecues lit by five-thirty, first load of salmon on the grill by six-fifteen, appetizers out at the same time, first tables of people coming up to the buffet by seven. Desserts served at eight. Snack trays go out at ten."

"Make sure you finish up the desserts by three at the latest. If those fishermen haven't cleaned the fish, we're going to have our hands full. Don't forget to get the coffee urns going in good time; they take forever." Dylan made a few quick notes.

Maryanne stomped across the hall and yelled down to Jeremy where he sat operating the sound system, "You'll have to bring up the sound on Izzy's mike; the doo-wop girls are drowning her out. And don't forget which part Justin is coming in on to play the harmonica. That middle mike will have to be adjusted. Write it down, Jeremy."

Darlene smiled at Dylan, "Now tell me one more time about the desserts you're making. And don't skimp when you're talking about the chocolate." Darlene fanned herself as Dylan described the desserts. She enjoyed every minute of working with this handsome young man whose broad shoulders made her sigh.

Izzy and her group came off the stage as Maryanne breezed by. She shouted at Jeremy, "Don't lay that music on so heavily when I get to the Lady Macbeth section ... I couldn't hear myself think the last time."

Lisa-Marie and Maddy collapsed into chairs near the back and hugged their sides laughing as Maryanne moved through a quick-paced version of fifteen minutes of Shakespeare. "Where on earth do you think she got that skull?" Maddy asked between chuckles.

They sat up straight as Darlene bore down on them, "Maddy, do you have the final drawing for the programs and posters? I want to have them at the printer tomorrow." Maddy ran off to get her portfolio.

Lisa-Marie picked up her camera and moved around the hall taking photos. She tried to imagine what it would be like the night of the event. Edward had explained to her the importance of being prepared. The light levels would be difficult – bright on the stage and low everywhere else. There would be people sitting at the tables in the front, possibly moving around and getting in the way. Edward was going to take photos of her and Izzy while they were performing. He expected a full logistical report when she got back to Crater Lake.

Jesse stood on the stage with Maryanne. Lisa-Marie pulled her camera up, focused on him and waited. Maryanne leaned over and tapped the piano bench with her clipboard, "You've got to jump straight up onto the piano bench and lean forward to start pounding the keys. Can you do that?" Jesse did a couple of knee bends and then sprang up on the bench like a cat burglar about to burst through a window.

The moment he bent his knees to launch himself into the air, Lisa-Marie started shooting. She was hard-pressed to contain her own amusement and hold the camera steady. She shot about twenty photos in quick succession, but then she had to stop. The sound of Maddy's hysterical laugher could not be ignored. After the leap to the piano bench, Jesse had thrown his head back, stretched his arms in the air a few times, flexed his fingers and leaned over at the waist to pound the piano keys. When he got up on his toes and his feet started moving to and fro, Maddy ran over to Lisa-Marie. They screamed, clutched each other and nearly collapsed.

When Jesse jumped off the piano stool, Maryanne smiled and thumped him on the back, "Excellent. That is exactly the effect I'm looking for." She turned quickly and shouted, "Jeremy, make sure you have Jesse's music set up correctly. We don't want him up here swinging his butt in the air, lip-syncing out of time."

Maryanne looked around, "Where is Willow? Oh, there you are dear. Come on up." She took a quick look at her clip board, "I know this song you've chosen is heartbreak central but the last time we went through it, you sang it like a dirge. Try to lighten up the mood a tad this time. We don't want the audience feeling as though they'd like to slit their throats. Away you go."

Maryanne kept her eyes on Willow at center stage but stopped beside Izzy to complain, "Why she insists on singing this song is beyond me. She'd have been better off doing the *Cosette* piece which is more upbeat and suitable for a young girl. I could have had her in a beautiful period piece costume. But no, she chooses this number and insists on standing on the stage dressed in rags. I mean seriously, we could have done so much better than sackcloth and ashes. I don't know why she won't accompany herself on the piano, either. We all know she's a virtuoso. Sitting behind the piano would give her some size and hide that horrid excuse for a costume."

"Let's try her with a stand-up mike instead of the hand-held one. That way she'll look sturdier."

"Izzy, you're a genius," Maryanne swung around and bellowed, "Jeremy, carry that stand-up mike out here."

Alex grabbed the meat mallet and flattened the chicken breasts on the cutting board in front of him. He was still laughing at the story he had just told.

Cynthia handed Robbie a mixmaster beater. She began to ice the chocolate layer cake she had baked earlier in the day.

Robbie slicked his tongue around the beater and asked, "Do you know any good stories about my mom?"

Alex threw a flattened piece of chicken onto a plate and started pounding another. "I know more than a few stories about your mom. I'll think of one I can tell." He looked over at Robbie, "Remember I told you I met your mom during all the trouble with the lobster fishing?" Robbie nodded, waiting until Cynthia wasn't watching before he dipped the beater back into the bowl of icing.

"Hey, I saw that," she told him.

"We were out on the water in the boats, circling around - making our stand about the way the commercial guys were cutting up our traps. Out of nowhere, this Department of Fisheries boat comes barrelling down on us - prow up in the air, churning the water, coming right at the boat your mom was in." Alex pulled out another cutting board and carved ham in thin shavings. "Your mom was one courageous woman, Robbie. When everybody else was jumping into the water left, right and center, she stood up in the boat and started screaming, *bring it on Fishery pigs*. The boat she was in got slammed and she went flying. I had a bad moment or two but we pulled her out of the water."

It was quiet in the kitchen as Alex set the ham aside and peeled off slices of Swiss cheese. Robbie put the licked-clean beater into the sink. "That wasn't the day my mom would drown but I guess you didn't know that." Cynthia looked up from her work. Her gaze went from Robbie to Alex. The bleak tone of Robbie's words made her swallow hard over the lump in her throat.

Alex pulled Robbie against his side in a quick hug. "Here's another story about your mom." He wrapped and skewered the chicken cordon bleu pieces and lined them up in a pan while he spoke.

"This story is about what happened the day you were born, Robbie. It was a Friday and your mom went into labour in the morning. She was all freaked out because there was no doctor around for the whole weekend. You were her first baby and all. Your grannie told her to give it a rest. The nurse practitioner was there; what more did your mom want? Your grannie always said doctors were overrated."

Alex reached for a pile of fresh herbs on the counter and sprinkled them over the chicken. "Like all first babies, you were slow. The labour dragged out all day. Come dinner time, your mom gets it in her mind that she's going to the Bingo Hall. She's rattling on about the jackpot being at least two hundred dollars in cold hard cash and she feels lucky. Off she goes down the road with your grannie following and screaming the whole way that your mom's a nut case. Now the labour was getting intense and your mom was suffering, but she was stubborn. She wasn't going to leave before that jackpot game. People were getting steamed about the way she was moaning and groaning through the contractions. Other players started throwing candy wrappers and bingo chips at her. She just hunched over the table playing her cards and telling them all they could go straight to hell. Your grannie tried to pull her by the arm out of the chair but it was a no go. She sent your aunt to get me. Then she hollered at your mom to go ahead and have her baby in the Bingo Hall, like a gambling junkie."

Alex put a lid on the casserole dish, "When I got to the hall, the place was in an uproar. No one could even hear the caller. Your mom was screaming with the contractions and screaming that she had paid decent money to be there so no one was going to make her leave. I jumped up on a table and told everyone to simmer down so we could get the game over with. And wouldn't you know it? Your mom was just waiting on *top of the house - O seventy-five*; the machine gave a final groan and out it popped. We hauled your mom over to the clinic and before the nurse even got there, you popped right out into my hands, just about as fast as the ball marked *O seventy-five* came out of that bingo machine. Your mom was crying and laughing, waving that jackpot money in the air, saying, I told you I felt lucky, I told you so - cold hard cash. Your grannie looked down at you and said maybe your mom should name you Bingo. I think your mom thought about it for a minute or two."

Izzy and Liam had come into the kitchen right after Alex began the story and by the time he finished they were laughing as hard as Robbie and Cynthia. Robbie looked over at Liam and then turned to their dad, "Tell us one about when Liam was born."

Alex shook his head and grinned. "Liam's mom and I were kids ourselves when he came along. It was that long ago but I remember it like it was yesterday." He put the chicken in the oven and stood with his back to the counter, his arms folded over his chest. He told Liam, "You were the kind of baby that gives his mom no end of trouble because you didn't want to get yourself born. Your mom's labour went on into a second day. Everyone was getting worked up. People were saying they better get a medevac chopper. I'll tell you, I was scared half to death, what with the nurse talking about hard decisions to make. The clinic was crowded but I could see your mom waving at me from across the room. I went over to her bed and she grabbed my shirt, dragged me up to her face and hissed, *Alexander Collins, this is your bloody fault. I'm not getting on any friggin' chopper and going anywhere. You better damn well make this whole mess come out right.*

"I was scared before, but then I was shaking in my boots. I guess I do my best thinking under pressure, because right at that minute I got an idea. I crawled up on the bed and straddled your mom's legs. I put my hands on her stomach and shouted, *Liam Samuel Collins, you get your ass out here right now.* This was before all the fancy ultrasound scans people have now. But me and your mom, we thought you were going to be a boy and we had your name all picked out. You can imagine, it went awful quiet in that room as everyone started thinking it might be a good idea to put me on the medevac and take me straight to a psych ward. Your mom laughed, one of those really deep belly laughs she had. Then she yelled at me to get off the bed because she had to push. In no time, there you were, Liam. You always were the kind of son who knew when to listen to his old man."

Liam laughed with everyone else, but after a moment he said, "You're making that up."

"Let's take a vote. Who doubts my story?"

Liam's hand shot up and Robbie laughed and put his hand up, as well. Izzy kept her hand down. When Liam raised his eyebrows at her she said, "I'm sorry, Liam but I've got to tell you ... I believe every word."

"I'm with you, Izzy," Cynthia agreed.

⚜ ⚜ ⚜ ⚜

Dear Emma:

It was so weird being with Justin down at the beach. I thought it would suck to have Robbie tagging along with us but the kid is a riot and it turned out it was good to have a third wheel. You can't be embarrassed about how your bathing suit looks with a crazy kid around doing cannonballs.

Every day last summer, I wanted Justin to be my boyfriend so badly I couldn't think straight. We're so close now but he's just a boy who's a friend. And that sucks, Emma because I love Justin. I can't ever imagine loving anyone the way I love him. Not in my whole, long life and you remember how I said I want to live a long, long time.

⚜ ⚜ ⚜ ⚜

Beulah lay with her arms around Bethany, holding her close in their bed. She couldn't believe how great it was to have her life back. It was as if the past year had dissolved like the remnants of a bad dream. Bethany was back in tip top

216

condition in all the ways that mattered to Beulah. The A-Frame was clean, the meals were on time, the bakery was running like a well-oiled machine and, to top the list, things were right in the bedroom. Beulah had to admit, a happy Bethany equaled a happy life for her.

"You should come into town one afternoon with me and Alex and watch these kids play baseball. Good for a laugh if nothing else." Beulah chuckled, "They are making progress, though."

"Sure, I'd like that." Bethany cuddled into Beulah's side and asked, "What do you think of Alex?"

"He's the real deal ... like Caleb."

Bethany sat up and stared at Beulah, "He's nothing like Caleb. What do you mean?"

"Caleb was exactly what he seemed to be. So is Alex."

"So, Alex really is a warrior?"

"In every way," Beulah laughed.

"No wonder you like him."

Beulah folded her arms behind her head and let her thoughts wander. "I've been thinking Beth ... I'm still not feeling good about Izzy picking up the tab for Lisa-Marie."

"Oh, Beulah, come on. You know as well as I do that Izzy has more money than she'll ever need. How on earth can it matter to her?"

"It seems wrong is all I'm saying. The one who pays the bill is the one who calls the shots. That's the way the world works. Are you willing to turn over to them every decision that has to do with the kid?"

"You're overreacting as usual. I'm Lisa's guardian, not Izzy and she knows it." Bethany pulled the blankets up and scrunched her pillow under her head, "I've got to get some sleep. I'm tired and it seems like five a.m. comes pretty early these days."

THIRTY-ONE

Dylan leaned against the kitchen door of the Dearborn Community Hall. His arms were folded over his chest as he watched the last table of diners make their way through the buffet line-up. Already others were coming back for seconds. Several people gave him thumbs up as they passed. He smiled and nodded.

His special recipe chicken appetizers, wrapped in bacon then drenched in brown sugar and chili powder had been popular. The barbecue sauce for the salmon had combined the perfect mixture of sweet and spicy. All the salads had come out of the kitchen crisp and well presented. Another huge pot of coffee was perking. Dylan could hardly wait to unveil the desserts.

Arianna walked up and threw her arms around his neck. She pressed her body tight against his, "Every single thing was delicious. People can't stop talking about what a great cook you are." She stepped back for a moment, still clinging to him, "I hope I'll be able to see you later, after the dance ... when we get back to the Camp."

Dylan looked down at the expression on Arianna's face. Her eyes were glowing. He couldn't hold her off much longer, not without raising questions. He had to make a choice. Get it over with; give it a try. He leaned in close to her, "I want to dance with you tonight and later, down at the boat shed, I want to do another kind of dance." Arianna backed up quickly, resting her hands on his chest. A smile lit up her face. Dylan pushed away from the wall, "I've got some finishing touches to do on the cheesecakes - chocolate drizzle and fresh peppermint garnish. Do you want to give me a hand?"

※※※※

As the performers assembled near the stage, Justin reached out to steady Willow who was looking more than a bit shaky, "Hey, what's up? Are you okay?"

"I'm worried I might make a fool of myself. Sometimes the song I'm going to sing makes me feel like crying."

"I'll keep an eye on the crowd when you're on stage. If it looks like some of them are going to throw rotten eggs, I'll escort them out." Willow laughed as she took her place in the line-up that Maryanne was overseeing.

Roland high-stepped across the stage, his tuxedo tails flapped against his legs. He spun his cane, twirled his top hat and announced that life is a cabaret. With a flourish, he threw back his head of slicked hair and proclaimed, "Welcome." He bowed and introduced the first act.

A spotlight appeared on the main floor in front of the stage. Mark, dressed in a red leather jacket and pants short enough to give a glimpse of his white socks, stood beside Arianna. She wore jeans rolled up at the calves and high heels that emphasized the shape of her legs. The opening notes of the Michael Jackson song, *Thriller*, filled the air. Mark lip-synched and danced to the music. When a dozen zombies shuffled out to complete the cast, the audience clapped in time with the music and sang along.

Watching from backstage, Izzy shook her head at the sight of Mark's star performance. No one knew the talents that lay hidden in some of these kids. She straightened the short black dress over her hips and winced when her shoes pinched her toes. Lisa-Marie and Maddy were catching glimpses of the show from around the corner of the stage curtains. The dresses looked better on the two of them and her backup singers didn't seem to have any problem prancing around in heels. Izzy had to admit, she was getting old. The zombies were slouching out of the hall, weaving their way through the people, to the sounds of whistles, cheers and table thumping.

Izzy called the girls over as she grabbed her purse and pulled out a spray bottle of perfume. She wafted a bit on her wrists and down the top of her plunging neckline. Turning quickly, she did the same to Maddy and Lisa-Marie. Justin came up the backstage stairs two at a time with his harmonica in hand. Izzy smiled at all of them as they waited for Roland to introduce their act.

They took their places on the stage. The opening notes of the song came out of the sound system and Izzy lost herself in the performance. Many were the nights that Caleb had plied her with wine and got her up on the stage for karaoke at the Dearborn Legion. Not that she needed all that much coaxing. She loved to sing; she always had. She was good but not great and that made performing fun.

The applause rang through the hall. Arms around each other's shoulders, the quartet took a final bow and left the stage. Justin stood back and watched Izzy walk straight into Liam's arms as he said, "Every guy in this hall wishes he was me right about now." Izzy laughed in a way that was intimate, low and husky, before her lips met his.

Justin walked down from the stage and across the hall. He headed for the bar where he could see Reg and Beulah lining up a row of shooters. He slammed a hand onto Reg's back, "How about I join the two of you?"

Jesse's impersonation of Jerry Lee Lewis came off without a hitch. When he leaped onto the piano bench, got up on his toes and began swivelling his hips and pounding on the keyboard, people were on their feet, screaming.

Willow was the last performer of the evening. She appeared on the stage under a single spotlight, gripping the stand-up mike with both hands. She wore a dress that was tattered, ripped off one shoulder and jagged at the hem. Her long blonde curls were twined up on her head, arranged to tumble down over one shoulder. Maryanne frowned from her place in the audience but the crowd was mesmerized from the moment Willow opened her mouth to sing *I Dreamed a Dream*, from the musical *Les Miserables*. As the final notes faded away Willow bowed and stood very still. A stunned silence gave way to thunderous applause.

Justin strode across the room from the bar to meet Willow as she came down off the stage. He leaned over and kissed her on the cheek and whispered something in her ear.

Lisa-Marie felt her stomach turn over as she watched the two of them. The speed with which Justin had disappeared after their number had surprised her. Then she'd spotted him over at the bar with Beulah and Reg. She had put him out of her mind as she grabbed her camera and immersed herself in the hard work of getting the right angles and shots for each of the performances. He smiled as he passed her, now. The slight waver in his step made her wonder how many drinks he'd had.

⚜⚜⚜⚜

The dance portion of the evening was in full swing. Jeremy had the music cranked up full blast. Izzy checked to see if Sophie was sleeping in the playpen that was pushed against the far wall. She was out for the count, with her baby thumb snuggly in her mouth. She had been passed back and forth, waltzed around the dance floor and fussed over for most of the night. No wonder she was fast asleep with no regard for the noise.

A slow song began as Izzy returned to the table. Liam reached over for her hand. Out on the dance floor he held her tight. Izzy spoke close to his ear, "Do you realize this is our first public dance as real partners." She felt his body press against her as they moved slowly together, in perfect time with one another.

Later, Lisa-Marie plopped into a chair beside Izzy and glared over at Edward. He was looking comfortable in the armchair Liam and Alex had carried in for him at the beginning of the evening. "Why on earth would you give Robbie a camera? He's driving everyone crazy popping up all over the place, taking God knows what kind of gross, unfocused pictures."

Edward sipped rye and Coke from a plastic glass, "I'll let you download them all. Then you can have first veto."

Robbie appeared at the table with the camera and tried to take a picture of Lisa-Marie and Izzy. Lisa-Marie blocked the front of the lens with her hand, "No way, the light is all wrong here and with the flash, you'll make us look like ghouls."

Izzy drew Robbie over beside her, "Can you go to the kitchen and ask Dylan when the snacks are going to be put out. I'm starving." She looked over at Lisa-Marie, "I was afraid to eat too much dinner in case my stomach stuck out in this crazy, tight dress." Izzy squirmed a bit on the chair to pull the dress down, "I'm sure it fit better when I first bought it."

Robbie hung his head and told Izzy, "I don't want to go to the kitchen and talk to Dylan. At the Camp, he gets mad if I come into the kitchen when he's in there. One day he called me a stupid pain-in-the-ass."

Izzy filed Robbie's story away for future reference and decided she would go herself. She slid out of her chair and glanced down the length of the long table of friends, drinking and enjoying themselves. Bethany and Beulah were sitting side by side; Reg and Josie had joined them. Alex and Cynthia were laughing together about something. Roland had removed most of his makeup but his hair was still slicked back. He had his arm around Jillian's shoulder. Edward looked as comfortable as they could make him. She had wondered about his insistence on coming because she was sure the late night was going to be hard on him. But her father was not to be denied when he made up his mind to do something.

The opening bars of the song *Footloose* blasted through the hall and Justin shot past Izzy to grab Lisa-Marie by the hand and drag her onto the dance floor. Several dancers were soon gathered in a circle around the two of them, clapping in time to the beat of the music. When the song ended, Justin pulled Lisa-Marie into a tight hug. She didn't have time to catch her breath before Misty grabbed Justin's hand and dragged him away for the next dance.

The hall was crowded as people moved on and off the dance floor. Some made their way to the bar while others stepped outside for a breath of air. Maddy was standing by herself near a wall, scanning the room anxiously for a glimpse of Jesse. She hadn't seen him for at least fifteen minutes. Mark touched her arm as the melancholic Cindy Lauper song *Time After Time* drifted across the hall. He reached for her hand. Out on the dance floor, he held her formally – one hand on her waist and the other resting against her back. The sweetness of dancing with Mark made Maddy cry. She leaned forward and rested her wet cheek against his shoulder as they moved gracefully together. She was glad of the dark. As the music died away, she dropped her mouth to Mark's and kissed him with a feathery touch of her lips. She wiped the tears from her eyes and smiled, "Thank you, Mark. That was the nicest dance I've ever had." She walked off towards the bathrooms at the back of the hall; her arms were crossed tightly over her body as she tried to hold back a fresh onslaught of tears.

Darlene leaned over the playpen and glanced at the sleeping baby. She turned and pulled up a chair across from Izzy and Liam. Jeremy was taking a refreshment break, so the music was down to a reasonable blare. She folded her arms on the table, "What's the story with you guys and the baby?"

Izzy stiffened but Liam remained relaxed, leaning back with his arm slung over her shoulder. He answered in the same easy manner, "We're helping out. Lisa-Marie's pretty young to be a mom and she has school to finish."

"Are you going to adopt the baby?"

While Izzy chugged down the rest of her drink, Liam said, "We're helping out, like I told you, Darlene." The music started up again with the opening bars of a polka and the mayor appeared by the table to claim his wife. Along with enjoying his ex-mayor status, Darlene's husband also liked to uphold his reputation for being the local polka king.

Roland walked over to the bar and glared at a couple of the residents who were hanging around nearby. He gestured with his hand for them to beat it away from the alcohol. All the residents were aware that drinking at a function associated with the Camp was prohibited. Not that the rules were going to matter much tonight. The kids could walk outside to the nearby ball diamond dugout and get their fill of whatever was being offered.

He watched Jeremy slide back through the hall's double doors with a couple of female residents trailing behind him. He was dressed in a pair of jeans and a bright red T-shirt with an image of Che Guevara on the front. Roland reminded himself to keep Jeremy on his radar. Rumors of pot use at the Camp were on the rise and he had his suspicions about who the supplier might be. Then there was the fact that Jeremy was spending a lot more time at the Camp these days, giving extra tutoring and hanging around for meals. He was probably lonely since his marriage break up but Roland knew he'd be wise to stay on top of the situation.

Darlene stuck her head into the kitchen and called out, "Come on, Dylan. That's enough. Whatever is left to do in here, someone else can take care of. It's time to have some fun. You promised me a dance." Dylan laughed and headed onto the dance floor with Darlene who managed to move with quite a lot of energy for a woman her size.

⁂⁂⁂⁂

Beulah was more than half-way to feeling no pain when she saw Abbey come into the hall on the arm of a guy who was probably the mystery-man husband. Beulah was prepared to ignore her but that proved difficult. Abbey was decked out in a satin green sheath dress that almost laid her breasts out on the table every time she leaned over. The woman drew attention to herself at every turn. But worse than any of that, when Bethany walked to the washroom, Abbey smirked at Beulah and followed right behind her. If Bethany got up to dance, Abbey walked onto the floor, as well. After an hour of this, Beulah was ready to explode.

She saw Abbey go outside to stand on the wide stairs at the entrance to the hall. Beulah glanced around for Bethany. She could see her on the far side of the dance floor with a group of women, so she followed Abbey out to the porch. She grabbed her arm, pulled her over to a dark corner and blocked her in. "Stay away from Bethany. If I see you following her one more time, you'll be sorry."

Abbey wrenched her arm away, "Oh, Beulah, honey ... you and I both know you can't do a damn thing to stop me from following your blonde sweetie around." She laughed and pushed herself against Beulah, grinding her body in time to the music that blasted out of the hall. Then she turned and walked off without a backward glance.

Bethany had left the crowd of dancers to get herself a glass of water. Even halfway across the dance floor, she could see Beulah walk out the double doors. Her short, spiky hair was easy to spot. She was about to follow when she saw Beulah grab a sultry redhead by the arm and pull her into a corner. Bethany froze and stared. Beulah's back was to her but it was obvious she was

223

angry; her head jerked up and down and her stance was rigid. Bethany moved out of the way of a group of dancers and kept her eye on Beulah. Before long, the other woman freed herself from the corner and strolled back into the hall. Beulah paused briefly on the porch before walking down the stairs and out to the parking lot.

When she came back to the table, Bethany asked, "Where have you been?"

"Having a beer over in the dugout."

Bethany stared at her, "I saw you out on the stairs talking to a red-headed woman. You looked pretty worked up. What's going on?"

"It's nothing for you to worry about." Beulah glanced at her watch, "I'm about ready to head out. Let's start saying goodbye to people." She pulled the truck keys out of her pocket and tossed them to Bethany, "You look a hell of a lot more sober than I feel. You're driving."

THIRTY-TWO

C ynthia hesitated on the trail as Lisa-Marie led Justin away. She turned to Alex, "Do you think they'll be alright? He's quite drunk." Justin staggered as he and Lisa-Marie disappeared around the corner. Cynthia giggled right along with the hysterical laughter that was coming from down the trail. I should talk about being drunk, she thought. She knew she was over the legal limit and she'd been quite relieved when Alex was available to drive her car back from Dearborn. In the back seat, Justin and Lisa-Marie had joked and laughed the whole way home.

She walked up the steps to the porch of the guest cabin and turned, hoping to find Alex behind her. He was still standing on the trail. She called out, "I think the blockade might have collapsed."

Alex came up the stairs and across to her in a couple of strides. He stretched an arm out to rest it against the glass door and leaned forward, "Are you sure, Ms. St. Pierre, that this collapse is not due to the many alcoholic beverages you consumed this evening?"

She stiffened, "I'm shocked, Mr. Collins, that you would presume such a thing. I am not the kind of woman who becomes intoxicated and invites a man to share the pleasures of her bed."

Slipping an arm around her waist he pulled her close, "The pleasures of your bed? That has a nice ring to it." He leaned in to kiss her.

Cynthia pulled back, "Maybe we should talk about what we're doing – what it might mean – or what it doesn't mean." Her heart was pounding. She was glad he had not altered the firm way his arm encircled her. She moved closer and reached up to touch his face.

Alex slid the glass door open with his free hand and pulled her inside the cabin. He kissed her and let his hands roam freely over her body, "We'll figure out what it means later. I find that it is often in retrospect that things make sense."

⅔·⅔·⅔·⅔

Lisa-Marie managed to steer Justin, falling and tripping, up the loft stairs to the bed. He flopped over in a heap, dragging her down beside him.

"Oh God, Leez ... I'm so drunk." Justin gripped onto the far side of the bed with one hand and held Lisa-Marie tightly with the other.

She struggled out of his arms and sat up, doing her best to get his long legs onto the bed. He tugged her down beside him again. "You could at least try to help me out here," she said as she pushed at his legs with her own.

"You smell so sweet," Justin said. His lips moved down her neck and his breath was hot against her skin. He pulled her close. She whispered his name right before he raised his lips to hers and kissed her – a kiss that turned every fiber of her being into a rush of longing and desire. He moved his lips from hers and murmured against her cheek, "Always so sweet ... like roses." Justin's head fell to one side. He breathed deeply and between that breath and the next, he passed out.

Every muscle in Lisa-Marie's body tensed when she heard the word, *roses.* The perfume ... Izzy's signature scent ... she had sprayed it on herself, Lisa-Marie and Maddy before they went on stage. For luck, she had said; let's break a leg and all of that. At least we'll smell nice when the paramedics arrive.

She stared over at Justin in disbelief; could it be possible that he still wanted Izzy? An overwhelming wave of pain hit her, rising up from her stomach, across her chest and into her throat where it threatened to break into a howl. She disentangled herself from his arms, moved off the bed and stumbled down the stairs. She wrapped herself in an old blanket on the couch. The tears came in waves. She collapsed into the cushions and buried her head to hide the sound of her sobs.

⅔·⅔·⅔·⅔

Dylan pushed Arianna up against the wall of the boat shed and kissed her. He was moving faster than he wanted to be but he had to make it through to the other side of his doubts. He slid his hands up under her top. As she raised her arms, he pulled her shirt over her head and let his hands come back to work at the clasp on her bra. He could feel her unbutton his shirt and drop it off his shoulders as she returned his kiss. Her body was grinding into his. He

226

had his knee wedged between her legs and she was pressing down on him. He felt his belt being undone and the fly of his pants sliding down. Then her warm hands moved over his skin.

It wasn't going to happen. No matter what he did, he couldn't make his body respond the way she had every right to believe it would. He pulled away and slammed his fist against the wall.

Arianna cringed away at the thunking sound. "It's okay Dylan. I was rushing things, I'm sorry."

He rounded on her in anger and desperation. He couldn't be the guy who dragged a hot looking chick like Arianna down to the boat shed and couldn't even get it up for her. "You aren't doing it for me - period - end of story. I thought I could buy into your *Indian princess* routine but I touch you and find out you're a dirty little squaw. God, you even stink. What is that smell, anyway ... bear grease?"

Arianna staggered back a step. Dylan knew his words were like a hand slapping her face. He turned away; he couldn't look at her. He stared out the window of the boat shed and waited for her to slam out the door. But he didn't hear anything and after a moment he felt her close behind him. She snaked her arms around him, spread her hands flat against his chest and held on tight, leaning her face into the naked skin of his back.

He heard her whisper, "I'm so sorry." He wanted to push her away and keep acting like a total bastard but he couldn't. His shoulders slumped forward. He felt her hands move down his chest toward his open jeans. He tensed and tried to push her away, "Stop Ari. You don't understand. It's no use. What do you want from me?"

Her hand kept moving and she whispered against his back, "Close your eyes, Dylan ... close your eyes and pretend it's Jesse touching you." His whole body stiffened and responded in a flood of pounding heat. He heard himself moan as he stretched his arms out to grasp the window ledge. He felt Arianna slide around him, her lips on his chest moving down in an agony of slow heat.

Afterwards, they ended up slumped on the ground, sitting side by side with their backs against the wall. Dylan said, "Why did you do that?"

Arianna crossed her legs lotus style. She pressed her hands down flat in front of her on the floor, "I couldn't stand to see how much you were hurting. It wasn't a big deal. It was good, right?"

"Ya, of course, it was good." He shifted uncomfortably, "How did you know ... about Jesse?"

Arianna stretched her arms over her head and bent to one side, curving her body in a graceful sweep. "Well, I've been hanging around you a lot, right? There didn't seem any good reason for you to hate Maddy so much. I saw the way you looked at Jesse a couple of times when he and Maddy were fooling around together."

Dylan heard his own voice tremble, "Do you think everyone knows?"

Her long hair swung across her face as she shook her head back and forth, "Of course not ... no ... absolutely not. I'm positive no one else has a clue."

He grabbed Arianna's hand and held it tight against his chest. Even if she was lying to make him feel better, he was grateful she was willing to make the effort. "If it was a girl I wanted, you know it would be you ... right Ari? You're really hot. Don't think about the horrible things I said. I was acting like a bastard because I felt so stupid."

She hung her head and nodded. It was quiet. He knew she was crying ... and trying not to cry ... and wanting to keep him from seeing her tears. He pulled her over close to him, "We won't ever do anything like this again. You said it wasn't a big deal. Well ... it is. I don't want to use you." Dylan stroked his hand down the long, glossy hair that fell over his chest. "I want you to know something, Ari." He waited until she had raised her eyes to look at him before going on. "I'm never going to forget that you didn't walk out on me, that you care so much about me."

⚜ ⚜ ⚜ ⚜

"Darlene sure knows how to ask some awkward questions." Izzy snuggled close to Liam.

He tightened his hold on her, "I guess people are bound to wonder."

"Let them wonder. When we adopt Sophie, no one has to know anything. I will be her mother and you will be her father ... end of story."

She felt Liam tense. Silence stretched out between them. The sound of Sophie's crying intruded. Liam withdrew his arm from around Izzy, "I'll go." At the door, he stopped and turned back, "Did I tell you how beautiful you looked tonight? I love you, Izz." Then he was gone and any discussion of their future went with him.

THIRTY-THREE

Lisa-Marie woke to the morning light flooding the small cabin. She looked over and saw Justin pulling the orange juice out of the fridge. He opened the carton and emptied it into his mouth like a man dying of thirst. He stood with his naked back to her in jeans riding low on his hips. The well-defined muscles of his shoulders stood out as he leaned against the side of the counter. The smell of booze came off him like a wave. He turned suddenly and jumped with surprise.

"Leez, you scared the crap out of me. What are you doing here?"

She sat up and pushed the blanket away, "I helped you get home last night, remember? I don't think I've ever seen anyone as drunk as you were. You passed out. It was late, so I crashed here."

Justin sat down in the rocker and dropped his head into his hands. He looked up at her and groaned, "The last thing I remember is doing shooters at the bar with Reg and Beulah, then that *Footloose* dance." He reached over to nudge her arm, "You're a real friend, Leez. Thanks for watching out for me." He looked down at his watch and moaned, "Shit, I've got to shower and shave. I have to be over at the Camp to write my friggin' English midterm this morning."

Lisa-Marie waved him off toward the bathroom, "You better hurry. I should get back to Izzy's before they send out a search party." Or something worse, she thought, as she imagined Liam's disapproval.

※ ※ ※ ※

Lisa-Maria walked into the cabin, still wearing her black dress from the night before and dangling her shoes over the fingers of one hand. She passed Liam without a word and headed straight for the shower.

Before she reached the bathroom door, she heard him raise his voice loud enough to demand her attention. "Where were you last night? Did you even stop to think we might be worried?"

Lisa-Marie answered without turning, "Watch it Liam. You're not my boss and you're sure as hell not my friggin' father."

"What about Sophie?" He gestured with his free hand to the baby in his lap sucking away on her bottle, "You missed your shift."

"I'm sure her father was around to take up the slack." She walked into the bathroom and slammed the door.

Liam got up and carried Sophie out to the kitchen. He could see Izzy out on the deck, drinking a coffee. He grabbed a tea-towel from the drawer and went out to sit beside her.

Liam threw the cloth over his shoulder, hefted Sophie up and started patting her back. "Did you hear that?"

"Hard not to ... you were both shouting."

"She's not even seventeen yet, Izz. Someone should be in charge of her."

"I'm guessing she doesn't think you're qualified for the job."

⋇⋇⋇⋇

Justin dropped his pen; it rolled off the edge of the desk and hit the floor. He was in the middle of writing his exam, alone in the small office where Roland had left him. He had let his mind wander for a moment. The memory of kissing Lisa-Marie came back to him, right out of nowhere with a tingling thump. He could feel the touch of her lips against his, the silkiness of her long hair, the warm softness of her skin when he held her. He shifted on the hard-backed chair and forced himself to stay with the rush of memory. Did anything else happen? He remembered flopping over after he had kissed her. Then he passed out. There wasn't anything else. What a thing to do – pass out like that. He was surprised she hadn't gotten up off the couch this morning and slapped him across the face.

He reached down to pick up the pen and tapped it against the side of the desk. It was strange that Leez had said nothing at all about the kiss. She hadn't been drunk; he knew that. She would have remembered everything. She must be over him; otherwise, she would have tried to get some mileage out of the way he had kissed her. She was letting him save face by not mentioning anything about what had happened. It was pretty decent of her. She was a good friend.

But when he thought of that kiss, he felt a rush of desire so strong and sudden he wanted to leave the office and find her. He would put his arms around her, kiss her again and make her think twice about getting over him. But he stopped himself. He thought about Misty and the open invitation in her eyes. Girls who wanted to have sex with him were readily available. To find a girl who wanted to be his friend, now that was a rare thing.

❦❦❦❦

Cynthia stepped up to the camper and rapped against the metal door. She heard Alex call out from inside, "It's open." She took a deep breath and turned the knob. Alex was shirtless, stretched out on the camper's small sofa reading another of her novels.

He raised his eyebrows over the top edge of the book, "Ms. St. Pierre. Just the person I was hoping to talk to." He sat up and pointed the book at her. "Had I read the steamy pages of this book before the delightful time I had with you last night, I think I would have asked you to put to the test some of what you've written here." He looked back at the page he had been reading, "On second thought, I fear I might have been a disappointment." He got up, tossed the book aside and asked, "Do you want coffee?"

Cynthia tried not to notice how sexy he looked as he pulled a T-shirt over his head and hid the well-defined muscles of his abdomen. Before she knew it, he'd set two steaming mugs of coffee on the table between them.

Cynthia cleared her throat, "I thought we should talk."

"Here's a better idea," Alex smiled at her. "We drink this coffee and then we test out a few of those passages in your novel – for research sake, if nothing else."

"I'm serious." She cleared her throat again, "I don't want you to think that last night was my attempt to hook you and that now I'm planning to reel you in because we've slept together."

"Maybe I should get that book. I'm sure I read something about hooks and I think handcuffs were mentioned, as well."

Cynthia went right on talking, "I like my life the way it is. I write when I want to write. I travel whenever and wherever I want. I didn't sleep with you because I want to change my life. And stop mocking me with that stupid grin." She banged her hand on the table in frustration.

Alex folded his arms over his chest and studied her, "We appear to have a great deal in common. I like my life, too. But change, my dear Cynthia, is inevitable."

"I wanted to be clear about what this isn't." She gripped the coffee mug in her hands, "I'm less sure about what it is." She stared down into the black liquid, "Do we enjoy a few good times together, then move on?"

"Is that type of behaviour normal for you?"

"Oh damn you, Alex ... you know that isn't what I'm saying. I've had relationships over the years. None of them lasted because a man usually wants a woman to adjust to his schedule, not vice versa. But they were all adult relationships. They were about more than sex."

Alex reached across the table and took the coffee cup from her. He turned her hand over and pulled it up to his lips to kiss the pulse that jumped in her wrist. "We can sleep together without it meaning either one of us wants to be tied down. I'd like to spend time with you, Cynthia. If that means a relationship, I'm not adverse to the concept."

She stared into his dark eyes and told him in a no-nonsense voice, "Don't read any more of my books. It's embarrassing."

THIRTY-FOUR

"Why are you crying?"

Arianna wiped tears from her face with the back of her hand, "I don't know. I really don't know." She had finished telling Izzy about what had happened in the boat shed with Dylan the night of the talent show. "I just wanted to help him."

"And did you?"

"I think so. He was so angry and hurting. Afterwards, he wasn't. He said we would never do anything like that again but he felt better."

"What about you ... how did you feel?" Arianna had a helpless look of confusion on her face.

"Let's do some work with this, okay?" Izzy pulled a chair over, "I want you to move back and forth between the chairs today. In this chair -" Izzy pointed to the empty chair, "you are the girl who is crying. And in that chair -" she pointed at the chair Arianna was sitting in, "you are the nosy counsellor who asks why."

Arianna sat up straight and gathered her thoughts. She addressed the empty chair in a sharp tone, "If you wanted to help him and you were so good at it, then what are you blubbering about?"

She got up, moved over to the empty chair and pondered the question. Tears washed down her face, "The things he said to me hurt. I like him a lot and I wanted him to like me, too."

Arianna moved back to her chair across from Izzy and wiped her eyes. She stared hard at the empty chair and pointed her finger for emphasis, "If you were so hurt by what he said, you should have walked out. He expected you to walk out. But no, you decide to give the guy a blow job ... a nice bonus

233

when he was treating you like a piece of shit."

Back on the other chair, Arianna leaned over and sobbed. Finally, she sat up and faced her accusatory self, "Even needing me like that ... letting me pretend I was someone else ... it seemed better than not needing me at all."

After a few moments, Arianna rose and took her seat across from Izzy once again. Her tone changed to one of compassion as she looked at the empty chair and said, "But it wasn't better, was it? This is all about you. You needed to help him way more than he needed that kind of help. It's never going to be better for you to be needed like that."

Arianna finally turned her gaze to Izzy. "I want people to care about me even when I can't do anything for them."

Izzy nodded slowly, "Let's work together to figure out what you can do to make that happen."

⋇⋇⋇⋇

Edward groaned as he tried to get comfortable in his chair. He thought back to the talent night. He had savoured each moment of the evening, knowing that it was probably the last time he would leave the lake. He'd been embarrassed because he had hobbled around on his cane and leaned on nearby tables when he got up to take pictures of Isabella and Lisa. But he bore it. The reward was worth the effort – the joy of holding a camera in his hand, capturing the moment, coordinating his mind and eye with his finger on the shutter.

Filled with a father's pride, he had watched Isabella throughout the evening. She was poised and elegant; her smile lit up a room. In the turn of her head and the line of her neck, with her dark hair whirling around her shoulders, she was so like her mother. On the other hand, Isabella was down in the trenches of life with people in a way her mother had never been.

He recalled the look of anguish that had crossed her face when he'd stood and held out his hand to her, "How about a whirl around the dance floor with your old dad?" She had hesitated and gestured to his cane. He'd told her he would be fine ... that he'd lean on her if he had to. It was no whirl he had offered her. He'd kept on though, for that dance was to be the culmination of a lifetime of things that he had not been there for.

Edward took a deeper breath as the pain found a resting place beyond him. It was an odd phenomenon. Part of his brain knew the pain was still there but the morphine made him believe it had retreated into a darkness he couldn't penetrate. He reached for his desk calendar and flipped it open to the month of July. His strength was slipping faster than he had imagined it would. He needed another month to see the book through to completion. His prescription of morphine would be refilled at the beginning of August. He would be ready when the time was right.

He opened the calendar and reached for the phone that Isabella always made sure was charged and beside his chair. He dialed the office of Dearborn's only lawyer and arranged a time for the man to make his way out to Crater Lake. Yes, he was aware it was highly irregular and inconvenient to ask a professional to give up most of a day to make such a trip. Edward assured the man that dying was also a tad inconvenient. The lawyer's misgivings gave way like a falling house of cards in the face of Edward's promise of monetary compensation for time lost.

He set the phone back in its cradle and let his mind drift out over the water that looked like a rolling mass of silver scales, an undulating and twisting dragon moving toward the mountains in the distance. He thought of Dylan Thomas writing that old age should rage against the dying of the light. A strange exhortation, for he saw no darkness on the horizon. Every moment was dancing with light.

※※※※

Dear Emma:

It's been forever since I could even stand to open this journal and write anything. If I tell you things then it makes them feel so real. Justin got seriously drunk at the talent night. I helped him get home and he kissed me. Sorry ... I had to stop writing. Even after a couple of weeks, the thought of how that kiss felt still makes me start shaking.

I know you'll be thinking, way to go Lisa-Marie. Well, it wasn't like that. He said something about rose perfume (Izzy's perfume) smelling so sweet. Then he passed out.

I don't know, Emma ... getting kissed like that by a guy who's that drunk when maybe he's thinking I'm someone else ... it isn't a lot to hang onto. But the way that kiss made me feel, he's the one, he'll always be the only guy for me.

I cried myself to sleep on his couch. I kept thinking – he still wants Izzy. But now I'm not sure about anything. Surely Justin couldn't be that crazy. Izzy is so in love with Liam. Everyone can see that. Anyway, the next morning Justin didn't remember anything, so I didn't say a word.

If all of that wasn't bad enough, I get back here and Liam snaps at me about staying out all night. I thought I would throw my shoes right at his head, and I might have if he hadn't been feeding Sophie. The baby's a pain but I don't want to smack her with a shoe.

Why does life have to be so hopeless? Edward is getting weaker. I do everything I can to get him to eat more but it's no use. He looks at me from over his glasses and I know he's thinking there's no point. I want to scream. What if a miracle cure comes along and you're too far gone to grab onto it? I don't say that, though, because I know he would feel sorry for me and think that I'm a total fool.

Oh shit, the baby's crying and I'm supposed to go to her. To hell with it. Let someone else look after her. They shouldn't count on me for anything. I'm going to put a pillow over my head and go to sleep.

✻✻✻✻

Izzy walked into the cabin and across the dark living room. Her father was asleep in the sun porch. Through the half-closed door, she could see a stack of papers scattered from the bed to the floor as if he had dozed off with the whole sheaf clutched in his hand. Sophie was also asleep in her cradle. Izzy glanced at her watch. It was almost midnight. She looked up to Lisa's loft to see if her light was on. All was dark and quiet. She went into the bathroom, brushed her teeth and tiptoed back across the living room to her own bedroom.

Liam was huddled under the blankets but she could tell he was awake and watching her in the dark. She took her time unbuttoning her shirt before she slipped it off her shoulders.

He looked up, watching her, "What on earth were you and Cynthia laughing about out there?"

Izzy unhooked her bra and tossed it on the dresser. She and Cynthia had just polished off an entire bottle of wine out on the cliff deck. She was feeling no pain. As it turned out, she found she got along quite well with Cynthia. It had been some time since she'd had another woman with whom she could talk so freely. She grabbed a sleeveless T-shirt out of her drawer and pulled it over her head as she answered, "Our sex lives."

Liam watched Izzy move toward the bed. The thin shirt she was wearing outlined what he'd always considered her best physical assets. He had been exploring her body for months and he wasn't close to knowing all he wanted to know. He frowned as her words registered, "You and Cynthia were talking about your sex lives?"

Izzy sat down on the side of the bed and pulled her pillow from under Liam's head. "Did you know your dad is sleeping with Cynthia?"

Liam moved away as Izzy fluffed her pillows wildly and tried to straighten

236

the top sheet, "I can live without knowing who my dad is having sex with. What did you tell Cynthia about me?" When Izzy didn't say anything, he added, "You did talk about me – right?"

Izzy laughed, then she hiccupped, "Sorry, Liam, I honestly can't divulge that. I don't kiss and tell."

"I'm the one you kissed. It's others you're not supposed to tell."

After some effort, Izzy managed to get the bedding the way she wanted it. She had just put her head on the pillow when she heard Sophie cry. "Oh shit. How does she always know the moment I lie down?" She sat up and slid her legs out of bed.

Liam reached out for her arm, "Let Lisa get up with her."

"Her door was closed and everyone's sleeping."

"It's her shift."

Izzy sat on the edge of the bed while Sophie continued to cry. "She's not going to get up, Liam. She doesn't want to look after Sophie. She doesn't want to be a mother. Why can't you see that?" Izzy got off the bed and grabbed her pants from the chair. She started pulling them on.

"She doesn't have a choice."

Liam's tone of finality, as if he would always have the last word on the subject, drove Izzy crazy. She took the pants off, tossed them aside and got back into bed, "Fine, have it your way. She's a mother and you're a father and I'm –" she paused for a beat, "not. You go and tend to your screaming daughter and I'll go to sleep."

Liam got up and left the room. He was back in a few moments.

Izzy looked over her shoulder and said, "Well, that didn't take long."

"She took her soother and went right to sleep." Liam climbed back into the bed. He moved close to Izzy's back and lifted her hair to kiss her neck. He slid his free hand up under her top to rest on the swell of her breast. As he moved his hand, he whispered close to her ear, "Did you tell Cynthia about this."

Izzy laughed and turned in the bed to wrap her arms around him, "No, I did not." She caught her breath as his hands continued to wander. She pulled his face towards her, "I should have told her I have some sort of sorcerer in my bed. I can't think of another explanation for why you can be so annoying one minute then so enticing the next."

THIRTY-FIVE

Justin pulled Izzy's Highlander into the parking lot of *The Sea Shed* and everyone piled out. Lisa-Marie adjusted the straps of the dress Izzy had given her for her birthday as she told Maddy and Jesse, "They have the best seafood here and the desserts are supposed to be fabulous. I can hardly wait. I'm starving."

Jesse elbowed Justin as they followed the girls towards the restaurant doors, "You'd never know that chick had a baby a few months ago, hey?" Justin ignored Jesse. He was better off paying attention to only half of what the guy had to say. It kept any irritation in check. Lisa-Marie did look hot in a dress and heels, with her long hair swinging around her like a streaked waterfall of honey coloured brilliance. The girls were waiting for them by the doors to the restaurant. Maddy had on her standard-issue, long-sleeved shirt. It looked elegant – white, with a crisp, turned-up collar. They were happy and carefree, giggling over some girl joke he knew he wouldn't even begin to understand.

Justin told himself to loosen up. He was out for the evening. He wasn't anyone's keeper. He didn't want to spend the night thinking about what he did or did not feel for Lisa-Marie, worrying about Maddy, or being annoyed by Jesse.

Maddy grabbed the wine list when they were settled at a table inside the restaurant, "Let's order a bottle of wine to celebrate Leez being seventeen whole years old and looking like a smoking-hot fox in that dress. It will be my treat."

Justin was sure that someone would challenge the fact that they weren't all nineteen but no one did.

Their server brought two baskets of bread over and smiled at Jesse as she excused herself and scooted behind him to leave a pile of plates in the middle of the table. He smiled back and said, "No problem, babe."

As the waitress walked away, Maddy glared at Jesse, "Real nice, asshole." She pushed her chair back, got up and walked towards the restaurant's main entrance. Justin and Lisa-Marie watched in stunned silence as Maddy went out the door. Lisa-Marie stared at Justin. She turned her gaze to Jesse, "What happened, what's going on?"

Jesse stood up and dropped his napkin on the table, "Hang on, I'll fix things up."

He walked out of the restaurant and caught up with Maddy on the sidewalk. She was pacing back and forth, hugging her shirt close. He reached out to grab her arm. She wrenched away and refused to look at him. "You're freaking out again, Maddy. That's all it is. Come on. We're going to walk back into the restaurant together and get on with having a good time." His voice was matter-of-fact. He saw her slender shoulders start to shake. He knew she'd soon be weeping uncontrollably if he didn't head that off. He pulled her over to him and wrapped her in a tight hug, whispering in her ear, "Don't cry now. It's Leez's birthday. We're all going to have fun tonight, you included."

Maddy nodded her head as it rested against Jesse's chest, "Okay, Jess. Sorry. I'm alright now, I promise." Jesse kept his arm wrapped around her waist as they walked back into the restaurant. He pulled out her chair and she sat down.

"There, problem solved. Now, where was I? Right, telling you guys about the awesome place they have lined up for me in Palo Alto." Jesse grabbed a chunk of bread and slavered on the chive-butter as he spoke.

Lisa-Marie got up, "Come on, Maddy. Let's hit the little girl's room." *The Sea Shed's* bathroom was a pleasure Lisa-Marie had discovered when she'd had lunch there with Izzy.

The restaurant was a converted house on Dearborn's waterfront and the owners had made the most of the opportunities each room presented to promote an ocean theme. A room on the main floor had been outfitted to resemble a luxury ship's washroom. Brass fittings glinted everywhere against dark wood. Small porthole windows were set high on the walls. At one end of the room, a magnificent ocean mural blended into a real fountain with a stunning mermaid statue curled atop. The counter near the sinks contained a mixture of soaps and hand lotions.

As they stood by the round mirrors and fixed their makeup and hair, Lisa-Marie asked, "You okay?"

Maddy tried out one of the lotions and put the back of her hand up close to Lisa-Marie's face so she could catch a whiff, "Nice, hey?... I'm fine. Sometimes I get feeling weird about things. It's nothing."

"Things with Jesse? What's going on with the two of you?"

Maddy fluffed her hair and peered at her face in the mirror. She leaned forward to remove a smudge of mascara from under her eye. "We're here to celebrate your birthday, Leez. Lighten up. Let's have fun tonight. Come on, we better get out there before those piggy boys eat all that bread."

A second bottle of wine followed the first and by the time they left the restaurant, Justin could see that Lisa-Marie was weaving slightly. The breeze blowing off the water made her dress dance in flirty waves around her legs. He pulled his eyes away and stared out at the ocean. A white blanket was settling down over the masts of the boats along the dock. The eerie sound of a fog horn echoed through the mist that swirled up and off the boardwalk.

"Hey, Justin," Lisa-Marie called out, "Let's head up to the hotel and see if they'll let me in. They've got a live band tonight." He looked over at the birthday girl as she pointed to the huge sign at the top of the hill. It advertised what was happening in the hotel. She twirled around, swinging her hips and swaying her arms over her head, "We could do some dancing."

Justin thought, why not? They were bound to refuse to serve Lisa-Marie. But he was wrong. They entered the Dearborn Hotel bar to the crashing beat of a back-to-the-eighties band. The small dance floor was crammed with people. Maddy and Lisa-Marie wove their way over to a small table in the corner. En route, they managed to get a good deal of attention from the local guys at the bar.

Jesse elbowed Justin and raised his voice to say, "Redneck central, hey?" The tone of the evening went downhill from then on. Justin watched with a degree of detachment as Lisa-Marie downed a glass of beer and danced out onto the floor with Jesse in tow. Before he knew what was happening a few more rounds of empty glasses cluttered the table and the whole place got out of control. It wasn't that Lisa-Marie stood out; it seemed as though everyone was drunk.

With sweat flying off his hair, the band's drummer smashed his way through a solo that appeared to be building to some kind of explosive ending. A chick climbed up onto a table near the stage and pulled her shirt up to shake her naked breasts in time with the music while she hollered, "Bring it home, baby."

Justin turned away from that spectacle to see Lisa-Marie in the arms of a tall guy, slow dancing despite the strong upbeat of the music. When the guy's hand came to rest on her ass, Justin decided it was time to pull the plug on that. He walked onto the dance floor and tapped the guy on the arm, "Hands off, buddy." He pulled Lisa-Marie close as the drum solo ended. The band swung into what was possibly the only slow song they knew. Lisa-Marie wrapped her arms around his neck and melted against him.

Back at the table, Maddy's eyes gleamed as she said, "Better be careful, Justin. You looked like a jealous boyfriend storming onto that dance floor." She laughed as she helped Lisa-Marie dig around under the table to find her heels and get them on back her feet.

Out in the parking lot, Lisa-Marie and Maddy giggled nonstop as they climbed into the back seat of the SUV together. The drive to the lake was a noisy trip filled with loud singing, uncontrolled laughter and repeated requests to turn up the music.

Justin dropped Maddy and Jesse at the Camp. He then drove down Izzy's twisting drive, thankful he had stuck to his resolution not to drink. He parked the vehicle by the back of the workshop. Lisa-Marie stumbled as she got out of the car. With a firm grip on her arm, Justin walked her towards the cabin door. The lights were on and he could see Liam outlined in the kitchen window.

"Do you want me to go in with you, Leez?"

Lisa-Marie shook off Justin's arm and drew herself up to her full height, "I am perfectly fine, Justin. Thank you for a nice evening. I think this might have been my best birthday ever."

He watched her disappear into the cabin. As he walked back to his own place he tried to shake off a feeling of guilt for bringing her home in such shape. But what the hell was he supposed to do? He wasn't her friggin' father. For that matter, neither was Liam, so why worry?

As he walked along the dark trail, Justin relived each emotion he had felt from the moment he had seen Lisa-Marie in another guy's arms. There had been a blasting surge of jealousy that had made his hand curl into a fist. That had been followed by pure lust as Lisa-Marie moved with him on the dance floor.

He knew that all he had to do was say the right words and she would change her mind about being just friends. But knowing he could turn on the charm didn't mean he should. They'd end up sleeping together. Then what? She was seventeen. He was only twenty but the difference in age between them seemed far more than three years. She had the whole mess of her feelings about Sophie hanging over her head. She was going back to school and to Europe in the fall. He'd be at university. A distance relationship with a high school girl was ridiculous. No ... they would go their separate ways after this summer, things would be no different than they'd been the previous year. Justin walked into the dark cabin and promised himself that he would take Misty up on her offer to go into town and see a movie. And he would do it soon.

✄✄✄✄

Lisa-Marie stumbled as she walked away from the kitchen door. She leaned against the wall, "Waiting up, Liam? You shouldn't have."

Liam stared at her, "I was getting Sophie's bottle. Have you been drinking?"

Lisa-Marie giggled, then she turned pale, "Oh my God ... I don't feel good."

Liam led her quickly to the sink and pulled her hair back, seconds before she got sick. He walked her over to a chair, "Sit down for a minute." He filled a glass with cold water, gave it to her and watched as she raised the glass to her lips with a shaking hand. "You better go to bed." As she headed past him towards the stairs, he handed her an empty bowl, "Keep this close, just in case." Liam cleaned up the mess before reheating Sophie's bottle and heading down to the living room.

✄✄✄✄

After feeding and settling the baby, Liam went back to the bedroom. He sat on the side of the bed and asked, "Are you awake?"

Izzy moaned, "I am now. Is something wrong?"

"Lisa-Marie just got home. She's drunk. She threw up."

"Oh ... yuck. Is she alright?"

"She's gone to bed. She shouldn't be drinking."

Izzy sighed and tried to get comfortable, "Well, she was celebrating her birthday."

"Her seventeenth birthday, Izz."

Izzy straightened out the quilt and thumped her pillow, "You might be a bit paranoid about drinking. Maybe this is more about you than her." She had settled her head on the pillow before she realized that the silence in the room had taken on a strained quality.

When Liam finally spoke his voice shook, "That is the shittiest thing you have ever said to me."

242

She considered his words before agreeing, "You're right. I'm sorry. It was an unfair thing to say."

Liam rolled over and pulled Izzy close. "I'm worried about her. Is there anything wrong with that?"

Izzy shrugged, "Seems pretty normal, all things considered."

THIRTY-SIX

The Crater Lake Timber Wolves and the North Island Tricksters warmed up on the ball field across from the parking lot of the Dearborn Community Hall. As Alex walked around the field securing the bases, Bethany ran after him, score sheet in hand. When she caught up, Alex brushed the dirt from his hands and shrugged helplessly, "You'll have to ask Beulah about the line-up. I have no idea."

She stared at him, "But you're supposed to be coaching the Tricksters. You have to know who's playing where."

"Beulah takes care of that side of things."

Over on the edge of the field near the dugout, Arianna hooted with excitement, "Oh man, Leez, look at how good Dylan is. We are going to smoke these wannabe ball players." She grabbed Lisa-Marie's arm in her own and did a do-si-do spin.

Dylan wound up and blasted the ball across the plate. Justin, who was crouched down behind home base, flung his arm out and the ball made a thunking sound as it landed in his glove. Arianna shouted, "Hey, Tricksters – feel like eating a bit of crow?" She danced across the field and past the other team's dugout, chanting, "Caw, caw, caw, we're going to beat you so black and blue your own mothers won't recognize you." The Tricksters booed right back at her.

Beulah had a wide grin pasted on her face, "Now that's what I call spirit." She shouted out to the rest of the team, "Let's pick up the chatter."

Izzy had unpacked the Timber Wolves uniforms and had them washed. As she stood in the field waiting for someone to throw her the ball, she looked over at Josie and saw her tugging at her baseball shirt. Izzy was glad she wasn't the only one who found the uniform a bit tighter than it had been three years before. On third base, Liam looked exactly the same as he always had and seeing him in that uniform was like walking back in time. She couldn't bring herself to glance over at the spot in the dugout where Caleb had always stood. She was afraid of seeing a shade of him still there.

Izzy's eyes were more than once on Justin. The first time she saw him crouch down and adjust the catcher's mask on his blonde hair, she had blinked back tears. She had turned quickly away, only to find Liam at her side. He dropped an arm around her shoulder and pulled her close.

As the warm-up time ended, Beulah called the Timber Wolves in for a huddle. "Justin, listen up; don't hold back when you're throwing to Cook on first. I know she's a midget and she looks as old and dried up as a prune but she can take the heat." Beulah turned to Cook and asked, "Am I right?" Cook smiled broadly and adjusted her ball cap.

Beulah continued, "Reg, I'm counting on you to be all over the outfield though I'll kick your sorry butt if I see you anywhere near Josie at shortstop. She might want your assistance in the bedroom but she sure as hell doesn't need it out here on the ball field." Reg tried to grab Josie and kiss her. She pushed him off and frowned as she banged her fist into her open ball glove.

"I know you can handle third, Liam. Now listen, Izzy and Lisa-Marie, unless that ball is coming right at you, let Reg get it. No offense, Lisa, but you're not much of a ball player, are you? And frankly, Izzy, you never were."

Izzy rolled her eyes at Lisa, "You'd think this was the bloody World Series."

Lisa-Marie grinned back. "If it was, you can bet I'd be planning on throwing it. A coach like Beulah is just not inspiring my loyalty."

Izzy hooted loudly and earned a frown from Beulah who shook her head and went on without missing a beat, "Arianna is going to be right behind you at second, Dylan. Feel free to fake out a pitch to her anytime you want ... the girl can catch." Dylan moved close to Arianna and gave her a quick hug.

"Okay, let's get out on that field and show those Tricksters what the Crater Lake Timber Wolves are made of." Beulah raised her hands to her mouth and intoned an unearthly howl. Soon Liam, Izzy, Reg, Josie and Cook were howling, as well. Arianna danced over to the older team members, dragging Dylan by the arm. She howled while Dylan did his best to join in. When it was obvious that the game wasn't going to get started until Justin and Lisa-Marie made an effort, they walked over and gave the howl a try. Beulah shook her head, "Pathetic, but you'll get the hang of it. Hit the field."

Beulah ran over to the Tricksters dugout. She snapped at Alex, "You're supposed to be giving these kids a pep talk ... you could hear a pin drop in here." Beulah pulled the kids into a huddle and got them raising their heads and cawing loudly. She stood back and studied her team. Alex had gotten the band to spring for uniforms, black with white trim. She hoped they wouldn't be mistaken for magpies.

Beulah turned to see several members of the Timber Wolves glaring at her. She whacked hands with a few kids and ran back to the other side of the field.

Jillian walked out from the backstop fence where she had been chatting with Roland and stood behind the plate. She shouted, "Play ball," and the game began.

Beulah kept Robbie busy running back and forth with messages for Alex about what he should be doing to coach her team. At one point, she was seen urging one of the Trickster players to head for home. The Timber Wolves howled for real when that happened but Beulah just laughed at them. At the end of the fifth inning, with the Tricksters down by two runs, she announced, "That's that. I'm jumping ship." She trotted off to the sound of loud boos from one side and rousing cheers from the other.

After switching over to the Timber Wolves' dugout, Alex said, "I can't help you guys out in the coaching department. To tell you the truth, I don't know that much about baseball."

Liam smacked his dad on the back, "They didn't play any baseball over at Springhill?"

Alex burst out laughing, "Nope, no baseball going on there. Believe it or not, I did manage to get a black belt in karate during my stay." He crouched down and raised his leg in a high kick.

At the bottom of the seventh inning, the Tricksters had the game tied. The older members of the Timber Wolves were coming in from the field feeling more and more winded as each inning passed. Dylan's pitching and Justin's catching had become a synchronicity of beauty but it wasn't enough. The Tricksters were young and hungry and they had Beulah biting at them the whole time.

Lisa-Marie stood on deck waiting her turn at bat. She elbowed Arianna, "You must have been in heaven staring at Dylan's butt the whole game. Nothing like baseball pants to make a guy look hot. I think second base had the best view in the park." Arianna shrugged and swung the bat to warm-up. Lisa-Marie went on, "I saw you guys laughing together and him hugging you. What's up? Spill the beans."

"We're friends, Leez. That's all it is ... nothing to tell. Turns out Dylan doesn't want a girlfriend." Arianna watched the next pitch and let out a loud moan as Josie struck out. She headed for the plate, but not before reaching over to slap Josie on the back, "No worries. We can still beat them. I feel a home run coming on."

Lisa-Marie waited her turn at bat, convinced that she would soon share Josie's fate. She glanced at Dylan who had the place behind her in the batting roster. Any guy who didn't want a girlfriend that looked like Arianna needed his head examined. A thudding sound as bat connected with ball drew her attention back to the field. She watched Arianna dash to first and then sprint to second base on the strength of well executed grounder.

After striking out, Lisa-Marie shrugged at Dylan's frown and made her way back to the dugout to scrunch in beside Justin. "I suck at baseball."

He nudged her, "Try a bunt next time. That should fake them out."

Lisa-Marie kept her voice casual when she asked, "How was your big date with Misty?"

Justin slid a bit further down on the bench and pulled at his ball cap. He had told Lisa-Marie he'd be going out with Misty. He figured if he didn't mention it, he'd look like an idiot since she was sure to find out. She had been quite nonchalant about it, telling him to have fun. She might as well have slapped him in the face.

⁂

The date had been a disaster. Misty was overly friendly from the moment he picked her up. She sat close beside him in Izzy's SUV on the way to town. She playfully grabbed fries off his plate when they had fish and chips at the outdoor café. He hated anyone eating food off his plate – a holdover from his group-home days. Then she cuddled close to him in the dark of the theatre. When the show finished and she suggested they take a drive down to the end of the road that ran along the waterfront, he was in no doubt as to what she had in mind. A few minutes into a bout of heavy kissing, he pushed her away.

"Misty, hold on. Listen ... I can't do this. I'm sorry."

She looked at him in utter disbelief, "You're joking, right?"

He moved over to the far side of the driver's seat, "There's someone else. We're not together and we're not going to be but I can't get my mind off her. I can't be with you when I'm thinking of someone else. It makes me feel like a total jerk."

Misty narrowed her eyes, "I think I would rather you had felt like a total jerk and made the effort. Why on earth did you ask me out?"

Justin stared at his hands gripping the steering wheel, "I wasn't sure about how I felt. I know that sounds lame. Sorry."

"Do I know her?"

Justin shook his head, "No, it's someone from Vancouver."

Misty slid over to her side of the car, "Well, let's not write off the whole evening. There's a bowling alley in town. We could go and play a game or two ... work off that popcorn since we aren't going to get any other kind of exercise."

⚜⚜⚜⚜

Justin sat up straight on the dugout bench, "It was a mistake. I shouldn't have asked her out."

Lisa-Marie felt a surge of relief wash over her as she said, "Oh ya ... well ... live and learn, right?"

Justin got up and grabbed a bat, "When did you become such a philosopher?" He nudged her as he walked to the edge of the dugout. "I should have taken you to the movie. We would have had fun together." Then he was walking out to home plate, swinging the bat while the catcalls of the other team surrounded him.

The Tricksters squeaked out a win. The Timber Wolves gave them a congratulatory howl and the Tricksters returned the kindness by running circles around them and cawing loudly; the exhibition game was over.

Alexander and Liam unloaded two gas barbecues from Beulah's truck and rolled them over to the picnic area beside the ball field. Some people helped to get tables set up and the food out; others hauled lawn chairs out of their vehicles. The smell of grilled hotdogs and hamburgers soon filled the area. Reg and Josie carried a huge pot of corn on the cob over from the Community Hall kitchen. Izzy had made a massive bowl of potato salad that she placed in the center of the table which was already loaded with piles of buns and dozens of iced cupcakes that Bethany had supplied for dessert. Liam dragged over a pair of coolers filled with soft drinks.

Arianna mixed in so well with the other team that she encouraged all the young people to mingle. The adults hung back in a circle of chairs. Reg pointed a can of Coke at Liam who held Sophie on his lap, "Our baseball days may be behind us, Liam. I know Caleb would be rolling in his grave at the performance we gave out there on that field." Everyone laughed.

Izzy looked around the circle and thought that Reg was right. Times had certainly changed. Liam was at her side while Robbie sat cross-legged at her feet eating what had to be his fourth hotdog. She smiled at Lisa who jogged by

248

on her way to grab a few Cokes from the cooler before joining Justin where he sat at a picnic table talking to a couple of guys from the Tricksters. Izzy thought about the way she and Liam had sped through a few months of honeymoon time before entering a freeway ramp that led directly to parenthood. And Sophie wasn't their only responsibility. There was Robbie to consider and Lisa. Both of them had become part of the family they were creating as they went along. No one had written a rule book for the connections that held them all together.

Izzy gazed across the field. Dylan stood close to Arianna. He had come to Izzy with his own version of what had happened the night of the talent show, not sparing himself or hiding the anguish he felt for having hurt Arianna. But Dylan shared something else of importance with Izzy. Arianna's gesture of compassion had broken something apart inside of him. He had lost the tough guy attitude and he couldn't seem to find it again.

When Beulah finished flipping burgers and doling out hotdogs, she plopped into a lawn chair in the circle of adults and waved a copy of *Shoeless Joe* in the air. "Let's discuss how baseball is a metaphor for life. This book is now number one on my list of great books."

Izzy laughed. She pushed her chair back, "Hold that thought, Beulah. I want in on this conversation when I come back." She grabbed the diaper bag and asked Robbie, "Want to walk over to the washrooms with me? I've got to change Sophie and heat up her bottle." Robbie nodded and jumped up from the grass.

✻✻✻✻

Justin found Jesse hunched over a table in the corner of the computer lab at Micah Camp. He pulled out a stool and rolled it over to the table. He watched the guy's hands fly over the keys as he asked, "When are you heading down south?"

Jesse didn't take his eyes from the screen, "A week from tomorrow."

"What happens with Maddy when you go?"

"I sincerely hope she gets her shit together. It's been how many months she's been here now, working with Izzy? And I tell you, I'm not seeing a big improvement. She still gets totally out of control and acts like a nut case." Jesse gave Justin a quick glance, "You saw her the other night ... you know what I mean."

"Are you going to break things off with her before you go?"

Jesse continued to type, "It's not like that with us. We're not a couple."

"Right," Justin narrowed his eyes. He shoved Jesse's arm to get his full

249

attention, "Who are you trying to fool? Lisa says Maddy thinks she's going to California with you."

Jesse turned from the computer and stared at Justin, "No fucking way did Maddy say that. She knows we aren't together like that. She's said so herself, over and over."

"Uh huh ... and girls always tell us the whole truth."

A stunned expression settled on Jesse's face as he stared at Justin, "Shit, you have a point there."

Justin hooked his hands under the stool, "I hate being the one to say this, man ... but she's using you. Don't get me wrong, I'm not dumping on her. She's messed up. Everyone can see that. She's got some kind of dream of the two of you going to California and it's all about hiding from her own problems. Why else is Izzy getting nowhere with her?"

Jesse grabbed a couple of pens and tapped them on the edge of the table. "How am I supposed to know why Izzy's not doing her job? I thought I was helping Maddy, for shit sakes."

"All you're doing is helping her stay screwed up. Break things off with her now. Don't wait until the last minute."

"I don't know ... I'm not sure that's a good idea. She gets pretty crazy."

"You'll be going soon, anyway. Go and talk to Izzy first so she can keep an eye on Maddy."

THIRTY-SEVEN

"I saw something a while back and I've been wondering if I should mention it to you." Jillian glanced over at Roland as she pulled a brush through her thick hair. He was sitting on the side of the bed buffing his shoes with a snapping twist of the beige material in his hands.

"If it has to do with anyone's private life, I don't think you should." Roland folded the cloth and put it in the top drawer of his night stand. He walked over to the closet and flipped through a rack of ties on the door; he pulled one out, held it against his shirt and frowned. The next one met with his approval. He turned towards his reflection in the bevelled mirror and whipped the tie into a knot.

"It has to do with Jesse and that Maddy girl, but it most certainly concerns what should have been an aspect of their private lives so I'd better keep quiet, as you say." Jillian sat down on the edge of the bed and watched Roland choose a pair of cufflinks and matching tie pin from the case on his dresser.

As he adjusted his cuffs, he said, "If it relates to a resident then that is obviously a different matter." Roland turned back to the mirror and inserted the tie pin.

"The night of the bonfire when I was coming over here, I saw Maddy and Jesse in a fight on the trail. She seemed out of control, slapping at him and screaming." Jillian followed Roland out to the kitchen and poured them both a cup of coffee. She sat down at the table.

Roland picked up his cup and went to the fridge to get the cream. Though Jillian would not mention his cream consumption, she refused to make it easy. He stirred the white stream through the coffee, "How did Mr. McAlister respond to her behaviour?"

"He was just so sweet to her. He held her back from slapping him until she started crying, then he put his arms around her. There was something about the way he held her ... it got to me. I've always liked him."

Roland frowned at Jillian's reaction. The assumptions she made about people had him questioning her research ability. What she didn't know about Jesse McAlister would fill a book and yet she liked him and thought he was sweet. Admittedly, the young man had changed during his time at Micah Camp but calling him sweet was a stretch. "Thank you for telling me about this incident, Jill. Did you collect your mail yesterday? I noticed there were three letters from the university."

Jillian grabbed a dry piece of toast and munched on it, "My supervisor sent me a teaching contract. He says I have more than enough data now for two dissertations. He wants me back on campus for the fall semester. He says I can write it all up and teach while I'm at it. The idea of teaching again makes me shudder."

Roland was standing with his back to Jillian as he spread butter over his slice of toast. Before he turned, he composed his face and resolved to speak in a nonchalant tone. He walked to the table, sat down across from her and asked, "Have you begun making plans to leave?"

She stared at him, then got up and put her coffee cup in the sink. "If that's all you have to say to me, then I guess I'll start." She walked out without a backward glance.

※※※※※

Dylan stood in the doorway of Izzy's office. "I heard you wanted to talk to me." He had come straight from the kitchen and he was still wearing his white apron.

"Yes ... do you have a few minutes right now?"

"Sure, what's up?" Dylan sat down in the chair and slapped his cook's hat against his leg. "I've got about a half an hour before I need to start putting the pizzas together."

"I wanted to talk about whatever problem you seem to have with Robbie."

Dylan's voice took on a defensive tone, "I don't like little kids. He's always hanging around the kitchen ... under foot. He could get hurt. The kitchen isn't a friggin' playground and I'm no babysitter."

Izzy took a deep breath. Dylan had more than one demon haunting him and it was about time to bring this particular one out into the light. She looked him in the eye, "I think I know what's going on and it has nothing to do with the kitchen being a dangerous place."

252

Dylan got out of his chair and snapped, "So, now you're a mind reader, hey? What about me taking the lead and you waiting for me to say stuff?" He paced the office; the slapping sound of his hat against his leg picked up speed. He finally sat back down in his chair and stared at the floor. Silence stretched out between them.

"Do you trust me, Dylan?"

"Why?"

Izzy smiled, "If you trust me, you don't get to ask why."

Dylan shook his head in resignation, "Okay ... I trust you."

"Take a deep breath and tell me what you're afraid of when Robbie comes into the kitchen."

Dylan was up and pacing again, "I'm not afraid of anything. I don't have time to waste on this kind of crap. I don't want to talk about that kid. Why are you doing this?"

Izzy waited until the pacing had run its course. When Dylan looked over at her, she said, "Trust me on this one. I think it's an important next step for you."

He walked back to his chair and slumped into it. He twisted the hat into a tight knot and the words rushed out, "What if I wanted to hurt him and I couldn't stop? You wouldn't want me to take that next step, would you?"

Izzy watched as fear and anguish practically overcame the young man sitting in front of her. She reached out and placed her hands over Dylan's. She spoke slowly and clearly, "What you did to that other child was many years ago. You were too young to have been fully responsible for those actions. You are not that helpless boy anymore. You know the consequences of your actions." She removed her hands and sat back in her chair. "Have you ever had any thoughts or fantasies about touching Robbie?"

"No ... never. But how can I be sure I won't? Wouldn't it be better to play it safe and avoid the kid?"

"Since you came to Micah Camp, have you had any type of sexual fantasy about anyone?"

Dylan's face turned red and he shifted uneasily in his chair. "Only Jesse, but you already know about that."

"Jesse's an adult; you're an adult. You happen to be gay and you have a healthy attraction to another adult male. You're not attracted to a child. Give yourself and Robbie a break. Let him hang around the kitchen. Get used to being around him." Izzy got up to grab a piece of paper and a pen from her desk. She passed them to Dylan, "Let's work on some ground rules that will make you feel more comfortable."

Dylan scribbled something in large letters across the page and turned it so Izzy could read the words – *I don't want to be alone with him.*

"That's fine. I'll help you make sure that doesn't happen."

Dylan sat back in the chair and took a deep breath. He stared at Izzy, "I still might not like little kids. But I'll try."

⁂⁂⁂⁂

Later that afternoon, Izzy and Robbie were making their way home on the path through the thick trees. Izzy looked down at boy's dark head of hair, "Robbie, Robbie, McBobby ... I think you need a haircut soon. Maybe we should get Willow to give you a trim next time she comes over to cut Edward's hair."

"Only in the front though, I want my hair long like Dad and Liam."

Izzy smiled at the thought of the three of them, like peas in a pod. After a moment, she spoke in a serious tone, "I don't want you to go off anywhere alone with Dylan ... alright?"

"That wouldn't happen. He hates me." Robbie bent over to pick up a pine cone. He examined it and then threw it to the side of the trail. "How come I can't be alone with Dylan? He wouldn't hurt me."

"How do you know that?"

"I just know ... I knew when the dog was going to hurt my baby cousin."

"Whew, that sounds scary."

"I saw the light change. It went crazy, spitting all over the place around that dog. Like those sparks you see when guys are welding. Anyway, I knew that dog was heading straight for the baby."

Izzy kept her voice curious and asked, "What happened?" Her heart was thumping at the images Robbie's story raised.

Robbie pulled up his shirt to reveal a thick white scar running along his forearm, "I grabbed the baby but did that dog ever take a bite out of me. I needed a whole bunch of stitches and my mom raised hell with my auntie for keeping a dog who would do something like that."

Izzy glanced at the scar on Robbie's arm, "I believe you know things. But I still don't want you to go off alone with Dylan."

"Okay. Want me to tell you what happened in the new Spiderman comic? It's pretty awesome."

⁂⁂⁂⁂

"I was thinking that maybe you and I should cool things. I'll be leaving in a week and I have a ton of stuff to do before I go." Jesse blurted out this idea as he and Maddy were lying in his bed together.

There was a long, awkward silence before Maddy said, "Sure, if that's what you want." She slid out of bed and started grabbing her clothes from the floor.

"Hey, you don't have to leave this second."

Maddy yanked her pants up, "I get that you're busy. No problem."

Jesse jumped up and reached for her arm, "Look, we both know you're not yourself and things aren't getting better. I talked to Izzy this afternoon. I told her you're not going to California with me. You know we never once talked about that happening but Justin says you've been telling Lisa-Marie it's a done deal."

Maddy jerked her arm away and pulled her shirt over her head, "Thanks a lot for running to Izzy behind my back and making me look like a complete idiot in front of everyone." She pushed her hair out of her eyes, "Like I said, Jess, it isn't a big deal. You don't have to rub my face in the fact that I have problems. I get it ... you wouldn't want to be tied down with a psycho like me when you fly off into the sun to become a famous gamer."

"It was you that never wanted us to be a couple."

Maddy whirled on him and smashed her hands into his chest, "What a cop-out. You make me sick. Tell me to my face, right now ... would you take me to California with you if you thought I wanted us to be together like a real couple?"

Her words hung in the air between them. Jesse couldn't hide how obvious the answer to that question was. He wouldn't want to be stuck with Maddy the way she was now, especially when his life was heading for the fast lane.

"Ya, like I thought." Maddy glared at him one last time before she slammed out the door.

THIRTY-EIGHT

Bethany pulled up a chair across from Jillian in the deserted dining room. She sipped her coffee and said, "Jill, let's say – hypothetically speaking – you see your partner in a very heated argument with another woman. They're both pretty worked up and when you ask what's going on, your partner says it's nothing for you to worry about and walks away. What would you think?"

Jillian snorted as she riffled through a stack of papers, "He's definitely sleeping with her. Why else the emotion? Why else wouldn't he explain?"

"That's exactly what I thought."

The room was quiet. Jillian glanced up at Bethany and saw the distressed look on her face. "Oh my God, Beth, I'm sorry. I shouldn't have said that. Listen, I've had a few crappy relationships and I'm jaded. I don't know Beulah at all; maybe what you're talking about means something totally different with her. I should never have been so flippant. Don't pay any attention to me." Tears shone in the corners of Bethany's eyes as she looked down at the table. Jillian reached across to squeeze her hand, "Talk to her, Beth. That's the best thing to do."

❧❧❧❧❧

"I want to know who she is, Beulah ... that red-headed woman you were talking with on the night of the talent show."

Beulah gazed up over the top of her bifocals and frowned. Bethany was sitting across from her. Lunch was finished and Beulah was about to head out to deliver the bread. "That was weeks ago and you're asking me now? I said it was nothing for you to be concerned about."

"I've decided I am concerned. I want you to tell me who she is."

THE LIGHT NEVER LIES

"What is your problem, Beth? When did we enter a twilight zone where I can't talk to anybody I want to talk to?"

"My problem is that you won't answer my question."

Beulah pushed back her chair and shoved a pile of invoices into the briefcase, "She's someone from the bowling team. There, are you satisfied?"

"No ... why would you be arguing with someone from your bowling team? What's her name?"

"Her name is Abbey Greene. She was pissed off because I decided not to join up for the spring league."

"Ya, right ... that sounds totally believable." Bethany paused to be sure she had Beulah's attention. "Look me right in the eye and tell me there's nothing going on between you and that woman."

Beulah laid the briefcase down on the table and walked around to Bethany. She drew her up and into her arms. She tipped her chin up, kissed her and said, "There is nothing going on between me and Abbey Greene."

After Beulah left the A-Frame, Bethany sat outside and watched the light dance off the rippling water of the lake. She would never take the boat out again but she missed being on the water and the peace that she had felt while fishing. Dan's actions had ruined all of that for her. As she considered his betrayal, she suddenly knew that Beulah had cheated on her and had looked her straight in the eye and lied about it. Over the years, there was one thing Bethany had learned very well – she knew how to recognize betrayal when it was right in front of her, but she had never figured out how to see it coming. She got up and went into the bedroom to haul out her old suitcase.

⚘⚘⚘⚘

Beulah walked into the quiet A-Frame a few hours later. Even the dogs were subdued. Looking morose, they curled together in the corner. A single sheet of paper lying on the middle of the kitchen table caught Beulah's eye. She went over, picked it up and read the words.

I know you lied – I know you slept with that woman. I've moved over to the Camp and I'm staying in Jillian's cabin until I decide what to do. I'll be at the bakery each morning, as usual. If you try to bully me even a bit, you'll be on your own there, too.

Beulah put the paper down in the exact spot where she had found it. She stared at it for a minute or two. Then she walked into the kitchen and grabbed a bottle out of a high cupboard. She uncapped it with one hand while using the other to grab a glass. She poured the whiskey and took a long, deep drink. She walked into the living room and sat down. It was Saturday – no need to worry about lighting the fire in the bread oven. Good timing, all things considered. There was nothing at all to stop her from giving one hundred percent of her attention to that bottle.

❧❧❧❧

"Beth, I'm so sorry," Izzy reached out to place her hand on Bethany's arm as she passed her the box of Kleenex. "Are you sure about all of this? That she lied?"

"She admitted all of it when I showed up at the bakery this morning. You know how high-handed Beulah can be. She thinks I'm pulling a tantrum by moving out. She threw her affair in my face as if it was all my fault ... I was the one who went crazy after the accident ... I was the one who wouldn't have sex with her ... I was the one who changed all the rules by wanting something more out of my life. She'd been sleeping with that woman since February, when I had to go down to Victoria to see Lisa-Marie, and she didn't stop until almost the end of April. And get this, Izzy ... Liam knew all about it. Did he say anything to you?" Izzy shook her head. "I know Beulah thinks she can get away with all of this because she doesn't believe I'd actually leave her."

"Is she right about that?"

"At first I wasn't sure myself. But, you know what? I'm not a stupid woman, no matter what Beulah thinks about me. Since I've been working with Jill, I see other things that my life could be. I know I had a hard time after the accident and that I grabbed onto the idea of having a child like my life depended on it. Maybe people think that taking courses at my age is more craziness. But it isn't." Bethany sat up straight, "I know I can't stay on here at the Camp forever. Right now, I feel more desperate about leaving Crater Lake than I do about leaving Beulah. This has been my home for so long. I love it here."

Izzy sat back in surprise before she said, "Listen to me, Beth. No matter what happens between you and Beulah, you don't need to leave here. We have plenty of land. We'll build you your own cabin if that's what you need. Never think you have to leave."

"I couldn't let you guys do something like that for me."

"You would have let Liam father your child but you won't let us build you a place to live? That doesn't make much sense."

"I guess if you put it that way, it does sound kind of silly. Thanks. It makes

258

me feel better to know I have choices." Tears were running down Bethany's face again.

Izzy got up and drew her into a tight hug.

After Bethany left the office, Izzy sat staring out towards the lake. Her clenched hands and tight neck muscles made her realize something was wrong. She willed herself to relax. Beulah hadn't cheated on or lied to her. But there was something about the fact that Liam knew and hadn't said anything, that implicated him. Izzy's thoughts raced along to conclusions made inevitable by months of pushing down her feelings. *Beulah and Liam are two of a kind. They got to have their fun, didn't they? The rest of us should accept that and get on with our lives. They won't ever have to pay for what they did.*

Izzy caught herself as she heard the words running through her head - *like I had to pay with years of guilt for even thinking about cheating on Caleb.* She got out of her chair suddenly. Liam wasn't Beulah. Thinking like that, for whatever reason, was foolish; it wasn't right or fair, either. But she couldn't deny that Beulah's infidelity set her teeth on edge.

🙂🙂🙂🙂

"You told her what?" Liam's voice was strained.

Izzy held a sleeping Sophie in her arms and rocked back and forth on the cliff deck's swing chair. She saw the stunned look on Liam's face as he turned from putting a log into the chimney stove. "I know you heard exactly what I said, Liam. She shouldn't have to leave here because of what Beulah did."

"Don't you think it would be better to stay out of it ... let them work it out for themselves?"

"Obviously, I don't think that. And I'm not saying they shouldn't try to work things out. Don't twist my words. But just out of curiosity ... how exactly should Bethany work out the fact that Beulah cheated on her, lied about it and doesn't even appear to be all that sorry?"

Liam sat down beside Izzy on the swing. "You know how Beulah is. I'm sure she regrets what happened. It's going to take her a while to come around to that."

"Well, guess what? Maybe Bethany isn't going to be patient. And I can't say I blame her. Beulah thinks it was okay for her to have all the fun she wanted romping around in bed with Abbey Greene, then act now as though it doesn't matter, that there aren't consequences."

"Is this really about Beulah and Bethany, Izz?"

"Of course it's about them, what the hell is that supposed to mean? I think Bethany deserves to have options."

"What if those options make her think she doesn't need Beulah anymore?"

"Maybe that's been the problem in their relationship from the start. People shouldn't stay together because they need to; they should stay together because they want to."

"You make everything sound very simple."

A deep glow of anger had taken hold down in Izzy's gut the moment Liam hinted that her emotional investment might be about something other than Bethany and Beulah. He had no right to get in her head like that. "I know it isn't simple but I stand behind my offer to her."

"You could have discussed it with me first."

The anger leapt from her belly upwards to her mouth in a flash, "Right ... like the way you told me you knew for months that Beulah was screwing around? Or maybe like the way you kept quiet about what had happened between you and Lisa until I confronted you with it. Or what about this, Liam ... the way you've dodged every single discussion about what the hell we're going to do to ensure some kind of stable future for ourselves and this child," Izzy jostled Sophie a bit for effect. "Like those discussions we could have had, Liam?" She got up, thrust the sleeping baby into his arms and walked off towards the cabin.

THIRTY-NINE

L isa-Marie hurried to finish her bowl of cereal when she saw Liam coming into the kitchen. The less she had to interact with him, especially first thing in the morning, the better her whole day would be.

"You need to be back here by ten o'clock tonight." Liam was reaching in the fridge for the milk as he spoke. Lisa-Marie felt her stomach clench.

"Ya, ya, ya ...," she was out of her chair and moving away.

"Edward can't cover for you anymore with Sophie. With the amount of morphine he's on, it isn't safe."

She jammed her feet into her runners; her head was down and tears clouded her vision. Why did he want to say a shitty thing like that – trying to make her feel bad, throwing it in her face that Edward was getting worse? She felt a stab of guilt, followed by anger. Edward said he didn't mind filling in for her and Liam knew damn well that Edward never tried to pick Sophie up. He rocked her cradle or gave her the soother. It was none of Liam's business.

"Can you put your bowl in the sink? I feel like a servant around here some days." Liam slumped into a chair at the table.

Lisa-Marie's T-shirt rode up her side as she leaned past Liam to grab the empty dish. She banged the bowl into the sink, "Happy now?"

"Do you think that shirt is appropriate for work?"

Her eyes widened, "How the hell is what I'm wearing any of your business?"

She watched as a look of surprise flitted across Liam's face. He shrugged and looked uncomfortable, "It's pretty skimpy."

"That's the last friggin' straw. Who do you think you are? You don't get to make comments about my clothes." She could feel a flush of ugly red colour

261

spreading across her face. "That's it ... I've had it. I'm leaving and I won't be coming back." Tears blurred her way as she left the kitchen, crossed the deck and hurried along the orchard path.

Liam saw Izzy standing at the far end of the kitchen. She was staring at him with a look of startled disbelief. He pushed his chair back and stood up. "Don't say it, okay? Don't say anything." He walked out the door and headed for the workshop.

✂✂✂✂

Through the front window of Jillian's cabin, Liam could see Bethany sitting at a table, typing. She looked up and the sight of him startled her. A moment later the door to the cabin opened. Bethany came out and sat down on the top step, hugging her knees. "I don't have much time. I have a couple of interviews to transcribe before Jillian gets back." He caught the chill in her voice.

Liam had always thought Bethany was pretty, in a sweet and unthreatening way. Something had changed. She was like a photo he had gotten used to seeing somewhat out of focus. Now she was all sharp detail. He stood at the bottom of the stairs and shielded his eyes from more than the sun, "I was just over at the bakery to drop off the eggs. Beulah's in bad shape and that kid you have working there ... what's her name?"

"Arianna."

"Ya ... she said Beulah hasn't come out of the A-Frame for the last two days. No bread, no deliveries, nothing. When the kid banged on the door the other morning, Beulah opened it, threw a bag of dog food at her and told her to feed the dogs and clean the bakery. Then she disappeared inside again. No one's seen her since."

Bethany stared at Liam as a flush of red worked its way up her neck. She put her hands up to her cheeks and shook her head, "What has this got to do with me? Beulah has no one but herself to blame for ending up alone at the A-Frame and in the bakery. I told her I would keep working. She's the one who had to have the last word and bully me into leaving. Fine, she can go to hell."

Liam shifted his weight and dug his hands into his jean pockets. He squinted up at Bethany. If there had been a point to his remarks, he no longer had the words to make it.

Bethany's eyes shone now with tears of anger, "I don't appreciate you coming over here and taking her side. I still can't believe you knew about her

262

and that woman for months and never said a single word. I thought you were my friend."

※※※※

Liam slammed his fist against the back door of the A-Frame until he heard something crash against it. Probably a shoe, he thought. He banged again and heard Beulah shout, "Get lost."

"Open up, Beulah ... unless you want me pounding on this door all night."

There were sounds of someone stumbling and the door opened a crack. Beulah peered out, "Hey, Liam, old buddy, didn't know it was you." The door swung open and Beulah ushered him inside. The cabin felt closed in and hot but it was meticulously clean. Liam was sure that if the curtains were opened, everything would gleam.

Wearing only one shoe, Beulah wobbled over to the recliner and flopped down. Liam saw an open bottle on the table near her chair. He watched as she splashed whiskey into her glass. She raised the bottle to him, "I'd invite you to join me but I know you aren't a drinking man." She waved her hand towards the sofa, "Sit down; take a load off." Her words were slurred. She sipped from the glass and stared past him at nothing at all.

Liam sat down. The cabin was quiet. Except for the heat, he wouldn't have minded hanging out here for a while. He found himself wondering when he had last had the time to sit in a quiet room with nothing but his own thoughts to ponder. It must have been a lifetime ago.

Beulah stared into the glass, "Some days there is nothing that I wouldn't give to be able to sit down with Caleb and have a drink." She snorted, "Wouldn't work out too well for you though, would it?"

"If Caleb was still around, I wouldn't have fallen in love with Izzy. Everything would have stayed the same. Nothing would have happened between Lisa and me. There'd be no Sophie."

Beulah nodded, "No Bethany with her near-death experience making her think our life together was shit. No fucking Abbey Greene ... no pun intended." Beulah choked out the last words and shrugged at her own double entendre.

"If you could turn back the clock, would you?"

"Damn right, in a heartbeat." The cabin was quiet except for the sound of more alcohol splashing into the glass. "Why are you here, Liam? Do you think there's anything you can say that will help?"

"I know there isn't."

Beulah narrowed her eyes at him and frowned, "Are you going to sit there and make me give myself a good, stiff kick in the butt? You're a great friend, you are."

"Tell me what Caleb would have said. You saw a side of him that I never did."

Beulah snorted, "Ya, a drinking side." She was thoughtful as she answered, "Caleb would have said ... *What we have here, Beulah, best case scenario, is a temporary setback; worst case, a game changer. But there are still a few innings to play. Life is like a game of baseball. You never know when a grand slam is going to change the whole damn outcome.* Then he'd have offered me that lucky watch." She nodded her head towards the watch on Liam's wrist.

Liam found himself smiling. The imitation of Caleb's way of putting things into perspective did help. He got up, pulled the watch from his wrist and put it down on the table. "A loaner," he said as he picked up the bottle. He screwed the cap on tight and walked over to the cupboard to put it away. He went back and took the glass from Beulah's hand and rinsed it out in the sink. "Go to bed, Beulah. Get some sleep. I'll get the fire in the oven going for you." Beulah got out of the chair and staggered as she reached out to swipe Liam on the back. She wove her way to the bedroom.

After he lit the fire and hung around long enough to make sure it would burn for the night, Liam headed home. For a multitude of reasons, he couldn't shake the familiar feel of that bottle in his hand.

✻✻✻✻

Lisa-Marie knocked on the door of Justin's cabin and walked in. She called out, "It's me." He was standing in the middle of the room buttoning up his shirt.

"Hey, Leez. I was just going to head over to Izzy's for dinner. What's up?"

Lisa-Marie sank onto a kitchen chair, folded her arms on the table and dropped her head down. After a moment, she raised her head enough to say, "I've run away from all of them. I'm not going back."

Justin watched Lisa-Marie stare out the window to the lake. The afternoon light caught the honey-blonde streaks in her hair and they flashed like gold. When she glanced over at him, her heart-shaped face was filled with an anguish he wasn't used to seeing.

"I was going to go back to the A-Frame. I stopped by after work but I can't stay there now that Auntie Beth's gone. Beulah is one mean drunk. She wouldn't even let me in. It's all so depressing." Lisa-Marie looked down and added, "What could have happened between the two of them? Old people shouldn't be having all this break-up drama."

264

"Why are you running away?"

Anger and frustration flashed in her eyes. "Liam is making me feel like I want to drive a stake straight into his heart. I can't even look at him, he makes me so mad. He won't stop bugging me. He's always on my case about something. This morning he nagged at me about wearing this T-shirt to work."

Lisa-Marie got up, folded her arms tight across her chest and paced the floor of the cabin. Justin watched her and thought that Liam had a point – though the guy seriously needed his head examined to have mentioned it. Why was she wearing a T-shirt like that to work? He couldn't even tell now that she had been pregnant. She looked like the girl he had known last summer. The sound of despair in her voice brought him out of his thoughts.

"He yaps at me because I get home late and picks on me about cleaning up after myself, and I know exactly what's behind all of it. Why can't he get it? I don't want to be a mother. The baby was a mistake. I just want to get on with my life."

Justin winced at her words, "Don't call Sophie a mistake, Leez."

She stopped suddenly and stared at him, "You've changed your tune from when you were saying Liam ruined my life because I was pregnant. She's the same baby, you know."

"That was before she was real. Then it was easy to think things like that."

Lisa-Marie came back to the table and sat down. There was pain in her voice that twisted his heart when she spoke. "I don't want her. I want to be a kid going into grade twelve. Liam won't let me do that. It's like he has ten bloody claws sunk into me; every single one of them has Sophie's face on it and he keeps digging them in deeper."

"You've got to lay off the vampire novels, Leez."

"Ha, ha ... this isn't funny. But now that you mention vampires, it is like he's sucking my life essence right out of me and trying to turn me into," Lisa-Marie paused and shuddered, "someone like them – old people who think the most important thing that can happen in a whole friggin' day is that a baby, who obviously has gas, is smiling."

"But it's not always gas. She did smile at me the other day."

Lisa-Marie shook her head in disgust, "Ya, well they've already sucked you into their baby booster club. I'm just saying, you better watch out. Pretty soon you'll be thinking it's more exciting to stay home on a Friday night and watch a baby spit up her formula than it is to go out and have fun like a regular guy."

Justin thought it best to change the subject, "What about working with Edward on his book? I thought you guys were getting close to finishing things up."

"I'll still go and work with Edward ... when Liam isn't around."

"Where are you going to live?"

Lisa-Marie looked across the table at him, "Can I stay here?"

He sat back in his chair and stared at her. He had been sure she was going to say that she would stay over at the Camp with her aunt. "This place is pretty small, Leez."

"I don't mind sleeping on the sofa. I could help out ... clean up a bit."

"Sure you can stay here if you want but you better take the loft."

"No, I don't want to sleep there," Lisa-Marie looked away. "Besides, you're the one with the back-breaking job. You take the bed. I'll take the sofa." A frown settled suddenly on her face, "I don't want to be in your way, though. If you want to bring someone home, just tell me. I'll go stay the night at the Camp with Auntie Beth or Maddy."

Justin laughed, "I'm not in the habit of bringing anyone over here."

"Well, if you change your mind, tell me."

"Do they know you're not coming back?" Justin asked as he got up from the table.

"Liam and I had a giant fight this morning. I said I'd had it with him telling me what to do." Lisa-Marie shook her head, "I said I was leaving and not coming back but I bet he didn't believe me."

"I'll go over and tell them. If we don't show up for supper, they'll worry."

Lisa-Marie went to the fridge and peered inside, "See if they'll let you bring us something to eat. I'm starving and there isn't a thing in here that looks edible."

❧❧❧❧

Justin walked into the kitchen as everyone was getting ready to sit down. Izzy called out, "We were wondering where you were. Have you seen Lisa?"

"Can I talk to you and Liam," Justin looked around the room and added, "alone?"

"Sure, let's go out on the deck." Izzy put down the dishes in her hand and followed Justin outside.

When the three of them were grouped near the railing, Justin said, "Leez is at my place. She says she's not coming back here."

Liam looked stunned, "She doesn't mean that, Justin. She's upset right now. She can't walk out on Sophie. Tell her you think she should come back, she'll listen to you."

Justin caught the look of sympathy Izzy directed at Liam. He thought it would be best if he said what he had to say as quickly as possible and moved on. "I'm not going to tell her what to do. And she is serious ... she isn't coming back. When I first got here, Liam, you told me to stay because Leez needed a friend. That's exactly what I'm doing. She wants to stay at my place and I told her she could. It's done."

Liam jammed his hands into his pockets, "I'm sure you think you're being her friend, but helping her run away isn't right." Liam turned and walked to the far side of the deck.

Izzy looked at Justin and asked, "You're sure she means it?" When she saw him nod, she added, "Tell her that I'll bring some of her stuff over after dinner." Justin turned to walk into the house and Izzy called after him, "Tell everyone to start without us and get Alex to dish up a couple of plates of food to take back with you."

Izzy joined Liam on the bench under the arbor. He frowned at her, "You don't think sending him away with dinner-to-go was a bit over the top?"

"They might as well eat."

Liam sat forward on the bench, "The moment you decided to have her stay here with us, Izz, we became responsible for her. She's a kid. You can't think it's a good idea for her to move in with Justin."

"I'm pretty sure she isn't moving in with him, Liam. Not like that."

"It's not Justin's cabin. You could have told him she can't stay there."

Izzy gave Liam a sharp look. She could feel her one eyebrow rising in a dead-on impression of her own mother. She tried to relax her face as she said, "I fail to see how alienating both of them will help the situation."

Liam slumped back on the bench. "Go ahead and say it - *I told you so* - you probably want to, after what you saw this morning. I know you've said from the start that I was going to drive her away."

Izzy reached out and took Liam's hand in her own and held it up to her face. She watched the sun glint off the water. A hummingbird flew past and hovered near the honeysuckle. Its wings were a blur of movement around its tiny, green-striped body. "I don't want to say anything like that."

"This whole thing is such a mess. What are we going to do?"

"Give her some space. I'm hoping that I can convince her to come over every day to work with dad on the book and have dinner. I'm sure she and Justin don't have cooking high on their priority list."

"We're giving her permission to do whatever she wants."

"More like we're accepting that we never had the right to tell her what to do in the first place."

FORTY

Izzy went in search of Liam and found him out in the greenhouse. Lisa-Marie had been gone for a couple of days and Liam had done a disappearing act of his own - withdrawing into himself and speaking only when necessary.

The baby was fussing in the swing that sat in the open doorway of the greenhouse. Izzy stopped to put the pacifier in Sophie's mouth before she held up an official brown envelope, "Beulah just brought this over - a registered letter from vital statistics for Lisa-Marie. She took the liberty of opening it and I'm glad she did. A baby's birth must be registered by the parents within thirty days. Did you know that?"

Liam stood back from the work he was doing, pruning and tying up the tomato plants. Izzy could see that he was startled by the sudden way she had of throwing words at him but she ignored his reaction, "According to this, Lisa has already received three notices saying she has to fill out the paperwork." Izzy shook the letter in question, "It says here she could be subject to a fifty thousand dollar fine and since she's a minor, I guess that would bounce back on Bethany."

Liam stared from the envelope to Izzy, "That sounds a bit ridiculous."

Izzy's eyes narrowed, "Sophie can't go through life with no birth certificate and no official name. We have to make some decisions and get this damn paperwork done."

He stared at her before answering, "I'm sure Lisa will fill out the forms. Maybe she doesn't realize how important they are."

"Or maybe she doesn't want to be bothered with the responsibility of caring for a child ... like she's said from day one. Sophie's almost three

268

months old, Liam. Lisa will be returning to school soon. What's going to happen when she graduates? Do you think she'll turn around and say – oh goodie, goodie, I can hardly wait to be a mother now? Isn't it more likely that she'll want to travel or go to university? What then? Do we all just live in limbo forever?"

Liam frowned, "How would we be living in limbo?"

Izzy decided that this time she would just say the words and keep on saying them until the message got through. "I want us to adopt Sophie and raise her as our own. That will have a definite impact on what her last name is. I want to be her real mother. You can't keep avoiding what I want." The words were out, hanging in the air, malodorous, like they'd been carried downwind from a pig farm.

Liam's reaction was quick, his words rushing out, "You're talking about pushing Lisa-Marie out of Sophie's life for good. I know she doesn't want a baby right now but she won't be a kid forever. She's going to grow up. When she does, she's going to want her child."

"But don't you see, Liam? That's exactly what I'm afraid of. Think about the kind of life you're asking me to live. No guarantees about anything. I'll love and care for Sophie and make my life revolve around the three of us being a family. Then Lisa-Marie will walk in one day and take her away from me. If we adopt Sophie now, with Lisa feeling the way she does, she'll move on with her life and she won't look back."

"It's wrong."

"How can you be so certain that this isn't the best choice for Lisa and Sophie ... for all of us?"

Liam's voice slipped into a range of quiet desperation, "I know if you ask Lisa to give up Sophie, she'll say yes. All she wants is to get away, like any kid would and she'd do anything to please you. I'm not blind. I can see how close the two of you have become since Sophie was born. But Lisa is too young to understand what she would be giving up and you would be asking her to do it for the wrong reasons. It would be about what you want, not about what's best for her. Can't you see that?"

Izzy refused to give up on her argument, "Girls her age give up babies for adoption all the time, Liam. They move on with their lives. There's nothing wrong with that."

Sophie spit out her pacifier and began to howl. Liam looked hopelessly from the baby to Izzy before saying, "She needs to be changed." Izzy glared at him, turned and walked away.

〜〜〜〜

After changing the baby and settling her down for her nap, Liam joined Izzy out on the cliff deck. Her arms were folded tightly over her chest and she wouldn't make eye contact with him. "I need to tell you something, Izz." His voice shook slightly, "I'm not going to change my mind about this adoption thing. You probably got the impression that the subject was open for discussion because I didn't speak up sooner. I'm sorry about that."

Izzy's eyes widened, "I can't believe this." She brushed away a tear with an abrupt sweep of her hand as she rose from the chair. "I stood by you every step of the way. I never threw any of this in your face. I never judged you. I've spent the last three months running around holding people's hands, telling them to be calm and taking care of their emotional needs ... as if I didn't need someone to hold my hand now and then."

Izzy gripped the deck railing. "I've tried to make the best of a situation that neither of us ever anticipated when we got together. And I saw a future in all of this, for you and me and Sophie." Her voice rose, "Is it so bad that I want to be a real mother?"

Liam stood beside her and pain filled his eyes, "No ... it's not so bad. I just can't make myself believe that in this case, it's the right thing. I know what I'm asking of you is hard but I'm asking anyway. I don't have a choice. I can't walk away from you or Sophie."

"Spit it out, Liam. Let's be clear with each other once and for all. What do you expect of me?"

"Love Sophie and help me raise her for as long as we need to do the job."

Izzy's eyes held onto Liam's in a cold stare. "It's not like I have a choice, either. I love you, I love the baby. So, that's that. I'm to be a fill-in until Lisa grows up and wants to be a mother. Then I'm supposed to be overjoyed when she walks in and takes Sophie away from me. It's easy for you, right Liam? No one is going to be taking anything away from you. Sophie is yours. You'll always be her father."

"I never, ever meant to hurt you like this."

Liam reached again for Izzy's hand but she drew back, "Go away. I don't want you here. I don't want to look at you right now and I sure as hell don't want you holding my hand and telling me how sorry you are."

Liam turned away. The sound of Izzy's sobs made him feel like dropping on the ground and rolling in agony. He couldn't turn around and go back to her. He knew she meant what she said and he felt as though his increasingly tenuous grip on any kind of equilibrium had just snapped.

🎔🎔🎔🎔

Robbie heard Liam enter the cabin, go into the bedroom and shut the door. He got off the couch and looked out the living room windows to the cliff deck. He could see Izzy, sitting, bent over on the swing chair. Her hands covered her face and though he couldn't hear her, he knew she was crying. The light flashing around her made tears come to Robbie's eyes.

He had once seen light that colour moving in exactly the same way. One year his cousin had wanted a new bike so bad that he made himself believe his dad was getting him one for his birthday. But his dad never showed up at all and Robbie heard his auntie telling his grandma, "I've got no friggin' idea how the kid got it into his head that his good-for-nothing father would get him a bike." Dark spikes inside waves of deep purple light had surrounded his cousin that day.

Robbie had been a little kid then. He didn't understand all the different types and patterns of light. He asked his grandma what the light around his cousin had meant. She shook her head, "That's a hard light to see, Robbie. It's about feeling sad, as if your heart's breaking for something that you're never going to have."

🎔🎔🎔🎔

When Izzy left the cabin the next morning, after a restless night of tossing and turning in Lisa-Marie's empty bed, she spotted Alex standing in the driveway near his camper. He was stretching. His hands were on his hips and he was leaning his body backward with his face upturned to the sky. She checked her watch and decided she could spare the time to talk with him. "Hey, Alex," she called out, "Got a minute?"

"Sure, I just made a pot of coffee."

Izzy followed him up the metal stairs and into the camper. She slid onto the bench seat behind the small table and Alex handed her a cup of coffee.

Sitting down opposite her, he asked, "What's up?"

Izzy opted for full disclosure; anything else would have been a waste of time for both of them. "Liam says he will never agree to our adopting Sophie. He's given me a few things to think about when it comes to my own self-interest on the subject and the influence I could have over Lisa-Marie." Izzy sipped her coffee and studied the view from the camper's tiny window. She felt drawn into the thickness of the trees that grew along the edge of the drive. "He acts as though it's a given that adoption would be the wrong choice ... almost as though it's wrong in general. Obviously, every situation has to be examined carefully but surely giving a baby up for adoption can't always be a bad idea. What am I missing?"

Alex leaned back and leveled his dark eyes at her, "It's a worldview thing and I'm thinking it's a world you've never been in." Alex waved his hand, "I've walked down dirt roads on dozens of reserves all across this country and everywhere I go, I see kids Lisa-Marie's age or younger, pregnant or pushing baby strollers. Aboriginal people have the highest birth rates in this country right now and the babies are being born to younger mothers. Those are the stats. I'm not claiming it's a great idea. I'm not judging it one way or the other. I'm just telling you the way it is."

Izzy's face wore a puzzled frown, "In case you hadn't noticed, Alex, Lisa-Marie is not Aboriginal."

"Ya, I did notice that ... but Liam is."

Izzy put her cup down with more force than she intended, a frustration at her inability to grasp the meaning of his words edged her voice, "Keep talking, Alex, I need to understand and I'm not there yet."

"In my experience, you'd have to go a ways to find an Indian girl who didn't want to keep her baby. Sure, a lot of people would tell that girl she should give the baby up, but she won't do it without a fight. She'll leave the baby with an auntie or a grannie or an older sister but she sure as hell won't give the baby away for good. If a girl made that choice it would feel wrong to me and I suppose it does to Liam, too. We come from a different world." He stared at Izzy as a note of impatience sharpened his words, "You talk about adoption as if that white-man legality means something to us. It doesn't. We've plenty of reason to distrust anything that comes out of that system. We don't believe in owning kids. Care for them, look after them, teach them by showing them the way - but you can't wave a piece of paper around and change who they are, where they come from or where they belong."

Izzy slid out from behind the table and stood with her back to the tiny counter, "Jesus, Alex, I'm not thinking of owning Sophie. What kind of person do you take me for? I love her." Alex stared back at her in silence. "I've been trying to think about what's best for everyone. I think a child deserves to be raised in a stable family."

"It looks to me like Sophie has a stable family. What makes you think it will be more stable because of an adoption?"

Alex delivered this question in a tone of curiosity that made Izzy feel even more off-centre. His tone softened as he said, "I know you want to be a mother to that child. What do you think that takes?" Izzy looked away. There were tears in her eyes. "Caring and loving - no piece of paper is going to

272

make you do that anymore than you're already doing. And let's face it ... kids always leave, it's only a matter of time."

Izzy wiped a tear away with her hand, "It's hard to let go of the picture I have in my own head of how it should be for Liam and me, with Sophie."

"Better to let it go of your own free will. Sometimes you've got to know when to fold. The stakes are pretty high and you don't have the cards to win this hand. And even if you did, I'm not sure you'd want to live with the consequences.

Maddy walked across the dining room towards Jesse where he sat hunched over a plate of bacon and eggs. As he raised a piece of toast to his mouth, she leaned in behind him and whispered close to his ear, "Want to meet me down at the boat shed tonight?"

Jesse jumped and turned to look at her. She hadn't spoken a word to him for days. He saw a smile on her face that was filled with bad-girl fun and he found himself smiling back.

She kissed his cheek before she stood up, "Once more, for old time's sake?"

He nodded as she strolled away.

As Izzy passed Roland's office she saw him get up and gesture for her to come in. He pushed open the door, "Izzy, I need to talk to you."

He had already turned and walked back towards his desk before she could answer. She followed him into his office, "I hope this won't take long. I have a session in less than half an hour, I haven't had lunch and it's already after three o'clock."

Roland unbuttoned his suit jacket and sat down, "I'll try to be brief. It's about Ms. Sinclair."

"What about Maddy?" Izzy could feel her defences going up. She forced herself to take a deep breath. "Go ahead, Roland. I'm listening."

"It has come to my attention that Ms. Sinclair has been displaying some erratic behaviour." Roland pinched the bridge of his nose, "Jillian told me that she witnessed Ms. Sinclair in what appeared to be a violent altercation with Mr. McAlister outside his cabin. She said that Mr. McAlister was holding Ms. Sinclair's wrists while she slapped and screamed at him."

Izzy matched Roland's stare, "I'd be the first to admit that Maddy's emotional state has not stabilized. I've been dealing with a host of complex issues in her treatment. I have considered the fact that she needs more help than I can give her and I've been looking for a program that will meet her needs."

"Ms. Sinclair is not a resident here. Micah Camp is not legally responsible for her care. In reality, she is a private client of yours who happens to be staying here. You are working without the safety net you would ordinarily have as an employee of the Camp. That's the first point I want to make. Second, I would not want to see her behaviour compromise the care of the residents for whom we are responsible. I'm sure you wouldn't want that either."

"Is there a bottom line coming in all of this?" Izzy stared pointedly at her watch.

"The bed she is occupying will be required in two weeks. That gives you time either to arrange alternate accommodations if you want to continue working with her, or to wrap up your sessions and prepare her to be referred out to another program."

Izzy got up; her eyes narrowed with frustration. She didn't like being handed a deadline. "Is there anything else?" Roland shook his head and she walked out of his office.

FORTY-ONE

Izzy forced her voice to remain calm as red flags flew up in her head like a scene from a semaphore training video. "Willow, are you saying no one else knows about Jonathan's violence towards you," Izzy leaned forward in her chair, "not your social worker or your foster caregivers in Kamloops?"

Willow shook her head. She was holding the collage she had made in her first session and tracing her fingers over the central picture of the guy in the leather jacket.

"I need to ask you a question and it's important that you answer me truthfully. Have you had any contact with Jonathan since you left Kamloops?"

Willow twisted the paper in her hand. "You said what I told you would be confidential ... right? I don't want you to tell anyone about Jonathan. I don't want him to get in trouble."

"I understand that. Do you remember what else I said about confidentiality?" Willow shook her head. "I explained the limitations. I am legally required to break confidentiality if you are in danger."

Willow held onto a rigid silence for a moment but in the face of Izzy's stare, she bowed her head and mumbled, "I haven't had any contact with him at all. I promised I wouldn't. I won't do anything to get him in trouble. It isn't his fault, he can't help himself. He loves me. I love him. I only left him because of how much I love him."

"So, as far as you know, Jonathan has no idea where you are?"

Tears slid down her face as she asked, "How could he?"

After their session, Izzy pulled Willow's file and combed through it to see if she had missed anything, but there was nothing about a boyfriend named Jonathan and no mention of any abuse or violence. If what Willow was saying was true - that she had feared for her life at the hands of this young man who professed to love her - and that no one at Social Services knew a thing about it, her situation had the potential to become dangerous. No one should be handing out information related to Willow's whereabouts. Izzy was particularly careful to always follow the well-established protocols about not releasing personal information on youth in care. But it isn't a perfect world and she knew from experience that in the absence of a specific threat to personal safety, rules get bent.

Izzy went in search of Roland and ended up looking through the glass doors of his empty office. Why wasn't he ever where he should be when she needed him? She walked through to the kitchen. Cook had a roasting pan open on the top of the stove and was checking the meat thermometer buried inside a huge slab of beef. Izzy asked, "Have you seen Roland?"

"Jillian said they were going into Dearborn for dinner but they'd be back by seven or so. Is something wrong?"

"No, I'll talk to him tomorrow. Thanks." She made her way back to her office to scribble a quick note.

✻✻✻✻

Maryanne sat at her desk and wondered what she was going to do about the matter of Willow's high school transcripts. She had arranged for her to fill out applications for various post-secondary programs but those transcripts had to be attached. She had already brought this up with Izzy and Roland and had received nothing but vague suggestions about making another request.

She checked back in her notes and found the name of Willow's high school in Kamloops. She googled the school and found a phone number. A quick call to the school counsellor solved the problem. Willow's transcripts had been mailed to the address of her former foster home in Kamloops instead of being sent to Micah Camp. The school counsellor gave Maryanne a phone number which she called. She reached a polite but busy woman who said, yes, she had Willow's transcripts, both sets. She'd had no idea what to do with them. Maryanne gave her the Micah Camp address and the woman promised to forward the transcripts.

Maryanne smiled. The whole situation had been resolved in less than fifteen minutes. She should have phoned the school herself from the start rather than counting on Izzy or Roland. Both of them were far too busy. Micah Camp needed a full time career counsellor; she had said so time and time again.

❧❧❧❧

Jonathan knocked on the screen door. The woman was folding laundry at the kitchen table. She smiled at him, "Come on in, Jonathan. Is it hot enough out there for you?" She pointed behind her, "There's a jug of iced tea in the fridge. Help yourself."

He grabbed a clean glass out of the open dishwasher. As always, he scanned the front of the fridge before he opened it. A scribbled note was fastened to the door. *Willow's transcripts – Micah Camp, Box 874, Dearborn, BC.* He forced his hand to remain steady as he grabbed the jug of iced tea. He turned to watch the woman fold a brightly coloured T-shirt. All of her actions were sure and swift, as if she were performing a dance she had done a million times.

"It sure is a hot one, you got that right." He sipped his iced tea with gratitude as he thought about never having to mow that fucking lawn again.

FORTY-TWO

Izzy woke up, disoriented in the dark and overwhelmed with the feeling that something was wrong. Her skin turned clammy with sweat. She glanced at the clock on the night table of the sunflower room and realized it was still early, not even ten-thirty. She got up, pulled on some clothes and went downstairs. The cabin was quiet. She looked into the cradle. Sophie was sleeping, her tiny fist jammed against her mouth.

Through the window she saw a flicker of light from the fire in the chimney stove on the cliff deck. She scrunched her bare feet into her runners and went outside. Liam was sitting on the swing chair facing the lake. Positioned on the railing in front of him was an unopened bottle of whiskey. The orange glow of the fire gleamed off the liquid inside. As she sat down, she could feel the waves of tension coming from him; he was coiled tight as a spring with his hands in fists on the knees of his faded jeans.

Izzy reached over and put her hand over his, "Hey."

"Hey." The silence hung between them like a shroud.

"Where did the bottle come from?"

"I bought it in town today."

"Oh," Izzy took a deep breath as her hand curled around Liam's fist.

"You know I'm not a praying man, Izz. I've never had much faith in the whole higher power thing. But I've been sitting here for the last five minutes praying with everything in me that you would come out here," Liam stopped talking to look at her in wonder, "and here you are."

"Yes, I'm here."

Liam forced his fists to unclench. He flexed his fingers and laid his palms flat against his knees. "I told myself I could wait to open the bottle until the

278

moon had gone down behind those trees. I've waited a good many years. I could wait that long. But now the moon is behind those trees and I couldn't think of another bloody reason to put it off." Liam's eyes were on the bottle and he was shaking his head, "Some days I don't even recognize myself. Where did he come from – this guy who's telling other people what to do? It feels as though everything around me is unravelling like some crazy coil of wire. I want to know how life got so screwed up."

He spoke with mounting defeat in his voice, "I'm disappearing under all of it ... like before. I dream about the baby dying in the fire – over and over – and this time it's Sophie." Liam's hand clenched tightly under Izzy's. They were both silent as they watched the firelight glint off the bottle on the railing.

Izzy wanted to smash that bottle and drag Liam away ... to scream at him that he couldn't start down a road that would surely destroy him; but she knew she couldn't. Liam had to choose. If he decided to open the bottle and have a drink she would sit right here beside him. No matter what happened next, she wouldn't leave him. Her heart had been squeezed in her chest like she might double over in pain when he'd said he was having dreams about the baby dying in the fire. She knew better than anyone how Liam had suffered trying to exorcise the guilt he felt about living when that baby had died. She couldn't even imagine the horror of compounding that guilt with the fear that something so terrifying could happen to Sophie.

She filed away for future consideration the fact that over the last couple of days she'd had no idea that the man she loved was walking so close to the edge of a precipice. She could have been the one to push him right over.

Liam turned and pulled her into his arms and held her tight against his chest. His voice trembled as he whispered in her ear, "I want to go inside the cabin and make love to you. I want to bury myself so deep inside of you I can't remember how it felt to buy that bottle or what a living hell the last hour has been. And I don't ever want to spend another night in that bed without you."

Izzy pulled away from Liam's arms and stood, dragging him up after her. She held tight to his hand. Liam pulled them back toward the railing. He picked up the bottle and hurled it over the edge toward the lake. They both watched as the bottle snagged in a tree that jutted out from the cliff face. It lay there suspended in the green network of branches where its contents still reflected the thin light of the dying fire. As they turned toward the cabin Izzy said, "I guess there was a good reason Caleb never let you pitch for the Timber Wolves."

꙾꙾꙾꙾꙾

Maddy waited until the sound of Jesse's shoes on the gravel outside the boat shed faded away. Once more for old time's sake had turned out to be nothing more than that. It hadn't changed anything at all. She reached into the pocket of her jeans and drew out the razor blade. She unwrapped it and held it between her fingers as she lay back down on the floor. She didn't falter or hesitate. She drew the blade swiftly and deeply across her left wrist; then she transferred the blade to her other hand and did the same to her right. She let the blade slip from her fingers. She stretched her arms down beside her and watched the blood drip across her hands to collect in a pool on the floor. She could feel the pain inside slide out with the rush of the red flow. She relaxed and let it happen. All she had to do was lie still and let it happen.

꙾꙾꙾꙾꙾

Justin was waiting for Lisa-Marie in front of the main doors to the Camp building when he saw Jesse walking across the grass towards him. He called out, "Hey man, what's up?"

"Not much ... you?"

"Waiting for Leez. So you're heading off in two days. Are you ready?"

"Ya sure, can't wait."

"Well say it like you mean it." Justin studied Jesse's face in the light that was coming from the building.

"I was with Maddy down at the boat shed – her idea. Goodbyes suck."

Justin looked around, "Where is she?"

Lisa-Marie came out the door and stood beside him. "Where's who?"

Jesse shoved his hands in his front pockets, "Maddy. She said to go ahead without her ... that she'd be heading back to her cabin for some party Arianna is throwing."

Justin stared at Jesse, "You left her down at the boat shed?"

Lisa-Marie looked in surprise from Justin's face to the confused look on Jesse's. "I just saw Arianna in the TV room. She didn't look like she was planning any kind of party."

"Oh shit," Justin turned and grabbed Lisa-Marie's arm, "Run as fast as you can to Roland's cabin and tell him I said he should start one of the vehicles and wait in the drive." He could tell she was getting ready to question him. He shook her, "Don't ask why, just do it." Justin wheeled around and started running across the drive toward the boat shed. He called back over his shoulder to Jesse, "Come on, man, hurry up, we've got to get down there."

Justin saw Maddy the moment he got inside the boat shed. She was lying curled up in a small ball with her arms down in front of her resting in a dark, thick pool of blood. He could hear Jesse shouting but the sound faded into the background. Everything went still; time slowed down. He pulled off his overshirt and ripped it down the middle as he moved. Jesse had rushed past him and was already kneeling in the blood, pulling Maddy up into his arms and against his chest. Justin knelt beside them and checked for a pulse in Maddy's neck; it was weak but it was there. He wrapped her wrists in strips of his shirt.

"These cuts are bad. This wasn't for attention. Shit, she really meant to do it." Justin was working fast, checking that the tourniquets were tight but not too tight. "Have you got her? Let's go."

Jesse rose with Maddy draped in his arms. He and Justin ran up the slope to the driveway. Maddy's head lolled back on her slender neck and her face shone ghostly white in the moonlight. As they came up in front of the main building, they saw Roland and Jillian by the driver's door of his car, the engine was running. Jillian held a blanket over her arm.

Lisa-Marie stood near the edge of the grass. She ran toward Jesse screaming, "What happened, what happened to Maddy? Oh my God, no, no."

Justin let go of the grip he had kept on Maddy. He had been holding her wrists together by encircling the hastily wrapped bandages with his own hands – holding his warmth against the fabric that was already seeping blood. He pulled Lisa-Marie away. Roland had the vehicle door open and was bundling in Jesse, who was still holding Maddy tight against his chest. He draped the blanket over both of them.

"Let go of me, Justin. I want to go to her. I need to be with her."

"No ... listen to me. You have to get over to Izzy's and tell her what's happened. She'll want to come to the hospital. Someone will have to stay with Sophie. Go there right now." Justin was already moving back toward the vehicle.

Roland pushed Jillian toward Lisa-Marie, "Go with her, Jill."

Justin jumped into the back seat and grabbed onto Maddy's wrists. He willed the energy that flowed through him to reach her and slow the bleeding. He could hear Jesse whispering over and over, "Stay with me, Maddy, stay with me. Don't leave like this, please."

Lisa-Marie burst through the kitchen door of the cabin. She ran down into the living room as Izzy and Liam came through the back door. They were holding hands.

"What is it, Lisa? What's wrong?" Izzy moved through the entry and across the living room towards her. She saw Jillian at the top of the stairs to the kitchen.

Lisa-Marie threw herself into Izzy's arms sobbing and choking out the words, "It's Maddy, oh God, Maddy cut her wrists down in the boat shed. There was blood everywhere, all over her arms and on Justin and Jesse."

Jillian spoke up, "Roland just left, driving them to the hospital. Things didn't look good."

Izzy had paled visibly. "We have to get there right away." Liam was already grabbing the keys to the SUV.

Izzy looked over Lisa-Marie's head to Jillian, "Can you stay? The baby's asleep in the cradle and my dad is down in the sun porch. He's already had his nightly meds, so he'll be pretty groggy. Robbie's upstairs asleep, too." Izzy looked down at Lisa-Marie, "Stay here with Jill in case she needs help with anything." Lisa-Marie nodded with tears streaming down her face.

FORTY-THREE

Liam and Izzy rushed through the doors of the emergency room. Dr. Rosemary Maxwell was standing by the nurse's station with a chart in her hands. She looked up in relief, "Liam, I've checked the database and you're a match. Go through," she pointed behind her. "A nurse will be there straight away to take your blood."

Liam moved away past the curtained-off beds as Izzy looked anxiously at the doctor and asked, "How is she?"

"She's lost a lot of blood. We got lucky; one of the nurses on shift tonight was a perfect match. The transfusion helped and if Liam crossmatches, that will be great. We've got fluids going in but I'm concerned. Her blood pressure is still dangerously low and her heart beat isn't as steady as I would like. She was serious about ending her life. If she had managed the second cut as well as she did the first we would be having a different conversation right now." Rosemary reached out and squeezed Izzy's arm, "I've got to get back in there. Maybe you can see to those young men," she pointed to Justin and Jesse in the corner of the waiting room. "They look a sight. One of them seems pretty shaken up. Is he her boyfriend? Sounds like some fast thinking on Justin's part - they got her here in time - that's all I can say for now."

Izzy walked over and knelt down in front of Jesse. His hands were caked red with blood and the knees of his pants were stiff with it. His face was pale. She took his hands in hers and rubbed them together. She looked up at Justin and asked, "Could you go across the street and get us coffee?"

"Roland's already gone to do that."

Dried blood streaked up the back of Justin's forearms. She got up and went to him, "Take a minute and get yourself cleaned up." She touched his arm and looked up into his eyes. The adrenalin was still running strong; his muscles tensed tight under her hand. He nodded and walked toward the washroom. She turned her attention back to Jesse.

Liam returned from giving blood to wait with them and the minutes dragged by in anxious silence. Finally, the doctor came out to the waiting room and pulled up a chair. "I like the looks of her vital signs. She's stable."

Izzy clutched Liam's hand as tears gathered under her lashes. "What's going to happen now, Rosemary?"

"We'll keep her overnight and send her out tomorrow."

"Where?"

"Medevac down to a psychiatric ward in the city."

"Oh no. She'll be drugged and wait forever for an assessment. You know how overloaded those places always are."

"We don't have a choice, Izzy. I'm sorry." The doctor motioned to Roland, "They've got a slew of paperwork for you to sign." Roland looked up in surprise and glanced at Izzy who was staring down at the floor. He nodded at the doctor and walked away.

Rosemary turned to the rest of the group, "You should all go home."

Izzy and Jesse shook their heads in protest, "I'm staying," they both declared at the same time.

The doctor raised her eyebrows, "There's no point. She's going to be out for at least six hours. You can't do anything here. Go home and get some sleep and come back in the morning. That's what I plan to do."

※ ※ ※ ※

Lisa-Marie jumped out of the chair and hurried into the entry when she heard the sound of the back door opening. Izzy stepped toward her but Lisa walked right past her and into Justin's open arms. "She's going to be okay, Leez. She's going to make it." He held her tight, resting his head against hers. "Let's go home." Izzy and Liam watched wordlessly as the two young people walked out of the cabin without looking back.

Jillian came into the entry holding Sophie in her arms. "She's been a bit fussy since we gave her the bottle about half an hour ago. Probably knows something's up."

Izzy took the baby, "My dad and Robbie ... did they sleep through everything?"

"Not a peep out of either of them."

"Liam will drive you back over to the Camp, Jill. Thanks so much for taking charge here."

"Is Maddy going to be alright?"

"Her physical condition is stable. She isn't going to die. As for everything else, I don't know."

⚜⚜⚜⚜

Lisa-Marie sat on the sofa with her knees drawn up to her chin and her arms wrapped tightly around her legs. She couldn't stop crying. Justin had gone straight into the shower when they got to the cabin. He felt desperate to get the flinty smell of blood out of his nose. Even a prolonged stay under the hot water hadn't totally done the job.

He walked over to the sofa, sat down beside Lisa and put an arm around her, "She's going to make it. We wouldn't have left the hospital unless we were sure of that."

"I know ... it's just ... when I saw Jesse carrying her and she looked so white and her blood was all over everyone, I was so scared."

"Ya, it's a pretty gruesome thing to see."

"How were you so sure she had done that?"

"I know Maddy and I've known other girls like her. What Jesse said didn't fit - that everything was over between them but she was okay with that."

"You were so calm. Weren't you scared?"

"No ... not scared. I want to tell you something." Lisa-Marie looked up at him, her eyes on his. "When things get intense, the way they did tonight, time slows down. I guess everything keeps moving fast but for me, it's all slow motion. My mind goes clear and sharp. I feel like I have all the time in the world."

"You make it sound like you do this stuff all the time."

Justin's arm tightened around her, "When I was nine, my sister got hit by a car in front of our house. My mom was working in the flower bed by the driveway and Angie was riding her trike. I guess my mom lost track of her for a minute because Angie pedaled out into the road and a car slammed right into her. I was on the tire swing in the backyard when I heard the screech of the car's brakes and my mom screaming. By the time I got out there, my mom was hysterical and the woman driving the car wasn't much better. Angie was in bad shape, broken up and blood everywhere. It happened the way I told you. Time slowed down as I moved from one step to the next. But I couldn't stop the bleeding and Angie died before the ambulance got there." Justin's voice shook when he said, "She was only three. Sometimes, when I hold Sophie, I remember what it was like when Angie was a baby."

285

Lisa-Marie reached over and rested her hand on his chest. The small cabin was still with the sound of their breathing.

"My mom never got over it. She started taking pills and everything fell apart. She overdosed a couple of times before they locked her up. I tried to see her when I turned eighteen – just before I came to Micah Camp. It was a mistake. She's didn't even know who I was." Justin stared at the floor as he explained, "She was one of those supermoms, Leez. My dad took off right after Angie came along. My mom worked two jobs just to be able to keep the house. She never took a break. She'd be up half the night, icing cupcakes for a bake sale or sewing a costume for Halloween. Until I saw her like that, in that place, I thought the social workers had lied to me all those years when they said she wouldn't even know me."

After a moment of silence, Lisa-Marie looked into Justin's eyes and said, "I never even met my mom. She died of a drug overdose right after I was born." She took a deep breath and rushed out the words, "Remember last summer when you said that I was an immature, screwed up kid?"

"Don't remind me." Justin slumped down on the couch, "I've thought about that night over and over." He asked the question that had been bothering him for three months, "Why did you go to Liam the way you did? I know you were upset. I know you said you were trying to get back at Izzy and me, but it must have been more than that."

"It's because you were right, Justin. I was screwed up ... really screwed up. Before I came to stay with Auntie Beth, I tried to kill myself." Justin tensed beside her and reached out to grab her hand. "Not like Maddy. I took pills and polished of a big bottle of vodka. Then I had to get my stomach pumped. The kids back home, they picked on me a lot. I was that girl, Justin – the girl that everyone hates. Kids were always pushing me around and saying horrible things to me, stealing my stuff and hitting me on the head with textbooks when the bus driver wasn't looking. I was that girl." Her voice rose, "Then I went crazy, letting guys do whatever they wanted to me. I believed all the terrible things everyone said about me. I believed I was a worthless piece of crap. After a while, I couldn't take it anymore. I wanted it all to stop. But when I saw Maddy tonight and what it would be like to come so close to dying, it scared me so much I could barely get my breath."

Justin pulled Lisa-Marie closer. He heard her say, "Last summer, Liam was the only person who saw all the pain that was still inside of me. I was swimming out into the lake that night and I wasn't going to stop. It wasn't because you left me, even though I thought it was. It was because I was screwed up and I hadn't forgotten about all the other stuff that hurt so much. I didn't have anywhere else to turn. Liam and I were connected in some crazy way. He cared about me. I wouldn't be alive right now if it weren't for him." Lisa-Marie wrapped her arms around Justin and held on tight.

Justin felt her slide down against him. After a short time her crying leveled off and her breathing slowed. He could tell she was almost asleep. He shifted on the sofa and Lisa-Marie whispered, "Don't go, please don't leave me alone."

"No, Leez ... I won't leave you." He stretched out on the sofa and drew her close. The words she had spoken of last summer played through his mind. She was wrong about one thing. Liam hadn't been the only one to see something was wrong. Justin had left her alone, out in the water, and he had known all along something wasn't right with her. He tightened his hold on the girl in his arms. If anything worse had happened to her that night, it would have been his fault.

❧❧❧❧

Izzy was sorting through a pile of files on her desk and stuffing things into her briefcase when she looked up to see Roland at her door. She quickly explained, "I'm here for only a few minutes. I thought I would grab some work to do. I have to get back up to the hospital. I'm taking Jesse with me. He wants to see Maddy before they send her out."

Roland came into the office and closed the door behind him. "Izzy, I need to talk to you. Can we sit?" He gestured to the two chairs on the carpet in front of the window. Izzy joined him.

"First point – you are not to blame yourself for Ms. Sinclair's suicide attempt."

Izzy stared at Roland in disbelief, "Isn't that what you're doing ... blaming me? From the start, you didn't think she should be here or that I should be working with her."

"I'm doing nothing of the sort. I didn't see this coming any more than you did. Yesterday, I was just carrying out my job as director of this facility when I discussed with you my concerns about Ms. Sinclair. At no time did I doubt your professional judgment and I still don't. We may disagree on our ideas about treatment options but, when it comes to this type of work, there are no guarantees. We aren't playing at crystal ball gazing. No one holds you responsible for Ms. Sinclair's choices, least of all me."

Izzy sat back in her chair and looked past Roland to the morning sun glinting off the water of the lake. "Thank you. I appreciate knowing that. The truth is, I do feel responsible and it seems almost too much to bear."

287

"I would encourage you to keep your feelings in perspective. Learn from them, certainly, but don't let them take you down a path of self-recrimination that can help no one." Roland brushed a non-existent piece of lint from the knee of his trousers, "Second point - I have a colleague who is the head of a treatment program for women diagnosed with border-line personality disorder. The facility is located on one of those Gulf Islands, off Vancouver. They use multi-modal treatment options and the suggested stay is eight months to a year. The articles I've read show some impressive results but the waiting list is as long as my arm. I spoke to my colleague this morning. He owes me a favour from the time we did our graduate work together, before he went on to psychiatry. He had quite the struggle running advanced statistical analysis, as many do." Roland shrugged his shoulders, indicating he couldn't imagine why that was the case. "If funding can be arranged, they'll fit Ms. Sinclair into the program immediately."

Izzy couldn't hide her shock. She swallowed hard and looked down at her hands folded in her lap. She would never have considered asking Roland for help or imagined that he might be willing to pull strings and call in favours for one of her clients. She glanced up at him, "Would it be a good fit for Maddy?"

"It would be a perfect fit, except for the matter of the price tag. As I said, it's a private clinic and the provincial Medical Services Plan will cover only a fraction of the cost of her stay."

"Cost is not an issue at all, Roland. Can we set up a transfer directly to this facility?"

"They say they can have an ambulance meet the plane – all at an additional cost, of course. We can arrange the transfer through Micah Camp – from our facility to theirs via the hospital. That should take care of the legalities. I filled out the paper work last night as if she is still a resident here. Rosemary assumed that was the case."

"I can't tell you what it means to me to know that she won't lie in a hospital bed in restraints for days. Thank you so much for arranging this."

Roland got up, "Please stop by my office before you go. Ms. Delacourt got all the residents together and they have created a rather large card for Ms. Sinclair. I hoped you might deliver it." He paused at the door to add, "I got your note about Willow Donaldson. I've been in contact with the Ministry. They assure me that all privacy protocols are strictly in place."

Maddy's long, artist fingers stretched beyond the thick, white gauze around her wrist to lay on the hospital bed's yellow sheet. Her face was as white as the bandage. She looked past Izzy, who was sitting on the chair by the bed, and saw Jesse standing in the doorway. Her eyes held a silent plea.

Izzy turned and rose from the chair. "Jesse, come in. The ambulance is going to be here soon. I'll leave you two alone." She walked out of the room.

Jesse sat down and pulled Maddy's hand into his. He leaned over to rest his face against the thick bandage. The room was quiet. After a few moments, he looked up to see tears washing down Maddy's face.

"I'm so sorry for putting you through this, Jess. You never deserved any of it."

"You're the one that doesn't deserve this, Maddy."

She shrugged and brushed the tears away with her other hand. Her slender arm was awkward with the weight of the bandage. The sleeve of the hospital gown rode up and revealed all the scars that marched up her arm in a relentless line, each cut a tiny rehearsal for the final act. Her voice shook, "You stuck with me through all the crap I pulled on you. No matter what I did, you were still there. I thought that meant something. I went over the edge when I found out it didn't."

Jesse rubbed the back of her hand along his cheek, "It did mean something. Every minute of it meant something. I put up with all of it because I love you. I've loved you from the start." He reached over, ran his finger along the neckline of her hospital gown and pulled free the tiny, gold cross she always wore. He held it in his hand, "Since that first day, remember? When I asked you if you were a good little Christian girl, or did you like to come out and play." He smiled at her and saw the merest hint of a Maddy grin flit across her face. "You were the first girl who saw right through all my bullshit. What did you always call it? Oh ya, I remember ... my crazy stud-boy routine." He tucked the cross back inside her gown and held her face in the palm of his hand. "For me, it was always exclusive – no matter what you said or thought. It all meant something." Jesse pulled Maddy up into his arms and held her close to him, "Our timing is wrong, that's all it is. You need help right now. I need to go to California and take my shot. We'd only pull each other down if we were together."

At a sound in the hall, he turned to look over his shoulder. The medevac guys were outside the door with the stretcher. Maddy clung to him, "I'll never forget how you came back to the boat shed for me."

"You remember that?"

She nodded, "I felt you holding me; I heard you calling me, Jess. You asked me not to go."

Jesse and Izzy stood in the hallway and watched as the doors of the emergency room swung closed behind the stretcher that carried Maddy away. Izzy put her hand on Jesse's arm, "The program she's going to is the best there is. Don't blame yourself for what happened."

Jesse heard Izzy's voice tremble over the last words. He watched as she leaned against the wall for support and covered her face with her hand. The quiet choking sound of a sob escaped. He moved to put his arms around her and hugged her tightly, "Don't blame yourself either, Izzy. Maddy would never want that."

Fusion

FORTY-FOUR

Beulah walked out the back door of the A-Frame. The dogs scrambled to get past her. She brushed them aside, "For the love of God, are the two of you trying to send me ass over tea kettle down these bloody stairs?" A movement by the bakery door caught her eye. Bethany stood there, waiting. The dogs pelted towards her and she knelt down to greet them.

She looked up at Beulah, "I'm here to work. It isn't fair to dump the whole bakery on you when you have no one to help but Arianna."

"I know you would have been here every day, Beth, if I hadn't tried to blame you for my own mistakes."

Bethany stood up and brushed the dog hair from the front of her shirt before folding her arms over her chest, "You've got that right. Anyway, I'm here now so let's get to work."

Later that morning, they were standing side by side shaping the loaves for the first batch of bread. Beulah flipped a loaf from the board to a large stainless steel tray, "Arianna told me about what happened over at the Camp the other night, with that Maddy girl. What a hell of a thing, hey?"

Bethany nodded and dropped a round loaf of bread onto her own tray, "It's terrible. A lot of the kids are pretty rattled. Roland called all of us into a meeting. He and Izzy talked about the kind of things we should do to help."

"Like what?"

Bethany turned to lean against the table, "If the kids want to talk about what happened, we shouldn't do anything to discourage them from sharing how they feel. You know ... like offering them platitudes or telling them everything is fine. Izzy said that if a kid is talking to an adult, that's a healthy sign."

Beulah came back from placing her tray in the warming cupboard. She grabbed the one that Bethany had filled, "I did the right thing then."

"What do you mean?"

"When Arianna came to work yesterday she had this other kid with her - a guy with dark hair sticking up all over the place - the kid she did that Michael Jackson number with at the talent show. She said she didn't want to leave him on his own."

"Mark ... she hangs out with him. I guess you could say she's taken him under her wing."

"She went on for a while about what had happened to this Maddy girl. She and Arianna were roommates, right?" Bethany nodded. "Now and then, he chimed in his two bits worth. Sounded like he worshiped the ground the girl walked on. Arianna started crying a couple of times. It wouldn't have surprised me if he did, too. I just let them talk but I kept saying it was a shocker, for sure." Beulah set the timer on the warming cupboard, "For a small guy, that Mark kid can pack away the food. He ate most of a loaf of bread while he was here."

Bethany stared at Beulah. "That was great listening, Beulah, exactly what Roland and Izzy were telling us to do. You're good around kids."

Beulah shook her head, "I got no time for kids."

"That's not true. What about the kids on that ball team? I saw how well you got along with them." Bethany smacked the flour off her hands and headed for the sink, speaking back over her shoulder, "I don't know why you try to deny it."

❧❧❧❧

"Do you ever have nightmares?" Liam leaned against the work bench in the shop and asked his father this question. Alex slid out from under Caleb's old Dodge. They were changing the oil ... *they* being a relative term since Liam had never had any inclination to take up do-it-yourself car maintenance.

Alex rolled over and jumped up from the ground like a Chinese gymnast. He grabbed a paper towel to wipe his hands. "You'd think I would, the things I've seen over the years. Can't say I ever do, though. Pass me that funnel and crack open a quart of oil."

Liam handed over the funnel and the oil. His father was already working back under the hood of the truck when Liam said, "I dream about a fire that happened up north. A baby died. My mind gets all mixed up with images of something like that happening to Sophie."

Alex emptied the quart of oil and reached for the next one from Liam's hand. "Dreams can tell you what to pay attention to ... tough to figure out what a dream like that is trying to say."

Liam looked beyond the doors of the shop to the winding driveway along which evergreens bowed over in deference to the slash carved through their territory. "I bought a bottle the other day; the idea of taking a drink had been growing on me."

Alex screwed the oil cap back on the top of the engine block. He closed the hood and leaned back against the truck to study Liam's face. "You ever hear that phrase ... *a change is as good as a rest.?* Someone over in Cedar Falls told me about this hike up to the lighthouse at Cape Scott. What do you say we take Robbie and go on that hike? We'll camp out for a couple of nights, sleep under the stars."

Liam snorted loudly, "Camping under the stars on the West Coast is as close as you'll get to begging for a downpour." But he found himself thinking it would be good to get away.

Alexander pointed at the Dodge, "She's done." He pulled a set of keys out of his pocket. "I'll drive my truck in and we'll tackle her next."

ᑫᑫᑫᑫ

Jonathan stepped off the Greyhound bus in the parking lot of the Dearborn Hotel. He shrugged his large duffel bag up and over his shoulder as he walked away. He mixed in with the tourist crowd around the boardwalk and along the boat docks.

He leaned on the counter of the take-out window of a small restaurant and ordered halibut and fries. As he handed over a twenty-dollar bill, he asked, "Could you give me some directions out to Crater Lake? I'm looking to do a bit of hiking and camping."

The woman smiled as the till's cash drawer popped open and she handed him his change. "The turnoff is back up the highway, maybe two kilometers or so. You'll see the sign. Once you get on the gravel road, you'll come to a bigger sign with a map that shows the entire area. Make sure you take the turn to the right. If you don't, you'll end up on the other side of the lake. There isn't much out there except a few private cabins and a sawmill –" she turned to grab a cold Coke out of the cooler, "and that Micah Camp place."

Jonathan thanked the woman and took his food over to a picnic table. He ate quickly, then he walked up to the grocery store he'd seen when the bus arrived in Dearborn. He went down the aisles, choosing a few items – crackers, a chunk of cheese, a few small cans of devilled ham with flip-top lids, four large chocolate bars. Outside the store, he stuffed the food into his pack

294

and shifted his duffel bag over his shoulder. He hiked back out to the highway.

ﻪﻪﻪﻪ

Izzy sat by her father's worktable and flipped through the pages that were laid out in front of her. "These are the final proofs?"

Edward smiled at her from the recliner, "Almost ... I've made note of a couple of minor changes. Lisa will attend to them." Edward looked out the window to the light dancing on the water. His mind wandered. He had to work at staying focused these days. He shook his head to clear out the morphine-induced fogginess, "Isabella, I want to talk to you about my will."

Izzy swung the rolling chair away from the work table and turned it until she faced her father. He watched as she stretched out her tanned legs, sipped her tea and met his gaze with a studious look. Her dark hair curled around her face and down over her shoulders. This daughter of his was a beautiful woman; she took his breath away sometimes. He forced himself to collect his thoughts. "I wish to be cremated and have my ashes spread around that Mountain Ash tree near the stairs down to the beach. I have watched that tree leaf up so magnificently over the last couple of months ... very impressive. I'd like to be part of that in the years to come."

Edward's eyes wandered to the view of the tree and the lake beyond. "No formal service ... maybe a gathering of a few people. Something along the lines of your delightful book club meetings with good food, alcohol and conversation." He pointed to the drawer of the end table, "You'll find an envelope in that drawer marked *The End.*" He smiled and went on, "Somewhat dramatic, I know. My London solicitor's contact information is there, as well as a copy of my will and some other small things you can take care of for me." Edward took a deep breath. He had one more important point to cover. "The sale of the flat in London brought in far more money than I had anticipated. Besides that, I've never touched the funds from the sale of your mother's house. There's quite a tidy sum of cash." He finally looked over at Izzy and noticed the concerned expression on her face. "Am I upsetting you by talking about all of this?"

Izzy shook her head, "It's not that, honestly. I'm afraid you're going to say that you're giving me the money. The truth is, I don't want it or need it. I was worrying about how to tell you that without sounding rude."

"I already have the impression that you are not short of money. That's why I wanted to have this conversation." Edward took a sip of tea and set his cup on the end table by his chair. "Are you aware of the talent Lisa has for photography?"

"I've always thought her photos were good. If you say she's talented, I believe you."

"I would like to leave my money to her. It would give her the freedom to explore her ability. She'll find that hard to do if she's always scrambling to make a dollar. I hope you would not object to such a decision."

Izzy smiled with relief, "Whatever you decide to do with your money is fine, as long as it doesn't involve giving it to me." She frowned, "But she's underage. How will you handle that?"

"My solicitor will set up a trust fund and allow her to draw from it for legitimate reasons until she's older. I'll be counting on you to steer her in the right direction when it comes to managing the money." He reached into the drawer of the table beside him and pulled out a small jewellery box. He opened it to raise a locket and chain from inside. "Your mother refused to have this in the house after we separated. In fact, she threatened to garrotte me with it. I was nostalgic, I suppose. I kept it. I thought you might like it." He handed the necklace to Izzy.

The filigree chain draped over her hand as she studied the locket. It was a beautiful thing, a small heart with a diamond sparkling in the center. Izzy glanced up at her father with a look of surprise, "I remember this; I remember mom wearing it." She opened the locket and ran her finger over the two tiny photos inside.

Edward's attention wavered again; the wind was rippling the surface of the lake in short, glittering lines of movement. After a moment, he forced his gaze back to Izzy. "The pictures were done the day your mother and I were engaged to be married."

Holding the locket in the palm of her hand, Izzy said, "I've always wondered why you left and why neither of you ever seemed to move on. Her diaries certainly detailed how much she detested you. She never wrote a word about why."

"I imagine it was all too painful for her." A sad look settled onto Edward's face. "Your mother had an extraordinary sense of pride. She was more easily wounded than other people realized." He let out a sigh, "There was another woman - someone I worked and travelled with. Not someone I would ever have considered marrying and I'm quite sure she felt the same way about me. The affair had gone on for years and I assumed your mother knew. We were both civilized people. I thought she was involved with someone else, as well. We were apart so much of the time." Edward picked up his tea cup and took a sip. "She hadn't a clue, and when she found out she was quite beside herself ... understandably, of course." He shrugged, "I regret an assumption that caused her so much pain. After all the acrimony, the sight or even the thought of me devastated your mother, so I stayed away. I always knew it was an unfortunate state of affairs for you."

Izzy brushed a tear from her face, "I understand what you mean about regrets."

"If you value the advice of a dying man, and a father who loves you, deal with them while you can."

⁂⁂⁂⁂

Justin and Jesse walked along the shore from Micah Camp to the fire pit on the beach in front of Izzy and Liam's cabin. Justin lit a fire before he dug the half-sac of beer out from under the log where he had stashed it. He passed Jesse one. They clicked their bottles together and sat down in front of the small blaze to drink in silence. The moon was full, gliding in a stream across the still surface of the water. After the festivities of the August long weekend, the other side of the lake was quiet. There were only a couple of campfires to reflect an orange glow on the water.

Jesse grabbed a stick and leaned over to poke at the flames. "Does Leez think what happened to Maddy was my fault?"

Justin tipped his bottle back for a long drink. "Nah ... she's broken up about all of it but she knows there's no point in blaming anyone. Shit, if she wants someone to be responsible, she might as well pick me. I'm the one who told you to break up with Maddy."

"You were right, though, man. The way she was acting, I wasn't ever going to take her to California." Jesse peeled at the label on the bottle in his hand, throwing the paper into the fire; each scrap flared up briefly, curling in on itself and dying away. "It's like I told her at the hospital when I said goodbye, we would have dragged each other down."

Justin passed Jesse another beer. "It couldn't have been easy, the way she was acting all the time. Why did you do it?"

Jesse twisted off the cap and tossed it into the fire. He glanced over at Justin and asked, "Do what?"

"Stick with her through all the shit she pulled on you."

"I thought I was helping her. Fucking pathetic ... right?" Jesse took a drink and shook his head.

Justin reached over for a chunk of wood and threw it on the fire. The sparks glittered up into the black sky. "Maybe you did help. If you hadn't

297

brought her back to the Camp, she might have managed to kill herself. Lots of girls do. At least now she's got a second chance."

A comfortable silence fell between them. After a while, Jesse glanced sideways at Justin and said, "You'll think I'm an idiot; shit, most of the time, I think I'm an idiot. I stuck it out because I love her. There isn't any other reason."

"Will you try to see her again?"

Jesse drained his beer and reached for the last bottle. "Izzy says Maddy won't be allowed to be in touch with anyone for months. If she did try to contact me ... right now, I feel as though I'd want to hear her voice more than anything ... but who knows? My life is about to change. I don't know how I'm going to feel next week, let alone in a few months."

The mountains loomed dark at the end of the lake. A wolf howled up in the hills behind them. In a moment, the cry was taken up again and again. Jesse looked over his shoulder, "That sound always freaks me out." He raised his bottle to salute the lake and added, "I never thought I'd be saying this, but it's hard to think of leaving here."

"I hear you, man. I feel the same way."

Jesse pointed his bottle back in the direction of Micah Camp, "It's a good program. At first I thought Jeremy was a dimwit for volunteering to work here. I get it now ... I get why he believes in the program and wants to give back."

"I'd never want to be any kind of teacher, but I get it, too."

"Last dead soldier," Jesse said as he dropped his empty bottle into the case. "What comes next for you?"

"University, for my second year. I think I'll be coming back here again next summer to work. Reg has promised me more responsibility and a pay raise."

"What about, Leez? Seems pretty cozy the way the two of you have been sharing that cabin."

"Complicated man, fucking complicated."

Jesse laughed, "I hear you on that one. I better get back; I've got an early start tomorrow."

Justin stood up and threw the nearby bucket of water over what was left of the fire. He turned quickly and wrapped his hand over Jesse's to pull him close enough to slap him on the back. They both stepped away.

Justin grabbed the case of empties and said, "Good luck, man. Make us proud. Remember the little guys when you get to the top."

Jesse chuckled, "I'll do my best. Tell Leez I said goodbye."

FORTY-FIVE

"**B**eulah, I was wondering ... would you mind if Lisa-Marie and I come over today for lunch?" Bethany asked the question as she pulled her apron off the hook that protruded from the bakery wall and tied it around her waist. As she turned, she saw Beulah's look of surprise and hurried to finish, "She's received all this information about the exchange trip and she wants to talk to both of us about things."

Beulah stood back from the giant vat she had wheeled into place under the mixer. She went to the wall to hit the on switch. The double mixing arms swung into action, plunging up and down through the dough. "I'd like to hear about the trip. I won't have much time to prepare anything for lunch and I'd have to leave to make the deliveries. How about we do dinner instead?"

A frown crossed Bethany's face as she said, "Okay ... dinner tonight."

Beulah smiled, "I'll bring Chinese food home from town."

❧❧❧❧

Robbie leaned out of the window of Caleb's old Dodge and yelled, "Come on, Liam. Dad says hurry up already, kiss her and get it over with." Robbie laughed and Alex pulled him back into the truck.

Liam grabbed Izzy and leaned her back over his arm to plant an impassioned kiss on her lips. He raised her to her feet and smiled, "I better get moving. I'll miss you. Are you sure you can manage with Sophie and your dad?"

Izzy laughed and shooed Liam away with a gesture of her hand, "Of course I can manage. Lisa is going to stay over with us and Cynthia will come by more often. Everything will be fine. Go ... have a good time hiking, getting

299

soaking wet and smelling from wood smoke. Have fun eating food covered with sand. Live it up sleeping on the cold ground." Izzy made a face, "Seriously, Liam ... enjoy yourself and don't worry. I mean it. We'll be fine."

Liam's dark eyes lingered on her for a moment before he turned away to trot across the gravel to the driver's side of the truck. She heard him tell Robbie, "Get your seatbelt on kid. Let's roll." Robbie leaned out of the window and waved one last time. The truck honked and moved forward to disappear into the thick trees.

⚑⚑⚑⚑

Jonathan scrambled down a bank and slid into the thick bush near the road. He'd been camping out rough for almost three days, always making sure to give a wide berth to the sawmill and the dogs that roamed the yard. In the daylight hours, he circled Micah Camp over and over with the dull black assault rifle close to his side. He had discovered a couple of well-concealed vantage points where he could stop and observe the comings and goings around the facility. He hadn't seen Willow yet.

Later that afternoon, his patience and constant movement were rewarded. A flash of blonde hair caught his eye and he spotted her as she came out the door of one of the small cabins that ran in a row at an angle away from the main building. Jonathan forced himself to lie still on the ground of the small jutting bank that overlooked the Camp. Every muscle in his body had tensed at the sight of Willow. He pulled a cartridge out of his pocket and jammed it into the gun. He squinted down the scope as he brought Willow's blond head of curls into the cross hairs. She walked along a path, across the open space in front of the chalet-style building and up the steps. He held his finger lightly against the trigger and thought about the way the small bullet would drill into her head. As she disappeared through the wooden doors, he lowered the gun. Blood pounded in his ears.

People came and went from the building while Jonathan waited. A couple of hours later, Willow finally came out. A tall guy was beside her. She stood close to him and the guy reached out to touch her arm. Then he waved, walked off across the drive and onto a path that led into the bush on the far side of the Camp.

Jonathan stroked the length of the rifle at his side. His eyes locked on Willow where she stood on the steps of the building. He saw her squeeze her arms around herself as she looked past the driveway and up into the trees on the hill. A rush of anguish slammed him in the chest. He rolled into a tight ball and tried to catch his breath. Pain and rage and an overwhelming desire to possess her ripped through him.

He thought about jumping up from the ground and screaming so she would see him, know he was there watching her, know that he had come for her. Then he would shoot the little whoring bitch. But he held himself tight on the ground, digging his hands into the earth. He looked up in time to see her turn to go back into the building. Her curls made a halo around her head in the afternoon light.

Jonathan considered sprinting back through the bush and running along the trail across the drive to catch up with the tall guy. When he found him, he'd blow his brains out. A deep fury burned down through his entire being. How dare another guy put a hand on Willow?

He forced himself to concentrate. The guy had at least a five-minute head start and Jonathan had no idea where the trails around the Camp led. He knew he would get only one chance to do what he had to do. He needed to make it count.

The idea of killing Willow was so confused with the dream of holding her in his arms again that he lost track of time as he played one wish after the other in an endless loop. It was dark when he pulled himself up from the ground and moved with stealth through the trees. It was time to explore the whole area.

✻✻✻✻

Beulah reached for the bottle of wine and topped up Bethany's glass. Everyone was stuffed with Chinese food but they were still picking away at what was left.

Lisa-Marie riffled through the stack of papers beside her, "London, Paris, Rome, Berlin ... a few weeks in each city with tons of side trips. The family I billet with in Paris have twin daughters my age."

Bethany sipped her wine and pointed to the itinerary, "So, you leave in the middle of September and you're back before Christmas. We better talk about the money part."

Lisa-Marie dipped a piece of egg roll into the plum sauce. She checked her information package, pulled out another sheet of paper and passed it to her aunt. Bethany slid the page over so she and Beulah could look at it together. Beulah got up and grabbed her glasses from the end table. She stared over at the figures and whistled.

Bethany pointed to the top line, "We've already paid for the flights."

Lisa-Marie spoke around a mouthful of food, "I've got enough saved for my rail pass and spending money."

"Do we send the rest to the school?" Beulah asked.

Lisa-Marie bit her lip, "Ya, a cheque, I think. I know it's a lot of money."

Beulah took off her glasses and sat back down. "It is, but this trip is a great opportunity for you. We can manage, don't worry about it." The word *we* hung over the table and caused an awkward silence. After a moment, Beulah added, "Whatever happens between your aunt and me, we both took on the responsibility of looking after you and so far, we're not winning any awards. This will be a chance for us to get back on track."

Bethany's face was pale and she chewed her lower lip nervously. She got up quickly to clear the dishes. Lisa-Marie felt like getting out of the A-Frame as fast as she could. She picked up the papers and put them back into the large brown envelope. "I've got to get going. I promised Izzy I wouldn't be long. She has her hands full, looking after Sophie all on her own."

The sound of the back door closing behind Lisa-Marie echoed through the cabin. Beulah held the wine bottle over Bethany's glass and waited for her to say yes or no. When Bethany nodded, Beulah poured the wine and asked, "Can we sit for a minute and talk?"

As they sat down in the living room, Bethany noticed Beulah's empty hands, "You aren't having anything?"

Beulah shook her head, "I'm off the booze for the foreseeable future. I did a bit of an overdose after you left ... I've had enough to last me awhile."

Bethany stared down at her glass and ran her finger around the rim. "It's good that we're talking now."

"I've thought a million times of what I would say to you if I ever got a chance. Sorry isn't good enough; I sure as hell know that. It goes way deeper, all the way back to the beginning of you and me being together. It's all wrapped up with the way I've acted all these years, like I'm the boss ... behaving as if you have to toe the line for the rest of your life because I look after you ... like you were one of the dogs or something. I've thought a lot about this stuff, Beth. No matter how I look at, it's all wrong."

"I needed you to look after me ... then. Don't blame yourself for something we both created."

Beulah stood up and paced the living room, "I didn't want things to change. That's the bottom line. When you turned everything upside down, I got pissed off. I felt hard done-by. I thought I had a right to get involved with someone else."

Bethany flinched at the bluntness of the words.

"You might think this is stupid but I wasn't trying to replace you. To be honest, I didn't consider the possibility that you would find out and, even if I had, I didn't think you would leave me, no matter what I did. Another example of how arrogant I've been." Beulah stopped pacing and stood in front of Bethany. "It was sex, pure and simple, nothing else." She settled back on the recliner and shook her head, "I know that's bad. I know that. But I never cared about her ... not the way I care about you."

The A-Frame was quiet until Beulah said, "One last thing, Beth ... remember when you asked me to look you in the eye and say there was nothing going on with me and Abbey Greene? That was the truth. Whatever the affair had been, it was over. I had pushed her so far away, I didn't even see the lie for what it was. I know it sounds like splitting hairs, but I want you to know that."

Bethany finished her wine and set the glass down on the coffee table. "I need more time, Beulah. There are things I want to say to you as well but for now I'd like to be on my own and think over everything you've said. Would you walk me back to the Camp?"

⚜⚜⚜⚜

Izzy flopped onto the couch, "I thought she'd never settle down."

Lisa-Marie was curled up in the recliner, reading. She closed the book, "I hear you. Sophie's a lot of work without Liam or Robbie around."

"I'll say. How was the dinner?" Izzy struggled up and grabbed the full basket of clean laundry just begging to be folded.

"It was good. We had Chinese food. Auntie Beth stayed after I left, so maybe she and Beulah talked. I wish they would just get over whatever is going on between them." The cabin was quiet. Lisa-Marie turned the book over in her hands a few times before asking, "Is everything going to be okay for me to go back to school?"

Izzy looked up in surprise, "Of course. Why do you ask?"

"I thought, in the beginning, that there might be some legal stuff to do about Sophie. But no one has ever said anything."

Izzy kept her eyes on the folding task as she said, "Liam thinks things are fine the way they are. I've been meaning to talk to you about an envelope Beulah brought over last week. Have you been getting letters from vital stats about not registering Sophie's birth?"

Lisa-Marie made a face, "I guess. After the first one, I just threw them in the drawer with all the stuff from the hospital."

"The paperwork is serious, Lisa. Sophie's birth needs to be registered. It's

303

up to you to apply for her birth certificate, an official medical card, the government child allowance, even her social insurance number. Vital statistics have sent a whole bunch of new paperwork and you'll have to get a notarized affidavit explaining why you didn't fill out the other forms earlier."

Lisa-Marie's shoulders slumped forward. "I did look at the stuff the nurse gave me at the hospital but I didn't know what to put down for Sophie's last name. No one said anything to me. I still don't know what to do. "

Izzy glanced over at the confused look on Lisa's face, "Think about it for a couple of days. You've waited this long – another short delay won't matter. When you decide, I'll be happy to help you figure out the rest. The new forms are upstairs in the middle drawer of my desk." Izzy pushed the laundry basket away, "I borrowed a DVD from Jillian; she's says it's a total chick flick. Want to watch it?"

Lisa-Marie got up, "I'll make the popcorn. Let's just hope *Miss Cranky Pants* stays asleep."

FORTY-SIX

Liam strolled out to the kitchen deck where Izzy sat on the bench, sipping her morning coffee. She was dressed for work and her briefcase was tossed to the side.

He and Robbie had returned home late the night before. He had dragged the kid into the bathroom with him. After Robbie ran out with only the first layer of camping dirt scrubbed away, Liam had stayed in the shower for a long time, letting the comforting stream of hot water soothe him. He had fallen into bed with a heavy sigh of satisfaction, having only the strength to pull Izzy into his arms before he dropped off. Sleeping on the ground was hard on the old bones. He had been amazed at the way his father had sprung out of his sleeping bag each morning as if he were Robbie's age.

Izzy smiled at Liam as he sat down beside her. He took the cup from her, drank a little of her coffee and passed it back. She reached over to lay her hand against his face, "You were sleeping so soundly when I woke up, I didn't want to bother you. I'm glad you're home, I missed you."

Liam watched as the sun climbed up the mountains on the far side of the beach. The day was probably going to be another hot one. He felt Izzy's fingers intertwined with his own. She sipped her coffee and asked, "How was it?"

"Good, exhausting but good. I had a lot of time on my own, hiking on the beach and sitting out on the rocks and watching the ocean. Robbie had a riot."

"I can imagine. Promise me you'll go through that bucket of shells and things he brought back. I think I saw something squirming in there."

"I will. It'll probably take most of the day to sort out the camping gear and

305

the laundry. And I still feel as though I have sand stuck on me." Liam squirmed a bit.

Izzy sat up straight and handed him her coffee, "I've got to get going. If anyone wants the SUV today, it'll be over at the Camp. I'm driving into Dearborn this morning to pick up a few things. I'll go straight into work from there." She leaned over and kissed Liam, lingering before she straightened up, "Can you remind Dad, when he wakes up, that I'm bringing Willow over this afternoon to cut his hair?" Izzy grabbed her briefcase, waved to Liam and strolled off towards the driveway.

✦✦✦✦

Lisa-Marie walked out to the cliff deck. Liam was relaxing on the swing chair, staring out at the water. She had avoided talking with him for long enough. She stood in the corner leaning her back against the railing, "Are you still pissed off at me?"

Liam shook his head, "I'm not mad. I acted like a fool, kiddo. I'm sorry. I was way out of line, trying to tell you what to do." Lisa-Marie decided to allow the nickname. She could feel herself choking up at Liam's words and her reaction surprised her. For the first time since she had returned to Crater Lake, he seemed like the man she had met the previous summer – the person who listened when she talked.

Liam sat forward on the swing, "I still believe it would be better for you to stay here instead of over at Justin's. I think it's the best thing for Sophie to have her mother living under the same roof with her for as long as she can. But I can't make those choices for you."

Tears clouded Lisa-Marie's eyes. She blinked and swallowed hard. "I can't be what you want me to be. It's too hard. I'll be gone to school soon –" now her voice was cracking and she couldn't stop the tears. "I don't want to be Sophie's mother. I don't want to love her. I get that you love her, Liam ... that's great, but what about me?" She stared at him with tears streaming down her face, "Why don't you see me anymore? You used to listen to me. What happened to you? Why don't I matter anymore?" She lost the battle with the tears that made her choke out her next words, "You said nothing that happened between us was my fault, but I feel like you're making me pay."

Liam got up from the swing chair and moved over to her. He put his hands on her arms. She leaned into him, so the top of her head rested against his chest. He could feel her sobbing out her relief at finally being able to describe how she had been replaced in his mind and heart by Sophie.

"I do care about you, Lisa. I've never stopped caring. Everything's gotten

306

so complicated with the baby, but you're right; I shouldn't have let myself stop seeing you."

She pulled away and wiped her eyes with the back of her hands, sniffing and taking a deep breath. Liam let go of her arms as he said, "I know how you feel now. I won't pressure you anymore. But I want to ask you one thing ... okay?" She nodded and he went on, "Are you sure you'll always feel about Sophie the way you do right now?"

Lisa-Marie shook her head so forcefully that her hair flew wildly around her face, "How do I know what I'll always feel. I want to have my life back. I want to go to school and go to Europe on the exchange trip. Is there anything so wrong with that?"

"No, there's nothing wrong with that. I think you're going to grow up and change your mind about Sophie. I want you to know that when you do, she's going to be waiting here for you."

"But what if I never change my mind? What if I can't ever love her like you guys do?"

"Then Sophie will have a life here with Izzy and me ... we'll help her understand."

"That's great for her. That baby has it made, doesn't she? What about me? Where is my home? Everything has fallen apart at the A-Frame. Who knows if Auntie Beth and Beulah will get back together."

"This is the place you can always come back to – next week, or in a few months, or next year, or ten years from now. This is your home." Liam had a faraway look in his eyes as he said, "Caleb always used to tell me that I belonged here, that I shouldn't ever leave. I never understood how he was so sure about that. Now I get it. He saw the part of me that needed this place and now I see that part in you. What comes around, goes around." He smiled, "I've got to get moving if I'm going to get all the eggs gathered up before Sophie's done napping."

As they walked back toward the cabin, Lisa-Marie told Liam, "I'll get her bottle and stuff if you aren't back by the time she wakes up. I'm not going anywhere. I've decided to stay here until I go back to school."

❧❧❧❧

Jonathan had pushed himself to the limit exploring the whole area around Micah Camp. His food was long gone; nightmares stalked him every time he closed his eyes. He heard strange sounds in the bush all around him. He ran his hand over the stubble of a beard on his chin and flicked his tangled hair out of his eyes.

Next door to the Camp, he'd watched the two women who worked at the bakery. The smell of fresh bread made his mouth water and he considered breaking into the bakery at night. But every time he came close, he set the dogs to barking up a storm. One evening, the tall woman came out on the back porch of the A-Frame to shout, "Gertrude, Alice ... what the hell is the problem. Bloody bears again, I bet."

He had circled the largest cabin more than a few times, staggering the time of the day. He had spotted a woman working in the garden, an older woman coming and going between a small cabin and the bigger place, and a young woman moving to and from the Camp. The woman who worked in the garden sometimes appeared outside on the decks with a baby. He lurked in the evening dusk near the edge of the garden and ate raw beans. They caused his empty stomach to heave. He tried to sneak into the greenhouse but once again, a chorus of barking sent him back into the bushes.

Furthest from the Camp, a cabin perched out on a cliff; this was the place where the tall guy lived. Jonathan had followed him one morning all the way to the sawmill. He fantasized about sneaking into the cabin and blowing the guy's head off. But he knew he couldn't take the chance. He had to know he had Willow first before anything else went down.

He moved one of his daily stake-out spots to more risky ground in the trees near the far edge of the Camp driveway. He lay there as the afternoon sun dipped toward the mountains, and he saw Willow. She was walking beside the gardening woman, towards an SUV that was parked in the drive. The blood hammered in his ears. He held the gun close to the side of his body. Willow turned when a girl ran across from the main building calling out to her, "Are you going to be back for dinner? Dylan's made quesadillas."

Willow raised her voice to answer, "I'm going to Izzy's to do a haircut. I'll be back in plenty of time for dinner." She got into the car with the woman and they started up the drive.

Jonathan slithered backwards into the trees. This was the chance he had been waiting for. He knew the woman would be driving over to the large cabin. He jumped up and headed for the trail, moving quickly in a low crouch with the gun banging against his side.

⚜⚜⚜⚜

Izzy parked the SUV, got out of the vehicle and waved to Liam who stood in the workshop, fiddling with the weed eater. When Dante and Pearl ran out to sniff at her, Willow backed up with a look of fright on her face.

Liam called the dogs back into the shop, "Go ahead, I'll make sure they stay in here with me."

As Izzy and Willow entered the cabin, Cynthia called out to them from where she stood behind Lisa-Marie's chair at the dining room table, "Edward's ready, Willow. We even wrapped a towel around him for you. We're double-checking the final proofs of the book." Edward sat at the end of the table. He glanced at Izzy and Willow with a bemused, faraway look in his eyes.

Izzy walked past Sophie's cradle and stood beside Cynthia to glance at the pages Lisa-Marie was turning. Willow pulled her scissors out of her bag. Smiling at Edward, she picked up the spray bottle on the dining room table, spritzed his head of silvery hair a couple of times and started to snip.

✥✥✥✥

Robbie had dozed off upstairs with his head on Izzy's desk. He had been watching the path through the apple trees hoping to catch the first glimpse of Izzy when she came home from work. The cabin was like a clock that had stopped ticking when Izzy wasn't around. No one had bothered to tell him she would be driving around from the Camp. He woke up, raised his head from the desk and wiped away a small puddle of drool that had formed on the wooden surface. He was surprised to hear Izzy's voice down in the dining room. Sophie cried and Izzy said, "You go ahead with what you're doing, Lisa. I'll get her."

As Robbie got up from the chair, a flash of movement outside the window caught his eye. A man he had never seen before was hunched over, running across the kitchen deck. In his hands was a large gun. The light that surrounded the stranger made Robbie's stomach lurch with pain and he gagged. He turned to yell but before he could produce any words, he heard the kitchen door open and hurried footsteps running through the cabin. He dropped down to the floor.

✥✥✥✥

Izzy put Sophie's soother back in her mouth and tucked the thin sheet around her. She turned and her eyes widened at the expression of horror on Willow's face. The girl was looking past Izzy and up the stairs to the kitchen. The scissors in Willow's hand snapped shut, echoing loudly in the sudden and complete silence that hung over the room. Izzy watched a piece of her father's hair flutter to the floor a split second before she spun around to see what Willow was staring at.

309

Jonathan moved quickly down the three stairs, backhanding the woman who stood in his way. Izzy dropped with a thud onto the floor. He hefted the gun up and aimed it into the cradle, "Don't anyone move or this baby will be the first to die."

FORTY-SEVEN

Robbie crawled across the upstairs room and slithered down the stairs, keeping his body tight against the wall furthest from the kitchen landing. He slipped off the bottom stair and crawled through to the pantry. He got out the door, cleared the two steps in a leap and ran. His heart pounded a crazy beat in his chest. He could see his father, Liam and Justin standing in the driveway.

Alex had come out of his camper moments before. He had been having what he referred to as his afternoon catnap – twenty minutes, no more and he was refreshed. He planned to head into the cabin and start dinner. Liam walked out of the workshop and told his father, "I've been working on that damn weed eater for most of the afternoon and I still can't get the thing going." Alex shook his head at Liam's inability to tinker tools into action.

They both looked up the driveway when Justin called out, "Hot one today, hey. I'm heading straight for the lake."

Liam opened his mouth but before he could get out any words, he spotted Robbie running towards them with a look of sheer terror on his face. Alex moved forward and knelt down in the gravel. He pulled Robbie close to him and said, "What is it?"

Robbie gasped for breath, "There's a guy in the cabin ... he has a gun. He says he'll kill Sophie if anyone moves." Robbie turned away and leaned over to heave the contents of his stomach onto the gravel.

Alex stood up, "Justin, get up to the sawmill. Take the Dodge. Get them to call 9-1-1." He turned to Robbie and pushed him towards the camper, "Get in there and lock the door and stay put." He grabbed Liam's arm. Their eyes met for a moment. A silent message passed between them. "Come on," Alex said as he drew the hunting knife from the sheath at his belt and moved towards the open pantry door.

ขขขข

Lisa-Marie scrambled up from her chair when she saw Izzy fly away in front of the guy with the gun, as if she were some sort of toy. A scream started its way out of her mouth but then the dull black rifle was pointed into the cradle at Sophie, and the scream lodged tightly in her throat.

Jonathan crooked his finger at Willow, "Get over here."

The scissors dropped out of Willow's hand and skittered across the floor. As if in a daze, she walked around the table towards Jonathan. Cynthia watched the scissors slide to a stop. She tried to think straight, to keep her rising panic at bay. Could she get to the scissors? If she did, what could she do with them?

Edward was also desperate to focus his thoughts. He wanted to shake his head but worried his movement might draw too much attention. He flexed his hands against his legs and shuffled his feet. Adrenalin was pumping through his bloodstream. He hoped it could negate the sluggishness of the morphine that made him feel as though he was moving underwater.

The moment Willow was within reach, Jonathan's free hand wrapped around her throat. He raised her off her feet, "You thought you could walk out on me?" He shook her hard and brought her face close to his, "I told you I'd never let you go. Who's the guy I saw you with, Willow? Who is he?" His features twisted with rage. He threw Willow onto the floor. Her head made a sickening thud as it smashed against the edge of the table on the way down. Jonathan spit out his words, "You cheating little whore." He pulled his leg back and kicked the still body at his feet.

Izzy was having a hard time focusing, her vision was blurred and there was a loud ringing in her ear. She saw Jonathan drop to one knee. The gun hung in his hand, away from the cradle. He drew Willow's lifeless body close. He seemed almost oblivious to the rest of them as he spoke, "Willow, baby, come on, wake up. I've come for you. I missed you so much. I love you, Willow. Say something, please, wake up."

Izzy thought about trying to grab the gun. She looked over at her father and he caught her eye and shook his head.

Jonathan suddenly dropped Willow's body on the floor. He raised the rifle to swing it around and point it at Edward, "You're first old man."

Edward caught a blur of movement at the top of the kitchen stairs. He looked into the crazed eyes of the gunman and knew that the moment for a diversion had come. He jumped up, gripped the edge of the table and tried to flip it over. The table didn't move; his intention had outstripped his strength.

The gun went off - a deafening roar in the small space. Edward slumped over the top of the table and slid down to the floor. Alex sprang down the stairs as the sound of the spent shell pinged off the hardwood floor. He grabbed the gunman around the neck and twisted his head back. His other hand came down in a sharp chop near the young man's wrist. The gun dropped to the floor. Alex swung the long, lethal blade of his knife up to glint against exposed skin and spoke in the guy's ear, "Don't move or I'll cut your throat wide open."

Jonathan tried to push back against Alex. Drops of blood sprang up bright red along the edge of the knife. His eyes widened and he stood very still.

Lisa-Marie let loose the scream that had been lodged in her throat. She fell down on her hands and knees and crawled over to Edward's body. He lay on his side as the bullet's exit wound in his back pumped blood onto the floor. She leaned over him, trying to staunch the flow with her hands.

Cynthia slid the gun forward with her foot. She leaned over, picked it up and ran down to the sun porch to set it gingerly on the work table. She dashed back up the stairs and knelt down beside Willow's motionless body. Izzy got up, reeling on her feet and shaking her head. She stumbled to the cradle. Sophie had begun to scream.

Alex kept an arm wrapped tightly around the assailant's neck. He held the blade between his teeth as he tugged the stranger's arm high up on his back and pushed him the rest of the way to the floor with a thud, pinning his other arm underneath him. Alex got a knee in the middle of the man's back and crouched there, breathing like a large cat over his prey. He looked up at Liam, "Get me a piece of rope to tie this guy up and something I can use to gag him." Between bouts of profanity, Jonathan had been shouting at Willow to wake up. Alex leaned close to his captive's ear, "Shut the fuck up or I'll break your arm." He emphasized the threat with a sharp tug that made the man under him groan.

✻✻✻✻

Justin burst into Reg's office and told him to get on the phone and call the police. Then he careened back down the driveway. As he jumped out of the Dodge, he heard the gunshot. Hunched over, he ran to the front deck of the cabin and raised his eyes to the window ledge to peer inside. He could see Alexander on the floor with his knee pressed into a body underneath him. He

313

could hear Lisa-Marie screaming. He ran across the deck, around to the entrance door and into the cabin.

Robbie had been hiding under the blankets on the upper bed of the camper when he heard the gunshot. He peered out of the camper's window and saw Justin running towards the cabin. He climbed down from the upper bunk. His heart thudded with fear as he opened the camper door a crack to look out. Justin ran up the stairs to disappear inside. Robbie thought for a second about what he should do. He knew his father had meant it when he'd told him to stay put, but his need to find out if Izzy was alright overrode everything. He jumped down the camper's three metal stairs and ran towards the cabin.

Once inside, Justin went straight to Lisa-Marie. He reached out to see if Edward had a pulse, then he shook his head at Cynthia who had looked over at him with an obvious question in her eyes. He pulled Lisa-Marie away. Her hands were dripping with blood and she was hysterical.

With Liam's help, Alex got the attacker's hands tied and a gag in his mouth. Alex dragged the guy to his feet and told Liam, "I'm taking him outside. Have you got things in here?"

Liam nodded and moved to Cynthia where she knelt beside Willow. Cynthia whispered to him. "Stay with her. I've got to check Edward and do something to stop Lisa from screaming like that." She jumped up and motioned for Justin to pull Lisa-Marie away. She quickly examined the lifeless body on the floor. It was too late – something she had known from the moment she had seen Edward take a gunshot to the chest.

She got up, ran down to the sun porch and made her way over to Edward's bed. She opened the night stand drawer and grabbed a small bottle of pills. After checking the label, she returned to the dining room and told Justin to bring Lisa-Marie over to the living room couch.

Cynthia pressed a small pill under the girl's tongue and told Justin, "Put your arms around her and make her stay put. She should settle down in a minute or two." She frowned, "We can't have her that hysterical right now. The pill is a mild sedative Edward uses to help him sleep; it should do the trick."

Holding Sophie, Izzy turned away from the sight of Willow's motionless body to stare at the blood on the floor where her father had fallen. She wanted to go to him but the baby was clinging to her and crying. Izzy's attention was suddenly diverted as the entry door burst open. Robbie stumbled inside, panic written all over his face. She ran over and turned him away from the scene in the dining room. He clutched at her waist as she said,

"I'm okay, Robbie. Don't look. Just don't look."

Before heading back to Willow's side, Cynthia grabbed an afghan off the back of a chair and draped it over Edward's body, pulling it up to cover his face. She knelt down beside Willow and whispered to Liam, "Edward's dead." He nodded and moved away to call 9-1-1. He told the dispatcher that they were out of danger; that the guy with the gun was tied up. He explained that they were going to need an emergency medevac chopper. It appeared that Willow might have internal bleeding. She was unconscious, no doubt because of a head injury.

Liam walked over to Izzy, "I'm going out to help Dad. The police and ambulance shouldn't be long. Keep Sophie and Robbie away from everything." He swung his arm back to indicate the carnage in the dining room.

Though she knew the answer the moment she had seen Cynthia cover the body, Izzy grabbed Liam's arm, "My father ... is he dead?"

Liam pulled her tight against him; he could feel Sophie's tiny body in Izzy's arms. Robbie pressed up against their legs. "Yes, I'm so sorry."

⚜⚜⚜⚜

The police four-by-four slammed to a stop, spewing gravel under the wheels. Liam ran across the back space from the kitchen deck to the driveway. He reached out to grab the RCMP officer's hand, "Thank God it's you Casey. Come with me. We've got the guy tied up over here on the deck."

Casey Donavan had been a police officer in Dearborn for almost ten years. He had played baseball on the Crater Lake Timber Wolves. His son worked part-time at the sawmill. With his hand on Liam's back, Casey was walking and talking fast, "What can you tell me?"

"Not much. This guy walked into the cabin with an assault rifle, he shot Izzy's father and seriously injured a girl from the Camp."

"Was he on his own? Is everyone else still inside? Where is the gun? Is anyone doing emergency first aid?" Casey was gesturing for the officers behind him to take charge of the gunman who was trussed up against the edge of the arbor on the kitchen deck.

Liam nodded to the first two questions, "I saw the gun sitting on the work table out on the sun porch. One of the women inside is a nurse."

Casey barked out orders, pointing as he spoke, "Get that guy in the truck. You, keep watch on him. You, come back and help me secure the scene."

The radio on Casey's belt crackled to life. He moved off and held the device to his ear. He snapped out, "Give us five minutes."

315

He turned to Alex and Liam, "The chopper has landed up at the sawmill. We'll have the paramedics down right away." One of the officers ran back from the four-by-four. Casey called over his shoulder to Liam, "Stay put while we check the perimeter of the cabin. Then we're going in."

✤✤✤✤

Holding the two children, Izzy collapsed into the recliner. She glanced over to the couch where Justin sat with his arms around Lisa-Marie. Her eyes were glazed but a steady stream of tears continued to track down her face. Cynthia still knelt on the floor beside Willow, monitoring her vital signs with a worried look on her face.

When Casey came down the stairs from the kitchen with another RCMP officer, followed by Alex and Liam, Izzy felt her whole body begin to shake with relief. Alex came over and took Robbie at the same time that Liam put out his hands for Sophie. Casey drew Izzy aside while the paramedics moved in to deal with Willow. "Tell me everything you can, Izzy."

She took a deep breath and forced herself to speak slowly and clearly, "The injured girl, Willow ... she knew this guy in Kamloops; he was after her. She called him Jonathan. I don't know his last name."

"And the man this Jonathan guy shot, he's your father?"

"Yes –" Izzy stifled a sob, "I think he was trying to create some kind of diversion. He stood up and tried to tip the table over and the guy fired the gun right at him."

"The injured girl, she's from the Camp?"

"Yes, she's a resident there."

Casey wrapped an arm around Izzy and squeezed her shoulders, "Let's call Roland, he'll need to be here."

Izzy nodded and as Casey followed her over to the phone, he asked, "Why was she here ... the girl from the Camp?"

Izzy handed him the phone, "She was cutting my dad's hair. He didn't get out much. He was dying of cancer." She turned to find Liam standing close. He put his arms around her.

Casey hung up the phone and did a quick head count. "I need everyone to stay put, don't anyone leave the cabin." He turned to Liam, "Why don't you get Bethany and Beulah over here, too. I think you're going to need some help for the next few hours."

A second paramedic crew arrived and knelt beside Edward's body. After a moment, one of them shook his head in Casey's direction. They moved Edward onto a stretcher. Izzy broke away from Liam and walked over to kneel beside her father's body. Pushing the hair out of his eyes, she stroked his face and kissed his cheek. She stood up and buried her face against Liam's shoulder as the stretcher was taken from the room.

FORTY-EIGHT

The police had questioned all of them individually. Casey had allowed Liam to stay with Robbie while he asked the boy to go over what he had done from the moment he had spotted the gunman on the kitchen deck. Alex's questioning took the longest, but he had walked away unscathed, receiving a slap on the wrist for taking things into his own hands and a pat on the back for his fast thinking. Casey told them that the questioning would start all over again the next day when a criminal investigator arrived from Courtenay.

It was quiet in the cabin. Izzy and Liam were lying in their bed with Robbie and Sophie tucked in between them. Izzy had an ice pack pressed to the side of her face. She felt only a far-away throbbing, thanks to the pain killers Cynthia had given her. It seemed to Izzy that Cynthia had been everywhere at once, attending to everyone. All she and Liam had to do was cling to one another and the two children that now slept between them.

She tried to recreate the sequence of events that had occurred but her mind kept skittering away from the details. The terror of a madman waving a gun and screaming at them had seemed to go on for hours. Yet Liam told her it had been less than ten minutes from the time she and Willow entered the cabin until he and his father had burst in.

Liam reached past Sophie and Robbie to stroke Izzy's hair back from her face. He watched as her eyes grew heavy. He thought about the words he and his father had exchanged as they stood guard over the trussed-up man on the deck.

Alex had held Liam's gaze, "You doubted. I saw it in your eyes."

"I did."

"I know it wasn't lack of courage, Son."

"No, I'd have died to protect all of them. I did wonder if we should wait for the police. I worried we might make things worse."

"There are times when you take care of your own. This was one of them."

"I saw that in your eyes."

Alex reached out to pat Liam's arm, "You were always a son who knew how to listen to his old man."

❦❦❦❦

Alex walked across the living room towards Cynthia. He had two squat glasses balanced in one hand and a bottle of whiskey in the other. He screwed off the lid of the bottle with his teeth and poured the alcohol into the glasses as he walked. He handed Cynthia a drink and sat down beside her.

Sipping with appreciation, Alex pointed down to the bottle he had placed on the floor between them, "It's the damnedest story about that bottle." He shook his head, "I was standing out on the cliff deck yesterday morning, enjoying the view, thinking it was good to be alive on such a fine day, when I caught the sun reflecting off something down in the trees. I stared down there for a bit and ... would you believe it? This unopened bottle was perched there, pretty as a fancy ornament on a Christmas tree." Alex savoured his drink before adding, "Took some doing to retrieve it, what with crawling down that cliff and up into the tree, but I considered it my duty."

Cynthia shivered, "I sense there is a part of you capable of doing whatever has to be done. And I'm not talking about climbing down a cliff to retrieve a bottle of booze."

"Under the right circumstance ... context is everything."

Cynthia reached out her hand and turned his face towards her, "Would you have done what you threatened if he hadn't given up?"

"Ah, Cynthia, what a question ... are you after ruining my warrior act?" He drained his drink and grabbed the bottle to splash another ounce or two into his glass. "If you mean would I have cut his throat open with the knife, there was never a need for such brutality, to say nothing of the mess it would have made. I could have disabled him in any number of ways. But he didn't need to know that, did he?" Alex smiled over at her, "And you have to admit, the knife did add a sense of drama."

❦❦❦❦

Justin was lying beside Lisa-Marie on the bed in the sunflower room. The pills Cynthia had given her had knocked her first into a state of stunned, silent

319

sobbing, then into a restless sleep. She whimpered and tossed her head on the pillow beside him. Justin held her in his arms and willed himself to take long, slow breaths. He wished he could drop off to sleep, but every time he closed his eyes he relived the moment when he had heard the gun shot and recalled how he had pulled Lisa-Marie away from Edward's body, blood dripping from her hands, her eyes wild and hysterical.

He didn't want to let himself imagine *what if*, but it was impossible not to do so. What if Robbie hadn't been in the house to run out like a mini commando and warn them? What if Alexander hadn't been there to take charge? Justin knew he was good in a tight situation but he couldn't have acted as swiftly as Alex had. What if that crazy maniac with the gun had hurt Lisa-Marie or Sophie? His fists clenched and once again he forced himself to relax.

Before he finally dozed off, Justin made a decision. He would talk to Reg the first chance he got, tell him he had to go back to Vancouver earlier than he had planned. Reg was a good guy, he would understand. Izzy and Liam, her Aunt Bethany and Beulah would rally around Lisa-Marie to help her get through this. He couldn't trust himself to keep his feelings hidden. Her need for comfort would break him down, it was that simple.

ɤɤɤɤ

A loud knock on the cabin door made Arianna jump up off her bed and shove her fist against her mouth to stifle a scream. She walked out to the living room and called out, "Who is it?"

"It's Dylan. Let me in."

Dylan took one look at Arianna's face and opened his arms to pull her close to him, "I came over as soon as I heard. Grab your stuff, you can come and stay with Mark and me. You can bunk in Jesse's old room. You shouldn't be alone."

Arianna looked confused, "How did you find out? Roland said he wouldn't be telling everyone until the morning."

"From Mark ... he made this radio that picks up emergency calls. He listened to the whole thing over in the maintenance shed - all the police and emergency dispatcher stuff. When he didn't come in for dinner and he wasn't in our cabin later, I went to look for him. He was wedged into the corner of that room Jim has out there, holding onto the radio, looking like a ghost. I got the whole story out of him."

"All Roland said was that Willow had been in a bad accident over at Izzy's.

He said she had to have surgery." Arianna's eyes were wide, "What really happened?"

"Best I could get out of Mark, some guy with a rifle broke into Izzy's and threatened to kill everyone. He shot a guy who was dead at the scene – Edward Montgomery – must be some relation to Izzy, right? The paramedics were rushing Willow down to Vancouver for surgery. The cops had the guy in custody. Mark said his name was Jonathan something."

Arianna's eyes widened, "He's Willow's old boyfriend. She told me all about him, how he beat her up. She left him because she thought he might kill her."

"Come on, let's get going. Mark is pretty much a basket case over at the cabin. I don't want to leave him alone for too long. I'm hoping you can help him get his mind off things."

Arianna threw a few things into her pack and followed Dylan out the door. As they walked across the quiet Camp, she said, "I know this is terrible of me but I kept thinking ... what if I'm next? They say bad things happen in threes, first Maddy, then Willow, then me, just like some summer camp horror movie. I was thinking about myself instead of caring whether Willow was going to be okay."

"Most people think about themselves when bad things happen, Ari. It's normal. And you could do with more thinking about yourself. Isn't that what you're working on?"

"I wish that things could be different, like you wanting me to stay at your cabin for other reasons. I can't help it. I'm so pathetic sometimes."

Dylan put his arm around Arianna's shoulder and pulled her close, "I know, sometimes the way things turn out really sucks."

✦✦✦✦

When Roland came in, Jillian looked up from the couch where she sat reading through a pile of research interview transcripts. She picked out two and set them aside before she said, "Oh babe, here you are at last. Was it awful?"

Roland had gone straight over to Izzy and Liam's cabin. He had answered as many questions as he could, then an officer had followed him back to the Camp where he'd handed over all the paperwork they had on Willow. After that, he'd had the unenviable task of informing Arianna that her only remaining roommate would not be returning to the Camp. When Arianna had burst into tears, he wished he'd delegated the responsibility to Jillian.

He sat down on the couch and gave himself up to Jillian's ministrations as she fixed him a stiff drink and stood behind him to massage the tension out of his shoulders. He set the empty glass down on the table, "Thanks, Jill. Come and sit down." When Jillian had settled in beside him, Roland took her hand, "I need to talk to you about something important."

Jillian reached over to grab the two transcripts, "I know what you're going to say. I should have known something like this could happen. I was so stupid, babe."

Roland shook his head in confusion, "What are you talking about?"

"Willow ... in both the interviews I did with her, she spoke about a guy named Jonathan and how violent he was. It didn't occur to me that no one else knew."

Roland took the files and set them on the table; tomorrow he would get to the bottom of who knew what and when. Right now he did not want to be deterred from what he had been planning for over a week to say to Jillian. "That was not what I wanted to talk to you about." He took a deep breath, "I've been giving our relationship careful consideration. I wasn't expecting that after such a short time, you would have become so important to me, but you have. I want to talk about our future."

Jillian clapped her hands in delight. She threw her arms around Roland's neck, "Oh babe, nothing on this earth would make me happier."

⁂

Beulah and Bethany walked back to the A-Frame together. Bethany didn't hesitate; she followed Beulah up the back steps and into their home. They sat close together on the couch. Beulah put her arm around Bethany and pulled her close before she said, "I want you to stay."

Bethany snuggled close, "I want that, too. I had already decided I would."

"The last time we talked you said that there were things you needed to say. I'm ready to listen."

Bethany pulled away and sat up. "I want to own up to my part of things. It takes two people to make a relationship work. I know that. When I came here, I did need you to take care of me. I got lazy. I never tried to move beyond that. Then the accident happened and everything changed. I felt desperate to do something with my life. I know I acted nuts over the whole baby thing, emotionally manipulating you and Liam. I'm ashamed of myself. Then I threw myself into the work with Jillian. I never considered the impact it would have on our relationship. You said it - I changed the rules. I owed it to you to talk about that but I didn't even try. It was easier to see you as the enemy. You were holding me back. That way I didn't have to face up to my own responsibility."

Bethany folded her arms across her chest and looked sternly at Beulah before adding, "My behavior doesn't excuse you for running off to sleep with someone else or for lying to me."

Beulah pulled Bethany close again, "I love you, Beth. I know I'm no prize of a partner, but I do love you." She ran her hand along the side of Bethany's face, drawing her closer as she kissed her. Beulah smiled, "It's going to take me a hell of a long time to show you how much I've missed you but ... first things first. Circumstances are going to change around here, starting with some legal issues." Bethany frowned as Beulah kept talking, "Your name is going on the deed to this cabin and that includes the bakery business." As Bethany's eyes widened at this idea, Beulah laughed, "And since same-sex marriages have been happening in the province of BC for some time, I think we should get on with that, as well."

Bethany gasped, "Are you asking me to marry you?"

"I am. Seems like a good time to make legal partners out of the both of us."

Bethany ticked off items on her fingers as she spoke, "I'll want a ring, a nice dress, flowers, a dinner out and some kind of honeymoon trip. Palm Springs in January might be nice."

Beulah pulled her wife-to-be back into her arms. "I think we could manage all of that."

FORTY-NINE

I zzy held the chain of the diamond pendant that graced her neck, twisting it slowly around her fingers. Looking around the cabin jammed with people, she experienced a strange sense of satisfaction. She could imagine that her father might smile and say, "Isabella, this is a smashing affair. You've done all things well."

The days since Edward's death had been an up-and-down blend of busyness and suppressed grief. Everyone needed her to do something and there wasn't a moment for her to think about how she felt. She touched the side of her face carefully. At least the swelling had gone down; she could cover most of the bruised discolouration with makeup. The corner of her eye was still bright red from some burst blood vessels but Rosemary had assured her that her vision would be fine.

Robbie had only been able to go back to his own loft to sleep the previous night. Though he had been lauded as a hero for his quick thinking and had not seen the full extent of the violence, the afternoon had affected him. One day Izzy had been sitting in the reclining chair with him and he had burst into tears. It was the first time she had seen him cry. He had sobbed out his wish that Spiderman could be real because he would have saved Edward and protected all of them.

Then there were the kids at the Camp who needed her help. Mark had been sent reeling by Maddy's suicide attempt and by the way Jonathan's actions had been revealed to him as he hunched over the radio, listening to emergency calls. It took a lot of support from Izzy, and the growing friendship Mark had with both Dylan and Arianna, to coax him out of the maintenance shed each day and back into the mainstream of Camp life.

There had been numerous phone calls to make and things to arrange in regard to her father's death. When she contacted his solicitor in London, she had learned that the man would like to attend Edward's memorial. He had gathered a couple of other old cronies – not Izzy's words, that's what they called themselves – and the group of them had flown to Vancouver. From there, the three men had rented a car and driven up the Island to Dearborn.

Izzy had made all the necessary arrangements for the cremation and had signed the papers that needed signing. She had tried to quell the memories of the echoing sound of the gunshot, the sight of her father's body collapsing over the table, the blood and the heart-stopping fear she had felt. Distraction was possible whenever she kept herself busy. At night, the whole thing came back to her. She clung to Liam, her heart pounding as she told him over and over exactly what had happened. He seemed to understand her need to organize the events in her mind and he didn't try to stop her.

Izzy sat on the piano bench and forced herself to look away from the slightly off-coloured patch of wood filler that marred the frame of the nearby French door. She had watched Liam patiently dig the bullet out of the wood, sand down the hole and apply the filler. Whenever she crossed the cabin her eyes sought out the only evidence left of what had happened. She couldn't help herself.

Casey Donavan and his wife walked past her carrying plates filled with food, and she returned their smiles. She saw Rosemary chatting with Alexander. Everyone was here – Cynthia, Roland and Jillian, Beulah and Bethany, Reg and Josie, teachers from the Camp along with Cook and Jim. Arianna sat on a chair beside Lisa Marie holding Sophie; Dylan and Justin stood nearby talking. Darlene had arrived from Dearborn with the mayor. Her father's friends were circulating and sharing stories. Robbie had regained his appetite and was in the process of grazing his way over the entire food table. Liam was doing a wonderful job as an attentive host. Izzy took a deep breath. All she needed to do was relax and enjoy an afternoon of fulfilling her father's last wishes.

She looked over to see Maryanne and her husband coming down the stairs from the kitchen. She got up and walked over to give Maryanne a tight hug, "Thanks so much for coming." Izzy watched as a look of anguish washed over Maryanne's face. Then the woman squared her shoulders and made her way across the living room to study one of several photo montages that highlighted Edward's career. Izzy's sympathies went out to her. She was well aware of the way guilt could weigh a person down.

꙳꙳꙳꙳

The day before, Izzy, Jillian and Maryanne had met with Roland. He had told them, "I've asked to have this meeting in Izzy's office. On neutral ground, so to speak. I want it to be clear from the very beginning that nothing we talk about today is related to blame."

Izzy and Jillian nodded while a look of confusion passed over Maryanne's face. She obviously had no idea why Roland had asked her to attend the meeting.

Looking down at a piece of paper in his hand, Roland said, "The police investigated all of the movements of Mr. Jonathan Burns. They went back to the time that Ms. Willow Donaldson left the Kamloops area." Roland shifted in his chair and crossed his legs. He studied the paper and went on, "In May, Mr. Burns obtained a job doing yard work for a Mr. and Mrs. Franklin – Ms. Donaldson's former, foster caregivers."

At the mention of the city of Kamloops and the name Franklin, Maryanne's eyes widened and her face became pale as she sat forward in her chair. Roland continued to speak, "When the police questioned Mrs. Franklin, she told them that Mr. Burns was always friendly; she had no recollection of him ever mentioning Ms. Donaldson. The police reported that they found a note on the fridge with the address of Micah Camp. When they brought this note to Mrs. Franklin's attention she explained that she had written the address down when someone from the Camp called and asked that she forward Ms. Donaldson's high school transcripts. The police ascertained that Mr. Burns left his job with the Franklins at about the same time as Mrs. Franklin received the phone call." Roland looked past the three women to stare at an arrangement of flowers on Izzy's desk, "About two weeks ago."

Maryanne's voice shook, "I did this. I caused this; that's what you're saying, Roland."

Izzy reached out and put her hand on Maryanne's arm, "You didn't cause this anymore than the rest of us did. If we're going to dish out fault, then I'm to blame, too. When I discovered what Willow's relationship with this Jonathan person had been, I was distracted by work issues and personal problems. I tried to talk to Roland but he wasn't here, so I left him a note. I thought he could handle it the next day. I should have tracked him down so we could both deal with the situation immediately."

Jillian cleared her throat, "I've got my share of blame, as well. In both of the mapping interviews I did with her, Willow mentioned how violent her boyfriend had been. I listened like a good researcher. I had Bethany transcribe her words. I coded them and filed them away. It never occurred to me that she hadn't discussed this with you." Jillian glanced at Izzy.

Roland set the paper on the table in front of him, "I phoned the Ministry and asked that all privacy protocols be enforced but I didn't believe it necessary to speak to the teachers here at the Camp, or the rest of the staff, or any of the residents. Ms. Delacourt has confessed that, months ago, Ms. Donaldson confided to her all the details of the violent relationship she had been in with Mr. Burns."

"How is Willow?" Maryanne asked.

Izzy spoke in a matter of fact tone, though images of Willow's body on her dining room floor haunted her, "She's had an operation to repair some damage to her spleen. The doctors are still worried about a serious head injury but she's awake and responding to various tests."

Roland picked up a yellow legal pad from the table, "We need to learn from this set of unfortunate circumstances. I would like to hear ideas on protocols that we can put in place to ensure we do not step into a tragedy like this again."

⚜ ⚜ ⚜ ⚜

Lisa-Marie looked up when she heard Sophie crying. She was showing Edward's book to an older man who spoke with such a thick Scottish accent she could barely understand a word he said. She excused herself and walked across the crowded living room to take Sophie out of Liam's arms. The baby was in obvious need of a diaper change and a nap.

Lisa-Marie took care of the diaper, carried Sophie into Izzy and Liam's room and shut the door. She tried to copy what she had seen Izzy, Liam and even Robbie do. She laid the baby down on her back in her cradle, put the soother in her mouth and tucked the blanket up under her arm close to her face. She stood back and watched as Sophie spit out the soother, kicked her legs out from under the blanket and scrunched her little face into a look of baby anger. Lisa-Marie frowned and tried the whole process again, all to no avail. Sophie was not about to settle down for her.

She shrugged with frustration, reached into the cradle and picked the baby up. She opened the bedroom door and walked out of the room. Robbie was standing in the living room stuffing a piece of cake into his mouth. She waited until he looked up, then she waved him over.

327

Lisa-Marie pointed to the baby squirming in her arms, "She won't settle down for me. You and Liam and Izzy can always get her to sleep. How do I do it?"

Robbie wiped his mouth and cake crumbs fell on the ground. "Izzy isn't as good at it as me and Liam."

Sophie was crying in earnest now. Lisa-Marie frowned down at the baby, "She acts like she hates me or something."

"You have to hold her different." Robbie reached out and repositioned the baby in Lisa-Marie's arms. "Do it like that so her head is tucked in tight beside you."

Lisa-Marie adjusted her grip on Sophie but the baby continued to squirm. "What now, smart guy?"

"Walk around with her for a while." Robbie watched as Lisa-Marie tried to get the soother into Sophie's mouth but the baby spit it out. He caught it before it hit the ground. "Do you know *Puff the Magic Dragon?*"

"The song? Ya, I guess. Why?"

"You have to sing that song to her."

"Sing to her." Lisa-Marie frowned, "What do you mean?"

"Dah ... walk around with her and sing the song to her."

"Why that song?"

"My grannie told me that every baby has a song. You have to pick it out right after the baby's born. No one else was doing it, so I chose *Puff the Magic Dragon* and now Sophie's stuck with it."

"I can't start walking around and singing. People will think I'm nuts."

"You can do it real quiet. Don't be such a fraidy cat. She's just a baby. It's not like you're trying out for *Canadian Idol*." Robbie made a face at Lisa-Marie. He slid over to the food table to grab another chunk of cake.

✻✻✻✻

Izzy walked through the garden towards the cabin. She had driven Rosemary up the road to her car. It was kind of the doctor to take time from her busy schedule to come out and be part of their farewell to Edward. Izzy's steps slowed and she took her time about going inside. The house was still full of people. She stood at the top of the garden and admired the way the lush arrangements of plants and flowers were making their burst of summer energy count.

As she entered the back door, her footsteps almost faltered in surprise. She could see Lisa-Marie walking to and fro in the quiet of the bedroom off the entry. Sophie was in her arms. She was singing to the baby and it looked like it was working. Sophie seemed to have fallen asleep.

Izzy went into the crowded living room and spotted Robbie sitting in the recliner. She scooted in beside him and tickled him, "Hey, Robbie, Robbie, McBobbie." She waited a moment, then she tickled him some more before adding, "Say it ... come on ... you know you want to."

Robbie giggled, "Izzy, Izzy, McLizzy."

Izzy dropped her arm around Robbie and sat back in the chair, "You gave away Sophie's song."

Robbie shrugged, "Leez needed it." He looked up at her; the smile faded from his face and concern edged the depth of his dark eyes, "Are you still sad that Liam said you can't be Sophie's mom?" He stammered, "I wasn't spying or anything. I heard you guys talking, then I saw you out on the cliff deck. I could tell from the light that you were crying. I knew you were sad."

"I was sad, but now I know why it matters so much to Liam that Lisa-Marie should always be Sophie's mom. Understanding why helps."

Izzy and Robbie sat together – their chair a private island in the midst of the gathering around them. Robbie drove the little red car in his hand up and down the arm of the chair. His voice was quiet when he finally asked, "Do you think Liam would let you be my mom?"

He glanced up at Izzy and she saw his face fill with a look of longing that only a child could feel for the end of searching. Tears filled her eyes. She pulled Robbie close and hugged him tight against her side. "You know what Robbie, Robbie, McBobbie? I'm pretty sure we could convince him."

⚜ ⚜ ⚜ ⚜

Beulah stood in the center of the room and tapped a spoon on the edge of a glass to get everyone's attention. "I would like to propose a special toast." She waited while Liam circulated around the room passing out plastic wine glasses and Jillian followed with a large bottle of champagne in one hand and a bottle of some non-alcoholic fizzy drink in the other. Izzy had no idea where the champagne had come from but she held out her glass like everyone else. When all the glasses were filled, Beulah looked over at Bethany and nodded her head.

Bethany smiled around the room at everyone, "We aren't trying to steal Edward's moment but you said this was a celebration of life, Izzy." Bethany paused and met Izzy's eyes. She looked over to Liam and smiled. She raised her glass, "Beulah and I have decided to get married right after Christmas. Let's drink to moving on."

329

Lisa-Marie had been standing in the doorway near the entry; she had been half listening to her Auntie Beth because her other ear was tuned to making sure Sophie had gone to sleep. Her eyes widened when the meaning of the words sank in and she moved across the room to throw herself into her aunt's open arms. "Oh Auntie Beth, I'm so happy for you, and thanks for waiting so I can be here for the big event."

Bethany smoothed Lisa-Marie's hair away from her face, "Well, I'll need my maid of honour, won't I?"

Roland stepped forward and raised his glass, "A final tribute to the person we have come here today to remember. Edward Montgomery ... he made the ultimate sacrifice for those he loved. No such action is ever lost in the karmic circle of life. Rest in peace, Edward, you served well, all those you cared for." Friends and family raised their glasses to drink to Edward.

❧❧❧❧❧

"Are you watching that movie again?" Lisa-Marie walked past Robbie who was sprawled on the couch near Izzy's desk, laughing at the cartoon antics of Timon and Pumbaa in *The Lion King*. Robbie waved at her to get out of the way of the television.

Lisa-Marie sat down at Izzy's desk, opened the middle drawer and saw the folder with the words – *Sophie and Robbie Important Papers* – written on the front. It was right where Izzy had said it would be. She opened the folder. A brown envelope with Robbie's name on it sat on top of the stuff from Vital Statistics. She held up the envelope, "What's this?"

He glanced over and intoned, "Important Papers."

Lisa-Marie made a face at him as she slid the papers out of the envelope. Robbie's birth certificate was on the top. "*Robert Anthony Collins-Albert.* Quite the name you've got there kid. Albert – was that your mom's name?" Robbie nodded. "And Anthony?"

Robbie pulled his Spiderman quilt up around him, "My grandpa – he died when I was little."

Lisa-Marie put Robbie's papers away and took from the file what she had come for. She left the boy on the sofa rolling around and making farting noises in time with Pumbaa, the wart hog.

❧❧❧❧❧

Izzy gently closed Robbie's door and walked down the short hallway to glance into the sunflower room. Lisa-Marie looked up from her bed where she sat

330

with her journal open in her lap. "Is Robbie asleep?" Izzy nodded. Lisa-Marie pointed at her desk, "I decided on the name and I started to fill out the new forms ... for Sophie. Can you help me later, with the rest of it?"

Izzy reached over and picked up the pile of papers. The name jumped off the top page at her - *Sophie Leanne Collins-Shannon.* The hyphen sent a message loud and clear. Liam was linked to the young woman who sat cross-legged on the bed. They had started out on a path together long before the sharp turn that led to Sophie's conception; today that path continued and it stretched out into a future no one could see.

She glanced up from the papers in her hand and read the emotions that raced across Lisa-Marie's face. Izzy couldn't count the number of young people who had looked at her over the years with those pleading emotions – accept my choice, love me no matter what, don't leave me even if you wish I would decide differently. As an experienced counsellor, she recognized those moments as a turning point in a therapeutic alliance – a turning point that could lead to change. In every instance, Izzy had given what was required. At the same time, what made her a good counsellor is that she knew how much of herself to hold back. A degree of objectivity was necessary in order for her to do her job effectively.

She gripped the letter she had come to deliver in her other hand and realized that Lisa was as linked to her as she was to Liam. Lisa wasn't a client and she didn't need objectivity from Izzy any more than Robbie or Sophie did. She could love all three of them without holding back. She smiled as she pulled out the stool near the desk and sat down, "Sure, I'll look them over and we can get them in the mail. Make *Sophie Leanne Collins-Shannon* official – it's a beautiful name."

Lisa-Marie smiled back and closed the book in her lap. "You guys don't mind if I keep Sophie up here for tonight, do you?"

Izzy shook her head, "I have something to give you, Lisa." She passed over the envelope in her hand. "Edward asked me to make sure you got this."

Lisa-Marie studied the envelope with a confused look on her face. The room was quiet as she opened the letter.

Dearest Lisa:

If you are reading this letter, then I am gone. The race has run its course; I have reached the finish line. I wanted to tell you myself that I have named you as the beneficiary of my estate. That will seem very complicated and stuffy to you. It means that you will receive, when all matters are settled, a sizable amount of money.

Money, my dear girl, is a curious thing. If you have it you will never think twice about what it means, but the lack of money can create all sorts of obstacles best not even considered. Money allows people to maximize their options and choices – it's as simple as that.

But money alone is not enough. What is also needed is someone to promote your best interests. In this way, we old people serve the next generation. To that end, I have written a number of letters on your behalf to associates who still owe me a favour or two. I am confident that you will be offered more than one internship opportunity after you have graduated. My advice would be to lean towards the BBC. It seems I am sentimental to the end.

I want to thank you for all the help you provided on the book project. I hope you will treasure the part of the dedication that refers to you. Always remember, in good times and bad, that you are a gifted and talented young woman. Best wishes Lisa.

Your devoted mentor – Edward Montgomery

Lisa-Marie read the letter through twice, tears clouding her vision. She folded it up and asked, "Do you know what it says?" Izzy nodded and Lisa-Marie asked, "You don't mind ... about the money?"

Izzy shook her head, "Liam and I don't need any more money." As she got up to leave, she turned to say, "I'm so grateful for the way you helped my father make his dream of finishing the book come true. I'm going to miss you when you go back to school. It won't be the same around here without you in this room."

FIFTY

J ustin sat at the kitchen table of Liam's old cabin and stared at his duffle bag tossed in the center of the room. Shades of the day he had arrived came back to him. The place felt empty enough since Lisa-Marie had gone back to stay at Izzy and Liam's. He didn't need the presence of his bag to remind him things were coming to an end. As if the thought of Lisa-Marie had conjured her, he heard footsteps and her voice outside the door.

"Justin, you'll never guess what's happened –" Whatever she had meant to tell him stuck in her throat when she saw his bag in the middle of the room. "Why are you packed already?"

"I'm heading back to Vancouver a few days early. Liam's taking me to the bus tomorrow morning." Lisa-Marie bit down on her bottom lip to stop it from trembling. Justin's own resolve almost wavered when he saw how hard she was trying to control her emotions. He pointed to the chair across from him, "Sit down. Tell me your news."

Lisa-Marie walked over to the table. She pulled her gaze away from the bag and all that it represented. "It's about Edward's will." With her eyes downcast, she continued, "He left me a letter. He wrote to people at the BBC about me and there's a good chance they'll offer me an internship when I graduate – a year of taking photos and learning everything from the ground up ... that's what Edward told me once." Her voice dropped to a whisper, "And he left me a lot of money, too. I don't get control over it all until I'm older but his lawyer says I can use it for things that make sense until then. All I have to do is ask."

Justin sat back in surprise, "Leez, that's amazing news."

333

A tear traced a line down her cheek, "I know it's crazy, right? I had no idea he cared that much about me or believed in me like that." It was quiet in the cabin. Justin imagined they were both thinking about Edward and how this gift was going to pave the way to a great future for her. He was wrong.

Lisa-Marie raised her eyes to meet his. She took a deep breath and the words rushed out, "I'm so sorry, Justin. I swear I won't do anything stupid like last year but I have to say this ... I lied when I said I was over you. Don't be mad at me. I've been crazy in love with you all these months. I know I'll never love anyone the way I love you."

Justin saw the coming year mapped out in front them. He could meet her somewhere in Europe for Thanksgiving or reading break. Then they could spend Christmas together; they'd come here for her aunt and Beulah's wedding. Victoria was only a ferry trip away from Vancouver. They could see each other every weekend throughout the rest of the school year and when school finished, they'd come back here together and share this cabin for real.

The vision faded away as suddenly as it had risen up. It was wrong for the same reasons he'd told himself all along that it was wrong. Her life was just beginning, she was too young; he had school and his own future to work out. In a way, it was like what Jesse had said about himself and Maddy – they'd pull each other down. As long as Justin didn't let Lisa-Marie know how he felt, she would get on with her life the way she was supposed to, the way Edward had foreseen that she could.

Justin reached across the table and covered her hands with his own, "Don't say you're sorry. I'm not mad at you. We're friends. We'll always be friends."

Lisa-Marie nodded, "We'll keep in touch like last year, right?"

Justin stood and reached over to pull her up beside him. "Don't tie yourself to the past, Leez, and that includes me. Everything in your life is just starting. It's your senior year; you've got this incredible trip to Europe. Grab onto all of it with all you've got and don't look back."

"I can't stand the thought of losing you."

Justin cupped her face in his hands, "Let's make a date ... your eighteenth birthday ... dinner at *The Sea Shed*. Are you in?"

Lisa-Marie smiled through her tears, "Only if there will be dancing at the Dearborn Hotel afterwards."

Justin nodded and pulled her close. He leaned down and kissed her on the cheek. "I love you, too. Remember that." She didn't need to know the restraint he'd used to keep the kiss and the tone so brotherly.

After Lisa-Marie left the cabin, Justin moved over to the rocker and sat down. The creaking of the chair going back and forth was the only sound in the cabin. He watched the play of the fading light on the worn floor boards. Emptiness opened and yawned inside of him. He thought of the day his sister had died, the way his mother had left him, how the closeness he had felt with Izzy had turned into something that could never be. He imagined Maddy's impossible despair and how nothing Jesse could have done would ever have saved her. He recalled the way Willow had lain on the floor of Izzy's cabin, like something tossed out on a trash pile. He remembered every word of Lisa-Marie's story, her high school pain and anguish caused by being the girl everyone picked on. Justin sat with the compounded sorrow of one loss after another. He wondered how he could bear to let Leez walk away when she might be the only person who would ever choose to stay.

❧❧❧❧

Liam and Justin leaned against the side of Caleb's old Dodge, waiting for the bus to chug up the hill to the Dearborn Hotel. With his arms folded over his chest, Justin said, "I never apologized for trying to take a swing at you that first day."

"No need. I'd have done the same thing in your shoes. You were looking out for someone you cared about. There's nothing to apologize for."

Justin studied the pavement in front of his feet. "Only she's more than someone I care about. I'm in love with her and I didn't tell her. I knew if I told her, she wouldn't get on with her life the way she has to."

"Sounds as though you did what you thought was right."

Justin glanced over at Liam, "Maybe so, but it hurts like hell."

Liam sighed, "Ya ... the hurting is the worst part about doing the right thing."

The bus turned into the parking lot. Justin pushed away from the truck and grabbed for his bag. He stretched out his free hand to shake Liam's. Their eyes met in silent understanding before Justin said, "Thanks for everything. If you want me to work here again next year, I want to come back."

Liam smiled, "That news is going to make Reg's day. You take care, Justin. You've got a life to get on with, too. Don't forget that."

❧❧❧❧

Cynthia let a sideways glance linger on Alex's face. He was off to Victoria later

335

that morning to take up his visiting professorship at the university. Despite what he had said about not being thrown off by being in a relationship, she felt as though things were up in the air between them. She had no idea how to broach the topic – neither what to say nor how to express it.

Alex smiled at her, "I was looking out over the water and thinking about what a fine woman you are, Cynthia." Unexpected tears filled her eyes. His comment was as appropriate for a final goodbye as it was for a declaration of commitment. She hadn't realized until that moment how much she didn't want to say goodbye.

Alex got up and moved over to her chair to pull her up next to him. "I'm thinking that I'd like to come back here for Thanksgiving. Would you be able to fit me into your busy schedule?"

"I'm sure I'll be able to find time for you, Alex." Cynthia laughed as she reached up to kiss the man who held her tightly in his arms.

⚜⚜⚜⚜

Lisa-Marie stood in the driveway behind the cabin. Her bags were packed and stowed into Alex's truck. She was catching a ride back to Victoria with him. She had spent most of the morning over at the A-Frame saying her goodbyes to her aunt and Beulah. Now she had to walk away from the baby.

She was holding Sophie, singing to her, gazing into the baby's dark eyes. With every bit of self-control she could muster, she tried not to burst into tears. By the time she saw Sophie again her daughter would be seven months old. The baby information book she had borrowed from Izzy said Sophie would be sitting up by then, maybe even getting ready to crawl. She would be starting on solid food. She would change in so many ways. Everything would be different and Lisa-Marie wasn't sure how to let go and walk away.

Since the moment the madman had pointed a gun in Sophie's cradle, Lisa-Marie had found inside herself a well of love for her daughter that she hadn't known was there. The love would have been alright; she figured she could find a way to handle that. It was the crushing anxiety and concern for Sophie's continued safety that made Lisa-Marie's mouth go dry. What if something happened to Sophie?

She looked around for Robbie and gestured for him to come closer to her. She scrunched down with Sophie in her arms and Robbie followed suit. She bent her head to him and whispered, "Look at her, Robbie. Look close. Is she okay? Is she going to keep being okay?"

"I'm no superhero, Leez. I can't see the future."

Lisa-Marie nudged him with her shoulder, "Come on ... don't be like that. You know things. Tell me what I want to know or I'll dump you right into the lake, clothes and all."

Robbie grinned and studied Sophie, "She's bright and shiny, Leez. Don't worry. We'll look after her. I'll watch her. Cross my heart and hope to die."

Lisa-Marie got up and told Robbie, "You behave yourself and don't go freaking people out all the time with those powers." She stared at the boy in front of her, "And don't be too sure you aren't a superhero." She walked over to Liam and handed the baby to him, being careful to avoid the look of concern on his face. She turned to Izzy and hesitated. Then she let go and threw herself into her open arms; the tears she had been holding back came out in a sobbing torrent.

Izzy reached up to stroke the back of Lisa-Marie's hair, "Hey, it's going to be okay. Don't worry; everything is going to be alright."

Liam watched the woman he loved, hold and console the mother of his child. He felt a familiar pain grip his heart, a combination of lingering guilt and fear, all swirled within a happiness that seemed impossible to hold onto. He had confronted this same juxtaposition of emotions when he'd sat alone by the fire on the coastal beach, hearing the sounds of the wind in the trees and the pounding surf. He knew he could live with all of it, with anything that was to come; he was strong enough. The love he had for these people who had become family to him was strong enough to keep it all together, deep enough to help him live with the fact that he couldn't control anything. He walked over to his father who stood with Robbie.

Alex reached down and swung Robbie up into a huge, fierce hug. Setting the boy back down on his feet, he took Sophie from Liam's arms, bent his forehead to hers and said, "Goodbye little Sophie. Live up to everything your name implies." He handed her back.

Liam gave his father a stern look, "You're not the littlest hobo. You know that, right? It's time to give up on the wandering from town to town crap. We need you to come back."

"I hear you, Son. I've got a few compelling reasons to find my way back. Seems like the whole bunch of you can use the wisdom an old guy like me can dish up. I'll see you at Thanksgiving."

Lisa-Marie walked across the drive and got into Alex's truck. In a moment, they were headed up the steep drive and she was on the way to getting on with her life. She was thankful that Alex was the kind of person who knew when it was prudent to ignore a woman's silent tears.

The fire crackled in the chimney stove on the cliff deck. Izzy sat on the swing chair holding Sophie. Liam was close beside her. She could feel the warmth of his arm against her own. Robbie was scrunched down near the stove, roasting marshmallows

"You're going to burn that one. I'm not taking a burnt one," Izzy told the boy. He laughed and pulled the marshmallow back from the flames. "I've been thinking about school for you, Robbie, Robbie, McBobby," Izzy bounced Sophie on her knee and the baby chortled happily.

Robbie turned a glum face toward Izzy and Liam, "Do I have to go to school? It's boring and I won't know anyone."

"For this first year, I was thinking about home schooling. There are lots of people around here and at the Camp to help out. I think we can keep it from getting too boring." She shook her head and pointed at the marshmallow on the end of the roasting stick, "It's on fire, Robbie. Good grief, I'm not eating that. I'll have to take the next one."

Izzy watched as Robbie settled down cross legged on the deck and shoved the burnt marshmallow into his mouth. His hair was a tangled mess, his face was dirty and sticky and every day he wove his way tighter and tighter into her heart. She smiled down into Sophie's face and wondered at the power both Robbie and Sophie had to make her want to move heaven and earth to ensure their well-being.

Liam leaned forward to speak to Robbie, "I've got an idea about you and me joining a few activities in Dearborn. There's a fall bowling league we could try out and maybe baseball in the spring. Beulah's dying to get back into coaching." They both laughed at the idea of being on a team coached by Beulah.

Robbie looked over at Izzy. His eyes widened and his eyebrows shot up. Izzy jumped and looked behind her. She turned back and glared at Robbie, "What the heck? Don't do that. It's not funny. You looked like you'd seen a ghost or something. You scared the crap out of me."

Robbie shook his head, "It's your light … it's different … it changed."

He kept staring at her and Izzy felt a cold shiver creep up her spine, "Different … how? What do you mean?"

Robbie glanced from Liam to Izzy to Sophie. He shrugged his thin shoulders, "You have family light. I never knew light could change like that."

Tears filled Izzy's eyes. Robbie had turned away and stabbed two more marshmallows onto his roasting stick. Her voice trembled as she asked, "Are you sure, Robbie."

Intent on the activity at hand, he didn't even look up. His voice held all the confidence of youth, "Ya, of course I'm sure. The light never lies.

ACKNOWLEDGMENTS

My first thanks go, as always, to my husband, Bruce. You are my companion through all stages of this amazing writing journey.

Next, I acknowledge a debt of gratitude to my brilliant editor, Louise. I am a writer fortunate enough to have found an editor who brings a keen understanding of my unique voice, a love of my characters, a finely tuned sense of language usage and a truly amazing eye for detail to my work. In the editing stage, Louise and I become true collaborators and this book would not be what it is without her input. Many thanks, dear friend.

Thanks to my son, Doug who provided much needed design assistance and my daughter-in-law, Maggie who loves my stories. To my daughter, Kristen and my two beautiful granddaughters, Emma and Britney – you three give me the gift of daily laughter and that type of support is invaluable. Thanks to my son-in-law Matthew who walked me through some detailed technical information. I'm not sure I could have gotten such a hands-on demonstration elsewhere.

Heartfelt thanks to friends who offer their own valued connections and skills to promote my work.

I am thankful for the support received from my local North Island community. You gave *Disappearing in Plain Sight* a wonderful reception. Much gratitude goes out to the businesses that agreed to carry a new author's debut novel.

To all my readers – so many thanks. To my blogging friends – you never fail to shout out my achievements both large and small.

Finally, to my beta readers – you know who you are. Your input is valued and appreciated.

ABOUT THE AUTHOR

Francis Guenette has spent most of her life on the west coast of British Columbia. She lives with her husband and finds inspiration for writing in the beauty and drama of their off-grid, lakeshore cabin and garden. She has a graduate degree in Counselling Psychology from the University of Victoria, British Columbia, Canada. She has worked as an educator, trauma counsellor and researcher. The Light Never Lies is her second novel. Francis blogs over at http://disappearinginplainsight.com and maintains a Facebook author page. Please stop by and say hello.

DISAPPEARING IN PLAIN SIGHT
Don't miss the first book in the Crater Lake Series

Endorsed by Dr. Anne Marshall – Prof. of Educational Psychology, and Director of the Centre for Youth and Society at the University of Victoria.

"Disappearing in Plain Sight is a novel that deals with the timely themes of bullying and emotional trauma through the voices of young people, adults, and the caregivers who surround them. There is much to learn on both sides. I recommend this book for mental health care workers, teachers, and parents.

EXCERPTS FROM AMAZON REVIEWS:

"It's quite rare for me to encounter a story that stays with me for months afterward. This book did just that rare thing for me. The beautiful prose made me yearn for the rugged west coast."

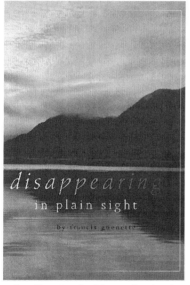

"A beautifully constructed novel – I couldn't put it down."

"Steeped in a vivid sense of place, this is a penetrating novel with adult characters and sensibilities. It will linger in your mind well after you're finished it."

"A beautiful read with fascinating, complicated characters and a setting you will be dying to visit by the end of the book."

"A story of real life problems and the often unforeseen consequences of the choices we make. It explores the themes of friendship, love and loss, grief and healing, and ultimately, the human capacity for forgiveness."

"This is no ordinary book; I was struck by Guenette's deep understanding of human nature and emotions. I loved this book and highly recommend it. A stellar accomplishment for Francis Guenette."

"I can't remember the last time I cried at the ending of a book, but boy, this one did it for me."

Made in the USA
Charleston, SC
17 February 2014